THE TRIAL WAS A DEVICE TO ROB CHARITY OF HER INHERITANCE.

When she testified in her own defense, Charity was cut off, not allowed to say much, but she managed to tell how her aunt had locked her in and her cousin had raped her.

She looked right at the magistrate as she said that, and thought she detected a gleam of sympathy in his eye. In that she was mistaken. The gleam was a purely lascivious one. He was imagining what she would look without the red dress, without her petticoats, without—he imagined her nude, climbing into his bed smiling. He scarcely heard Charity's testimony, so full was his mind of flashes of long shapely legs and snowy breasts and rounded hips and a temptingly parted mouth.

The room was silent for some time before it came to him that she had finished testifying and, startled, he ordered the court recessed. She must have bewitched him too, he decided. Burning was the cure for that. A girl like this one would only make trouble. His duty was clear.

He sentenced her to death . . .

This Loving Torment

Valerie Sherwood

WARNER BOOKS

A Warner Communications Company

WARNER BOOKS EDITION

Copyright © 1977 by Valerie Sherwood
All rights reserved

ISBN 0-446-82649-9

Cover art by Jim Dietz

Warner Books, Inc., 75 Rockefeller Plaza, New York, N.Y. 10019

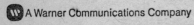 A Warner Communications Company

Printed in the United States of America

Not associated with Warner Press, Inc. of Anderson, Indiana

First Printing: August, 1977

10 9 8 7

Contents

This Loving Torment

Prologue

Cornwall 1666

I

Moll Whitten hurried down the dark wooded
path that led from the inn late one summer night.
As she came out of the deep shade of the overhanging branches, the moonlight struck her, and it
could be seen that she was a beautiful young woman
of no more than twenty, with amber eyes that
flashed gold in the moonlight and a heavy mane of
lustrous red-gold hair.

To her right—a half day's march—lay the
rugged smuggler-haunted Cornish Coast and the
stormswept seas. Behind her lay the sleepy little
village of Lawden and, on its outskirts, the Inn of

the White Stag where she worked—though not for long, if her plans went well.

A twig snapped behind her. Someone was following her. Moll tossed her mane of tawny hair, and her amber eyes lit with triumph. Young Lord Trelawney had been at the inn tonight and he'd been feasting on her with his eyes—and him owner of that great castle up on the hill! Moll had been sent packing from that same castle six months before for casting her eyes too brightly on young James Trelawney. His mother, an upright woman, had no mind for him to be scattering hooked Trelawney noses about the countryside as her late husband had done. When Moll was dismissed, old Mistress Rollins, an impoverished gentlewoman had taken her in to work for her keep. But then Mistress Rollins had died and, now, her relatives were allowing Moll to stay on as caretaker only until they sold the small cottage. Moll had found work as a barmaid at the inn since Nelly, the regular barmaid, was too near her approaching labor to serve. The job was temporary, but that was all right with Moll. Young Trelawney was still unmarried and Moll had eyes above her station. Why couldn't a titled lord marry a serving wench? Many another had done it!

Coming to another patch of moonlight at a dip in the path, Moll paused and deliberately pulled up her full skirts as if to examine her legs for briar scratches. She displayed a long sweep of handsome leg, brushed away an imaginary thorn, and then strolled on.

When she reached the shadowed doorway to her cottage, Moll peeked behind her to make sure he was still there. A shadow moved in the trees and her eyes kindled again. She'd been right to taunt him by flirting with the stranger at the inn. It had made him jealous! Lord Trelawney had come to the inn looking glum, and Moll knew this was her chance. She'd heard he'd been jilted by that London chit with the big dowry, and wasn't that just the right moment to nab a man?

10

So, Moll thrust out her full shapely breasts, edged down her white blouse so that they gleamed white in the candlelight, and smiled right into his eyes as she served him his pint.

He hadn't noticed.

Irritated, Moll had looked around her, wondering how to snap him out of his lethargy. At that moment, the wind slammed the door shut, and she turned to watch as a tall stranger, clad in a big sweeping cloak, entered the inn.

The tall man looked about with an arrogant air. His strong hard face and brilliant topaz eyes flicked over the room, quickly taking in who was there— and who was not.

The excisemen were not.

The stranger was a smuggler by trade, and sudden leavetakings were a hazard of his profession. So he settled his long legs at a table conveniently near both a door and a window, and ordered a pint of ale.

He was served by Moll, who tossed her head and posed as she served the pint. Leaning over to clean off an already clean oak table, she managed to brush her soft warm breasts against him. Then she jumped back coquettishly and gave him a look of saucy confusion, followed by a long, slow, meaningful smile.

The tall smuggler had seen that kind of smile before. It was an invitation. His eyes followed handsome Moll around the room.

Lord Trelawney, who never held his liquor well, held it no better this night. Moll kept close watch on him and when Trelawney got up to leave, tumbling over a chair as he did so, she announced to the innkeeper that her poor head was "near bursting" and she'd be bound if she could stand to work a minute longer what with all that pain.

The innkeeper sighed. He knew that Moll had an eye for Trelawney, but he had a soft spot in his heart for the girl, for all her insolent ways. Still he frowned as she flounced out through the front door.

Getting above her station, she was; she should have left by the back way—he'd have to speak to her about that.

Out in the open air Moll spotted Trelawney's horse tied to a nearby hitching post. And then she heard the young lord himself, singing a ribald song to the moon as he walked unsteadily through the night. He had obviously forgotten his horse, and it gave a disconsolate whinny as its master moved off down the path.

Moll passed James Trelawney with a bright smile and a hitch of her skirts, then moved on ahead of him, swaying as she walked in the moonlight. Trelawney staggered after her, she was encouraged to note, though the same path was also the way to the castle until it forked at the patch of woods.

Humming a little tune, Moll plunged into the woods, forcing herself not to look back so she wouldn't seem too obvious. But he had followed, oh, yes, he had followed! That shadow in the woods . . .

Moll unlatched the cottage door and hurried inside, leaving her wooden door ajar. Flinging back the covers on the bed, she hastily took off her shoes and stockings and tried to decide whether to take off her clothes. No, let him do that. It would make it seem more of a conquest. And tomorrow when he woke up in her arms, she could cry that he had seized her and torn her clothes—which of course would have to be replaced with better ones.

She lay down on the bed and closed her eyes, pretending to be lying there exhausted.

Overhead the moon, on a fitful path, scurried behind a cloud and for a moment the birdsong stilled as a darker shadow appeared in the doorway.

Moll could hear him moving toward her, but she kept her eyes determinedly closed.

A low laugh caused her eyes to fly open, and a voice said, "Well displayed, wench. You're a sight to tempt a king!"

Moll sat up in dismay. It wasn't Lord Trelawney —it was the stranger from the inn!

12

"Go away!" she cried. "I'm expecting someone!"

"Ah, yes, and I'm the one you were expecting," he said in a steely voice, sweeping off his cloak. Moll leapt up and tried to run away, but he barred the door. Laughing, he caught her running figure and dragged her panting back to the bed.

"Now you don't want to keep these lovely things in prison," he said, and gave her already loosened blouse a jerk so that her breasts tumbled out. "I see I've made a good choice for the evening," he added, bending over her and burying his face in her breasts, kneading them with his hands, his lips.

Moll screamed and kicked at him.

He stood up, surprised, holding her pinioned like a butterfly with one hand firmly on her stomach. "You're a fighting wench?" he muttered. "It's the struggle that pleases you?"

"No!" cried Moll loudly. "Go away and leave me alone."

"Ah, now that I can't do. Not yet anyway." He replaced his hand on Moll's stomach and with his knee held her down firmly as he unfastened his trousers. When she struck at him, he slapped her face hard, first on one side and then the other, so that her head spun.

She subsided, glaring up at him.

"You play too rough, wench," he said softly and caressed her throat with a none too gentle hand as he lowered his long body onto hers.

There was real fear in Moll's eyes now.

"Don't," she cried hoarsely. "I'm not what you think. I'm a virgin! I—"

He chuckled as if she'd made some great joke. This sultry tavern wench a virgin! He parted her tightly held legs and holding down her flailing arms, thrust his hardness against her.

Moll screamed.

His head went up in astonishment. "Damned if you aren't!" he said, amazed, and studied her face for a minute.

"Damn you!" cried Moll, twisting away.

"Ah, that's no way to talk to a man you've led on all evening!" he admonished, and thrust again, with deliberate pressure.

Moll writhed at the sharp violent pain inside her. Her breasts were crushed down by the weight of his body, her rounded hips felt the hardness of his narrow hips.

"Easy," he said in a soothing tone. "Easy now." As if he were riding a horse!

Hatred and fury and pain and something else, something new, welled up in Moll. She had guarded her virginity like a treasure to be brought to the feet of some earl. Though twice she had nearly lost it: once at a summer festival and once in the shade of some yew trees on a spring evening when the grass was wet with dew. And now to be taken like some whore!

She groaned and writhed under him, and unexpectedly desire woke in her and she felt a shivering of passion along with the pain. He felt this change in her and laughed softly, triumphantly. When he had done, his passion spent, and she lay sobbing with helpless fury, he kissed the hollow in her throat and trailed his lips down to her heaving breasts, nibbled at her pink nipples, tasted them exploringly.

She struck out at him, but halfheartedly.

"I'd stay with you tonight, wench," he said reflectively. "But methinks I've tarried too long already." He'd had an odd feeling all day that the excisemen were trailing him, but no need to tell the girl this. "I'll be back," he said, and patted her bare stomach.

She quivered at his touch. "No, you won't!" she screamed. "You've used me and now you'll be on your way to the next one!"

"As you like." He shrugged, drawing on his trousers. Suddenly, he grew alert. There was a sound outside, the breaking of a twig. He looked around, but the cottage was a deathtrap with only one door!

He threw his cloak about him and unbarred the

14

door. As he swung it open, Moll reached down one arm and snatched up a heavy chamberpot and threw it at his head.

It missed him but caught the man who had leaped into the doorway full in the face. He staggered back with a howl, and the smuggler slipped through the door. With a laughing, "Thanks, wench!" he ran into the darkness.

But there were too many of the excisemen, and they were ranged all about. They must have spotted him at the inn and sent for reinforcements.

He hid in the shadows and considered what to do. The gold! If he were caught with the gold on him, that would convict him. A solid purseful—and how could he explain it? What if they had already discovered the shipment of liquor he'd delivered to the butler up at Castle Trelawney?

He had to get rid of his purse.

He noticed the well that was used to draw water for the cottage and, as an exciseman crashed through the bushes, he dropped the purse in it. The splash was lost in the sound of heavy boots. Then he dodged instinctively as a musket exploded nearby and the ball went past him too close for comfort.

He turned, meaning to sneak past the cottage, through the trees, and head in the other direction. But an exciseman who had been squatting patiently under cover of a bush rose up and fired at him point blank. The ball crashed into his chest and felled him.

"I've got him!" crowed a voice, and feet came running from all over.

"The gold!" someone cried. "Where's the gold?"

"Drag him into yon cottage," growled someone else. "We can search him there."

His blood spilling on the ground, the smuggler groaned in agony as they dragged him to the cottage. They laid him on the bed he had so lately left and searched him. Moll drew a sheet around her, for she'd had no time to dress, what with men with guns running about outside the windows.

15

"The gold!" Someone prodded the smuggler with the butt of a musket. He moaned, opened his eyes and saw the disheveled girl with her tearstained face staring down at him. His expression softened. She'd been a good lay, she had, and he'd have come back to her right enough—foxy little virgin that she was! But now he knew he was never coming back, knew he'd never tell her his name was Johnnie O'Riordan, late of Ireland, knew he'd never see her again . . . or the stars . . . or the sea . . . or the great billowing sails that had carried him to this coast.

But the girl deserved something.

"Let me tell my wench goodbye," he gasped, "and I'll tell you where the gold is."

Somebody snorted, and somebody else gave Moll a shove so that she landed on top of the fallen man.

With the last of his strength he threw his arm about her and drew her face down to his, pressed his lips against her mouth and turned her head so that his lips traveled across her cheek to her ear.

"Well . . ." he whispered. ". . . the well . . . ."

Moll heard but did not understand. Then someone gave her bottom a whack and rough hands jerked her up, causing the sheet to fall to the floor.

All but one turned to study her naked body as she scrabbled for the sheet, but that one prodded the dying smuggler with his toe. "Where's the gold?" he said.

But he was too late. Too late to beat it out of Johnnie O'Riordan. Before the smuggler's eyes rose a blood red mist, and out of it rode a white ship with billowing sails, and beyond it a landfall, a green land of peat bogs and cloudy summer skies and great rocks and old castles and a smiling dark-haired girl who had spurned him and, now, had come magically back, wafted on the blood red sea fog. . . .

"Where's the gold?" repeated the voice.

"In Ireland," murmured Johnnie, and death rattled in his throat, as his head lolled.

He was dead.

The one who had prodded him—a big swashbuckling fellow—now gave a mighty oath and swung on the trembling girl.

"Bring her along to the castle," he said. "We'll make Trelawney tell us where it is."

"Unless *she* knows," said an evil voice.

"I know nothing," babbled Moll. "I'm barmaid at the inn. This man came in to drink his pint, and followed me home and leaped on me and raped me! I know nothing about him—not even his name."

"His name we don't know either," said the swash-buckling one carelessly, "but his type we do. Bring her along."

He turned on his heel and went out the door into the night.

So it happened that Moll made her return to Castle Trelawney, not as the happy bride of young Lord Trelawney, but attired in a rough bedsheet and dragged along in the firm grip of an exciseman.

At first, the butler did not wish to open the heavy door. But after the men threatened to break it down, a woman's strident voice called, "Open the door at once, Sedley!" and the butler reluctantly drew back the bolts. His face was very white as the excisemen charged into the hall.

"James," called the woman. "Come down here." Moll looked up to see a frowning Lady Trelawney, James' mother, standing at the head of the stairs in a faded muslin wrapper.

There was a drunken roar from upstairs as young James got himself on his feet and staggered down. Bleary-eyed and still dressed in the clothes he had worn at the inn, James cast a wild look at Moll in her bedsheet and at the assembled faces below.

"What's wrong?" he asked, sobering.

"God's teeth!" cried his mother. "These men come bursting in, in the night, and is that all you can ask? Order them out!"

Young James looked warily at the grim faces ringed below. "What d'ye want of us?" he demanded weakly.

They told him what they wanted. James grew

17

pale, knowing full well that the shipment of liquor had been delivered earlier. That damned smuggler! How dare he get caught and bring calamity down upon them!

"I know nothing about it," Trelawney said sulkily.

Moll, in custody of the butler and forgotten for the moment, had time to look around her. The castle was "great" only in Moll's eyes. It was sadly in need of repair, many of its rooms unusable. But to a serving girl it was magnificent. She looked about her at the great hall with its stone fireplace, so big a man could stand in it, and at the tall ceiling crisscrossed by heavy beams. She crouched, shivering in her bedsheet, as the men began their search. For a wistful moment she remembered what it had been like to work there, to walk through the awesome rooms every day. How she had hungered for the monogrammed silver, the snowy linens, the "yes, m'lady," "no, m'lady," the spices and wines and perfumes. . . . And now she'd been dragged back in a bedsheet, looking wild and tumbled—no one even cared that she'd been raped—and Lord James Trelawney was ignoring her.

She could hear him roaring about "improper search" as the excisemen combed the house. Beside her, the butler's eyes rolled wildly. But the excisemen did not find the large nook behind the fireplace where he had cautiously hidden the liquor, and eventually, tiring of the search, they were persuaded that they had come to the wrong place. The innkeeper might have received the shipment, someone suggested. After all, the smuggler had been spotted at the inn, hadn't he?

The excisemen made apologies of a sort to the Trelawneys, and turned away, still dragging Moll with them. The girl turned wildly toward her former employers.

"Make them let me go!" she gasped. "I know nothing of this business!"

James Trelawney looked worried. He stepped forward uncertainly. His mother's arm pushed him back.

Moll gave him one last look from large reproachful eyes as the excisemen jerked her along with them, and down to the inn. The surly innkeeper almost came to blows with them as they searched his establishment thoroughly from top to bottom.

"Think you it could be in the girl's hut" asked one of the men thoughtfully.

"Nay," said another. "He'd probably not set eyes on her before tonight. He'd made many deliveries from that wagon we found. This was his last stop. Who'd leave such a sum with a barmaid?"

"That's true," agreed the other.

It was morning before they completed their search, and Moll sat, shivering, tied to a chair until they had done.

"Well, it's not here," said one at last. "But all's not lost. We can have a bit of fun with the girl."

Moll shuddered, thinking what their "fun" would mean to her, and her pleading eyes sought the innkeeper's.

He appeared not to see her, but said instead in a surprised voice, "Are you tarryin' here then? I'd ha' thought you'd be off after the other one!"

"What other one?" asked the leader sharply.

"You mean you didn't go after him?" demanded the innkeeper incredulously.

"After *who?*" roared their leader, grabbing him by the throat.

"Him, the one that came by just after your men left," growled the innkeeper, "and asked about his friend. He waited a bit and then went off that way." He jerked his head toward the coast. "Could be you could overtake him."

The innkeeper staggered as the big man let go of him and led the rush to the door. As they rode away, the innkeeper called after them, "He had yellow hair and was wearin' a Manderville coat."

He stood in the doorway, the sound of hooves fading in the distance, then turned grimly to Moll and untied her.

"Get you gone, girl," he said gruffly. "When they

come back empty-handed, they'll be in a mean mood."

Moll stared at him, enlightenment washing her face of everything but surprise. There was no "other one"; the innkeeper had lied to save her!

"Hurry away now, Moll," he said more kindly. "Have ye a place to go? Will they take you in up at the castle?"

Moll shook her head. "I'll hide in the woods till they've gone," she said.

He sighed. "Raping of virgins, I wouldn't have thought they'd stoop to it. Shows you what we've come to under the Stuarts! Take some food and a flagon of ale with you, Moll, to warm your spirits."

Moll smiled at him wistfully. Saying thank you came hard to her; she hadn't had much occasion to use the words and mean them. She scooped up her sheet and, impulsively flinging her arms around the square-built older man, planted a warm kiss on his mouth.

A little shaken by the feel of her firm young breasts thrusting through the thin worn sheet, the innkeeper unwound her arms from about his shoulders. "I'll walk through the woods whistling a tune when the excisemen have left, Moll," he promised. "Go on now."

So, with some bread and meat wrapped in a napkin slung on one arm, and a flagon of ale balanced carefully in her hand, as she struggled to hold the sheet around her, Moll walked warily into the woods. This time, she left by the back door, and this time she looked behind her not coyly but in fright.

She stayed two days, crouched in a little copse whose leaves and branches gave total concealment, before she heard the innkeeper's rollicking whistle. Staggering out, stiff and sore, she returned to the cottage and sank down in misery onto that bed where she had lost her virginity, and where her attacker had lost his life.

"Well. . ." he had whispered to her. Well what? Well done?

Moll looked around her with vacant eyes. Soon the heirs would sell this place and she'd have nowhere to go. Although she could keep her job at the inn for a while, Nelly would be coming back after her confinement, needing work worse than ever.

She moved stiffly out into the yard to draw some water to cool her hot face. Looking down into the water's glittery surface, she lowered the oaken bucket.

The well! That was what the smuggler had been saying to her, and she had been too frightened to take it in. The gold was in the well!

Trembling, Moll peered down. The sparkling water fascinated her. It wasn't a deep well but still there was water in it. How to find out if he'd thrown the gold in?

Suddenly she remembered a big iron hook that held the pots over the fire. If she fastened a long rope to that—!

Hours later, her arms aching with fatigue and her dress torn, her waist rubbed raw from leaning over the well's rough stone edge, she felt the hook bite into something heavy, at last, and pulled it up. It was a dripping leather pouch, the hook had caught on its drawstring.

Moll pounced on it.

Laughing and crying at the same time, she counted the golden coins in the leather pouch. A fortune!

The smuggler had also left her something else.

Fertility ran in Moll's family. Her mother had said her father had only to hang his britches on the bedpost for her to conceive. Moll was the spitting image of her mother, and she had little doubt that in nine months' time there'd be another mouth to feed. Moll began to plan.

She packed her few possessions, hiding the gold in various places—a coin or two in each shoe, the remainder stitched into her petticoat except for one golden coin in her shabby purse, to keep her, and to represent her total fortune in case robbers fell upon her.

21

She was waiting at the inn for the stage when Lord Trelawney rode up. He was sober and he looked dismayed at the sight of her standing there. Plainly he felt a little guilty too, for word of the hard usage the girl had gone through had reached him via the local gossips.

"Are you off to somewhere then?" he asked Moll, reining in his horse.

She nodded, surveying him with steady eyes.

He hesitated, taking in regretfully the warm curve of her breasts, the gentle rise of her hips under the rough brown cloth of her skirt. "There's no need to go, Moll," he said. "I'll speak to Sedley up at the castle. He'll find a place for you in the kitchen again."

Moll's eyes gleamed. Now she had the smuggler's gold, she felt rich. She was through with kitchens!

"And," he cast a look around, saw there was no one within earshot, and grew bolder, "there might be a moment for us to dawdle together, eh?"

How she had yearned to hear him say that, all the time she had worked as a scullery maid at the castle. How sweet the words would have rung on her ears! And this was the man who could so easily have helped her. A word from him, that was all that would have been needed. But no, he'd let his mother fire her, and the excisemen drag her around. For all he cared, the lot of them could have raped her!

She lifted her head and smiled sweetly into his face. He looked pleased, waiting for her thanks.

"Go to the devil, James Trelawney," she said evenly. "I've no time to dawdle with you."

"What? What?" He was so startled he jumped and his horse reared, nearly knocking Moll to the ground.

The coach thundered into the courtyard and Moll turned disdainfully away from him to walk toward it.

Her child would not be born here. She would be born in London. And she would grow up to be a lady.

II

August had ended by the time Moll reached the outskirts of London. On advice of the stage driver, who realized Moll's innocence of city ways, she had found decent lodgings near the Boar's Head Tavern and, pulsing with excitement, set out to explore the great sprawling city that was London.

She did not have long to explore it.

For Moll, having escaped the year of the Great Plague, had arrived in London in time for the Great Fire.

She awoke one night to hear cries of "Fire, fire!" Dressing hastily, she hurried downstairs to learn that all of Pudding Lane was ablaze. Moll rushed out into the street, which was a sea of carts and running, shouting people, and heard there the rancor expressed at Sir Thomas Bludworth's contemptuous remark about the fire, "Pish, a woman might piss it out!"

Driven back by heat and smoke, Moll returned to her room, but stayed awake, listening to reports shouted from the street: the Star Inn on Fish Street Hill was alight; St. Margaret's Church was burning; the fire had consumed London Bridge. Moll knew that England was at war with Holland, and her heart thumped as someone rode through the streets crying, "Arm! Arm!"

Frightened by the ever-increasing heat and smoke and noise, Moll packed her few belongings in the sturdy square of linen cloth and started out to find safer lodgings.

Rumors were now abroad that a French army had

come to crush the city, and Frenchmen were attacked wherever they were found—one of them was suspected of carrying fire balls, when in truth he had only tennis balls.

Moll was swept by the crowds this way and that, and at last sat down, exhausted, in a doorway. Clutching her possessions and using them for a pillow, she fell into a fitful sleep.

She awoke to more carnage. The great clouds of yellowish-gray smoke had rolled over the outskirts of the city to the west, turning day to night. With nightfall, the city became brighter than day, and towering pillars of flame lit up all the streets and alleys as if a red sun shone in the sky.

Completely lost, driven this way and that as hoarse cries warned that the mighty Guildhall was in flames, this church or that one burning, the Thames awash with boats filled with refugees fleeing the charred waterfront, Moll felt frightened and helpless. Great fiery sparks carried three furlongs through the air, to set new fires where they landed. Tinder-dry London was ready for the torch and the strong east wind had brought it. All around, houses were being pulled down to make firebreaks, or being blown up with gunpowder. Added to the fearsome roar from the fire itself, the giant crackling and smashing as timbers fell and stone burst from the heat, was the incessant din of the fire alarms—parish church bells, pealing out the discordant sounds that meant "Fire." There was fear for the White Tower—its keep jammed with gunpowder—sitting above most of the nation's archives.

White Towers did not trouble Moll. Tossed about on a sea of shouting, struggling human flesh, she felt that she had descended into hell, and began to gasp out prayers as she tried to fight her way out. Tumbled carts with locked wheels had jammed the entrance to the city gates. There was no water, women screamed in terror, babies cried lustily, and all about her the air was heavy with choking smoke. She tried to make her way through the churning avalanche of goods as people fought to save their earthly possessions.

The prisons were burning, and old St. Paul's Cathedral—all 600 feet of it—was a furious sea of flames, as the melting lead from its roofs ran down the building causing the great stones to explode and fly with killing force in all directions. Next, molten lead crept out of its doorways to run down Ludgate Hill in a stream of fiery red as if a volcano were erupting.

Eventually the east wind lessened and halted the conflagration, but before it did Moll had been swept along in the human tide pouring out of the old city. She found herself surrounded by a great crush of carts, horses, wagons, every kind of conveyance—and by people on foot, carrying on their backs their most treasured possessions, who shouted to one another in wild excitement, asking where the fire had reached now. Against their voices was a great crackling roar as the flames advanced, and sometimes their cries were drowned in explosions as men from the dockyards, under orders from the king, sought to demolish houses with gunpowder and thus establish fire-breaks.

Night found Moll camped with thousands of other refugees on Hampstead Heath. Leaning against somebody's wagon in exhaustion. Drinking water from a borrowed cup, she listened to the wails of children, mothers calling for lost ones, occasional curses and snores.

Once again she had to find a little space where she could curl up under her cloak to spend the night.

When the fire had burned itself out, four-fifths of the old city lay in smoldering ruins and more than a hundred thousand people were homeless. The fire was on everybody's mind—and on everybody's tongue. A thin old crone cast a significant look at a fat friend across from her. "Mark you," she said disapprovingly, "any fire which begins in Pudding

Lane and ends in Pie Corner is a judgment on those who gorge themselves!"

"You're thin as a rail," scoffed the other, her pendulous chins bobbing, "and the fire burned you out too, didn't it?"

Moll, who was quite hungry by now, ignored their exchange. More bewildered than most, since she was a newcomer, she had just decided to walk as far into the country as possible when her left shoe came apart, spilling its golden coin. Moll snatched up the coin and sat down in the dirt and wailed. How far could she walk barefoot? And where was she to go?

A wheedling voice behind her said, "If you'll be givin' me that gold coin, I'll find you a cobbler, that I will."

Moll looked around at the ragged, rat-faced speaker in amazement. A gold coin to find a cobbler, indeed!

"Carts that be reg'larly hired for ten shillings be hirin' today for as much as fifty pound," he said with a smirk. "Tis a fair price—and _I_ know where a cobbler's to be found."

With a rueful sigh, Moll surrendered the coin.

"You can stay here," he said. "I'll bring back the cobbler."

"Nay, I'll go with you," said Moll grimly, hobbling after him. He led her on a crazy-quilt path through a horde of dazed-looking people, sitting among their remaining possessions, people who, to the idle gaze, might appear to be camping out on some great public outing.

She soon realized he was outdistancing her, and called sharply for him to wait, but he hurried on. She stumbled after him, shouting, but he eluded her rounding a maze of carts. She sat down and began to cry.

An old woman plucked at her sleeve to ask what was wrong. Moll poured out her story, and the old woman clucked her tongue. "Newgate Prison has burned," said she, "and the inmates they be taken to Southwark, but many escaped. Your trickster could be such a one. If you go now and cry out that you are in sore need of a cobbler, there'll be people here that may know where one is to be found."

So Moll got up and hobbled along crying out for a cobbler. After a while, a little group of people all turned and pointed at once, telling her that there was a cobbler to be found in that direction. As Moll advanced, limping, a pale thin man rose from a group sitting dispiritedly on the ground and said in a quite kindly voice, "I be a cobbler and my tools are here beside me. Give me that shoe and I will fix it."

In silence, Moll handed over her shoe and watched as the man, who was thin-shanked and plain-faced and exceedingly sober in dress, opened a wooden box of cobbler's tools beside him. Smiling at her, he proceeded to make her shoe whole again. He disdained her money, and instead offered her a seat beside him on the cobbler's box and a slab of cheese and coarse bread from a bundle that he carried.

Moll, who was nearly famished, sank down beside him and, between munches, asked him about himself.

His shop had burned, he told her gloomily, but by the grace of God he had been able to save his tools.

Moll liked him. Her recent experiences in Cornwall had made her like men in general rather less, but this man seemed different.

He was indeed different from the men she had known. His name was Increase Woodstock, he was a Puritan, and he had never seen anything so beautiful as the spirited girl who sat beside him, her amber eyes flashing with lively interest as he told her the simple story of his life.

When at last Moll sighed and said she must be getting on, though for the life of her she didn't know where to go, he offered to walk with her and give her protection on the road until they could find

27

decent lodgings. He had friends who lived some miles down the road. He was sure these friends would take them in, although their house might be filled and they would have to sleep in the barn. Sleeping in a barn sounded fine to Moll at this point. She looked around at the swarming quarreling humanity on Hampstead Heath and gratefully accepted his offer of protection that night.

Within a week, she was equally grateful to accept Increase Woodstock's offer of marriage. She was certain that she was pregnant. Her child would need a name, and should be born in wedlock. If the baby were a daughter, Moll dreamed that she would grow up and become a duchess; if a son, that he would grow up to wed one.

In the meantime, Moll would have to make do with a cobbler.

Increase was trusting by nature. He had never known a woman and, when Moll had cried out on their wedding night, he honestly believed that he had pierced her maidenhead. He was good to Moll and he worked hard. His health was fragile, though, which was why he had remained in England when his older brother Jason and his sister Temperance's family had gone to the Massachusetts Colony some years before.

The man was overjoyed when Moll offered him her small store of wealth. With it, he moved them back into London and into a new cobbler's shop that had living quarters above it. By that time, Moll had learned that her "fortune" was small indeed by London standards, and she congratulated herself on having had the foresight to marry such an indulgent, hardworking husband. In her way, she loved Increase, and she was ever faithful to him.

Moll, now a "lady" by her own lights, was determined never to serve a flagon of anything outside her own house or empty anyone else's chamber pot again. She worked with driving energy to keep their house spotless and comfortable. Increase was an avid reader of the Word of God from a well-thumbed

Bible. At her insistence, he taught Moll to read and write.

It was to change her life.

When Moll went into labor "prematurely" and gave birth to a lovely daughter, whom they named Charity, Increase was immensely proud. He never doubted that Charity was his own daughter. Cheerfully, he set about trying to keep up with the few demands his small family made on him.

Happy though he was, his health did not improve. In fact, marriage to a lusty young woman who made constant demands on his failing strength, and long hours at his trade, caused him to grow quite frail. He began to cough more often and was a partial invalid before little Charity could toddle about on her own.

Three years later, Increase died of consumption aggravated by the climate, leaving a tiny shop with living quarters, some cobbler's tools, a handful of coins, a scheming wife, and a daughter who had inherited her real father's brilliant topaz eyes and her mother's thick shimmering hair—although it was pale gold instead of red.

When Moll's own robust health began to fail, she started thinking uneasily about her daughter's future. She sold the shop and the cobbler's tools, forgot she'd ever been wed to a Puritan, left London attired in a rose-pink mock-velvet dress, and bought a tiny house in Torquay on Devon's lovely south coast. Her health would improve in the sea air, she told herself, and once she got her strength back, she'd see about Charity's future.

But her health continued to be poor, and somehow she'd lost her taste for men and good times. She stayed at home, trying to survive in genteel poverty. Their small house was set into the tiers of houses that climbed up the waterside streets, almost overwhelmed by a subtropical profusion of flowers, with gay mimosas and fuchias and flowering palms.

There in those narrow streets, her glowing blonde

hair blown about by the sea wind, little Charity had scampered, playing with a favorite kitten, delighting her mother. But as she grew older and the lads began to cast admiring glances at the ripening figure of this slender beauty, her mother had jealously kept her away from fairs and public gatherings. Moll frowned away any local lads who might have shown interest, fearing her pretty daughter would marry "down," as she put it—blithely ignoring the fact that she herself had started life as a chambermaid and would end it as a cobbler's near-impoverished widow.

But everything changed by chance one day when Moll, who never lacked for courage, heard a scream on the way to market and saw, hurtling down the hill toward her, a runaway team (whose driver, she later learned, had pitched off senseless from a heart attack). Leaning out of the driverless carriage, was its sole occupant, a white-faced, velvet-clad woman clutching a plumed hat.

Moll dropped her market basket and sprang into the street. She managed to seize the reins—to the accompaniment of a wild scream from the carriage—and brought the horses to a gradual halt.

Moll herself had collapsed in a coughing fit when the lady in velvet made her shaky exit from the carriage and reached for her smelling salts.

"Are you all right, *chérie?*" inquired the woman solicitously, as others sorted out the nervous horses, the injured driver. "Perhaps we could find somewhere a glass of wine?"

In this way, Moll made the acquaintance of Countess Stéphanie de la Croix, an impoverished French aristocrat. The countess confided, over that glass of wine, which was served in Moll's small spotless sitting room, that she had recently left Paris to live in Bath. Through her wealthy connections, she supported herself by teaching French and deportment and other useful things to four orphaned girls whose guardians wished to be rid of them for long periods of time.

Moll thoughtfully considered the fashion plate in her living room, noting with interest the countess's long-waisted gown with its low décolletage, its sleeves full to the elbow opening widely with a fall of lace, and its voluminous lavender velvet skirt. She was delighted when Charity came flying in the door, the sun behind her turning her fair hair to sunlight itself, and the countess drew in her breath and said, *"Mon Dieu,* what a lovely child!"

Moll bridled proudly, asserting that she expected Charity to grow into a great beauty, with which Stéphanie instantly agreed.

Stéphanie, her gaze still following Moll's unexpectedly gorgeous daughter in some amazement, thanked Moll effusively for saving her life. She insisted on taking them to dinner at the inn where she was staying. Over a tasty joint of mutton, she poured out the story of her various pupils' problems with their guardians, to Moll's utter fascination. Finally, Stéphanie asked again how she could repay Moll for stopping the carriage.

Moll saw her opportunity. She took a deep breath—which almost set her coughing again—and asked whether her own daughter could hope to become one of Stéphanie's charges?

Astonished, Stéphanie set down her glass, opened her mouth to say, indeed, no, remembered that but for the woman before her she might have been thrown to the street, her beauty marred forever, and hesitated. After giving the matter a moment's thought, she replied regretfully that the girl's background would have to be cloaked, she must have a fine wardrobe and arrive in a coach.

"But had I the means for that," pursued Moll, "you would accept my daughter and teach her to be a fine lady?"

"Why, then," said Stéphanie, her voice ringing with the recklessness that had brought her into her present straitened circumstances, "I would gladly accept her and teach her all I could of gentility."

That night Moll sat down and wrote a letter to America.

31

BOOK I

Massachusetts 1686

CHAPTER 1

The girl who stood in the dock waiting to be sentenced was barely nineteen years old. She was not dressed in the usual Puritan manner, but wore instead a torn and dirty dress of dark red cambric (the same dress she had been wearing when the authorities had seized her a week ago). Its skirt was full. Its long tight bodice seemed to the eyes of the men in the courtroom, as they feasted on the sight, barely to hold in bounds her firm young breasts, now rising and falling with emotion. Her face, however, was remarkably impassive, considering the fact that she was on trial for her life. She stood with her feet planted firmly on the floor planks, her head held high, her thick pale gold curls a shimmering tumbled confusion (she had not been allowed a comb). Her brilliant topaz eyes, with their dusky dark gold lashes, were fixed on the magistrate who sat above her. She looked like an adventuress. She looked wild.

The magistrate frowned down upon her, taking in the dark red dress, the disheveled, enticing appearance of the girl.

"Charity Woodstock," he thundered, and the buzzing voices in the great room of the meeting house, now serving as a courtroom, fell silent. People in the sober garb of Puritans leaned forward tensely, waiting.

As he paused, the girl herself now cast a look about her. There sat her accusers, looking smug: her Aunt Temperance, her Cousin Patience, her Cousin Matthew. *Now they would see!* the girl thought. After that farce of a trial! Now she would be exonerated and the real culprits punished! Not for witch-craft, as she had been charged, but for rape and false witness! Her gaze passed balefully over her Cousin Matthew's heavy face, and he shifted his feet and looked away uneasily. Charity gave her head a toss and turned back confidently to face the magistrate.

The magistrate had noticed this digression of attention on the part of the accused. His frown deepened.

"Charity Woodstock," he began again, "you are found guilty of the crime of witchcraft and this Court hereby sentences you to be burned at the stake on Tuesday next at—"

Charity did not hear the rest. She paled but she did not flinch. She simply stared at the magistrate as if she could not believe she had heard him aright. Her knuckles, gripping the folds of her dirty skirt, whitened and for a moment she swayed. Then somebody in the crowd giggled and her back straightened. She turned and looked coldly around the courtroom as if she wished to remember all their faces. Composed, she turned and let the jailers lead her back toward the filthy jail from whence she had come.

The crowd followed her, goggling, irritated by the prisoner's cold manner, her defiant gaze.

A little party of horsemen stopped to let them pass. They went streaming across the muddy road, the jailers and the girl and those gawkers who followed them.

The tallest horseman, the one whose hands were tied firmly with rope, one end of which was fastened to the saddle of the man beside him, watched the scene with interest.

"Witch!" cried a ginger-haired woman hoarsely and threw a clod of mud at Charity. It spattered on her already dirty red dress. Charity turned and gave her attacker a look of contemptuous disdain. Enraged by that look, the woman stepped closer. "Be ye gone daft?" she hissed. "Quick, confess ye're a witch; admit ye lied when ye said yon poor boy raped ye!"

"I'll not confess I'm a witch!" cried Charity. "Nor did I lie when I said he raped me!"

"Then ye'll burn," cackled the woman evilly. "And myself will light the faggots!"

The old woman had stepped too close. Suddenly Charity lunged forward and grasped a handful of ginger hair and tugged. Her jailer gave her arm a rough jerk, but not before the ginger wig came away in her hands and a balding head of sparse gray hair appeared. Her tormentor screeched and ran, while the crowd roared its laughter.

A young boy who had been with the ginger-haired woman leaped forward, livid, fists balled, and Charity swept him away with a backhand blow that stretched him out on the ground. Ugly now, the crowd gathered around, and the jailer, looking uneasy, gave the slender girl a hard cuff on the side of the head that jerked her head back and made her wince.

"That do be too gentle a blow," bawled someone. "Cuff her ears again!"

Charity stiffened, expecting another blow, but none fell. Her jailer only muttered and gave her another jerk.

"I'd applaud you, m'lady," called a light-hearted voice, "but as you can see, my hands are tied!"

Charity turned toward this first friendly voice and saw, astride a dark horse, a man with hair of sandy color that cascaded down from a sweeping hat with a broken plume. His audacious smile split a handsome gold mustache and a well-trimmed Van Dyke beard. He sat easily in the saddle with a natural grace that came of strength and well-being, and his pale gray velvet coat was stained with claret and perhaps with blood.

They had only a moment to consider one another before Charity was hurried on.

"Faith, she's a beauty," he muttered as the crowd straggled across the path. "What's her crime?" he shouted after them.

"Witchcraft!" an excited young lad in buckled shoes

turned to shout back. "She'll burn on Tuesday next!"

"Will she now?" he murmured, and turned with a genial smile toward the big fellow whose saddle held the rope that bound him. "But they won't be burning me along with her, I take it?"

The big fellow nudged his horse with his heel.

"Thou wilt hang," he said expressionlessly. "Like all highwaymen."

The highwayman, whose name was Thomas Blade and who was known in the trade as Lucky Tom, shrugged. "We'll see," he murmured. "We'll see. Could be I'll cheat the hangman yet."

The big fellow snorted. "Not this time! This time we've got you dead to rights! You'll swing, all right."

They moved on, and ahead of them, Charity had already forgotten the highwayman in the nightmare of catcalls and thrown clods of earth that surrounded her. She heard a nasty laugh and a rip and felt the material of her bodice pull outwards. She closed her eyes and prayed they would not strip her here in the street, prayed she might reach the comparative safety of the jail fully clothed. Pelted and humiliated, she was jerked along, often stumbling in the mud of the street, sinking once to her knees only to be yanked up with a curse.

The fact that she was going to die didn't really sink in until she was back in her dirt-floored cell and the jailers had left her. She had been too occupied with facing down the cruel crowd. But once she was alone, she looked at the dank slimy walls hopelessly. She was only nineteen, alone in a strange land and convicted of a crime she did not even understand. Witchcraft! To be burned as a witch. She imagined herself raised high on a pole so that all could mock her, imagined the wood piled in a heap below her as they set about making the fire burn, imagined the searing orange flames rise up around her as the black smoke blotted out the sky.

It could not be true. It was a nightmare. She was going to wake up!

As she sat with her head in her hands, seeing her young life slipping away from her, she heard the noise of feet, clanking keys, excited voices.

"Tis said they've caught the highwayman," came an awed voice from a nearby cell. "They've caught Tom Blade at last!"

"He'll swing for sure," said another avid voice. "Think ye they'll bring him by this way so we'll get a look at him?"

"Nay, they be putting him next to that young witch," sighed the first speaker.

Charity looked up to see men peering in at her as they opened the neighboring cell. She straightened at once and lifted her head. They wouldn't see *her* cry!

After a lot of loud talk and coarse jokes and scuffling of feet the men left and a voice she remembered as the horseman's said, "Is that you next door, little witch?"

"I'm not a witch," snapped Charity, glaring at the wall between them.

He chuckled. "Spoken with spirit," he approved. "What's your name?"

Charity was silent.

"Come, come," he wheedled. "You may as well talk to me. Remember you won't have much of anything to say after next Tuesday."

She grimaced. What he said was true.

"Charity Woodstock," she said. "I'm from Devon."

"Ah, I thought I knew the sound of that voice. A Fair Maid of Devon . . . How long have you been in America, Charity?"

"About a fortnight."

He whistled. "A fine reception you've had then, being thrown in jail and branded a witch."

"You're in jail too," she reminded him tartly.

"Ah, but for crimes I committed. There's the difference."

"How," she asked curiously, "do you know I'm *not* a witch?"

He laughed. "Bewitching, yes—witch, no. I don't

39

believe in witches or ghouls or goblins, fair Charity."

"What are your crimes?" she challenged.

"Like Robin Hood, I rob the rich and feed the poor," he said in a bantering tone.

"And what will happen to you?" she asked.

"They say I'll hang," he said in a bored voice.

"It's better than burning," she said morosely.

There was a little silence.

"Yes," he said softly, "it's better than burning. . . ."

And once again Charity seemed to see the flames rise, to feel the heat, to smell her own flesh burning.

"Perhaps," he mused, "we'll live to dance a jig on all their graves."

It was too much, this note of unwarranted optimism. As his voice came around the wall and through the bars, Charity dropped her head on her hands and dry sobs wracked her body.

CHAPTER 2

Charity Woodstock had come a long way in the few months since she had left England bound for a new life in the Colonies. She had stood eagerly at the ship's rail and felt the strong wind blowing over the Atlantic, making her cheeks pink and her eyes sparkle. The voyage had been planned at school, where word had come to her of her Uncle Jason's death in America. A communication from a lawyer in Boston informed her that she was the sole recipient of her uncle's estate, and that it would be in order for her to journey across the water to claim the property, which was considerable.

Just how considerable it was, he had not informed her, but her mother had said that it was Uncle Jason's money that was keeping her in her fancy school.

Moll, her beautiful, tawny-haired mother, full of dreams. . . . Charity leaned pensively on the ship's rail, her feet resting on the swaying deck, with its planking of Norway pine, and remembered her mother, dead these twelve months.

"Stay in school, Charity," her mother had pleaded on her deathbed, her eyes fever-bright with the consumption that wracked her now emaciated body. "It's all paid for through the term. Soon, you'll be a fine finished young lady, as the countess promised me, and you'll end up marrying some titled lord."

Charity had nodded through her tears. A fine finished young lady she might become, but marrying a titled lord was far above her reach. Her foolish, ambitious mother, dreaming wild dreams, had never

41

understood that. Moll naively believed that the countess's expensive school would bring Charity everything other wealthier girls had.

It had brought her nothing but a surface polish and a deep unease about her future.

Snubbed at school, she'd never been able to bring herself to tell her mother that the "grand young ladies" receiving their education at Stéphanie's house in Bath didn't consider her their equal, that they looked down on her background. One of them, Margaret Yorking, had an aunt who wintered in Torquay (where they had moved after Increase's death) and the aunt had told *her* that Charity and her mother lived in a *hut!* There had been general titters all around when the girls learned that, and Charity, standing rooted in the doorway behind them, had flushed bright with shame. She realized that, by comparison with Margaret Yorking's turreted castle in Kent or Jane Millwood's vast manor house in Sussex, she did indeed live in a hut. Her mother called their home "Cheltenham House," which looked good on letters, but it was only a tiny house ablaze with flowers and warmth and love. What did it matter that she lived simply, she asked herself violently. Wasn't she as bright, as pretty, as well educated as her schoolmates?

So she held her head high and faced them down, ignoring the two truly wealthy girls who set the pace —and being in turn ignored by them.

But her true position in life was brought home to her most forcefully when her carefree roommate, Priscilla Walsingford, whose guardian was a country squire in Hampshire, invited her home for the Christmas holidays. Priscilla's brother, home on holiday from Oxford, fell head over heels in love with Charity in a happy puppy-dog way and asked her to marry him. His guardian had got wind of the proposal and the lad was promptly whisked back to Oxford. When they returned to Stéphanie's house in Bath, Charity had found herself with a new roommate.

It was all very well for Priscilla to laugh and gossip

with Charity, but not for her brother to consider marrying such a girl.

Charity fell back on the company of her new roommate, the school's other "outcast," a Spanish girl named Mercedes Ramirez, whose uncle was in the English court. Due to the bad relations between England and Spain, the uncle found his Spanish niece an embarrassment to him and had placed her with the obliging Countess Stéphanie de la Croix, to be educated.

Unhappy Mercedes, homesick for the sunny lands of Spain, insisted on speaking Spanish. Trying to think in this new language helped Charity forget the sting of condescension she must live with. So, she bent her efforts to learn the language under Mercedes' tutelage. Charity's Spanish became fluent, and she grew very fond of her. Mercedes would never be a beauty, for she was much too thin, her nose too sharply pointed, but her black hair coiled thick and lustrous, and her big eyes flashed darkly as she spoke with the controlled emotion that was so distinctively Castilian.

The two of them grew very close and Charity would have invited Mercedes to visit her in Torquay, but her mother rejected that. "Let those girls think you live in a palace," she said flatly.

Charity sighed. The girls at school already knew she didn't live in a palace.

But her mother mustn't know that, her sweet, foolish, doting mother, growing frailer day by day, dreaming happily of that good marriage that would never come to pass. . . .

Charity buried her mother and, as a memorial to her, forced herself to endure her last year of schooling.

She had no clear picture of what would happen to her after that. Too well educated to go into service; too pretty, she'd been told, to get a job as a governess; from too low a class to marry well . . . what did a young woman in her position do?

Stéphanie had delicately mentioned she might find a "protector," but Charity shrank from that, sincerely

43

believing such a course was wrong. She had been brought up to look forward to marriage, as had the other girls at Stéphanie's, and she felt she would somehow be letting her dead mother down if she accepted less. So Stéphanie had shrugged her delicate French shoulders and dropped the subject.

It was all solved for her by the letter from America informing her that Uncle Jason, whom she'd never met, had died in America and left her everything he owned.

Her path was clear. After Charity sold the house in Torquay and her mother's few small possessions, she returned briefly for a last consultation with her mentor, Stéphanie, whose advice centered mainly on clothes. Then she journeyed across the Salisbury Plain to Southampton and purchased passage on the good ship *Bonaventure,* a merchantman bound for Boston, stowing aboard two trunks full of stylish dresses that couldn't have been more unsuited to Puritan life in Massachusetts.

The *Bonaventure* was slow in leaving port. Charity chafed at the delay that kept her in the bustling port town and obliged her to spend most of the remainder of her little store of funds. Sometimes she went down to the docks, and standing amid the screaming seagulls, watched the men loading, their big muscles bulging as they stowed salted pork and beef and fish and bacon and boxes of cheese and biscuits into the hold of the sturdy oaken ship. Wine casks and hogsheads of fresh water and beer were snugly fitted in, and at the last minute fresh vegetables and fruits to ward off the dreaded scurvy. She was surprised to discover that, while food was to be severely rationed, there was a plentiful supply of beer for each adult. The sailors explained, eyeing her handsome young female body, its curves hardly to be hidden under her trim broadcloth dress, that beer would help ward off fatigue and make damp nights on the ocean more bearable.

At last the great day came and Charity, hardly able to suppress her excitement, boarded the ship.

She picked her way daintily through the live chickens and pigs and goats lashed down in crates on the piled-up deck, feeling pity for the sad frightened animals which would supplement the monotonous diet of biscuit and salt meat on the voyage.

She found herself squeezed with the other women and children into tiny cabins between decks. The men passengers shared a large common cabin. The forecastle housed the crew, while the ship's officers boasted tiny cabins on the quarterdeck.

Packed to the gunwales, the *Bonventure,* with her sister ship the *Archangel* (for it was considered safer to travel in pairs), sailed down the Solent River to the Channel. The two overloaded merchantmen, crowded with goods and people eager to try their luck in a new land, pointed their stubby prows toward America.

The voyage was rough. From the choppy Channel, the two tall ships sailed out into the broad sweep of the Atlantic. Life aboard was dismal. Rats scuttled about, running over people, nipping ears in the night, and there was always the overpowering stench of bilge. In good weather the passengers cooked at an open fire on deck, the smoke billowing up to sully the white sails, and in bad weather they ate cold food and lay about retching from seasickness. Charity spent all the time she could on deck breathing in the fresh salt air because the air below decks was so foul.

On deck she became a favorite with the seamen because she took their rough admiring glances and words in the spirit given. She enjoyed watching the crew play cards on the planking, between watches, though she kept her distance from their rough-and-tumble wrestling matches. They told her that she had "got her sea legs," which most of these lubbardly landlubbers had not, for passengers were sprawled out over the decks, hanging over the rail, seasick from the steady rocking-horse roll of the little ship.

Charity shared her crowded little cabin with a fat old woman going out to join her son in Boston, and a young pregnant wife who, with her husband—he slept in the common quarters with the other men—was going out to the Colonies in hopes of rising above the hand-to-mouth existence that had been theirs in Scotland and later as servants in England. The wife's name was Janet MacTavish; she was a grave, pleasant woman of medium height, who looked at Charity in surprise when she learned the girl was traveling alone and asked candidly in her soft Scots brogue, "Is it a husband you're looking for then, lass? Sure, there must have been men aplenty who would want such a face as yours to gaze at over their morning porridge."

When Charity explained she was going to Massachusetts to claim her inheritance, Janet looked impressed.

They grew friendly, exchanging confidences. Janet and her husband were fleeing religious persecution. They had had a terrible time in Scotland, and Charity seethed to think how this gentle creature had been subjected to public humiliation. In England they had nearly starved. Charity hoped Janet and her Ian would find happiness in the new world to which they were going. But when a round of fever swept the ship, the luckless Ian died of it. Charity grieved with Janet and felt almost as if she too had lost a husband.

"And what's to become of me? And of the bairn when it's born?" asked Janet bleakly, standing by the rail with the strong east wind blowing her much-mended dress (one of two she owned). "It's a strange land. I've no kin to take me. To be bound out is all that's left—that or the streets."

"That won't happen to you," said Charity quickly. "You're to come with me to Dynestown. My uncle's farm can support us all and your baby will grow rosy in the country."

"Woudst really do that, lass?" asked Janet wistfully. "And me no better than a stranger?"

"You're much better than a stranger," corrected Charity, squeezing Janet's hand encouragingly. "And I've still some limes left that I bought on the dock when we left. You're to eat some—we can't have

46

you getting sick, with a baby coming!"

Janet smiled gratefully through her tears, her heart too full to allow her to speak.

The long, slow journey began to seem endless. Charity stood with the other passengers, one day, and watched as a sailor was punished with the ferula, that flat stick that ship's officers used to discipline their crews. The man had made a bawdy remark to one of the women passengers and she had complained to the captain. The captain—a dour Cornishman—had decided to make an example of him. Charity felt sick as she saw the man slip, unconscious, to the deck.

When, a week later, a sailor, who had broken into a barrel of wine and was reeling from the effects, slipped up behind her and suddenly ran his hand up under her modish long skirts and pinched her bare bottom so hard that she cried out, she turned and slapped him in the face. He reeled drunkenly away, laughing, but she did not complain to the captain. A passenger who had witnessed the incident said indignantly that if she complained the sailor would doubtless be "keel-hauled." Charity turned away with a shudder. She had no desire to have a man dragged, cut and torn, around the sharp-toothed barnacled hull because of her.

After that she kept her distance from the dice games on deck and the lingering eyes of the crew. For as the days went by, the sailors had taken to watching hungrily when the women came up out of the foulness below for a breath of fresh sea air.

Though some passengers kept diaries recounting each detail of the voyage, Charity did not, but instead brooded on the new life that lay ahead of her in a raw new land.

She was sure she had done the right thing. Would she not now be a woman of property, able to determine her own future? And in England what would have become of her with nothing to recommend her except a knowledge of French and Spanish and good manners, and a handsome wardrobe. . . . She told herself stoutly that she would never have accepted

Stéphanie's hesitant suggestion of a protector, nor would she have allowed herself to be forced into marriage merely for security. But she might very well have been forced into service. And life as chambermaid, or at best a housekeeper, after living as a counterfeit young lady in Bath, would have been galling.

The Atlantic crossing was a voyage to test one's courage, for they endured not only two minor squalls, but a sudden violent storm that boiled up out of the south and threw them off course. How the gallant little wooden ship rocked and pitched in the gale, cresting enormous waves in violent gusts of rain that darkened the sky, sliding down into seemingly bottomless troughs of giant waves, heaving in heavy seas that crashed green and foaming over the deck. Penned down below, the passengers rode out the storm in darkness, to the accompaniment of crying children and low-voiced oaths and howls of pain as goods and heavy items of furniture careened about, causing many a bruise and at least one broken leg. Charity often braced her own body to protect Janet who was near her time. When leaks sprung and the women rallied to stuff the openings with bits of clothing, most of Charity's cherished petticoats and chemises went into the breach.

At the height of that storm, Janet went into labor. Charity assisted at the birth, grimly bracing Janet's straining body with her own, and muttering soothingly as the frightened midwife did what she could. In spite of their exhausting efforts, the baby died and Janet weakened and slumped back in Charity's arms. Shaken with sobs, Charity held Janet's frail body for a long time in the darkness before she knew for certain that her friend was dead.

There, weeping in the darkness of that plunging ship, Charity promised herself—as one might when waking from a nightmare—that in New England everything would be better, in Massachusetts everything would be all right.

CHAPTER 3

When the storm cleared away, the tired passengers who crowded up to the decks of the battered *Bonaventure* discovered that they were alone on an open ocean. Their sister ship the *Archangel* had foundered and sunk. They found but one exhausted survivor, lashed to a floating spar, who gasped out the terrible tale of the ship breaking up, of screaming women and children trapped in the cabins below, tales of heroism and tragedy.

The stunned passengers listened and knelt down on the decks and gave thanks for their own salvation. Miraculously, the *Bonaventure* had endured only some damage to the sails, a repairable number of leaks, and a cracked mast that had now been securely lashed together.

In a sad little ritual, which was very painful to Charity, the shrouded corpses of Janet and her baby were consigned to the deep amid muted sobs.

They sailed on.

Charity felt she had lived a full lifetime before a roar of joy and the cry of "Land! Land!" was heard aboard ship. She arrived on deck in a tumbling struggle with the other passengers to watch as the mysterious shores of Massachusetts stretched out before them.

The ship docked in bustling Boston harbor on a beautiful windswept day, while seabirds cried raucously as they swooped among the white billowing sails and over the busy crowds at the dockside. Charity, as excited as the other passengers, stared curiously at the jumble of buildings, the fields and woods and the distinctive triple peaks of the Tri-mountain. She disembarked amid a hail of farewells, and was able to find a cart and driver for hire at the dockside. She bought an apple and munched on it happily as the jogging cart, with her two trunks sitting in the back, took her through narrow winding streets to an inn. From there, she sent a message to the gentleman who had written to her about her inheritance.

The attorney came around later in the day, a big florid man dressed rather too conspicuously for a Puritan. When Charity greeted him in the inn's public room, he looked startled indeed to see her. Refreshed and dressed modishly in a sweeping dress of fine twilled sarcenet, deep green and trimmed in black ribbons, she was an appealing sight to behold.

"*You* are Mistress Woodstock?" he stammered.

Ignorant of Puritan ways, Charity mistakenly ascribed his surprise to her youth and, remembering her instruction in deportment at Bath, tried her best to charm him. This met with such success that his blue eyes took on a kind of glaze, and he took her out and gallantly showed her Boston. He informed her that much of the city had burned in 1679, but rebuilding was moving apace. He showed her Fort Hill, the South Battery, a remarkable Triangular Warehouse, each corner topped by three-story hexagonal towers topped by pyramids and further surmounted by stone balls. To cap their tour, he proudly pointed out handsome Province House, a dormered brick laid in English bond, its weather vane an Indian archer standing proudly atop an octagonal cupola.

Although she was interested in the guided tour, Charity was impatient and bursting with questions about Dynestown and the propery her uncle had left her.

A good farmhouse, she was told gravely, on small but productive acreage, lying somewhat outside the village of Dynestown, and now the residence of the widowed Goodwife Arden and her two children, Matthew and Patience.

Goodwife Arden? Ah, that would be Aunt Temperance, her father and Jason's widowed older sister who had lived with Jason as his pensioner. Matthew and Patience would be her children. Charity expressed her eagerness to know them and said she hoped they would like her.

The attorney bit his full lower lip and his eyes rested somberly again on her fashionable hairstyle (although Charity herself considered it quite plain and suitable only for travel) and her deep green sarcenet dress. He cleared his throat and told her in a dry voice that her relatives were country people, rather staid in their ways. Charity took note of that and determined to dress her hair even more plainly and to wear her simplest dress on arrival. She had no wish to appear to preen in the eyes of less fortunate relatives, and she desperately wanted them to like her.

He sighed when she admitted she had brought to America only her clothing and toilet articles, no plows or seeds or useful tools or items of immediate salability. Then looking down into her fresh face he suddenly bestirred himself and remembered that he had a wife who would scold him if he was late getting home. And, so, after promising Charity that he would find her a guide and packhorses to transport her and her goods to Dynestown, he took his leave.

Charity ate her dinner in the common room of the inn, savoring the baked codfish, the bread made of rye and Indian corn, and the numerous fresh vegetables—all most welcome after her dull shipboard fare. She spent her first night in months in a bed that did not rock and pitch beneath her and went to sleep planning the gifts she would give her relatives in Dynestown: for Cousin Patience, a lovely swatch of rose silk, for Cousin Matthew a length of russet woolen fabric, and for Aunt Temperance a large quantity of glossy black silk lutestring.

The ride to Dynestown was made on the back of a sorrel mare, following a laconic guide who bestrode a big gray horse. Two packhorses carrying her trunks labored along behind her. It seemed a daunting venture to Charity as they plunged into the trees that rose up like a green wall before them, picking their way along a narrow trail. Surprisingly, there was an inn or "ordinary" tucked into a bend of the trail at the end of their day's journey, which served a satisfying dinner of wild turkey and carrots, pumpkin bread and apple cider.

Her guide, Goodman Tolliver, a middle-aged man of grumpy appearance who by now, under the influence of large flagons of hard cider, had become quite friendly, opened his mouth as if to speak, closed it again, and then said suddenly, "Methinks you do dress dangerous, to be goin' where you do be goin'."

Flagon in hand, Charity puzzled over this. "How so?" she asked.

He nodded at the sober dark blue serge of her full-skirted dress, which she had worn against the rigors of riding side-saddle through brush and briars. "I'd be takin' off those ribbons afore we reach Dynestown," he said dryly.

Charity looked down at the dress's sole decoration, a gay little fringe of yellow ribbons trailing down the bodice, and stared at him. "Why?"

"They be puttin' women in the stocks for less," he said. "Last fall old Goody Bennington, and her all of seventy-six year, were put in the pillory for speakin' ill of her husband. And Mistress Phoebe Blackwood, and her not yet eighteen, was whipped twenty lashes for wearin' a red petticoat."

"How did they know it was red?" demanded Charity tensely.

"Mistress Phoebe tripped and fell in the churchyard," he said in a moody voice. "So then everybody knew." He took another great draught of cider.

Charity thought uneasily of her own petticoat, which was of a light-hearted yellow to match the ribbons on her dress—and which Goodman Tolliver undoubtedly had seen as she swung up onto the back of the sorrel mare.

"It be a fierce upright town, Dynestown," he mused. "Last December . . ." His voice trailed off.

"What happened last December?"

"Two Quakeresses walked naked up the church aisle."

"Naked?" asked Charity weakly.

"Stark naked. It was their way of sayin' the preachin' was nonsense and should be shucked off, y'see? I were there," he added with a sigh, "and what happened to them weren't pretty."

Charity swallowed, waiting.

"They let those women put on their petticoats, but kept them stripped to the waist, tied them to a cart's tail and walked them through the snow right out of the Colony. Eleven times they stopped the cart and gave them each ten lashes on their bare backs."

Charity shivered.

"You do well to say not too much, nor yet smile too much, if you would live in Dynestown," he reflected.

"But surely—" cried Charity.

"There's some as has been branded on the forehead, and others as has had their ears nailed to the pillory and then cut free—cut their ears off, that is. And many terrible whippings."

Charity no longer felt hungry. She pushed away her wooden plate and went off to her bed, which was in a loftlike upper room of the tiny inn. She did not think of gifts that night. A fear of the place she was going to had taken root and was growing.

Leaving at dawn the next morning, they once again plunged into the woods. Charity, who had removed the yellow ribbons from her dress and changed her yellow petticoat for a white one, noted the approval of her guide as she swung up on her mount. It sobered her as they rode through the dense forest. Twice they crossed water, fording it, the horses splashing through the shallows, slipping dangerously on the rocks.

The monotony of the ride, the jogging gait of her horse, made her brood about a dream she had had the night before. She had had the same dream many times in England, had dreamed it intermittently from the time she was twelve years old. It always brought blushes to her cheeks, for in that dream she stood stark naked in some strange place, her bright hair rioting about her white shoulders, her whole body trembling with desire—and walked into the arms of her lover.

As always, his face eluded her. Would he be dark or fair? Rich or poor? Would she find him easily, would she know him at once? Or would her search for him be long and difficult?

She only knew deep in her heart that some day, some wonderful day, she would live out that dream, and it would have beauty and meaning for her beyond anything she had ever known.

Her face softened, thinking of it.

Then her horse stumbled in some berry bushes and she got a long scratch on one arm. The lover-yet-to-be was forgotten as she came abruptly back to reality.

Looking about, she saw that they were approaching cultivated fields, and in silence they rode into the village of Dynestown.

They passed a handful of cottages made of wood with big chimneys and high sloping roofs and a few small windows with leaded panes that seemed somehow to peer after her as she passed. Several dogs wandered listlessly in the streets. Near the meeting house, a large and forbidding building, stood the stocks and the pillory.

There was no victim. Charity gave a sigh of relief. Goodman Tolliver might have been trying to scare her for reasons of his own; perhaps he had told her tall tales because he enjoyed seeing her look frightened.

When he turned and gave her a sardonic look, she wasn't so sure.

"This be Dynestown," he announced unnecessarily. "You'll be to Goodwife Arden's, which is t'other side of town."

After that pronouncement, he rode forward with Charity following.

She passed two women in sober Puritan dress, and smiled at them.

They did not smile back.

Charity rode on through the village, feeling rather forlorn. As she reached the end of it, she turned and looked back. Several people, both men and women, had come out of their houses and were staring after her.

She told herself uneasily it was because she was a stranger, and nudged her horse with her knee to move closer to her guide. She rode the rest of the way close beside him through the dappled sun and shade of the New England afternoon. He turned off after a bit and they plodded down a green country lane thickly shadowed by tall trees, and came at last to her inheritance: Uncle Jason's farm.

The house was a disappointment. Built of weathered wood and innocent of paint, its graying boards exposed to the weather, it loomed before her out of the trees. She took an instant dislike to its steeply slanted roof, its bulging overhang and tiny windows that peered down from the second floor.

As they entered the yard, aflap with running chickens and geese, a woman came out of the house. She was dressed in the plain garb of the Puritans, dark brown holland, full-skirted, with a white collar and cuffs and white cap. Her expression was noticeably dour.

Could *this* be Aunt Temperance, wondered Charity uneasily, hoping against hope that this was a maid-servant and Aunt Temperance would be a rosy-cheeked, bustling, kindly soul.

Her guide stopped his horse and said gravely,

"Good even', Goodwife Arden. I do be bringin' your niece from England."

Charity slid off her horse and her aunt stepped forward, eyes narrowing. She was a big woman, tall and spare, with turned-down mouth and pale smoldering eyes.

"You do not look to be from Cheltenham House," she muttered.

"Nevertheless I'm Charity Woodstock," said Charity, taken aback at her tone of welcome. "And you're Aunt Temperance?"

The woman nodded, her gaze sweeping critically over Charity's lissome young figure in the tight-bodiced dress. She compressed her lips, then turned to the driver.

"Wilt thou take a drink of cider, Goodman Tolliver?" she asked.

"Aye," he said, dismounting. "Twould ease my thirst some. But I must make it quick for I'm for Wyefield this night."

"And pray what's in Wyefield that you must hurry there so fast?" she asked, as the three of them—Charity feeling rather lost—went into the big kitchen where Aunt Temperance poured three flagons of cider.

Charity sipped hers gratefully, for she was hot and tired after the long ride. But she set her flagon down when Goodman Tolliver said grimly, "I'm to escort two Quakers to the border, tied to a cart end."

"Good riddance," said Aunt Temperance tersely. "Be they the ones that broke bottles in meeting there last Sabbath?"

"The same," he said heavily. "And now they'll be whipped to the border."

"Why did they break bottles?" wondered Charity.

"Why, 'twas to symbolize how hollow is our faith, so they said." He shrugged.

"They be the devil's brood," muttered Aunt Tempearance. "We'll be well shut of them."

When Goodman Tolliver had gone Charity felt

suddenly forlorn without him; he had at least tried to warn her what Dynestown was like.

Aunt Temperance, who was sparing of words, went to the door and called, "Matthew."

Cousin Matthew, a big bulky fellow with heavy features, strolled in, gazed at Charity with awe as he was introduced, and at Aunt Temperance's direction picked up the heaviest trunk. His big muscles did not even strain at the task as he carried it up the narrow wooden stairway to the second floor.

"Mother says she be puttin' you in my room," he said to Charity, who followed.

"But—where will you sleep?" wondered Charity.

He nodded down the hall. "The attic."

Charity protested, weakly. The house was a dark shivery place, for all its small size, and she would have been afraid to sleep in the attic end herself. "That's very nice of you, Matthew," she said gravely.

He grunted and went down for her other trunk, his heavy footsteps shaking the wooden stair.

After he had gone, leaving her to open her trunks and unpack, Charity sat down on the edge of the four-poster bed, which was the best article of furniture in the room. It had a hard lumpy mattress and a serviceable brown linen coverlet. A rude chest of sorts occupied one corner of the room, and a wooden straight chair. A little pine washstand held a bowl and a pitcher, and inside its door a chamber pot. Flimsy unbleached cotton curtains hung limply at the small window. No rug adorned the floor planks. Charity looked around her in dismay.

Was this the inheritance she had traveled so far to receive? This gloomy farmstead, peopled with her dour relatives, on the outskirts of a fanatical village that whipped young girls and put old ladies in the pillory?

With shaking hands she unpacked a few of her things and put them in the rude wooden chest—then in panic, grabbed them up again and replaced them in her trunk and closed it. She tried to find something suitable to wear to dinner, and settled at last

57

on a dove-gray satin with slashed sleeves that showed to advantage the frothy white lace of her chemise sleeves. Surely no one could object to *gray!* With feverish fingers she tore off the pink satin rosebuds that decorated the shoulders and skirt. There— completely plain! And elegant, as befitted her new position. Stéphanie had warned her that when she went to the New World she must at all costs keep up appearances. Now, wild laughter welled to Charity's lips at the thought. Appearances! Here in this savage place Stéphanie would probably be exe- cuted for the gorgeous, low-cut and diaphanous gowns she wore!

Her hair brushed and shining, Charity took a deep breath and, carrying the gifts she had brought, went down to dinner.

The family was ranged below stairs—ranged, she felt, against her—as she came down, and she could not know how sophisticated her gray satin dress seemed to them, or how evilly wicked her slashed sleeves.

Aunt Temperance stepped forward and cast a venomous look at Charity's sleeves. "Slashed sleeves be sinful," she declared. And peering further at the full froth of white lace chemise that issued fashion- ably from them, "Lace!" she cried as if she had dis- covered a viper hiding there.

Charity remembered again how, under Stéphanie's urging, she had sought to bring only the finest with her. She bit her lip. "I—have none without lace," she said, remembering how most of her lovely underthings had been torn to shreds in an attempt to staunch the leaking ship during the great storm.

"You have none without lace?" demanded Aunt Temperance incredulously and rolled her eyes to heaven.

"That's right," said Charity unhappily.

"Then thee will not go out of doors until more canst be made for thee," instructed Aunt Temperance se- verely. "Wouldst end up in the stocks!"

Charity blanched and looked nervously down at the offending lace that had seemed so lovely when

Stéphanie had touched it and said, "Ah, *ma chérie,* you will break all hearts when you wear this!"

"Well, no matter now, there's none to see you save ourselves," Aunt Temperance said, and abruptly introduced her to Cousin Patience, a pale, round-faced girl with dull brown hair pulled back severely under a cap. Patience, who also wore serviceable brown holland, stared at Charity with the same fixed attention one might give a snake.

Cousin Matthew continued to stare at her with his brooding gaze.

"What have you got there?" asked Aunt Temperance sharply.

"Why—gifts for you all," stammered Charity.

"Put them down," said Aunt Temperance in a more mollified tone. "After we've supped, we'll see them."

Somewhat nonplussed, Charity put down the three packages wrapped in tea paper and joined them at the narrow board in the kitchen. One of the two large downstairs rooms served as both dining room and kitchen, the other was a sitting room where presumably they would retire after dinner.

They were a long time saying grace, and Charity was quite hungry by the time she could sample her pigeon pie and brown bread and baked beans. She noted unhappily that the food was served on wooden trenchers with wooden spoons, although the flagons were of pewter. Plainly there was no great wealth here; possibly it had seemed more to the lawyer because the other dwellings in the village were so mean. It was wealth by Dynestown standards, perhaps, but it was not wealth to a girl who had lived in Stéphanie's home in Bath.

At dinner she learned that Cousin Patience had spent the day quilting at a neighboring farm. When Charity admitted that she had never "quilted," Patience looked at her as if she must be a liar.

"I saw no one in the stocks as I came through town," said Charity, still nervous from the ominous references to people being tied to cart ends.

59

"They will be there soon enough," said Aunt Temperance.

"What—what are their crimes?"

"Slothfulness, not keeping the Sabbath, wearing such clothes as are on thy back—such like."

"It seems—harsh," said Charity lamely.

All at the table looked at her, surprised.

"They do be receiving no more than their just due," frowned Aunt Temperance.

"I did tell Sally Fawkes today she would be in the pillory if she did wear the red petticoat she has been stitching in secret this past month," remarked Patience, with a spiteful look at Charity.

"You'll go no more to their farm then," said Aunt Temperance severely. "I did not know her to be about the devil's work."

Patience looked dismayed, then gazed meekly down at her plate.

After this exchange, conversation languished, and during the respite Charity studied Patience's clothing and asked herself if she could ever wear *that*. The draping of Patience's serviceable brown holland dress had, to Charity's eyes, a strangely old-fashioned look. She wore a corseted bodice over a too-thick waist, which was fastened with hooks down the center of the front. Her white chemise cuffs were folded sedately back over plain gathered sleeves. Over her shoulders flowed a shapeless white collar, and her thin mousy hair was tucked severely into a cap.

It was Charity's opinion that such trappings would ill serve Cousin Patience in getting a husband. As if she realized she was being scrutinized, Patience looked up and glared at her.

Charity turned to consider Cousin Matthew. He sat slightly hunched over, his mouth full of food, stolidly feeding. Perhaps, she told herself, Patience's clothes would not matter, for she might marry such a man as her brother. For him, a hard-working upright woman to do the chores and bear the children would be enough.

Suddenly, and quite inexplicably to Charity, her

aunt seemed to warm to her. Temperance began to ask her numerous probing questions about her life in Torquay. Most of Charity's answers were greeted with dismay by Patience, but were received stolidly by her aunt. Cheltenham House was mentioned more or less continually and Charity, remembering how modest it had been compared with Stéphanie's, found their reaction puzzling. She looked around her at their faces: her aunt's dour malevolent one, Patience's shocked round one, Matthew's big dull one.

"Why do you keep asking me about Cheltenham House?" she asked curiously. "I mean, Torquay was beautiful and we loved our house, but it was so tiny —only barely big enough to hold us. The countess's house in Bath that I told you about was much more interesting—a big place and old."

Her aunt and her cousins exchanged significant glances.

Dinner was finished almost in silence, and after the dishes were cleared away and everything cleaned up—Charity's offer to help was brusquely shrugged off—they retired to the sitting room. Patience led them, carrying a large candle, and they settled themselves on hard wooden chairs.

There Charity somewhat shakily presented her gifts.

Cousin Patience's hard young eyes softened, and she exclaimed with delight over her swatch of rose silk, but Aunt Temperance snatched it from her.

"D'ye wish to be put in the stocks?" she demanded grimly. To Charity's unhappy glance, she added, "Tis plain ye do not understand our customs or our ways. Tis plain ye've not been reared in them."

"I'm afraid not," admitted Charity. "You can dye the silk," she suggested eagerly.

"But ye seem not too wicked, despite your ignorance," continued Aunt Temperance. "This black silk can be of some use, and that russet wool and rose silk too, once they've been dyed more suitable colors."

Patience looked woebegone, eyeing the gleaming rose material.

"It would seem ye weren't in the plot," added Aunt Temperance, considering Charity thoughtfully. "But ye've been the devil's handmaiden nonetheless. He be using you for his own ends."

"Plot? Devil?" Charity stared at her, amazed.

Suddenly Aunt Temperance got up and moved to a large corner cupboard, opened the door and took out a bundle of letters tied with a piece of twine. Silently she thrust them into Charity's hands.

"When ye've read these and thought on them, we'll speak again," she said. "Do be takin' this candle up with you, to light you to bed and to read what's necessary."

Troubled and anxious, Charity read the letters by candlelight in her small uncomfortable room. They were a shock. They were in her mother's handwriting and had her mother's signature plainly on them, but she still could not believe what they said. They were a masterpiece of invention. In these letters Cheltenham House became a home for Puritan orphans in which they were instructed in the True Faith and set upon the True Path. Reading them, Charity noted that the names of the various "orphans" were the names of her former schoolmates at Stéphanie's establishment in Bath. Margaret Yorking would have been shocked to learn that her name had been appropriated for an "orphan" receiving instruction in the fictitious "orphanage" of Cheltenham House. How Jane Millwood would have howled with laughter to know her name was among those who had found "suitable posts" in the establishments of gentlefolk under Cheltenham House auspices! Each letter prettily thanked her dear brother-in-law Jason for his latest "contribution," which would, the writer added piously, be used for "the Lord's work."

This was what Aunt Temperance had meant when she spoke darkly of a "plot" and suggested that Charity might be innocent of it. Overcome with shame, Charity covered her face with her hands and thought of her mother, whose desire for the impossible had driven her to such extremes in her daughter's behalf. Wrong-headed her mother certainly had been—but oh, how much she must have loved her daughter to embark on a course that could have meant imprisonment and ruin!

Charity sighed to think she had offered poor Janet shelter here—here where she herself had no right to be! Her eyes filled with dismay. Somehow she must pay it all back. Somehow. But—her cheeks burned—her relatives knew all about this fraud now. Her aunt had wormed the information out of her as she sat unsuspecting at dinner. So, even if she did her best to make restitution—which of course meant giving up all claim to the property immediately—her mother's name would be sullied, and to Charity that seemed the worst of all.

That must not happen!

Her lips taut, she took the letters and burned them one by one, carefully, in the candle's flame, putting the charred remnants in the washbowl. Her mother's name would be protected, she would see to that!

Almost with relief, she told herself there was no longer any need to pussyfoot about. She was leaving here. She would turn over everything she had to them and somehow catch up with Goodman Tolliver and accompany him back to Boston. Perhaps she could even bring some comfort to those poor victims tied to the tail of the cart! But she would get back to civilization and somehow make her way to England. There she would find a way to make good the rest of the debt owed Uncle Jason and his rightful heirs. Even if it meant going into service.

Having decided that, she went peacefully to sleep on the hard mattress that, she was sure, must have given Matthew many a backache.

In the morning she dressed in a pretty dress of sprigged muslin, cut artfully low—after all, she was leaving, why should they care what she wore—and went downstairs with a firm step.

"I burned the letters," she announced, as she arrived in the big kitchen. "And—"

"I'd expected no better of you," cut in her aunt, who was in the act of serving breakfast, a big white ironstone pitcher in her hand.

Charity took a deep breath and disregarded that menacing tone.

"It's clear to me," she said, "that through my mother I've done you a great wrong and I intend to make it right."

Her aunt stared at her stolidly.

"I realize that Uncle Jason was unduly influenced—"

Her aunt cocked an eye. "D'you mean all those lies your mother writ to him?" she asked sarcastically.

Charity sighed. "I mean to forswear my inheritance, Aunt Temperance, and leave this place. I'll catch up with Mr. Tolliver—"

"No need to catch up. He comes back through here day after tomorrow."

"Then I'll wait for him and go back with him to Boston, and leave as soon as I can for England."

Her aunt's eyes gleamed. "It speaks decent of you that you be forswearin', but what of all the money Jason lent your mother? What of that?"

"I intend to sell my wardrobe in Boston and send you the money it brings. I've fifteen shillings in money which you can have on account." She laid the coins upon the table. "I've tallied up from the letters what's owing, and I—I'll find the rest somehow."

"Somehow!" cried her aunt. "By scandalous behavior is the only way you could be earnin' such a sum—and mark you, there'll be no niece of mine walkin' the streets or dallying in taverns!"

Charity stiffened. "I hardly think—"

"Sit down!" thundered her aunt.

Charity sat.

"Now look you, we've come to a decision," her aunt announced, nodding toward her silent son and daughter who sat regarding Charity with hard suspicious eyes. "Our decision be that you marry Matthew and get rid of those devil's rags you brought

64

with you—" she sniffed contemptuously, "and wear sober clothes like a decent woman and tuck your hair up under a cap—"

Charity found her voice. She said, astonished, "But I have no intention of marrying Cousin Matthew."

Her aunt banged the pitcher down on the table so hard a little of the milk splashed out. "It be not a question of your intentions! Your intentions don't signify! Tis a question of what's to be done! If you be seen in those clothes, they'll have you in the stocks for it."

Charity looked unhappily down at her sprigged muslin dress, which had seemed so correct for breakfast in the country.

"Since I'm going back to Boston it can hardly matter," she said bitterly. "Your horrible townsfolk don't assault strangers, do they?"

Aunt Temperance's head snapped back as if she'd been struck. *"Horrible townsfolk?"* she repeated stupidly, and cast a look at her son and daughter, who were gaping at this sacrilege.

"Well, what I think of them really doesn't matter," cried Charity, "since I'm leaving day after tomorrow!"

Her aunt considered her as if she were really seeing her as a person for the first time. "You be very young," she said at last. "Think you on what your life will be like if you leave here with no money and no place to go. Tis your own good luck Matthew's willing to marry you."

"I'm sure some girl will be very lucky to get Matthew," said Charity in an unsteady voice. "But I'm not that girl. I am leaving!"

Her aunt sneered. "You do be needing an older and wiser head to think for you."

She stomped out, leaving Charity to breakfast in the silent disapproving company of the rejected suitor and his angry sister.

At last, to break the uncomfortable silence, Charity asked Patience ironically if she had marriage plans, and the girl colored and compressed her lips. Matthew answered for her.

"Patience be promised to the new young preacher," he said. "When she leaves, Mother will be needing help with the chores."

So that was the reason Aunt Temperance wanted her to marry Matthew! To have a free servant!

Charity spent the day fuming, afraid to go to the village in any of the clothes she had brought with her lest the authorities promptly pounce on her and fasten her in the stocks. She knew she would count the hours until Goodman Tolliver came through and she could leave this miserable place. Meanwhile, she had one more night to get through.

CHAPTER 4

Charity awoke to see a shadow looming over her bed. As a scream rose in her throat, her Cousin Matthew's voice said, "Twon't do no good to scream."

She realized that he was wearing only a nightshirt.

"Get out!" she cried in fury. "This is *my* room, Matthew. Get out of here!"

"Aye, but now it be mine again," he said in a surly voice, moving as if to get into the bed.

Hastily, Charity leaped out of bed. If it came to a struggle between her and Cousin Matthew for possession of the room, there was no doubt who would lose. Matthew had the big bulging muscles of a farm boy who had spent his life working long hours in the fields.

"Then I will remove myself to the attic!" she cried. "But I can't imagine why you came bursting in here in the middle of the night. You could at least allow me to remove my things by daylight!"

Matthew reached out and took hold of her wrist. His grip was awfully strong. Charity tried unsuccessfully to wriggle away.

"Matthew," she panted. "Let go of me."

He let go.

She strode with as much dignity as she could muster toward the door. It resisted her. She shook the latch, not comprehending.

Behind her Matthew chuckled.

So he had locked it!

Charity swung around. "Give me the key this instant!" she cried.

He shrugged. "I have none," he said affably. "Twas Mother that locked it."

Charity stared at him in the half-dark, her mouth gaping. It couldn't be true! She turned to batter on the door. "Aunt Temperance, Aunt Temperance!" she cried.

"'Twas her decision that we become better acquainted," said Matthew, coming up behind her. "Since we be soon to marry, there be no harm. Not so sinful-like." He reached for her.

Charity whirled and struck him in the face. He hardly seemed to feel the blow. He surged forward, slamming her light body against the door, pinioning her so that she could not move. She could feel his heavy muscles flex, his straining thighs hardening against her.

"*Matthew!*" she screamed, clawing at his face.

"That be no way to treat your future husband," said Matthew heavily, grasping her arms. "Be ye daft? You must respect me and obey my will. Come to bed."

Charity tried to break loose as he dragged her to the big fourposter, moving along as easily as if he had no struggling burden, and plumped her down.

"Be ye not mindful, I'll be taking a paddle to you," he said matter-of-factly. "Hast ever done this before?"

"Of course not!" cried Charity in outrage. "What do you take me for?"

"Mother says you have a harlot's mind inside a virgin's body. She did peek inside your trunks. Red dresses and ruffles and plumes."

"Those clothes are fashionable," panted Charity, trying to beat him off. "*Ladies* wear them."

"*You,*" he said with calm logic, "be no lady. Will you take off that nightgown or must it be I tear it off you?"

"Matthew," pleaded Charity in rising panic, "get hold of yourself. This—this is punishable by law. You don't want to hang, do you?"

"None will know," he said in a surly voice, and with an angry gesture reached inside the neck of her gown and tore it straight down the center. Treacherously the moon came out just as the material ripped and Charity found herself lying in the moonlight, her body silvered by the light, her white breasts pink tipped, her stomach and hips and thighs naked and exposed under his gaze.

He whistled. "You do be marvelous pretty!"

With a sob she tried to scramble away from him, but one of his big hands caught her by an ankle and slid her bare back along the bed. Feeling the blanket rub across her buttocks, she lashed out at him with her fist. Both her hands were suddenly pinioned and held above her head as he looked down at her, his full-lipped mouth grinning broadly.

"This can be as easy or as hard as you like," he drawled, "but it do be goin' to end up just one way, so you make up your mind to it!"

He eased his heavy body down onto hers, sliding his nightshirt up and up until it was almost smothering her. She could feel his naked sweaty body pressed against her own shuddering slender form. As she tried to twist away, he said, "You be full of fight. That pleasures me!" His hands fastened on her breasts, squeezing savagely, and as she tried in revulsion to make a last great effort to break free, she felt a sudden sharp pain as his hardness entered her. She felt herself grow weak with pain and fear and a humiliation deeper than anything she had ever known.

The night became one long convulsive nightmare, with Cousin Matthew grunting and sweating above her, devouring her virginity, taking his fill. Charity managed to push his nightshirt from her face, and as she did she felt the wet streaks of tears on her cheeks.

Cousin Matthew, a lusty young bull in pursuit of a recalcitrant heifer, continued his labors until he was tired. Then he rolled off her.

Summoning her remaining strength, Charity eased herself out of bed and looked about for something to hit him with. Her hand seized a heavy pewter candlestick and she lifted it murderously.

Matthew, who seemed to have some sixth sense

about self-preservation, jumped up in time for the striking candlestick to miss him. His consternation was very evident. He had obviously considered that once "bedded" she would become docile and pliable. Now he found he had cornered a fighting wildcat not one whit tamed by his treatment.

He seized the candlestick and flung it away. "Mother," he yelled. "She did try to kill me!"

There were running footsteps outside. A key turned in the heavy lock and the door was flung open. Aunt Temperance stood in the doorway, looking enraged.

"He *raped* me!" Charity cried.

"Harlot!" hissed Aunt Temperance. "Standing there with no clothes on! Tellin' wild lies! You did lure that boy in here!" And as Charity opened her mouth to speak, "I bid you be silent! Come out of here, Matthew. This be no place for decent folk."

Dazed, Charity watched them go, heard the key turn again in the lock, and sank back against the bed, trembling. These people were mad! She must get out of here, she must escape. She ran to the window. It was not such a terrible drop. She hurried to the chair where she had left her clothes. It was bare.

Her trunks were gone too. All signs that she had occupied the room had been removed. Matthew with his great strength must have tiptoed in and carried everything out while she slept.

Well, she would leave in her torn nightgown then. She looked for it, but it too was missing. Matthew, she realized, had bent down just before he left. He must have scooped it up and taken it with him.

She sank down round-eyed upon the bed. She could not run out naked into the New England countryside. She was as much a prisoner here as if she were in a jail!

When morning came she wrapped a blanket around her and, pounding on the door called angrily, "Let me out! Let me out!"

Nobody came. She could smell breakfast porridge cooking downstairs and the aroma of hot bread, and

70

found she was remarkably hungry. Nobody brought her anything to eat.

They meant to starve her into submission, she thought grimly. Well, she'd see about that! She'd get out of here and she'd bring Cousin Matthew and his confederate, Aunt Temperance, to justice! She'd prefer charges! This was a civilized Colony under the English king. Rape of young ladies just wasn't countenanced!

She saw her chance when a man arrived on horseback. He looked like a parson, she thought, as indeed he turned out to be. *He'd* get her out of here!

She threw open the window and leaned out, not realizing in her excitement that the sheet had come open and her breasts were exposed.

"I'm Charity Woodstock!" she called down to the man on the horse. "I'm just over from England. I own this house and my Cousin Matthew has raped me and my aunt has locked me in my room. Send the constable at once!"

The rider gawked up at her as if he were seeing an apparition, his face reddening. Suddenly a woman darted from the house, with an apron flung over her head. Aunt Temperance.

"Oh, Pastor Williams," she cried. "Tis glad I be to see you. I be at my wits' end! There be my niece up there with no stitch of clothes on—get you back in!" she shrieked at Charity, waving her fists. "Can you not see you aren't decent?" She turned back to the preacher, wringing her hands. "She did come yesterday—and you should have seen the evil frumpery she was wearin'—and *worse* in her trunk, red dresses and satins and laces. And it were all a pack of lies about the orphanage; her mother was spendin' the money in evil ways. Pray come in, come in, do."

The preacher cast a last wild look upstairs at Charity's disheveled hair and distraught face—she had by now gathered the sheet around her—and shakily dismounted allowing himself to be led into the house.

Charity listened at the door. Downstairs she could

hear the murmur of voices, and then she could hear her aunt's words as she led the preacher upstairs to the attic. "Put her in here, I did, so she'd not influence Patience and Matthew with her evil ways. But down she came into Matthew's room *stark naked* last night. Jumped right into his bed, she did! And conjured him so's he can hardly talk."

Charity was white with fury.

"It's a lie!" she screamed, pounding on the door. "It's all a lie! Don't listen to her. Get the constable, get the magistrate, get *somebody* to rescue me from this place!

The door was unlocked and wrenched open so suddenly that Charity fell backward, tripping over her sheet and tumbling to the floor. The preacher, a vein pulsing in his forehead, his eyes bulging, stared at her long white legs as she struggled up and strove to cover her exposed breasts beneath the quickly snatched up sheet.

"What new mischief's this?" shrilled Aunt Temperance. "Do you look for whippin'?"

"How long be she like this?" he asked sternly.

"She did talk wildly at dinner last night," volunteered Cousin Patience with a spiteful look at Charity. Charity yearned to slap her face.

"This is *my* room," Charity said, finally getting the sheet back around her and struggling to her feet. "While I was sleeping they removed my things. Then Cousin Matthew came in and Aunt Temperance locked the door—I fought him, but he's very strong. He raped me, and I want it reported!"

The preacher looked at her with narrowed eyes.

"Calm yourself, Mistress Woodstock," he said. "There be no need to excite yourself or make wild accusations."

"You can see for yourself this room has Matthew's things in it. Hers be all in the attic," volunteered Aunt Temperance contemptuously. "She did come here into his room last night like I told you, and did crawl into his bed while he were asleep to tempt him."

72

"He *raped* me!" screamed Charity.

The preacher, who had just finished reading several impassioned works on witchcraft and was eager to find a case in his area, said sententiously, "Possessed. Possessed by the devil, if ever I did see such a case."

"That's right!" cried Aunt Temperance joyfully. "She be a witch, all right! And she's conjured up a spell on my poor boy!" She began to sob, watching him with bright eyes.

"It signifies," he said gravely. "Tis hard proof will be needed, however. Such evil as is centered in this woman could wreak havoc on us all. We must not countenance witches or demons in our midst. Of course—" he frowned—"if it should appear that her story be true, and the boy did rape her, it would make a very great difference, I am afraid."

"*I* did see her fly out of the window last night," cried Patience triumphantly. "She did change herself into a great bird and fly out on a poker!"

All were awed by this revelation.

"That is ridiculous," said Charity weakly. "I am no more a witch than you are. I came here to claim my inheritance from my uncle."

"That's another thing," cried Aunt Temperance, aggrieved. "She do intend to take this house from us! Where will we go?" She began to wail.

The preacher looked shocked. These three were his charges, members of his congregation—Charity was not. "What devil's trick be this, girl?" he demanded sternly.

"Go away," said Charity stonily. "Go away and send the law here. Let them deal with the situation. Or give me my clothes and let me go and fetch them."

"Send them I will," he said testily. "I will send them at once that they may see you in your present unstrung state and judge what black mischief you be about! Good-day to you, Goodwife Arden, Mistress Patience."

The door banged shut after they went out and

73

was again locked. In despair, Charity watched from the window as they had a long earnest conversation in the yard, which she could not hear, and then saw the preacher ride away.

She lay back down on the mattress but leaped up as the door was unlocked again and Matthew entered. Regarding him with fear and loathing as he approached the bed, she wrapped the sheet more tightly around her.

"No sense to act like that," he chided. "I did see you naked already. Now think on it, should we not come to terms?"

The law, she thought. The law was on the way here! Matthew was frightened! She had a momentary sense of triumph.

He reached out and caught her feet, slid her down toward him, ran his hands up and down her legs, feeling the soft flesh, as she tried to struggle away. "Your time be short," he warned. "They'll be here soon. But if you did agree to marry me right now, we could say you was took by a fit because we had a lovers' quarrel. Since Patience is promised to the preacher, he'd speak for you if we asked him—and maybe they'd let you go."

Let *her* go! *He* was the rapist! She struck at him in fury.

"When they come," he ruminated, "my intent be to save myself. I do be goin' to tell them that you said how Goodman Tolliver had you down by the river bank, and before that some sailors on the ship. And how I did try to fight you off but you overcame me—you witched me."

Her jaw dropped.

"They'll believe it," he said earnestly, "on account of you did come here wearing harlot's clothes and did talk so wild and crazy when the preacher was here. They'll believe you do be a witch, Charity."

Charity shivered. She had once seen a pillar of smoke from a nearby town and been told it was old Grandy Morreton being burned as a witch. . . . She

74

moistened her lips, her hatred for this pawing bully overcoming all other emotions.

"I'd rather burn as a witch than live with you!" she cried.

He let go of her as if her touch burned him. "I'll plead no more," he said in a surly voice. "'Tis your own life you throw away. You be the one that'll burn!" He went out, banging and locking the door behind him.

They came for her later in the day—the town elders and the magistrate. They gave due consideration to her "harlot's" wardrobe, her nudity beneath the sheet. They ripped off the sheet and, while she blushed red with embarrassment, searched her naked body for a "witch's mark." Finding none, they asked her endless questions. Finally, Aunt Temperance preferred charges against her and, to Charity's stunned astonishment, the men took her away, accused of the crime of witchcraft in New England.

Witchcraft!

Clad in her oldest dress (a red one, carefully chosen by Aunt Temperance and thrust at her so she could "leave decent"), she was taken to Dynestown and thrown into a cell. Aunt Temperance did not come to see her, nor did her cousins—which Charity accounted her one blessing. There was no doubt in her mind as to why they were doing this. For the inheritance. Judging her by what they would have done in her place, they had not really believed that she would forswear the inheritance. They intended to make sure, for if Charity were out of the way, they were next in line to inherit.

It put a grim light on her predicament.

CHAPTER 5

The trial was macabre.

Aunt Temperance testified that Charity had cruelly bewitched her son, and Cousin Patience added the "flying out on a poker" incident with embellishments. Cousin Matthew shyly admitted that Charity had "swarmed all over him in the night" while he "did try manful to fight her off" but she had "overcome him," adding under prodding the bits about Tolliver and the sailors. Her clothes were put in evidence and created a sensation. There was a great clacking of tongues as people peered at the contents of her trunks. But Charity grimly noted a certain wistfulness in the eyes of some of the younger women. Then a strange woman with wild eyes and a twitch came forward and testified shakily that her milch cow had gone dry the very night Patience had seen Charity fly out the window. The woman had looked out the window herself and seen a big bird fly across the moon, and the next morning the cow was dry. She insisted Charity must have put a curse on the cow.

Charity was speechless with indignation.

When she testified in her own defense, Charity found she was not allowed to say much, but she managed to get in the salient points, how her aunt had locked her in and her cousin had raped her.

She looked right at the magistrate as she said that, and thought she detected a sympathetic gleam in his eye. In that she was mistaken. It was purely a lascivious gleam. He was imagining what she would look like without the red dress, without her petticoats, without—he saw her nude, climbing into his bed. Bending over him with her blonde hair falling down, her nipples brushing his face. He hardly heard her testimony, so full was his mind of flashes of long shapely white legs and snowy breasts and rounded hips and a tempting parted mouth.

As silence pervaded the courtroom, the judge realized that she had finished and, startled, he ordered the court recessed.

Outside, he pondered that she must have bewitched him too. Something that must not happen to a magistrate. Burning was the best cure for that, he reasoned. A girl like this one with her challenging eyes and shocking ways would make desperate trouble in the community, turn neighbor against neighbor. His duty was clear.

So, sternly, he sentenced her to death.

To Charity it was all a nightmare. She waited to wake up.

* * *

In her cell, unable to eat the bit of tasteless gruel they had brought her, Charity finally drifted off to an exhausted sleep only to wake with a start at a small sound outside in the corridor. She tensed. The jailer had an evil face . . . Could that be him shuffling around outside her door?

She sat up, thoroughly awake now, and saw in the dimness a shape outside the bars of her cell. She opened her mouth, determined to scream loudly, but closed it as Tom Blade's voice murmured, "Shush, witch."

Was she dreaming it or was the door to her cell opening? She stood up uncertainly.

"Well, come on," he muttered. "Don't just stand there!"

And she stumbled through the door and into the corridor where he put a hand over her mouth and whispered in her ear, "Walk soft and we'll be out in no time!"

Clutching his hand, trying to still the mad beating of her heart, she tiptoed along the dark corridor, waited while he felt in his pocket for another key, turned it gingerly in the lock. Then they were out-side, breathing in the cool damp air of the summer night. She lifted her head; she had thought never to breathe the air as a free woman again. She turned to look questioningly at the man who had set her free.

He was beckoning, moving away like a shadow into the night, and she followed to where two horses were tied beneath a tree.

As she reached the tree a short broad fellow stepped out of the shadows and clapped a hand over Chari-ty's mouth, silencing her.

"She were going to scream," he grunted. And then, "Why'd you bring a wench, Tom? You know we've only got two horses!"

"We'll steal one for her then," said Tom.

The short man had inky black hair, a swarthy complexion and small black eyes. Taking his hand from Charity's mouth, he shook his head vehemently. "These farmers around here might not follow the likes of us," he said, "but they'd follow their horses clear down to Carolina!"

"She can ride with me," said Tom shortly, boost-ing Charity up to the saddle. "If I'd left her, they would have burned her as a witch."

"She'll be our death," muttered the other glumly, climbing aboard his own mount.

"Charity, this is Bart Symonds," Tom said. "If brib-ery hadn't worked, he was going to try to break me out."

Charity looked at them both with new respect. Plainly she was in the company of bold men. But her fastidious nature was repelled by the slovenly Bart; nor did she like the way he looked at her.

A moment later they were walking their horses over the soft sod, and moving quietly through the streets of the sleeping town. When they reached the last house there was a shout from a sentry who leaped up and fired a musket shot into the air.

"Ride!" cried her companion grimly to Bart, giving his horse's flank a whack, and they were off like the wind into the summer night.

Charity felt her hair blowing wildly, and her skirts billowing as she leaned forward, held onto the saddle only by Tom's arm. The men urged their horses on down the twisting lanes, and the hooves made a solid thumping sound on the rutted track.

Bart Symonds sped ahead of them, left the road and they followed, thundering through a moonlit meadow, across a cornfield and down a path that led through a clump of trees to a stream. They urged their mounts into the stream. The horses went reluctantly, picking their way carefully among the rocks, splashing water on Charity's torn red skirt.

After that their pace slowed to save their mounts' strength. Charity, perched on the saddle in front of Tom, swaying against him, could feel his hard thighs against her own. He held the reins lightly in one hand and kept the other around her slim waist. After a while he changed arms, and this time he placed his arm under her breasts so that their rounded softness bounced against his arm as they rode. Held so close against him like that, she had a strange feeling of warmth and security—and something else, a small tingling thrill she would not admit even to herself.

By morning Charity was reeling in the saddle, her blonde head drooping, a dead weight in Tom's arms. Finally, they pitched camp in a thick copse of greenery—which is to say they rolled off their horses, exhausted, and slept on the ground all day until the sun was low in the western sky.

"Time to go." Tom Blade tapped her on the shoulder and Charity sat up with a start. At first, she was unable to orient herself to the green leafy world around her, the damp earth under her torn dirty dress.

A little way from her, Bart Symonds was already mounted on his horse.

"The horses have been eating what grass they could find," Tom said. "And they've watered at the stream. I suggest you follow their example."

"In what? Eating grass?" Charity felt more able to face things today; her sense of humor had returned.

Bart frowned impatiently. Charity ignored him.

Tom laughed. "I see I've met my match," he said. "When you've had your fill of the water at the stream, we'd best get started. We've a long way to go before tomorrow morning. This isn't safe country for us—not yet."

She didn't ask where they were going. She didn't care. Away, that was all she cared about. Away from vile relatives and filthy jails and bigoted judges and derisive townsfolk. She dashed cold water over her face at the stream and rose up, still stiff from her unaccustomedly long ride.

That night they seemed to be riding in long slow curves. She guessed they were skirting little hamlets that had sentries who might be alert to challenge two men and a woman riding through the dark. Twice they crossed water, going downstream and out upon the opposite bank each time, and she guessed the men were considering that they might be tracked by dogs. It was a terrifying thought.

As the moon waned in the sky and a false dawn appeared, Tom reined in his horse and found them shelter in a cave behind a waterfall. Charity woke feeling painfully hungry. The jail fare had been terrible, but she had now been without any food for two days.

She staggered to her feet and looked around for Tom.

He was gone.

She ran from the cave and rushed out from behind the waterfall—and gasped as Bart appeared from nowhere and caught her arms, pinioning them to her sides.

"Don't go running out like that," he growled. "Look where you're going first."

"I was looking for Tom," she said. "Let go, you're hurting me."

His mouth curled in a nasty smile. His swarthy face was very close. "And if I don't let go," he said, "what will you do about it?"

"Let go of the lady, Bart," said Tom's voice. It had a cold ring to it.

Bart's hands dropped to his sides. He stepped aside and Charity saw that Tom was carrying some berries in his hat.

"Best I could find," he said briefly, proffering some to Charity. "But tomorrow we'll have us a feast."

Bart grunted. "We'd have had us a feast today if you hadn't been carrying double and slowed us down."

Charity hoped they would have a feast. She was certainly ready for one. Wearily, she dragged herself back onto the horse, and Tom swung up behind her as they started off through the gathering dusk. She was more aware than ever of Tom's sometimes tightening arm beneath her bouncing breasts. She wished fervently the material weren't so thin. She wished she weren't so aware of him, tingling at the touch of his lean thighs against her legs.

By morning the trio had reached a little out-of-the-way inn, which they studied from a distance and then approached quite openly. It was a small stone edifice with its chimney already smoking, telling the world the scullery maids were up and about.

"I've friends here," Tom said with a merry smile. "Here they know Tom Blade for his generosity—not for his misdeeds!"

He lifted her gallantly off the horse and, swaying against him, her eyelids heavy with fatigue, she followed him inside.

Only the innkeeper was in the public room as they arrived. His face lit in a broad grin as he saw Tom and Bart, and they nodded amiably in response.

"We'll be wanting two rooms," said Tom. "Food. Feed for our horses and currying—and the wench here'll be wanting a bath and a comb and to have her clothes washed and mended. Can you manage it?"

"Indeed I can," said the innkeeper, rubbing his hands together as if already they felt the jingling gold. "First room on your right upstairs, Mistress. Bath'll be right up."

Charity trudged up the stairs and opened the door on the right. It swung wide on a room that was small, clean, and had a tiny dormer window that overlooked the country road.

All she could see was the big comfortable-looking square bed that occupied most of the floor space. With stiff fingers she began unfastening her bodice, but whirled around as the door opened and a curious-eyed country girl struggled in with a wooden tub, which she set down in the middle of the floor.

"You can get in," she told Charity shyly. "I'll be back with the water. It's heating." She disappeared.

Charity dropped her clothes on the floor and sank down in the tub. In a little while the girl was back with a bucket of warm water which she poured over Charity, gave her a bar of rough homemade soap, and scuttled away for another bucket. By the time the second bucket of water had been poured over her fatigued shoulders, Charity felt a little better. She lavished soap on her eager body, rubbing away the jail filth and the dust of travel, and luxuriated in the warm water.

The girl returned with a large flagon of milk. "It's cold. It's been in the springhouse," she said. Charity thought she had never tasted anything so good. "There'll be breakfast later," the girl added.

She returned once again to pour another bucket of warm water over Charity to rinse her off, and to hand her a large linen towel and a comb. She picked up all of Charity's clothes from the floor and said, fingering the material of the dark red dress wistfully, "This'll look real pretty when it's washed and mended."

"I hope so," said Charity, smiling her thanks as she toweled herself. She wished that she had something more tangible to give the girl.

The door closed, the latch clicked, and Charity —the morning now well begun—combed out her long shimmering wet hair and sank with a sigh between the clean sheets of the big bed.

She came out of a deep pleasant sleep to feel something warm against her, a body. To feel hands gently stroking her breasts, sliding down her back and along the curve of her hips. She sighed happily and suddenly jerked awake, opening her mouth to scream.

Instantly a big warm hand was clapped over her mouth.

"You wouldn't be wanting to wake the whole inn, would you?" murmured Tom's lazy voice. "Not over a bit of lovemaking!"

Charity made inarticulate sounds against his hand and continued to struggle violently.

"In case you should decide to scream," muttered Tom, "I should tell you first that one of the king's men has just come into the inn; he's drinking ale with the landlord downstairs. It may be he's never heard of Charity Woodstock, the condemned witch who's just escaped, or then again maybe he has. He rode in from the north."

Charity stiffened in horror. If she screamed, if she attracted any attention, she might well be returned to Dynestown to burn!

Cautiously Tom took his hand away from her mouth, but retained his firm grip on her body.

"I thought you'd be sensible," he said.

Charity struggled grimly in silence.

With ease he turned her toward him and climbed on top of her. Charity looked up at him murderously, her eyes wild, her naked white breasts rising and falling with fear as she fought him.

Tom lifted his head and looked down at her, his long golden hair swinging down so that it lay along her cheek.

"Is rape the only thing you're used to, Charity?" he muttered with a frown. "Don't you ever give yourself fully to a man?"

Her teeth caught in her lower lip and she fought back a groan of rage, but he laughed and held her fast. His golden mustache tickled her face as his mouth closed over hers forcing her lips apart.

Her struggles increased as she felt his hand pry her legs apart, felt his tongue part her lips again insistently, felt his hands move leisurely. He held her arms

84

steady, as one hand slid down her back and caught one cheek of her writhing bottom, holding her still as he thrust deep but gently within her, probing, exploring.

It was different from that other time. She realized that at once and was startled. She was gasping as he took his mouth from hers, whispered soothingly into her ear. Against her will, she felt her body respond to that rhythmic pressure, felt her flesh burn and tingle as his hands caressed her. And then the banked fires within her own self burst loose and she was aflame against him, straining toward him, moaning, thrusting her breasts forward to flatten them against his chest, raising her hips wildly against his, panting with exertion, burning with desire.

When they had finished, she lay panting beside him, raging inwardly that her body could thus betray her, hating herself that she had responded so fully to him and that he had known it, had enjoyed it.

Finally, she said resentfully, "You were supposed to sleep in the other room with Bart! If I hadn't trusted you, I'd have locked my door!"

"You'd have had a hard time locking the door," he said, "since the inn has no keys. The keys were all lost long ago, the landlord tells me." He grinned. "Possibly so he can move about the rooms at night if he wishes, and make a fat purse leaner when he has a mind to. And anyway," he added, "Bart's got him a wench to warm his bed. She's from the kitchen. Mine's from the parlor." He chuckled.

He leaned on one elbow and studied her naked body, tracing little patterns with his hand across her stomach. Charity quivered.

"How could anyone think you a witch?" he murmured. "Except a beguiling one. Tell me, how did they happen to charge you with witchcraft?"

"My Cousin Matthew raped me," said Charity bitterly. "And Aunt Temperance, to cover up his crime and secure my inheritance charged me with witchcraft. At my trial, they all testified against me."

"I see." His fingers moved lower along her stom-

85

ach, gently stroking the triangle of gleaming pale gold hair that grew there. "So I take it I'm the second man in your life?"

She turned and looked him full in the face. "No," she said honestly, "you're the first. Matthew was an animal."

She thought he looked pleased.

"Well," he said. "Two people so made for each other should take advantage of it, don't you think?" And rolled over on her again so that she gasped at his sudden weight. She felt a flare of passion as his lips trailed down her throat and across her bosom to nestle in the valley between her breasts, then slowly, deliberately to climb those small soft hills and nuzzle their pink summits. Under his touch she felt desire racing along her body tinglingly, felt her arms open and her legs seem to spread themselves wide of their own volition, to allow him to enter her gently. She shivered in his arms, reaching a crescendo of passion that shook and surprised her.

With a sigh, Tom flung himself off her and fell asleep almost at once. She looked at his lean muscular shoulder, at his gleaming tawny gold hair that mingled with her own on the pillow, at his newly trimmed Van Dyke beard that gave him a devilish look, at the whole naked length of him that lay sprawled beside her, one buttock touching the soft curve of her hip as she lay on her back. She looked at him, troubled, and asked herself if what she felt was love?

Did she love Tom Blade that her body could respond so fiercely to his lovemaking?

CHAPTER 6

Exhausted, Charity slept deeply and woke ravenous and very troubled about the events of the night before. Tom was gone when she woke and she dressed hastily, nervously sure of what would happen if he came in and found her still lying in bed. Her dress, newly laundered, smelled sweet and clean and had been neatly mended.

She took a long time combing her hair. The very thought of last night, of how she had given herself to Tom with such abandon, made her blush. She frowned. Undoubtedly he had come to the wrong conclusions about her—a misconception that must be erased. She was not a tavern wench, his for a tumble. Last night he had taken an unfair advantage, but he must be made to understand that she was her own woman and did not belong to him or any man.

Of course, she had found as much delight in the warmth of his arms as he had found in hers but, for the moment, that was beside the point.

She must set matters straight.

Tossing aside the comb, she was about to go downstairs when the door opened and the little maid who had brought her her bath last night came in with a breakfast tray.

"There be king's men downstairs," she whispered. "Tom, he said to stay where you are."

And then Charity understood. This out-of-the-way inn was Tom's headquarters. Not only the landlord, but the help knew what he did for a living. She found that thought strangely relaxing and sat down to eat the large bowl of porridge and the venison on the pewter trencher.

"Have you known Tom long?" she asked the maid, who seemed determined to hover.

The girl shook her head. "He be not long in these parts," she said. "But," she dimpled, "he do be a fine gentleman!"

"Yes," said Charity with a sigh. "He is that—in his way."

His "way" was what occupied her mind right now, his way with women and especially with her. She sat there, remembering the naked length of him sprawled on the bed beside her, one arm flung carelessly across her quivering stomach.

"He said to tell you, when you'd finished eating, to slip down the back stairs, there's a path I'm to show you—so's you can meet him by the river."

Charity's heart quickened. By the river. Fighting against the impulse to jump up and go to him, she forced herself to chew slowly, drank a second flagon of milk in leisurely fashion and then, smoothing her skirts, she got up and followed her eager little guide downstairs and through a back door.

"That be the path." The little maid pointed into a thick grove of trees. "Just keep goin', the river be not so far."

The primrose path, thought Charity giddily, walking down a wildflower-sprinkled lane into deep shade between tall old trees that had been here before the first settlers landed.

She had her arguments all marshalled when she found herself standing on the grassy river bank, watching the cool sparkling water surge by, reflecting the blue of the sky. She sighed, feeling oddly disappointed. Tom wasn't there after all, there was some mistake.

There was a tiny sound behind her, a hand was clapped over her mouth and she was drawn backward to the ground to the sound of muffled laughter —Tom's laughter.

"I was lying in wait for my prey," he grinned as

he turned her over, gasping, and took his hand from her mouth. "And pretty prey she is!"

"I'm not your prey," said Charity firmly, striving for some dignity.

"Ah, now that's no tone to take with a man who stole away and let you sleep, lying there like Venus with your nipples sending out a challenge!"

"Tom," said Charity, trying to struggle up and failing, "this won't do. I mean, you have a misconception about me. I'm not the sort of girl who—"

He lifted his eyes to heaven. "Don't finish it," he groaned. "I have heard it before. You don't make love with every man you meet. Sure, it's glad I am to hear it! But don't insult me by suggesting I'm like 'every man you meet'. I'm not! I'm Tom Blade, a man of parts if I do say so." He grinned at her meaningfully. "At least, there've been wenches who've said so!"

"I mean, this can't go on," she protested, her breath coming faster, her mouth very close to his own. "Just because last night you got carried away—"

"Carried away, was I?" He pulled her over on top of him and looked up into her flushed face. "Sure, I wasn't the only one that was carried away!"

His hand slid down her back, finding where her buttocks parted through the thin material and casually moving about, making her squirm in his embrace. "Tell me I was the only one carried away!" he challenged as she tried unsuccessfully to pull away from him. She sputtered as he rolled her over so that she lay quiescent beside him for the moment. He began undoing her bodice.

She grasped his wrist. "That's what I mean," she said sternly. "That won't do, Tom!"

"Oh?" His eyes were blue and innocent. "What won't do? Is this what won't do?" Expertly he managed to undo the upper part of her bodice, gave the drawstring of her chemise a tug and gently freed one bare breast, examining it with interest. "Is this what you mean won't do?" He gave the bare nipple a caress that left her quivering.

"Tom!"

"Oh, but I must understand," he said earnestly, liberating her other breast from its restraint. "This *is* what you mean, isn't it?" He bent his tawny head and caressed that nipple with his tongue as he rolled the other one lightly between his fingers.

"Tom!" Moaning in spite of herself, she tried to push him away. "Tom, stop!"

"Ah, then there's more to understand? More that won't do?" He managed as he spoke to undo the rest of her bodice and lifting one of her arms, suddenly slid her dress off the other arm and down around her waist, and as suddenly pressed his lips against her stomach below her breasts and trailed his mouth down to her navel as she gasped and struggled, feeling little tingles of desire fan out from the pressure of his lips. He gave her a last squeeze and as she exhaled she felt her dress leave her other arm and in spite of all her protests and struggles, dress, petticoats and chemise slid down over her wriggling bare hips until she lay naked and panting on the grass.

"A lovely sight," he commended, eyes shining. "Now is *this* what we were talking about?" He tickled her stomach so that she involuntarily laughed. "Ah, that's the right attitude," he said gaily. "Be happy! Live!" And as she gasped from being tickled he suddenly entered her and she quivered as she felt his manhood plunging deep within her, softly tunneling. Weakness came over her and she stopped struggling and shivered in his arms, her own slender arms twining around him, stroking his neck, his hair, his back, murmuring brokenly against his chest.

When he had finished, he lay there beside her and for a time they were silent, listening to the soft murmur of the river drifting by, looking up at a patterned leafy roof above their heads. Then he stood up, arrow-straight in his nakedness, and swung back his tawny hair, his expression still roguish. She stirred languidly. From somewhere he produced a feather and leaning over, dragged it lightly across her lower stomach so that her muscles contracted with a gasp.

"Tom!" She sat up, laughing, as he continued to tickle her, grasping unsuccessfully for the feather—and then threw her arms convulsively around his knees so that he staggered and went over backwards into the river with a great splash.

She jumped up and, standing above him on the bank, saw him dive under and disappear. As she bent over and looked for him nervously, searching the green water, hoping he had not drowned or been pulled into some deep hole by the current, a hand snaked up out of the water, seized her ankle, and sent her flying from the bank into the stream, to land in the cold water with an equally loud splash.

Charity could swim. As the water closed over her head, she darted away from him, knifing through the water, and he pursued her, leaping after her like a trout. Grasping her around her naked waist, he pulled her underwater with him. They came up, gasping, near the bank, and Tom looked into her wet-lashed eyes and said solemnly, "D'you think it's possible to make love under water?"

And at Charity's squealing "No!" he seized her slippery arm and glided her smooth wet body toward him.

"We must try," he said chidingly. "How else will we know what's possible?"

He thrust his bare leg between hers, but the water made her light and she floated away from him. He tried again, but Charity tore free and swam rapidly away. He came after her with strong strokes, catching her by a flailing foot and almost drowning her. She came up gasping, her hair hanging in long wet mermaid streamers down her back, and splashed water in his face.

He pounced on her but the water was too much for him. The more he strove, the more he was kept from entering her, and at last, laughing, he let her go and they swam companionably back to shore to dry themselves in the summer air. They lay wet and exhausted on the grass for a while.

When they were dry, their bodies warm and

toasting in the sun, and only her long pale hair wet, still falling in long gleaming gold ribbons about her, he turned and held her more tenderly in his arms and made love to her slowly, gently.

Charity felt a warmth that was not the sun's creeping over her, singing through all her veins. She responded to him wildly, so that even he was surprised, and afterward she lay trembling, hardly daring to look at him.

When she did turn and look, he had his clothes on and was considering her soberly.

"You're too much woman, Charity," he said. "I don't deserve you."

With that cryptic remark, he seemed about to leave, so, she sprang up and dressed hastily. Together they walked back to the inn, holding hands, swinging their arms together, Tom stooping occasionally to pick a wildflower to put in her coiled wet hair.

Neither of them saw Bart scowling at them from the bushes, his hot eyes running the length of Charity's softly rounded figure.

Life was idyllic at the inn. The weather was lovely —warm days, cool nights. Light breezes ruffled the leaves that were changing from green to brilliant yellow and red and gold, and brought them rustling down. The days were clear but the horizon was dulled by a gentle, blue-gray haze, which Tom told her was called "Indian Summer."

Tom never mentioned marriage, and she never asked him if he were already married. She was too afraid of the answer he might give her, for she had found a streak of frankness in his wild nature, an honesty that sometimes surprised her.

As they ate their meals—wild turkey or venison or squirrel or fresh fish from the river—she smiled on him gently. He was her lover and she loved him. She no longer fought him when he made love to her, but responded as passionately as he could have wished.

In its way, it was a honeymoon, but it was to end abruptly.

CHAPTER 7

One day Charity, about to enter the common room of the inn, heard a conversation not meant for her ears. After the first words, she stopped tensely and listened.

"Guess who's back," said Bart grimly. "Gert. I seen her strollin' by. And I hear tell she's had a baby."

"Yours or mine?" asked Tom, concerned.

"Hers. Seems she's taken a dislike to men, consigned them all to the devil—especially us."

"She has her reasons," sighed Tom. "We should do something to help her."

"Why?" demanded Bart truculently. "Weren't there plenty of country lads around these parts that laid with her as well as us?"

"True, but you can never be sure," murmured Tom. "I've a few gold pieces to spare. How about you?"

With a surly look, Bart parted with a couple and Tom added them to a store in a small leather pouch. "I'll give this to the landlord for Gert," he said. "She's his kin. It'll reach her sure."

He got up, presumably to find the landlord, and Charity—realizing they hadn't seen her—slunk away, her heart beating double-time.

Yours or mine? he had said about Gert's baby. Who was Gert? By cautious questioning of the little maid who served her, she learned that Gert was a chambermaid of a sulky disposition, who had left her job at the inn abruptly when she found she was pregnant. She had, presumably, gone to stay with her

93

brother in Rhode Island. People said Gert was back, added the little maid, but Gert hadn't applied for her old job, which had been taken by a new girl.

Charity yearned to inquire further, but held her tongue. There were, she told herself, undoubtedly numerous "Gerts" in Tom's reckless life. He could hardly be considered monkish in his habits.

The next day Bart spoke openly before Charity. He stomped into their bedroom with only a cursory knock. Charity was sitting on the bed, sewing a button on Tom's battered velvet coat, while he stood, legs wide apart, in breeches and shirt, watching her with a broad smile on his face.

Charity looked up to see Bart's angry, blackbearded face glaring at them.

"She's gone," announced Bart savagely.

"Who's gone?" murmured Tom, his gaze on Charity's soft mouth.

"Gert's gone, that's who! I think we should get out of here. She knows you've got a new wench—she may be turnin' us in to the redcoats!"

"Nonsense," shrugged Tom. "I gave that money to the landlord for her. Since she wouldn't speak to me, it was the only way. She's probably out spending it at the next town for the things she needs."

"Not if you'd seen the daggered look she gave me as she was leavin'," said Bart.

"She'll be back in a day or two," predicted Tom idly. "Let's rest awhile. We work too much, Bart— that's how we got caught last time."

Bart shook his head, giving Charity a look of suppressed anger, and stalked out, slamming the door.

"Perhaps he's right," said Charity uneasily. "Perhaps we should leave. We're still in Massachusetts."

"In a day or two." Tom lay down on the bed and rolled over on his back and considered the ceiling. "Let's have another day or two of contemplation."

"Contemplation!"

"Why, yes. I want to contemplate your breasts, your thighs, your changeable disposition toward me," he said lazily. "I want to find your heart, Charity. Is this where it is?"

He moved a hand impudently up her skirts.

She slapped his hand away. "I'll not give my heart to a highwayman who may be hanged any morning!" she declared tartly.

"Ah, but that's unfair," he protested. "Anyway, I'm seldom a highwayman. Tis just a name that they give me. Bart and I mainly hijack boats, and any road work we do is just lightening the load of gold of those who're about to get back on those boats!"

"That's an odd profession," she said. "So odd that I doubt I'm hearing you right."

"You're hearing me aright, Charity. Truth is, pirate vessels put in near shore all along these coasts, and your high and mighty saintly-minded citizenry are eager to buy their goods—knowing full well they're come by in no good manner. So men in little boats slip out to the ships, or else the ships send boats ashore to be met by carts and wagons and pack horses. And it's those I steal from—the stealers themselves. That's why they're so hot to get me," he added. "Because I'm disturbing the balance of a community that's too hypocritical to admit how it lives!"

"They'll hang you high one day," she prophesied gloomily.

"Aye, that's what my mother always said," he grinned. "But it's not happened yet and maybe not for a long time to come!" He drew her to him, his mustache tickling her cheek. "You've given me a taste for witches, Charity. Could be I'd die of it."

"At least you won't die without buttons on your coat," she said sensibly, handing the garment back to him and getting up. "I must return this needle and thread to that new maid—what's her name?"

"Tess," said Tom immediately.

"That's the one, the tall redhead." She stretched and yawned. "I'm sleepy. Would you return them for me?"

He gave her a sweet smile. "Gladly, m'dear. Get

95

your beauty sleep so you'll be ready to romp later!"

She lay down on the bed and her eyes had a tender light as she watched him go, his shoulders swinging jauntily. Reckless Tom could be very gallant.

The tall redhead of whom they had spoken was named Tess and she was a voluptuous country girl at the height of her looks. A saucy seventeen with a ripe figure, she wore her thick red hair plaited atop her head and her green eyes challenged every man who looked at her. Charity had paid very little attention to Tess, realizing perhaps that the girl would rather hear a single sigh from any man than a long dissertation from her.

But two days later Tess was brought to her attention rather emphatically.

Not finding Tom inside the inn, Charity started outdoors to look for him when Bart's big form blocked her way.

"I'd be stayin' inside," he drawled with a nasty smile. "Might rain any time and you'd get wet."

Charity cast a quick look through the window at the cloudless autumn sky. She liked neither Bart's expression nor his tone. "Get out of the way, Bart, and let me pass," she said impatiently. "I'm looking for Tom."

He shrugged and stepped aside. "Could be you'll find him, and maybe it's best you do at that."

She ignored that mysterious remark and went outside. She was about to make her way to the river when a giggle from the barn attracted her attention.

She made her way carefully around the corner of the barn and peered in. At first she could see nothing because of the sun's glare in her eyes as she looked into the dark interior, but then she could see very well indeed.

Comfortably ensconced in the hay, their bare legs intimately entwined, were Tom and Tess. Tess' red hair was in disarray, her green eyes sparkling, her skirts up around her neck. Tess bounced about delightedly, giggling. as Tom, wearing only his shirt, strove manfully to stay on board this heaving vessel.

Charity's world rocked. She staggered and a sound almost like a moan escaped her.

Tom and Tess!

At the sound, Tom turned his head alertly and a look of sharp concern wiped the pleasure from his face. Tess gaped up at Charity, her cheeks crimsoned, and she made a futile effort to pull her skirts down over her long white body.

"Charity!" cried Tom, a stricken sound.

But Charity had whirled, white-faced, and was running blindly toward the river. The sight of them entwined would be forever emblazoned on her memory. She careened down the path sobbing, branches whipping her face, vines catching at her ankles, and collapsed on the river bank, crying her heart out.

She had thought him hers—her own true lover—and he had betrayed her with a mere chambermaid. Her Tom!

She didn't know just when she became aware that there was a pair of boots planted one on either side of her tear-stained face.

She looked up slowly and saw Bart smiling down at her in sardonic amusement. "Saw too much, didn't you?" he said. "Can't say I didn't warn you, wench. Now how's about giving old Bart his just reward for that?"

He reached down for her and Charity shrank back, but he was too quick for her and his big fingers closed down on her shoulder, biting into the flesh so that she winced. He dragged her to her feet, pulling her toward him roughly so that her quivering body slammed into his hard barrel-like chest.

"Now don't pretend you don't like old Bart!" he said wheedlingly.

"Let me alone!" cried Charity, beating against him, her voice rising to a shriek.

"Bart!" It was Tom's voice, with a dangerous note in it. "Let her alone. She's my girl."

"I'm *not* your girl!" shouted Charity, jerking away

from Bart's suddenly relaxed grip so violently that she stumbled and almost fell into the river. "I don't ever want to see you again!"

"Well, that's for now," said Tom laconically, his level gaze on the man beside her. "Bart," he said more softly. "Time to go. . . ."

With an angry look at them both, Bart departed, muttering.

"And time for me to go too!" cried Charity, stomping off down the path after Bart.

Tom caught her arm.

"Go back to Tess!" she cried violently, trying to shake him off. "She's waiting for you!"

Tom kept his grip on her. "No, wait till Bart's gone," he said softly. "No need to put more temptation than necessary in a man's path."

She shook free at last and stood trembling, hating for him to touch her, refusing to look at him, glaring steadfastly in the other direction.

"It's time we all go," he sighed. "Bart's right, we've tarried here too long. It's dangerous staying too long in one place in our profession."

"Damn your profession!" said Charity through clenched teeth. "You'll not add me to your harem again!"

Tom sighed. "I'm only human, Charity, and a ripe wench is a ripe wench. Maybe," he added sadly, "I'm too human. It's a failing of mine. But twas only a moment's diversion, while *you*. . . ." His expression spoke volumes.

She didn't deign to notice it. "Words will not move me," she said in an icy tone. "I'm leaving."

"Now that I can't allow," he said, and a steely note crept into his voice. "You're still in Massachusetts where you're a wanted woman. I mean to take you out of the Colony."

She turned and stared at him, breast heaving, eyes blazing.

"If I have to tie you up to do it," he added gently.

She burst into angry tears and ran ahead of him to

98

the inn, meaning to get a horse and ride away in some direction, any direction.

But Bart, obviously guessing her intent, stood squarely before the stable door.

"Time we depart," Tom called to him jauntily. "Let's eat hearty and take victuals and a bit of brew and be off!"

Bart, who was looking sour, brightened. "Good," he cried. "Let's be off now before we swing from a gibbet!"

Tom caught hold of Charity's arm, lightly but with a grip she could not shake off. "Now act pleasant," he muttered. "Don't shame me before my friends."

She wanted to bite him.

They ate—Charity hardly touching the succulent roast duck on her trencher in spite of Tom's urging —and were off, well provisioned, and this time riding three horses instead of two. They headed into the wilds toward Rhode Island.

After an hour or two of riding with Tom in the lead, Charity following and Bart bringing up the rear, Bart called, "Ho there, Tom, where d'ye mean to stay the night?"

"I thought we'd camp out until we reach the Connecticut coast," called Tom, "in case anyone *is* following. I'd have been happier if Gert had come back."

Another of his women! Charity sniffed audibly.

"Good thought," sang out Bart. "There's a good spring a couple of hours up ahead."

And ahead they plodded through the autumn woods, the brilliant vermilion red of the scarlet maples, the bright gold of the black-boled sugar maples, highlighting their path through the more somber oaks and elms.

When they made camp in a grove of birches by a fast-running stream, Charity broke her silence to ask rebelliously, "Why Connecticut? Aren't you wanted there too?"

"Right," said Tom with a smiling shadowed look at her. "But you aren't."

She bit her lip and gave him a black look. He needn't try to win his way back into her favor! She wrapped a blanket around her and rolled herself into an angry ball and went to sleep, intending to turn herself into a porcupine, all teeth and claws and spikes, if anyone so much as touched her.

The second night she took the meat knife, theatrically, to bed with her.

Tom gave Bart a droll look but said nothing. Bart glowered at her. Charity returned the glare.

She awoke feeling stiff, and as the morning mists cleared, she felt a great indignation rise up inside her. She was tired of riding, tired of hardships. She had had time to consider Tom's behavior carefully as she rode along this weary trail with his back ever before her, and the more she thought about it, the more she seethed inwardly.

Treacherous! He had taken her against her will, he had made her respond to him, he had let her fall in love with him—and then he had promptly discarded her for the nearest chambermaid in the nearest haymow! Damn him! He had girls everywhere! He didn't even know if Gert's baby was his—and now this new wench, this Tess! And he dared to act casual as if nothing had happened! Dragging her through this endless forest against her will on the pretext that he was saving her from the Massachusetts authorities. Why, they'd arrest her in Connecticut if she was found with him. And probably hang her alongside him for keeping bad company, even if they didn't know about her conviction for witchcraft.

That night she had a hard time sleeping, rolling and tossing in the Indian blanket Tom had given her. The next day with brooding eyes she studied his jaunty back as he rode ahead of her through a colorful stand of young maples. He was waiting for her to simmer down, she knew, and one fine night she'd wake up to find him inside her blanket with her, taking her at his leisure.

The worse part of that was that she wasn't sure what her own reaction would be. Her body had betrayed her with him before; she would die of shame if it betrayed her again.

Oh, to be free of him!

Her chance came a few minutes later when they came to a fork in the trail and Tom unhesitatingly took the path to the left. On a sudden impulse, Charity slapped her horse's flank and thundered down the path to the right. Bart yelled and Tom turned his horse. Instantly both men rode after her. Bart caught up with her first, where she had got her horse tangled in heavy brambles. The horse thrashed about, trying to free himself. Quickly both men dismounted and cut away the brambles, but her horse trembled from the deep thorn scratches and Charity's own dress was torn down her back; long scratches had drawn blood from her arms and half-naked torso.

She was sobbing when Tom turned her horse around.

"If you try that again, so help me God, I'll shoot you," said Bart viciously. "I'm damned if I'll have the Indians turned loose on us to please a tempery woman!"

"He means," explained Tom gently, "that the trail you were taking leads straight to an Indian village—and sometimes they aren't so friendly. We'd like to keep our scalps."

"What about my dress?" cried Charity forlornly, picking at bits of the ripped bodice. "It's torn to the waist!" She hugged her arms about her.

Tom sighed. "Here. Take my coat." He stripped off the gray velvet coat on which she had so lovingly sewn the buttons in happier days, and proffered it to her. She took it reluctantly. It had the very feel of Tom. When she slid her slender arms into those too-long sleeves, when the coat's material touched her breasts, she could feel again the touch of his hands caressing her, and with the velvet coat wrapped round her she almost felt his strong arms were embracing her. Angry with herself for thinking such thoughts, she buttoned the coat around her until her nakedness was hidden from their eyes.

101

Two hours later where the trail forked in a boggy place around a giant willow, Tom again chose the left fork.

"Hell's bells!" exploded Bart, behind them. "You aren't goin' where I think you're goin', are you?"

Tom nodded, but Bart subsided, grumbling. Miserable, Charity didn't care where they were going. Riding through the green and gold and scarlet walls of this endless forest, it had occurred to her that she was a woman with no future. Tom pretended to love her now but—he loved all women equally, it seemed. She would soon be supplanted by any likely wench. And then these highwaymen would shuck her off somewhere, and she would have nothing. She couldn't even return to Massachusetts to get her clothes without a lot of fanatics setting upon her and burning her. She had no money to return to England, and her talents were even more useless here than they had been in England. If only she were a seamstress, or a good cook, she might hope to find employment. But she was neither. Her knowledge of French and Spanish and elegant manners seemed ludicrous and out of place in this vast wilderness stretching endlessly before her.

Once, as they rode through a grove of swaying poplars, a flight of geese came over that darkened the sky and they stopped in awe to watch them. Everywhere around them there was game, some too unaccustomed to the sight of man to be afraid. Deer were everywhere, squirrels watched brightly from the trees, rabbits scurried out from under the horses' hooves. They saw turkey and opossum and badgers—and twice they turned aside for skunks.

"Great country for trappers," muttered Bart behind her, and Charity shuddered, thinking of the small trapped furry things, dying slowly, so slowly. She had heard in Boston of the vast number of pelts that were being taken, the fortunes that were being made.

She watched the two men as they stopped at a rocky stream to water the horses. Bart was a hateful sort of person, dour and menacing. And Tom, she told herself bitterly, was worse. Insidious. Two-faced. Treacherous—at least where women were concerned.

Imagine being married to Tom Blade! (And she had just very briefly imagined this.) Why, you'd never be sure he wasn't bedding half the neighborhood! She kicked a lichened rock viciously, and winced as she hurt her toe, bent over and massaged it mournfully.

She'd hardly noticed that Tom and Bart were quarreling.

"But we aren't known there," insisted Tom.

"How can you be so sure?" demanded Bart.

Tom shrugged. "It's a chance we take."

Bart spat. "For the girl," he said bitterly.

"If you like." Tom's face grew cold. "Want a drink of water, Charity? Last chance for a while."

She shook her head, not deigning to speak to him.

She was astonished when, soon after dark, they came to a little clearing in a tall stand of pines and there stood a small inn. Overhead a little screech owl gave its wild plaintive call.

"But—isn't this still Rhode Island?" she demanded.

"It is."

"I thought you said we'd camp out until we reached Connecticut?"

"So I did. I've changed my mind." He flashed a smile at her. "Now let me do the talking. They don't know us here."

Charity was silent as a sleepy innkeeper heard a loquacious Tom say that Bart was his brother "lately from New York" and Charity his "bride from Virginia"; they were heading north, he added gratuitously. Going to try living in Massachusetts.

"You won't like it there," the innkeeper told him sourly. "They're a bigoted lot. I lived among 'em myself. Lucky to escape with my hide."

Tom looked as if he'd like to agree with him, said, "Ah, well, we'll think on it. My wife's tired. Right now she'd like a good bed, but it's a bit of ale my brother and I'll be needing."

The landlord led the way up the small narrow stair.

103

There were two rooms. Bart took one, Charity and Tom the other.

As the door closed and Tom set down the candle the innkeeper had given him, Charity turned to face him rebelliously.

"Ah," he smiled, "tonight we sleep in a bed."

"Two separate beds," she said coldly. "You can sleep in Bart's room."

He gave her a surprised look. "And how would that look when I've just told the innkeeper we're man and wife?"

"I'll—sleep on the floor," she said hurriedly.

He looked astonished. "When there's a bed in the room? No, I can't allow that. Go on. In with you!" He gave her bottom a smack and herded her fully dressed toward the big feather bed. When she hesitated, he swooped down and swung her up and dropped her into the middle of it where she sank almost smothered by the feather mattress.

She tried to struggle up from the soft enveloping expanse of ticking.

"Take a nap," he advised. "Bart and I'll have a drink with the landlord, and I'll try to find you a dress."

To her amazement, she heard the latch click, and he was gone.

She considered jumping up and trying to run off, but her general state of exhaustion caused her to fall back. She was soon asleep. She did not even hear the latch when it was raised again.

She came awake with a start when a hand was clapped over her mouth and Tom said in a voice that was barely a whisper, "Up, quick! There are redcoats downstairs, looking for us. Be quiet." He took his hand away and pulled Charity up so that she slid quietly out of bed and glided with him to the open window. She climbed out and jumped down into Bart's arms waiting below. Then Tom perched on the sill and dropped lightly to the ground beside her. They ran for their horses, which were stabled and eating contentedly.

Behind them, as they mounted, there was a shout

and, as they reached the edge of the woods, a shot followed, but it went wild. Moments later they heard the hooves of pursuing horses.

"Follow close," called Tom and swung off in a zig-zag course between the tree trunks that led him rapidly downhill to a stream which they forded, then climbed another hill to meet the stream again. This time they did not ford it but walked their horses up it until they found a deep pool and climbed out to wait silently on the bank. Tom put his ear to the ground, listening.

"Hear anything?" asked Bart.

Charity knew the earth would seem to shake if horses' pounding hooves were near. She waited in alarm.

Tom shook his head and stood up. "Could be that we've lost them." He sighed. "Ah, well, at least we drank deep and Charity's refreshed by her nap." He peered at Bart. "Think we should make for Lizzie's place? We should have shook them off long before that."

Bart shrugged. "It's as good as any. And she might have word of a haul for us."

It was all very mysterious to Charity, but she decided not to ask questions. She felt vaguely that she had brought calamity on them by striking out for herself and getting her clothes half torn off. She was just as angry at Tom as ever, but . . . she did not allow herself to finish the thought, just jogged along doggedly after Tom as he wandered through the narrow, almost indiscernible trails in the dense forest.

"Twould be easier if we took to the rivers," muttered Bart, as they made camp after a long exhausting ride. The brambles and thorn bushes had made their clothing even more ragged and left a cross-hatch of scratches on their arms and legs.

"They might be watching the rivers," said Tom thoughtfully. "It's what they'd expect of us, and maybe," he added ominously, "shunning the rivers is the reason we've got this far. Gert must have alerted the redcoats, and they must have followed us into Rhode Island."

"Or told the local authorities we were here," said Bart with his mouth full. "We're wanted here too, remember."

"Is there any place you're not wanted?" asked Charity despairingly.

"New York," said Tom promptly. "That's where we're headed."

New York! Her head spun. But that was endless miles away through the wilderness. She sank into an exhausted sleep, despondently sure they'd never reach their destination.

CHAPTER 8

Tom had made no attempt to make love to her on the journey. Once he had laid his hand on hers caressingly and she had shrugged it off. So, he had sighed and let her be.

Once at a stream out of Bart's hearing, he had tried to make amends.

"It's my failing, y'know," he had explained with a rueful smile. "I've never been able to resist a wench who wants wooing."

"So you belong to all women," she retorted crisply.

"With none to call my own," he said a bit wistfully, and reached out to touch her hair, but she turned on her heel and stalked away from him. She was not, she told herself grimly, to be seduced by his soft-talking ways. It helped to be angry at Tom and brood about his wayward manner, for then she did not turn to even more troublesome thoughts about what the future held for her.

After what seemed an endless struggle through the timber, fording rivers—sometimes swimming their horses across—climbing hills, winding down them, the air seemed to change. There was a smell of the sea in the breeze that rippled Charity's blonde hair and she felt a small surge of excitement. They were nearing the coast at last! But where?

Up ahead, Tom reined in and she saw before them a tiny clearing and a habitation that, though mean and small, might be an inn. It appeared to be a rude two-room structure with a stable. From somewhere came the wild cry of a loon.

"Think it's all right?" Bart muttered.

"It's dangerous," mused Tom. "But—all looks peaceful."

"If it's dangerous, why don't we bypass it?" asked Charity nervously. "We're near the coast—I can smell the sea air."

Tom threw her a merry look. "You need a new dress, don't you? Unless you've grown so fond of my coat you won't part with it?"

"Shut up," growled Bart, who was edgy. "Either do it or don't."

"Wait here," said Tom tersely, and leaving them in the shelter of the trees he walked his horse to the inn, whistled twice. After a moment a shutter banged open and a head appeared, swathed in a ruffled nightcap, with a pair of long dark braids hanging down.

"Tom!" The woman gave a whoop and Tom said merrily, "Not so loud, Lizzie. Could be I've got company not too far back."

"That so?" The shutter banged shut, and a minute later the door of the inn creaked open and a big woman in the most voluminous nightdress Charity had ever seen burst out. "What do you need, Tom?" she demanded anxiously. "Food I've got. Ale I've got. A fresh horse?"

"Three fresh horses, and a dress for the lady." Tom nodded toward the darkness under the tree.

"Lady?" She sounded surprised. "What size lady?" she asked suspiciously.

"About the size of your oldest daughter," said Tom.

She muttered "Cradle robber!" and hurried back inside, returning with a dress of green cloth. "Go to the stable and take your pick of the horses. I'll be currying those you've got so they won't look so hard ridden, and I'll bed 'em down. You can change back with me next time you're up this way. But you'll have some vittles and ale first, won't ye?"

"Thanks, Lizzie." Tom gave her large bottom a whack, and she gave a happy giggle and trotted off. As the door of the inn banged, Tom waved Charity and Bart forward. They came across the little open space and dismounted. Bart led the horses to the

108

stable, while Tom took Charity inside, where she changed to her new dress.

In the kitchen, Lizzie, talking a blue streak to Tom, banged pots and pans as she prepared them a meal.

The dress was a shade of green much out of fashion, and made of stout cotton material, but it was clean and looked as if it would resist brambles. Although it was both a little tight and a little short, Charity breathed a sigh of relief as she got into it, and went into the next room to return Tom's much-the-worse-for-wear gray velvet coat.

"Sure, that dress becomes you," he said, his eyes sparkling as he slipped into his coat again. His roguish smile told her that he'd noted the way it hugged her figure. Lizzie, slapping down three pewter tankards of ale on a table that already groaned under a big roast joint on a wooden charger and three big wooden trenchers, nodded solemnly. "It do look better on her than it did on Betsy," she averred in a surprised tone.

"How is Betsy?" asked Tom.

"Now don't you be lookin' her way, Tom!" Lizzie roared with laughter. "Betsy and the rest are visitin' with my sister over the next town. Didn't you come through there?"

Tom shook his head. "We came through the forest."

"No wonder you look so done in," said Lizzie sympathetically. "Well, eat up." She lifted her head as Bart entered. "Bart," she cried. "It's been a long time since I seen you here."

Bart grinned at her. "Where's your husband, Liz?"

She shrugged. "My John? Out huntin'. Always huntin'. Or fishin'. Never did see the likes of that man. Always gone when there's firewood to be chopped or kindlin' to be split."

For a time they were silent while everybody ate and drank hungrily.

"So there's been no alarm for us?" asked Tom, after draining his tankard and letting Lizzie fill it up for him again. "That's surprising, seeing how far they chased us."

Lizzie shook her head. "Nary sign of redcoats here,

Tom. You know I'd tell you quick if there was. Sure, it be plenty safe to stay the night."

"I've a feeling it's not," he said restlessly.

"We'd be in the woods still had Tom not wanted a dress for the wench," growled Bart, and Lizzie nodded.

"Well, and so he was right. He can't have her ridin' through the woods half naked, now can he? And sure I've seen enough of his gold to let him have what he wants without askin' for ready cash."

Tom smiled at her. "You're the right kind of woman, Lizzie," he said. "But we'll not be tarrying here this night. I've a chill feeling in my bones that all's not right. We're for New York."

"Oh?" Lizzie was instantly alert. "Could be there'd be a boat down by the shore t'other side of the bluff that might take you there."

Bart guffawed. "So that's where your husband is? At the shore unloadin' contraband!"

Lizzie shrugged. "Well, you say they are after you, and I'm thinkin' that if you get took, then you can't tell them what you don't know, can you?" she said sensibly. "But if I were you, I'd hurry. Could be they're still there."

"Thanks!" Tom's smile flashed. "I won't forget you, Lizzie, when my pockets are lined with gold."

"No, I know you won't, Tom." She gave his shoulder an affectionate pat. All women loved him, thought Charity grimly.

Lizzie stood in the doorway and watched them ride away, a stout woman in a huge shapeless gown, outlined vaguely against the candlelight. And Charity thought how strange life was in these raw new colonies, as she thundered along with Tom and Bart through the moonswept night, heading for the coast.

Tom seemed to know his way well. He guided his horse smoothly, surely, between the trees. Behind her she could sense Bart's impatience as his mount's head almost nuzzled her horse's flank.

Soon they found themselves moving between two low bluffs on a single-file path, descending sharply.

The salt air was sharper now and she could hear the raucous call of birds, and hear the pounding of the surf even before the vista opened up before them. Moving out onto low dunes, they saw in the distance what appeared to be a merchantman lying at anchor, sails lightly billowing as if impatient to be gone. On the beach nearby were two piled-up longboats, swarming with men, and two wagons.

"There's John," said Bart excitedly. "Ho there, John!" He slapped his horse's flank and galloped across the dunes towards the startled men unloading the longboats.

Charity would have followed suit, but Tom stayed her. A musket was fired, and Bart reined up indignantly. "John," he roared, "you tell them I'm a friend. I've Tom Blade and a woman with me."

"Hold yer fire," called a hoarse voice which seemed to come from the heaviest-set man of the group. "Bart's a friend, like he says. Come on here, the three of ye."

Tom relaxed, and he and Charity cantered across the dunes, their horses floundering a bit in the soft sand. Then everyone was shaking hands and nodding. But greetings were abruptly cut short as Lizzie's John said, "Fall in and help, if ye like. We'd best be quick. Could be someone's seen the ship out there."

As Tom and Bart worked, they inquired about the chances of a ride to New York. It could be managed, they were told. A ketch out yonder was being loaded now and would sail in close to the coast and unload into hay wagons to be driven into the city. The bargain was quickly struck and they were half unloaded when there was a sudden rattle of musketry from the heights and the sound of, "Halt there, in the name of the king!"

"We been betrayed!" cried Lizzie's John in consternation. "Grab what you can, lads! Into the boats, quick!"

In the ensuing furor, Charity felt Tom lift her up and toss her into the nearest longboat. She crouched down, frightened, hearing musket balls whistle about as the men heaved mightily to launch the beached boats. Tom was the last to jump in. Others were already pulling at the oars as he did so. He landed with a sudden gasp at Charity's feet and in the moonlight she saw a dark stain spreading across the shoulder of his velvet coat.

Charity let out a cry.

Tom, clutching her about the legs, raised himself a little, painfully. "Faith, it's not so much of a wound," he gasped, and passed out, his tawny head falling on her lap.

"Hurry!" cried Charity. "Is there a doctor on that ship?"

"Aye," was the surly answer from a sturdy fellow pulling at the oars. "A pirate's doctor he be and good with wounds."

"Tom." Tears were running down her face now as she cradled his head and tried to staunch the flow of blood with a ruffle torn off of her petticoat. "Tom, can you hear me?"

"Best you leave him be," muttered the man beside her, sweating as he pulled at the oars. He ducked as a musket ball came across the water. The king's men on shore were cursing because they had no boats. Still, they had ended up with most of the contraband, the horses and wagons.

The boats were well out on the water now, too far for any kind of accurate marksmanship, and the men called back raucous insults at the uniformed men on the beach, which were answered by curses and a spattering of gunfire.

As they reached the ship's rounded side, Tom came to. He rallied and looked up at Charity with a smile. "Be not so mournful, m'love," he said jauntily. "I've lived through worse, and will again."

She stroked his hair and tried to smile back at him through her tears, but it was an effort. Bart, in the other boat, called over to them, "How's Tom?" for he had seen Tom struck down by the bullet, and Charity answered in a quivering voice, "I don't know."

"Living," amended a laconic voice.

112

"'Tis a scratch," called Tom and coughed. Charity winced, feeling Tom shudder as a sharp pain went through him.

Then they were swarming aboard the merchantman, which was no merchantman at all, Charity realized. The ship had many gunports which could be opened to fire on honest shippers. A great blackbearded man who seemed to be the captain rumbled, "Who be these?"

As the ship's doctor, a wiry rat-faced fellow, inspected Tom's wound, he muttered, "It's bad, I'm afraid."

"Couldst give me passage to Barbados?" asked Tom of the blackbearded captain.

"Near enough, if you've gold to pay for it," was the rejoinder.

Tom tried to reach for his belt, shuddered and said faintly, "Charity, there's a money pouch. Keep one gold coin for yourself. Give him the rest."

Charity found the pouch and surrendered the money—all but one coin.

"Nay," said the blackbearded man. "'Tis not enough." He eyed Charity.

Silently she handed him the last gold coin and took from around her neck the little gold chain that she had managed to smuggle even into the jail. It had been her mother's and her mother's likeness was in the locket. "It's all I have," she said pleadingly.

"'Tis enough," pronounced the captain. And added, "Free passage for you, Mistress Golden Hair."

"No," said Tom in a stronger voice. "She goes with Bart."

"As you will," the captain shrugged. "Are you loaded there?"

Bart called to one of the men on the ketch, "You've two passengers would like to go along. We'll help you unload."

"'Tis done, if you'll drive one of the wagons into New York," boomed a voice from the ketch. "I'm short a driver."

"I'll do it," said Bart. And to Charity, "Come along.

They can't be kept waiting."

Still Charity lingered, bending over Tom. "Oh, Tom, why can't I go with you?" Her voice broke. "The captain said I could have free passage. And I could take care of you. You'll need someone."

He spoke in a low voice, only for her ears. "If I die—and there's some chance of that—they'll draw lots for you. Or else all have you."

She shuddered.

"Best go with Bart to New York," he added, more loudly. "There you can find a job in an alehouse or passage to England somehow." He patted her hand, and her tears fell unashamed on his face. "There, there, Charity," he said softly. "Let's be off in good style. Sure, I've always been lucky. Why should my luck desert me now?"

She bent over and kissed him, heard his muttered, "Take care, m'love. Keep her safe, Bart." And then Bart was dragging her away and she was over the side and into the ketch, still sniffling.

The sails billowed and they were away on the wind under the fitful clouds. As Charity watched, the great ship seem to shiver and then run out to sea to be lost in the darkness that came across the moon.

She would never see him again, she told herself, the highwayman with the sunny smile. And . . . she had not been even civil to him these last days. But he would not now be lying on the deck in his own blood, dying perhaps, except for her. He had chanced two inns to get her a dress, and except for that they might be far from here, ploughing their way through the wilderness, and he'd be alive.

Tears ran down her face and were salt in her mouth and she knew bitter regret as the ketch sailed on, moving farther from the coast until the trees receded and became tiny things in the distance.

She put her head down on her arms and wept.

BOOK II

New York 1686–1687

CHAPTER 9

Charity was suddenly aware of Bart's heavy hand on her shoulder. Looking up she saw a small secluded inlet and two men waving at them from shore. The inlet seemed to be surrounded on three sides by dense woods and she shivered as she waited for more musket balls, but none came. Their boat docked and the unloading took place quietly and swiftly, then the ketch was off again into the night.

Charity and Bart were left ashore with the two strangers who had been waiting, and three wagons piled high with hay—and under that hay, contraband. Only two of the wagons had drivers, so Bart, as agreed, drove the other wagon, with Charity on the seat beside him.

"What are we carrying?" she asked Bart uneasily, hoping there was no gunpowder under that pile of hay.

"Bales of cloth mainly," he said. "I asked. Laces, ribbons. Try to look more like a farmer's wife, Charity. If we're stopped, let me do the talking. Just bob your head."

She looked at him resentfully. He was very cheerful and seemed to have forgotten all about Tom.

"Why didn't you go to Barbadoes?" she challenged. "I know you have gold for your passage—I saw you counting it."

"Because I'm wanted in Barbadoes," he said equably, turning the team of horses to avoid a rock in the road.

"Is Tom?" she asked fearfully, wondering if the light-hearted highwayman was sailing into a death trap.

117

"Tom? Wanted in Barbadoes? No, he's never been there far as I know."

"What did you do that you're wanted?"

He gave her an impatient look, his dark face suddenly evil. "I killed a man there," he said and laughed.

She shivered and sat back, sorry she'd asked.

"We'll go as far as need be to deliver this load," he said, making his plans aloud. "Then we'll drift toward the waterfront and find us an inn—that way we'll be far from the trouble, if trouble there be after this stuff's unloaded."

"Why would there be trouble? Nobody saw us, did they?"

"They'll be selling these goods," he explained patiently. "And could be some who buy are the king's men, checking on such as us."

"Oh," said Charity.

She sat back. She wasn't ready for a life of crime.

The unloading was done on the outskirts of town at an empty barn with big rafters and a strong odor of manure. It went off without a hitch, and Bart muttered, "Let's be taking our leave before there's any who come in to inspect the goods." Bart inquired the way upriver before they sauntered away.

"Why'd you do that?" asked Charity, once they were out of earshot, walking down a street just pinking with dawn. "We're not going upriver, are we?"

He gave her a look. "That's just why," he said coldly. "Then if they chance to look for us, it's upriver they'll be searching."

Bart, she decided, was ideally suited for the life he led. He had the true makings of a criminal: he was tough, he was wily, he was strong. Certainly he was strong. After they'd walked for a while she found it hard to keep up with him. Characteristically, he did not shorten his stride for her, but frowning, kept up his pace. She almost had to run to match his step.

At last they reached the waterfront, which Charity found picturesque in the morning sun. Ships of many kinds were anchored in the harbor, which bustled with activity as furs and grain and timber were loaded

118

for export, and rum and sugar from the West Indies unloaded, as well as delft ware and loom products from Holland, and a variety of goods from England.

Charity was still looking around her curiously when Bart, taking her firmly by the arm, led her into an inn, where he engaged a room. He looked at Charity thoughtfully, but told her that he was not going up with her yet. He planned instead to drink downstairs and get the "lay of the land." So, Charity trudged upstairs and indulged herself in a hot bath, with the door carefully latched. She looked wistfully at the inviting featherbed. She was afraid to nap there, afraid Bart would come in. She shivered at the thought of his big violent hands, the coarse bristly hair of his chest which she had seen when, on their journey, he had pulled off his shirt and splashed water on himself at streams.

She would have to find work quickly. She could not stay with as crude and violent a man as Bart.

When she arrived downstairs, looking fresh and tidy with her hair smoothed back, Charity asked a friendly-looking barmaid about work. She was startled when the girl shook her head and answered in Dutch.

"Her be from the country," volunteered an old man who sat, drawing on a long pipe. And Charity was reminded that New York had been New Amsterdam not so long ago, and that these people were not English but Dutch.

"I wanted to ask her if she knew where I could find a job," said Charity wistfully.

"They be few and hard to find," he answered in a thoughtful voice. "Do ye be a good cook?"

She shook her head, too honest to lie.

"Ye look not strong enough for heavy work," he said. "Be ye a seamstress?"

Again she shook her head.

"Then best ye marry," he observed bluntly, "and find some strong young lad to support you."

Charity turned away feeling hopeless and walked out to the street, determined to find some sort of job to support herself.

The sun blazed down on Manhattan Island, and sea

gulls and terns screeched overhead as Charity stepped out of the inn. Looking up and down at the yellow brick walls and red tiled roofs and step gables—which Bart had told her were called "crow steps" and were constructed to give the sweeps easy access to the chimneys—she decided the best chance of obtaining work lay away from the dockside, and walked along, hoping for inspiration.

Dutch burghers brushed by, well dressed men, and women in spotless white coifs and wearing big-skirted dresses of fine materials and rich laces, reminding her that Flanders grew the finest flax in Europe. Among the strollers there was a preponderance of blue eyes and fair hair, but there was also—much to Charity's surprise, for she had thought slavery confined to the South—a spattering of black slaves, just as there had been in Boston, and she realized that just as the Puritans had black slaves, so had the Dutch.

At a cobbler's shop, she stopped. Her father, Increase, had been a cobbler, she reminded herself. This cobbler, a sunny-faced Dutchman in worn breeches, round as a butter ball, smiled and shook his head, his eyes following her bright hair and trim figure as she again went out into the street.

Undaunted, she walked on, observing the shop signs which were interesting metal decorations hanging at the ends of anchoring irons. They were distinctive features of the flat-fronted row houses. Sometimes they were in the form of huge iron figures, sometimes they were large iron letters shaped into the initials of the shop's owner—or of the residents if it were a private dwelling. She smiled at the sight of the fierce little weathercocks perched atop the steep roofs, and noted with approval the split Dutch front doors, the top half of which could be opened to let in sunlight and air, while the lower half was left closed to keep the children in, the dogs out.

At a baker's, a hard-faced woman who spoke English turned her away.

"Could be, she'd have been good at the work," the baker said wistfully.

"Nonsense," said his plain-faced wife in a resentful tone. "She'd be good only to ogle the men, with a face and a figure like that. Back to the oven—your bread is burning!"

Charity wandered on, past close-set row houses of Holland brick, with their small windows.

It seemed little use to inquire at a smithy, or a wheelwright's. She turned away, sickened, from the squeals and smells at the butcher's.

She was about to inquire at a little dry goods shop when she saw that not one but two girls were lolling in it, looking bored. Since neither of them had anything to do, it seemed extremely doubtful that the management would add a third to join them in their idleness. With a sigh, she turned away.

By now she was tired, for she had had practically no rest in two days, but hope rose in her because she had come to a dairy. Although she was unfamiliar with cows, they had gentle eyes and milk was a clean wholesome thing. She thought she might enjoy a season of being a dairy maid.

Thankful that the owner—whom she found shoveling manure in his big spacious stone barn with its massive beams—could speak English, she inquired about work, too honest to pretend she knew anything about cows.

He thought it over, looked at her several times, seemed to consider and then nodded his head. Her heart leaped. She could get away from Bart!

"I'd take ye, if ye'd sign articles of indenture," he said slyly, "and consent to be bound, so that I'd know ye'd not be runnin' off with the first likely lad to walk by, leavin' me with the time wasted I'd spent trainin' ye."

Charity's heart slumped. Bound! To be a bound girl. It had a sad ring to it, almost like slavery. Still . . . it might be the only way.

For how long? she asked anxiously. For seven years, she was told, at the end of which time she would receive a calf and a respectable dress and in florins she would receive—

But Charity had already fled. Even the thought of getting away from Bart did not seem so tempting that she would sign away her freedom for seven long years. Seven years! A lifetime to one who was only nineteen.

She had no way of knowing that the crafty dairyman had only meant to bargain with her; assuming she knew that three or four years was the usual period of indenture, and had hoped to strike a bargain at five. Regretfully, he saw the girl hurry away; she'd been a healthy, rosy-cheeked maid, she had, and well spoken even if it was only English she spoke—far different from his own surly *vrow*. He sighed. Ah, well, times being what they were, perhaps the girl would be back.

Thoroughly upset by his offer, Charity sped away.

The light was fading and so were her spirits, which had started out so resolutely. Discouraged, she plodded back to the inn, her shoulders drooping, her mind filled with worry over Tom's fate, wondering whether he was still alive. In silence, she walked across the plank flooring and sat down to dinner with Bart, who was getting soddenly drunk in the inn's public room. Somehow during the day, he had acquired the companionship of a foursome of trappers. The trappers were having a high time in town before they departed once again for their life in the remote forests where they trapped the woodland animals for their pelts. The noisy men were also getting very drunk and one of them kept grinning inanely and pinching Charity's thigh under the table.

She kept edging away from him and, eventually, he took the hint and began talking to the barmaid, a buxom Dutch girl with a coarse full-bodied laugh, whose big breasts nearly popped out of her low-cut blouse as she leaned over to bang down their flagons.

Charity knew that there was no longer any hope of finding a job this day. She also knew with certainty that Bart had her staked out for a romp in the room upstairs. But she was determined not to go upstairs. She would simply sit at the table all night, seated on the hard wooden bench, and when everyone either passed out or left, she would fall asleep on the wooden table, and try again tomorrow to get a job. She had already decided that tomorrow she would take anything—even as a last resort the seven years' indenture. Bart's woman she would *not* become.

The trappers pressed drinks on her but she shook her head. She must not become giddy. She'd need her wits about her if Bart suddenly decided to drag her upstairs.

Numb with fatigue, she sat silently listening to the men talk. Sometimes she found their conversation interesting. One of the trappers told Bart that Manhattan was an Indian name which meant "the island," and that the Iroquois had named the Albany area *Ska-neh-ta-de,* which meant "beyond the pine trees."

Bart was curious about the Indians. Were they friendly?

Not always, was the reply. They blew hot and cold. Those in the Hudson Valley were the friendliest of the lot. The fiercest tribes, all agreed, roamed to the west of Albany—the Iroquois, the Five Nations.

One heavyset trapper who had been in the area longer than the others said that the friendly Algonquins of the Hudson Valley had given the Iroquois their name, which meant "real adders," but that the Iroquois called themselves the Ogwanonhsioni, which meant "long-house builders." They called their land the "Long House," since that was the shape of their territory, presided over from east to west by the Mohawks, Oneidas, Onondagas, Cayugas and Senecas.

Bart had heard of the Mohawks.

The Mohawks were so fierce, they had once forced the Delawares to lay down their arms and to dress as squaws. They exacted tribute from the Hudson River tribes. And it was their enemies who had named them the Mohawks.

Bart pounced on that. What did Mohawk mean?

His informant grew grave. The Mohawks called themselves "people of the place of flint," he informed them, which was the meaning of their musical name for themselves, Kanyengehaga, but their enemies had christened them "Mohawks" meaning "those who eat people"—as indeed they did.

Bart laughed uneasily, but Charity's smile wavered. Cannibals!

"Ye're scarin' the girl," objected another trapper. "She'll be afraid to come along!"

Bart gave him a fierce look and he subsided.

Come along. . . . Charity was very tired. She certainly wasn't going anywhere, she told herself. Furthermore, she intended to stay awake and make certain that nothing untoward happened.

But she was even more tired than she knew. Gradually the men's voices became a drone in her ears and resting her head on her arms on the table, she fell fast asleep. A furtive pinch on the thigh from the trapper on her right woke her so that she stirred ever so slightly, but she didn't raise her head from her arms.

Bart was rolling drunk by now, but not so drunk as to miss the main chance; he was having a low-voiced conversation with two of the trappers—the two who were still sober enough to talk—and the drift of that conversation froze Charity's blood.

They were talking about her.

"That's my lowest price," Bart was saying. "I'll sell her to you for that, no less, to warm your beds in the wilds."

Charity tried not to move, not to let them know she'd heard.

"Where would you find a woman like this one?" Bart wheedled. "Look at that shiny hair, those round breasts—well, you can't see them now, she's lyin' on the table, but you should see her naked! Skin like silk!" He paused to let them drink that in.

"You seen her naked?" asked one of them eagerly.

Bart's voice had sneaky laughter in it. "By the riverside," he said. "She belonged to my friend Tom then, and they used to roll in the grass there. I seen them there more than once."

Charity writhed inwardly. Bart had *watched* them!

He must have hidden in the bushes waiting for them to appear!

"But tonight? What about tonight?" cut in a hoarse voice.

"Tonight's mine," said Bart in a surly tone. "Tom never'd let me get near her, but tonight she's mine. Tomorrow you can have her."

"Where is this Tom?" asked another. "Will he come after her? And try to kill us maybe?"

"Tom's dead for all I know," said Bart heavily. "He were bleedin' like a stuck pig when I saw him last. Anyway, he's on his way to Barbadoes. If he comes back, you can sell her back to him when you've done with her—and make a fair profit!"

"Hell, we can always buy us a white woman from the Indians at their slave market up north on the lake. The Indians catch plenty of 'em, and they sell 'em up there—those that last that long. Some's real good lookin'. Hard for us to get in there, but we can always make a deal to have one brought out to us by the Frenchies—"

"But this one's English!"

"There's lots of English women at the slave market. Thought you knew that."

"But if the Frenchies have to go in and buy one for you," Bart pointed out craftily, "you got no guarantee what she'll look like. And you don't know how many painted savages has had her. Or what they's done to her. This girl was a virgin when my friend took her—and that was only a few days ago."

Charity's nerves shrieked as they digested it all. She sat tensely, her head on her arms, waiting for them to stop talking about it, so she could make her escape.

"A virgin you say?"

"Yep. And educated. You heard her talk."

"That ain't the kind of education I'm interested in," sneered one trapper. "The kind of education I want in a woman is all got thrashin' around under a blanket!"

"At your price we oughta have her tonight," grumbled the other. "I still say—"

125

"Why, ye'll *thank me* for beddin' her tonight," declared Bart intensely. "I plan to teach her some tricks twixt now and mornin' that'll make her worth more to ye. Don't mind none if y'hear her screamin' tonight—she's bound to kick up a ruckus at first until she is tamed, but she'll come round to it right enough and be real respectful and glad to go with ye come mornin'."

Glad to go with them! Teach her tricks! Warm their beds in the wilds! Horror washed over Charity in such an engulfing flood that she almost fainted. First Bart—loathsome Bart—and then this coarse crew. She pictured herself being dragged along with a thong tied around her neck—for that was surely the only way they could force her to accompany them— along a hundred dirty trails, with tree branches slapping her in the face; being forced to cook for them by day and to endure all four of their unwashed bodies by night. Horrible pictures flashed through her mind as she imagined herself struggling like the poor trapped animals slowly dying in their cruel snares. And if she became pregnant or if she could not keep up, she supposed she'd be left by the trail to starve, or traded off to the Indians in return for a strong young squaw!

"Another round here!" roared someone at the next table, and with her nerves taut as a drawn bowstring, Charity jumped. She sat up, deliberately yawning. "That man woke me up," she declared pettishly. "I'm going up to bed. Bart, you can stay down here until you fall off that bench for all I care!"

Bart laughed. "I'll accompany you!" He winked at the others.

"No, you won't," snapped Charity. "I'm going to take a bath first and comb my hair." She hoped he did not know she had already taken a bath; it would make him suspicious.

Bart shrugged. "Time for another round of beer then." He watched her lasciviously as she moved away from them. She could almost feel the naked lust in that stare.

Very pale, but moving with apparent aimlessness,

she had reached a point midway between the stairs and the door. She did not think there was a back stairway. At least she had not seen one. If she climbed those stairs she would be trapped.

She took a deep breath and strolled toward the door.

"Ho there," yelled Bart, his voice suddenly sharp. "You're goin' the wrong way!"

"I want a breath of air," she called back over her shoulder, moving steadily toward the door.

There was the sound of a table going over as Bart leaped up, as she streaked through the door and went flying up the street. She had turned down a dark narrow alley when she heard them come thundering and cursing out into the street.

"You go this way, I'll go that way!" she heard Bart yell. "She can't have gone far!"

Her heart sank. If the trappers were looking too, they would surely catch her. She nearly tripped over a sleeping dog in the alley. He moved with a growl as she jumped away, and she tiptoed on. If he had barked, she would have been lost. It brought home to her how dreadful was her position. These men were used to trapping animals—animals far more wary than she. They would have little trouble trapping a friendless woman alone in a town that was strange to her.

Turning a corner she gazed into an empty street that led straight down to the docks. Before her stretched a maze of boats and ships—*there* was her hiding place!

She slipped off her shoes and, holding them, ran silently toward the docks. Many of the smaller craft were drawn up there, side by side. Some would have cabins, all had sails and gear—she would find a place to hide.

Behind her there was a drunken shout. "She's headin' for the docks!" Footsteps pounded behind her.

Charity redoubled her speed, sprinted across the dock and leaped onto the deck of the nearest boat. Luckily the night was dark and the boat was deserted. She dodged behind a low sail, jumped from the deck to the next boat, landing silently on bare feet, scrambled to the higher deck of the river sloop alongside and hid, crouched down behind a huge pile of rope. The pursuing men ran cursing in both directions. On the sloop where she was hiding, heavy footsteps suddenly ascended to the deck and a voice as heavy as the footsteps growled something in Dutch. Though she didn't know the language, she guessed it was a sharp "Who goes there?"

One of the trappers gave a surly answer in English.

The heavy voice spoke again in thickly accented English. "No woman is aboard the sloop of the patroon!" the voice thundered. "Get you off or I'll split your gizzard for you."

There was some angry muttering, and one trapper growled, "Come on, Bart. She didn't go this way anyhow!"

Riveted with fear, Charity crouched where she was. The loud-voiced Dutchman, if he found her, might very well turn her back to her pursuers. After a time, the angry muttering receded. She was about to peer out when several sets of footsteps sounded across the dock. She kept her head bent low, hoping Bart and the trappers had not come back. From her hiding place, she could not see the men approaching, only hear them.

A voice of great authority gave rapid orders, footsteps hurried below, and after a few minutes she heard other footsteps. This time, only one man sauntered down the dock and came aboard the sloop.

"Ah, Mynheer van Daarken," said a deep strong voice.

"You are prompt," replied the voice of authority that she had heard before, now speaking English. "I suggest we speak only in English, as my crew speaks nothing but Dutch—save Jan, who is in my confidence."

"As you wish." The deep voice was refined, a gentleman's voice. "My ship lies off the point. Here is a list of the cargo. You will find all the goods of first quality."

"Yes, yes." Van Daarken's voice. "Let me see the

128

list. I think I can read it by moonlight. Yes, yes, this is excellent. Especially the wine. That I can use myself."

"And the rest you can sell to advantage since there will be no tax involved," the other observed sardonically.

Charity blinked. This was a smuggling transaction! Was everyone in the New World a smuggler? she asked herself incredulously.

"Send your longboats to the usual place around midnight," directed van Daarken.

"And the wine? Will you transport it upriver in this sloop? It is an easy distance."

"No," said the Dutchman thoughtfully. "There is some risk and I am a man who prefers to take no risks. Deliver it all ashore in the usual manner. My men will transport it upriver to me."

"Then the price is agreed?"

"Yes—although I find it a trifle high."

"It would be far higher if it were taxed." The deep voice took on a note of steel. "Besides, I take all the risks for you, Mynheer."

"That is true," said the other hastily. "The price shall be as you wish. Here—the moon is bright enough for me to pen it—here is a draft upon the Bank of Amsterdam. But tell me," he added on a note of curiosity, "how will you transport the money from Holland?"

"Mynheer van Daarken, the money will not need to be transported. It will merely be transferred from your account in the Bank of Amsterdam to my account in the Bank of Amsterdam."

"An excellent arrangement," said the patroon, sounding surprised. "So then we are agreed."

"Good. I will take my leave of you then, Mynheer."

"You must be a rich man," observed the Dutchman dryly. "Tell me, do you put all your money in Dutch banks? Holland must be bursting."

"My expenses are large, Mynheer van Daarken," was the cool answer. "And in my profession a man may need large sums at any time. I find it convenient to have money here and there."

The Dutchman sighed. "The world of business could have used you."

"My career is not of my choosing," said the other voice grimly. "I must make the best of what is offered."

Goodbyes were spoken, and the footsteps of the man with the deep voice resounded across the deck. The Dutchman gave another goodbye from the deck. Charity presumed van Daarken was watching the smuggler go. Then the heavy-voiced fellow joined van Daarken, and Charity heard him speak respectfully to the patroon asking about the departed smuggler.

"Did you mark his rapier, Jan?" murmured van Daarken. "It is said he has spitted more men with it than anyone since—" Charity could not catch the name.

"I will break his neck if he crosses us," growled the man called Jan.

"He will not cross us," said van Daarken comfortably. "It is known that his word is good. He is a man of honor, Jan. He would be a force today in his own country, but because of his politics, he cannot return home. So he makes his living as he can. Such men are to be pitied—and used." He sighed. "It might have happened to us, Jan."

"Not so," said Jan sturdily. "You would have found some other way. You would have bought someone."

Their voices faded a little, but they remained on deck. Charity knew she dared not attempt to leave while they remained there. She closed her eyes and sagged against the pile of rope. She was cruelly tired from her day of trudging through the town looking for work. She must look healthy and able to do a hard day's work tomorrow, if she were to have any hope of finding a situation.

Bits of their conversation played through her mind as she drowsed there. *He is a man of honor . . . he cannot return home . . .* and that deep cultured voice that had stirred her. She wished she knew what the smuggler looked like, she wished she had had the courage to lift up her head and peer out. But had she

130

done so and startled them, she might well have been spitted by that rapier of which the patroon spoke so admiringly. She shuddered and slipped down another notch into unconsciousness. Soon she was asleep.

When she awoke the sun was shining brightly and the sloop was moving. She sat up sharply and looked around her. Land was far away. They were moving up-river.

"Ah, I see you have awakened," said an authoritative voice.

Charity's breath caught in her throat and she scrambled to her feet.

The man who faced her was square-built and portly with stocky legs, big feet and hands and thick ankles, a peasant's build. Beneath bushy dark brows that now met in a frown, two small keen eyes of a pale watery blue considered her. An auburn periwig added to the ferocity of his demeanor and showed that, however coarse might be his appearance, he was not a peasant but a gentleman.

His clothes also were clearly those of a gentleman. A long coat of dark red broadcloth with wide black cuffs, a long waistcoat and knee breeches of the same dark red material. All of it trimmed with handsome gold buttons and black braid. Red stockings covered his heavy legs and ran down into red-heeled dark leather shoes with small buckles set high on the instep. His neckcloth was of snowy linen with lace ends. Beneath one arm he carried a plumed hat and his manner was entirely one of authority.

Even if she had not recognized his voice from last night's exchange Charity would have known that she was in the presence of the patroon.

CHAPTER 10

"Mynheer van Daarken," she said shakily, "I—I can explain my presence here."

"Pray do," he said, frowning. "And also how it is that you know my name?"

"Everyone knows your name," said Charity meekly, hoping to flatter him.

It was apparent that he was pleased with this reply. His broad chest expanded a little in its dark red broadcloth covering, but he took her remark only as his just due. "You speak as if you were gently bred," he observed with some surprise.

"That is true," answered Charity, choosing her words carefully. Hope was rising in her. She assumed her most genteel manner. This man at first glance might seem coarse, but he was a patroon and therefore had been gently reared. Like speaks to like. "I am come to unfortunate circumstances, being—" she almost said "newly come from Massachusetts," but remembered in time that van Daarken might take a dim view of having a convicted witch aboard—"newly come from England to find my relatives in Virginia," she said quickly, her inventive imagination racing ahead. "Once there, I was told that they were all dead, killed in an uprising of the Indians. A cousin was said to have escaped north to New York. But when I arrived to seek him in New York, some—some ill-bred men, much the worse for drink, pursued me from my inn, where they were trying to force their attentions on me, and I sought refuge on your boat. I—I was so tired I fell immediately asleep." There was sincerity in that last, and a touch of the hopelessness she had felt the night before.

"I see." His voice softened a bit. "You are young to wander about alone."

Charity sighed and brushed back a strand of bright hair that blew in her face. "My mother died in Torquay, and I came across the ocean seeking my relatives."

He pondered this. "Your trunks? Your belongings?"

"All lost," said Charity regretfully, remembering the pretty wardrobe Countess Stéphanie had counseled over. "I was set upon by bandits."

"And they took your clothes—and let *you* go?" There was an undertone of amusement in his voice as his pale blue eyes coolly roved over her soft feminine curves, saying plainly that given the choice *he* would have stolen the girl and let the clothes remain.

Charity flushed. "I escaped," she said tremulously. "And I have walked a very long way. I was lost."

"It is an interesting story," he said. "And it must have cost you something to invent it."

She winced. "My mother *did* die in Torquay," she said defensively, "I *did* come across the ocean to find my relatives."

"But the rest of the story is not quite right, is it? Trunks and belongings are cherished by women. And you are a long way from Virginia. But we will let that pass." He studied her. "You are no doubt hungry. Will you join me for breakfast?"

Charity was afraid to let him know how grateful she felt. Grief and fear had exhausted her, but now she had had several hours' sleep and had waked with an enormous appetite. She joined the patroon in his cabin. Seating herself in the chair he drew out for her with a sweep of her skirts, she ate with the delicate grace Stéphanie had taught her, and made polite conversation as if she were once again seated in the French countess's drawing room in Bath.

Across from her the patroon ate greedily, then sat and watched her in a detached way, but alertly, as if he hoped to catch some chink in the perfection of her manners.

It was a small success, but Charity came through

breakfast with flying colors. In an effort to pass what seemed a test for she knew not what, she entertained her host with stories of her life at school, with Stéphanie in Bath. And in these stories, she changed places with Margaret Yorking, wealthy, with much to fall back upon—held back only by a vengeful guardian and a delicate mother in failing health.

He listened in amusement and some fascination and when she had finished he said, "You speak an aristocratic brand of English. You say you have been instructed in French and Spanish as well. Please to address me in French."

Charity, mimicking Stéphanie's Parisian accent, spoke readily in that language. And when he next asked her to speak to him in Spanish, she felt as if she were again addressing her old school friend Mercedes, for she had not spoken Spanish since last she had been with the unhappy girl.

"You speak both languages quite well," he commended her, and sat studying her for so long that she was tempted to fidget, but managed not to, remembering Stéphanie's remarks about the dismal future of young ladies who fidgeted.

"You could pass for the daughter of a duke," he said suddenly, his manner at once cold and approving. Charity flushed, half with pleasure and half with alarm, for she did not like the crafty look in his eyes. "I take it you have no one to write to for funds?" he added in an offhand manner.

"No," she admitted. "All—all are dead."

"I see." He sat lost in thought.

"As you may have heard, I have an estate upriver," he said, finally.

"All have heard of it," lied Charity.

"I doubt it," he said. "But it is pleasant to hear. My manor is named Daarkenwyck, and there I have a wife and a son. My son Pieter is to go next year to Amsterdam, there to spend a year continuing his studies before he returns to us. He is a pleasant boy, a year or two older than yourself, but he finds it difficult to apply himself to his studies. Since I have business interests overseas which he will one day inherit, it is essential that he be proficient in languages. Dutch is of course his native tongue. French he speaks passably, English indifferently, and Spanish not at all. I would propose to you that you join my family in the capacity of, say, distant cousin? Thus you would eat with us at table and be present at our social gatherings, and could engage the boy in conversation. Pieter would not wish a prettty woman to find him wanting, and so it would be a great spur to his endeavors if you would converse with him in English, and at times, in French and Spanish. He will undoubtedly teach you our own mother tongue in return but that is not of interest to me. It is my desire that my son speak these three languages fluently, and with a patrician accent so that he will be instantly recognized in any company as a gentleman and the son of a patroon. Do I make myself clear?"

"Yes," said Charity, almost overwhelmed. By this weird turn of fate was she to have thrust upon her, at last, the life for which she had so yearned at school and which she had so envied Margaret Yorking and the others? She would live in a great house, eat at table with the others as an equal and—

"But I have not the proper clothes," she said with a sinking feeling. "I had a beautiful wardrobe, truly, all chosen by Countess Stéphanie de la Croix, but—I have lost it all."

"As to how you came to lose your possessions," his voice hardened perceptibly, "I make one condition. Since you are to eat at my table and live with my family as my cousin, I must know the truth about you. If you lie and I find it out, it will go ill with you, I promise."

Charity hesitated. He sat before her, square as a brick building in his dark red broadcloth coat. An almost malevolent figure. She remembered the sly way he had looked at her and was tempted to lie again—something more plausible. But if he should find out . . . Small fingers of fear pressed against her spine as she stared into those cold little ferret-like eyes.

Still . . . what chance was there for her if he did not take her in? Where could she go in this savage upriver country?

She moistened her lips.

"I would not wish you to harbor ill thoughts of how I came into my present condition," she said slowly. "The charges against me were false."

"Ah," he murmured, "and what were those charges?"

Charity's back stiffened. "I was charged with witchcraft in Massachusetts, and sentenced to burning. But I—I escaped."

He considered her, and she recoiled a little, realizing how hard those small ferret-like blue eyes really were. "And are you a witch?" he asked on a humorous note.

"Of course not," she said indignantly. "It was a ruse to gain my inheritance." She thought it best to go no further in that direction.

"Ah? An inheritance?" He seemed to see the light. "Yes, some men will take any advantage to gain money." His voice had a cynical note. "You will not of course speak of this matter to anyone?"

"Of course not," said Charity, shamed.

She was afraid of Mynheer van Daarken, but she told herself grimly that she had a weapon to use against him; she knew of his deal with the smuggler. If he pressed her too hard, she would confront him with that. Even a patroon must fear the authorities, for the king's tax was levied on all, and it would go hard with him if they learned he had evaded it.

"Everyone at Daarkenwyck must consider you a distant cousin, well educated but in somewhat impoverished circumstances," said the patroon. "I will say that your trunk was lost overboard, and Jan will back me up. It will then of course be necessary to replace your lost clothing because the fault was mine that I let your trunk fall overboard."

Her voice caught. "Would you really do that?"

"Of course," he said. "I wish you to decorate my table."

She felt ashamed at the harsh things she had been thinking of him and cast her eyes down.

He drummed his fingers, and frowned at the dress she was wearing. "You look like a servant in those clothes," he said. "You must by no means arrive garbed as a servant." He pointed toward the corner, where a stout leather trunk reposed. "In the top of that trunk you will find two dresses I was bringing home as gifts. The blue one should become you."

Charity hesitated. "But—won't your wife object?"

He shrugged. "We bring with us the mail from Holland. It is doubtful my wife will notice that I have brought along anyone at all."

Charity gave him a puzzled look. Was mail then so important to the patroon's wife?

"In any event," he added, "the two dresses were not for her. The length should be about right, but your waist appears smaller. Possibly you are clever with a needle and can stitch up the bodice."

"I am not clever with a needle," admitted Charity truthfully, "but I can certainly stitch up the bodice." As she spoke she lifted the lid of the trunk, sighing as she saw the lovely materials, silks and satins and laces, that lay within it.

She pulled out a misty blue broadcloth with an overskirt and tight bodice of paler blue velvet, with billowing slashed sleeves. It was a dress such as Stéphanie might have chosen for her. She held it up in delight. "Did you mean this one?"

He nodded, considering it critically.

She hesitated. She had glimpsed a chemise and petticoats peeping out from the lower part of the trunk. "My—my undergarments leave something to be desired. Could I—?"

He smothered a smile. "By all means. Take your choice." He rose. "You will find also needles and thread which I was bringing upriver. Come on deck when you have dressed."

Swiftly Charity stitched up the too ample waist of the bodice and tried it on. Not yet tight enough. She addressed herself again awkwardly to her needle and

138

again tried the dress on. Perfect! And how wonderful it felt to be rid of her torn undergarments and to feel against her skin the fine holland of her new embroidered chemise and petticoats! She snatched up the patroon's comb and began to work on her disheveled hair, training the curls so that they fell softly about her ears, fixing them with hairpins and pale blue ribbons which she had found along with the needle and thread.

Recklessly, she added a tiny diamond of black court plaster to her cheek in the manner that, according to Stéphanie, was all the rage in London and Paris. Pinching her cheeks to make them red, she went out on deck and looked around for the patroon.

He was leaning on the rail with his back to her, smoking a long pipe.

"Mynheer van Daarken," she said in a tremulous voice, and as he turned she swept him a low curtsy with all the grace at her command.

For a moment he looked stunned, and even big Jan turned to gape at her.

"You will do nicely," murmured the patroon. Then he bowed to her, his auburn periwig curls sweeping his shoulders as he did so. "Cousin—you did not tell me your name."

"Charity Woodstock."

"Cousin Charity, it is a pleasure to have found such a relative."

Their eyes met and they both laughed.

CHAPTER 11

At dinner, the patroon drank heavily of the wine and began to brag.

"I am a self-made man," he told her. "I have taken my life and shaped it. I began life humbly as a herdsman." He stopped and looked at her quizzically. Then abruptly he laughed. It was a discordant laugh. "I know that anything I may say is safe with you," he said in an almost sneering voice, "because if I am displeased, then *you* will suffer."

Charity felt a slight chill pass through her, as if she had been caressed by a whip.

He considered her, a slightly insulting smile on his face.

"I am curious to know," he said, "how you envision your own future. A woman like yourself, with no resources except beauty and an education."

Under that mocking gaze, Charity felt her hands on her lap clench nervously. The subject he brought up was one which had been engrossing her as the sloop sailed up the Hudson. It had been one thing, hungry and frightened and running from such men as Bart, to consider possibly even the life of a bound servant. Now, again well fed and well dressed and holding in her delicate hand a silver goblet of wine, her confidence had returned, and such a life was unimaginable. In spite of van Daarken's insulting manner, she could see mirrored in his small eyes a reluctant appreciation of that beauty which he seemed to mock.

Her topaz gaze flung back the challenge.

"I shall marry, of course," she said in a cold voice. Let him know now that she would not trade her body

141

for breakfast and a blue dress. Let him understand now that she did not intend to become his mistress. For she had no illusions as to where that road led. She had no intention of spending her life being passed from hand to hand through a succession of men.

"Ah." He raised his heavy eyebrows and amusement lit his small blue eyes. "I should have guessed it. You will marry. . . ."

Charity met his gaze unwaveringly.

He gave her a crooked smile and watched her as he continued to drink.

"You will like the life at Daarkenwyck," he said suddenly. "When the Hudson freezes over there is skating and sleighing on the river. Do you skate?"

Charity shook her head.

"Pieter will teach you," he said absently. "A face like yours should turn the head of all my neighbors' sons." He considered her, smiling expansively now. "And we set a good table. In the spring, striped bass are plentiful. They are very flavorful, a sort of white salmon. They are said to make the Indians very lascivious. . . ."

His sly look when he said that made her nervous.

"I have heard there are many sturgeon in the river," she said quickly.

He shrugged. "Sturgeon abound and are eaten by the Indians, but we Dutch do not like them."

Charity took a desperate sip of wine. The patroon's gaze was now concentrated on her round breasts, so nicely displayed in the blue velvet dress.

"I thought the houses in New York very pretty," she said. "The stoops, and the step gables, and those small quaint windows."

He snorted. "Those small quaint windows make a dark house. And past those *stoops,* you will find a confused pattern of austere little rooms with every cranny in use—though to the *vrowen's* credit they are very white scoured. And many a prudent burgher keeps his house down to a story and a half just to escape the tax which mounts with each story! You will like it better at Daarkenwyck where the rooms are large and the windows let in the light."

He drank deeply again and, to her relief, seemed to lose interest in her altogether. He sat moodily awhile, made a couple of disjointed remarks about his past in Holland, and then made an irritable gesture.

"I grow maudlin," he shrugged. "I am sleepy. There is a small cabin next to this one. It is Jan's, but you can boot him out."

"Suppose Jan does not wish to go?" she asked uncomfortably.

"Then you must sleep below with the rats and my crew or on the windy deck." He laughed and rose unsteadily.

She shivered as the dampness from the river penetrated her thin underskirts. With her old dress thrown around her like a shawl, she went to the cabin next door. There was no answer when she knocked so she opened the door. Big Jan lay sprawled in the only bunk, snoring noisily. Charity touched his shoulder, but he only growled and turned over.

She spent the night shivering on deck, wrapped in a blanket she had filched from Jan's cabin.

When at last it was light, Charity got up stiffly and stood by the rail to watch the sun cut away the morning mist.

The patroon strolled out on deck. "Did you sleep well?" he asked, his heavy face looking none the worse for his drinking bout of the evening before.

"The deck was a little cold," she admitted grimly.

He stared at her, noting the blanket that lay beside her. "Why did you not wake Jan as I told you?"

She looked away. In broad daylight it sounded silly to say, *Because I am afraid of Jan.* "He did not wake," she muttered.

He eyed her keenly. "Breakfast will warm you."

And she followed him gratefully to the comparative luxury of his cabin.

Charity voiced admiration for the boat as they ate breakfast. It was named the *Onrust,* which meant "Restless," he told her, and it was a river sloop like

143

the canal craft in Holland, its broad bottom suitable for river travel. Some sixty-five feet long, it had sides of red cedar which resisted decay, but a bottom of white oak, which though softer did not split so easily. He added that he was fond of white bottoms, and Charity quickly asked him about the sails.

Serviceable, she was told. The sloop had a large mainsail; its one mast was placed well forward, and the jib was small. Charity admired its high quarter-deck and its bright yellow color. It was very seaworthy, he told her, but the duration of their trip would depend both on wind and tide.

The Hudson, he told her, was divided into four-teen reaches between New York and Albany, the first being the great Chip Rock reach or palisades. Next the Tappan Zee and Haverstraw Bay reaches. He would point out to her Verdrietege Hook (Hook Mountain) when they reached the west shore between the Zee and the Bay. She asked what "Verdrietege" meant and he smiled and told her it was Dutch for "tedious," so named by impatient sailors waiting for the wind. As the river twisted through the Highlands there would be Seylmaker's Reach and Crescent Reach, and Hoge's and Martyr's or Vorsen's. From Wappin-ger Creek to Crum Elbow was Lange Rak or Long Reach. And on Long Reach lay Daarkenwyck—six-teen fair miles lying along the river to the east.

The winds, he added moodily, would be a problem, most particularly that northwest wind that roared through "Mother Cronk's Cove," that gap at the Highlands' north gate between Storm King and Crow's nest. More than one sloop had capsized there. But the most perilous stretch of the river as it wound through the Highlands was Martyr's Reach.

She frowned and he laughed suddenly at her con-cern. There was no need to fear, he declared with a slight swagger; he had made the trip many times and had yet to capsize.

For Charity it was a memorable voyage. Past the mountain ramparts of the palisades and up the wild deep river. She looked with awe on mighty Storm

King, its granite 600 million years old. Sometimes the tides seemed to sweep them backward, sometimes the current tossed them forward. Often they had to wait for the wind. To Charity it was a voyage of uncommon beauty. She was impressed not only with the scenery, but with the wild game she saw along the banks, and the occasional handsome manor, and once even Indians.

She told the patroon this, and he laughed and said that she would see many Indians about. He told her that October was the customary time for Indian women to bury their dried corn in rush baskets in the earth and go with their husbands and children on a deer hunt. The Indians did not return until December, when they brought the smoked meat back with them. The Indians hunted deer by forming a long line and howling like wolves as they pressed the frightened deer toward the river, driving them ahead, killing those who hesitated on the river bank with arrows, while those that tried to escape by water were caught and drowned by other Indians who waited in canoes.

Charity was silent for a long time staring upriver toward the savage wilderness, thinking of the Mohawks near Albany, those savage "guardians of the eastern door" of the Long House.

She began to think of the manor of Daarkenwyck as an oasis—and all outside of it as The Dark.

CHAPTER 12

Scarlet maples flamed among the tall oaks and sycamores that shadowed the lush green lawns of Daarkenwyck, while clumps of swaying willows overhung the water at the river's edge. Before her, on both sides of the small wooden pier set on pilings, Charity could see a pair of square blockhouses made of heavy logs and built obviously for defense. Beyond, through the brilliant vermilion of the maple branches, she could glimpse the house, an imposing stone structure, two stories in height, steep roofed and enormous, and her spirits rose. This was not Margaret Yorking's turreted castle in Kent nor Jane Millwood's imposing manor house in Sussex, nor yet the Moorish-columned *alcazar* surrounded by orange trees in sunny Spain that Mercedes Ramirez had described to her so often and so wistfully—but it was an aristocratic seat, and a far cry from the cramped wooden houses of Dynestown.

On the dock waiting for them stood several servants, and a soberly dressed older man who looked to be of some authority. As Charity watched, another figure raced down across the green lawns—a woman's figure, her striped pink skirts flying, her auburn hair flying too. The figure ran lightly across the wooden pier.

"Cousin Killian!" she cried. When she saw Charity, she came to a sudden stop, her expression almost ludicrous with surprise. Charity reckoned that the girl was about her own height, young, with a slightly fuller figure. And her eyes—her eyes were just the misty color of the blue velvet of Charity's new dress.

Charity stiffened. No wonder the girl looked shocked. The dress had been meant for her, Charity had no doubt.

The patroon looked amused.

"Cousin Annjanette," he said in an offhand voice, "this is Cousin Charity, whom I was fortunate enough to encounter in New York. She will be staying with us. In the room you formerly occupied. Please prepare it for her."

"Cousin . . . Charity?" whispered the girl.

"Yes," he said coldly, and turned his attention to the authoritative looking older man who bowed deeply, his wide-brimmed hat sweeping the pier's wooden flooring.

"My lord patroon," he said diffidently, "I have hastened to greet you with a matter of some importance. The wife of Godyn Wessel, who lives on one of your *bouweries,* has been caught weaving."

The patroon looked at him sharply. "You confiscated the loom, of course?"

"Of course, Mynheer van Daarken. Also the material she had woven and her flax. But of the punishment I would speak."

The patroon frowned. "Is not her husband that giant oaf who pulled the cart loose from the mud last year when the horses could not?"

The other nodded.

"Then say no more of punishment. Warn them sharply of the law, say that it is not to be flouted. Remind them that the company from whom I have my grant of land would protect the looms of Holland— but otherwise disturb them not. He is a strong man and valuable to the land."

His agent frowned but bent his head in obedience to the patroon's will.

Charity had paid little attention to this exchange. She and Annjanette had been measuring each other warily with their eyes, and Charity had detected in the other girl's face a look of profound shock that she was trying desperately to conceal. Cousin Annjanette was a pretty girl, with her misty blue eyes and small

148

turned-up nose and silky auburn hair, but just now her fair skin was flushed an embarrassed pink and there was anger in her eyes and something akin to fear.

Charity was puzzled. It seemed to her that Annjanette was over-reacting.

"Come with me, Mademoiselle," muttered the girl in French, finding her tongue at last. And tossed over her shoulder, "Jochem, bring Mademoiselle's baggage."

French, thought Charity, surprised. A French girl. . . .

She muttered something in French about not having any baggage. The patroon's voice cut in.

"Cousin Charity's baggage lies at the bottom of the Hudson," he announced coolly, "where a foolish oaf by the dockside dropped it. Perhaps you can find a dress or two of your own that she can wear while others are being made for her." It was not a question; it had the force of a command.

"Of course." Annjanette's eyes were snapping now and she pressed her full lips together angrily. She marched Charity across the sweeping green lawns toward the house without a word.

As they approached the house, Charity considered the wide stoop at the front, the generous small-paned windows. "Are there many in Monsieur van Daarken's family?" she asked, speaking in French as Annjanette had done.

The other girl turned. "You are his cousin and yet you do not know that?" she flung at her.

Charity frowned. She would have to be careful. "I am lately from England, and we have not had much time to talk."

"The patroon has a wife, Clothilde, and a son, Pieter," Annjanette said flatly. "There was a daughter, but she is dead. The grandmother keeps to her room and comes down only on occasion."

In silence she led Charity through the large front door and into a spacious hall that had large rooms on both sides of it and a wide staircase in its center. Up that stairway they went and down the hallway to their

149

left. At a closed door Annjanette paused and frowned. "We had best enter through here," she muttered. "Cousin Clothilde may be taking a nap in the other room."

Charity was mystified. She followed Annjanette into a large bedroom, handsomely furnished in the Dutch style, heavy, dark and carved, then through another door into a large dressing room that was also furnished as a bedroom, though not so handsomely.

"We came through Cousin Killian's room," said Annjanette in a defensive voice, "so we would not disturb Cousin Clothilde who sleeps next door." She nodded at another door leading from the dressing room. "I sleep here so as to be at Cousin Clothilde's side if she should wake in the night and need anything. She is not well and sometimes she—she walks in her sleep," she added hurriedly.

Charity was surprised to see that Annjanette's sleeping quarters could not be entered from the hall, but must be reached either from the bedroom of the patroon or his wife's. Still . . . if the patroon's wife were ill. . . .

Ungraciously, Annjanette pulled open the drawer of a chest. "What will you require?" she snapped.

"Mainly a nightgown and a dressing gown," sighed Charity. "Perhaps a cloak against the cold."

Annjanette snatched out a very expensive embroidered nightgown and an equally handsome dressing gown. She almost threw them at Charity. With compressed lips she jerked a blue cape from a chair, where it had been carelessly thrown, tossed it atop the other things, and turned and marched out. Over her shoulder she asked, "How long have you known Cousin Killian, mademoiselle?"

She was jealous! Charity realized. This pretty young thing was jealous of her, angry that Killian van Daarken had brought her home with him!

"I met him in New York," she said, adding in hope of soothing the other girl, "where is his son? I had hoped he would be at the dock to meet us."

"Pieter?" Annjanette swung around and looked at

her sharply. "What have you to do with Pieter, mademoiselle?"

"I am to assist him in languages," explained Charity patiently. "French and English—and to teach him Spanish, which I understand he does not know. It is why I was brought upriver," she added gently.

Annjanette's eyes widened. *"Mon Dieu!"* she murmured. "A language tutor!" Her whole manner changed. "I am—sorry, mademoiselle," she said haltingly. "At first I thought. . . ." She did not elaborate on what she had thought. "Wait, you could use some ribbons for your hair. And I have a yellow morning dress that will fit you; it has grown tight for me." She left Charity blinking over this sudden change of manner, and hurried away, returning with her arms full of clothing and blue and yellow ribbons, including a dainty white lace coif over which Charity exclaimed.

"I was living in France when my father became ill. When he learned he was going to die, he wrote to Cousin Killian and sent him my picture, asking if he would not take me in," she confided. "And as you can see—" she gestured proudly at the pretty clothes Charity held in her arms, "here I am treated as a daughter of the house."

Charity was not quite certain this was so, but she was grateful the French girl's hostility had ceased.

"You will be happy here," Annjanette predicted. Happy now herself, she led Charity jauntily down a short flight of stairs which, Charity realized, led to a wing that swept away from the house at the rear. Charity followed her pretty guide into a small room furnished with a narrow wooden bed, a small chest, a straight chair and a washstand.

"This was my room," Annjanette said, looking around her. "Until Cousin Clothilde needed someone to sleep only a whisper away from her."

Charity nodded, carefully appearing to accept the explanation at face value.

"It is too bad Pieter was not here to greet you," Annjanette added. "He has gone upriver to visit the van der Dooncks and will probably be bringing Ryn van der Doonck and his sister Cordelia back with him tonight. You will meet him at dinner."

Promising to send a maid with clean linens and water, Annjanette went out, leaving Charity to look around her room. The first thing she checked was the bolt on the door. It worked very well and seemed more than adequate.

From her small window, she could see fields and forest stretching out for miles. Killian van Daarken had told her that Daarkenwyck was comprised of some 165,000 acres. It seemed to her dazzled eyes that it must reach beyond the mountain mists and into the morning sun.

She turned as a stocky little maid knocked timidly on the door and came in carrying linens. The maid eyed Charity with frank interest as she replaced the bed linen and bustled about tidying up.

Fully intending to make an entrance and establish herself at once not as a servant but as a member of the family, Charity resisted the impulse to prowl about. She remained in her room until another round-eyed little Dutch girl in a white cap knocked on her door and told her in halting English that dinner would soon be served and she was expected downstairs in the dining room.

Charity, who had been sitting, dressed and waiting, rose at once to answer this summons and went downstairs to find five people awaiting her in the living room.

The patroon she already knew. And "Cousin" Annjanette, richly gowned in pink damask, who was his undoubted mistress if Charity was any judge.

Ryn van der Doonck was a wild-looking slender young Dutchman of around twenty with dark hair and a wicked smile. He looked stunned when he saw Charity, but quickly recovered himself—though during the whole of the evening his admiring gaze seldom left her face. His sister Cordelia, a sharp-eyed, round-faced, dark-haired girl of no more than seventeen, reacted to Charity's presence with alarm which hardened into dislike as the evening wore on.

But it was Pieter van Daarken who held Charity's attention. He stepped forward vibrantly, his hat held gracefully under his arm, and swept her a low bow as his father introduced them. His yellow hair fell over his eyes, and when he lifted his head and tossed it back, Charity felt her confidence rise at the naked admiration in his bold blue eyes. He was young—she guessed no older than Ryn—and of a handsome build; a stripling yet but he would develop into a strong man. There was something a little fretful in the set of his mouth, but this dissolved instantly into a bright smile for Charity's benefit. Pieter had a patrician look about him and an easy grace. Except for his coloring, there was little to indicate that he was the powerful, heavyset patroon's son.

They went in to dinner, which was served on a snowy linen cloth covered with heavy gleaming silver trenchers and tall brass candlesticks. The patroon's wife was conspicuously absent. *The mail from Holland has come,* mused Charity. *That was what Killian van Daarken had told her, and there had been something in his voice as he said it . . . something both cynical and dark. And as she had passed the door of Clothilde's bedroom on her way downstairs she had thought she heard weeping.*

Pieter said something to Charity, and she turned to give him her attention, noticing as she did the fine Flemish lace at his throat and cuffs, the richness of his dark green velvet coat with its silver braid and silver buttons, the thick blond curls—undoubtedly his own —that swung below his plumed hat. It was the custom for gentlemen to carry their hats under their arms as they walked about, thus keeping their elaborate wigs or curls in order, and to put their hats on when they sat down—even at dinner. Pieter looked the very essence of fashion and Charity was surprised to find so much elegance in this wild land so far from any town.

Their conversation was interrupted by a sudden

burst of laughter at the other end of the table where the young van der Dooncks sat on either side of the patroon. A deep blush suddenly stained Annjanette's cheeks and she was biting her lips. Charity asked what remark had occasioned the laughter.

"Ryn was saying that we van Daarkens are an international family—first a French cousin and now an English one," Pieter shrugged. "And for some reason his sister laughed and he joined in. Cordelia laughs inappropriately as you will soon discover."

But perhaps not *too* inappropriately, thought Charity, realizing that the sharp-eyed van der Doonck girl probably assumed Charity to be the newest addition to the patroon's harem on the Hudson. Charity shrugged and her eyes grew cold. Such thoughts would be proved wrong soon enough and Cordelia, like the apprehensive Annjanette, would come to realize that Charity's position here was actually that of a language tutor.

"There are several branches of our family," Pieter added hastily, as if fearing Charity might take offense at Ryn's barbed comment. "A French branch, a German one. I did not know about the English branch, but—" His manner said that he accepted the relationship without question.

Charity smiled at him and, to change the subject, remarked that the blue-claw crabs were delicious. Then she switched to French, asking him about the seafood they ate at Daarkenwyck.

All manner of seafood, he responded in flawless French. Mussels and clams, smelt, alewives and carp and eels—which were his favorite—scallops and lobsters. At Daarkenwyck they also ate much wild game. They set a good table, he told her proudly.

Charity studied him narrowly. That easy fluency in French . . . he had been conversing with Annjanette in her native tongue no doubt. She tried him in Spanish. He looked blank.

"I would love to learn Dutch," she said wistfully. "Do you think you could teach me? I would teach you Spanish in return," she added hastily.

He responded with great enthusiasm and, as they lapsed back into English, she realized that he was fairly proficient although his accent was faulty.

Charity was aware that the patroon was studying her with some amusement, that Ryn was watching her with dancing eyes, and that Cordelia had ceased to eat entirely, her teeth biting into her lower lip as she watched Charity and Pieter laughing and talking together.

Charity ignored them. She was here to instruct Pieter in languages and she could do so only by engaging him in conversation. If that offended Cordelia van der Doonck, that was Cordelia's misfortune.

From his easy manner, she gathered the patroon approved of her monopolizing his son's attention, which gave her a sense of relief. It was clear now that she would be accepted not as a servant but as a member of the family.

It would be pleasant, she told herself, to learn a new language while brushing up an old one. And speaking Spanish would remind her of Mercedes Ramirez, whom she had counted as her only real friend in Stéphanie's school.

She was still thinking these pleasant thoughts when they retired to the living room. There Cordelia van der Doonck, with only the slightest urging, swept up her ample skirts and, sitting down at the rosewood harpsichord, began to play. She had little talent and struck as many discordant notes as true ones, but she looked pretty and young posing there in the candlelight, with her dark curls swaying as she moved her hands lightly over the keys. The candle glow flattered her and complemented the rich dark wine of her big full-skirted wool dress with its heavy cream lace at collar and sleeves.

But no one was looking at Cordelia tonight. Nor at pretty Annjanette, who rose next to sing a little French ditty. Charity, sitting with her back straight and her hands folded primly in her lap, could not help but feel the pressure of three pairs of masculine eyes focused curiously on her. Only the patroon's glance made her feel nervous. She sensed in him a latent lechery that made her uneasy about her future here. It was all well enough to tell her that she had been brought here to polish up his son's proficiency in languages, but Pieter spoke French well already, his English was passable, and with relations between Spain and the rest of Europe being what they were, what chance would he have to speak Spanish? Probably very little.

So Charity's color heightened nervously as she felt Killian van Daarken's small brooding eyes rest upon her. She was almost glad when the younger man asked her if she played or sang. Charity had never mastered a musical instrument, but she had a sweet clear voice and young ladies were expected to exhibit some talent in the drawing room. She rose willingly to stand by the harpsichord beside a flushed, rebellious Cordelia, who thumped out an accompaniment as Charity, her pale gold hair caressed by the candlelight, sang a simple love song.

In an attempt to avoid looking at the patroon, she looked toward Pieter as she sang it, and saw his blue eyes kindle. After the song was over he sprang up to escort Charity back to her chair, and Cordelia van der Doonck began waving her fan so fast it blew her dark curls about.

"I am sorry not to have met your mother," Charity told Pieter, ignoring Cordelia. "Is she ill?"

He shrugged. "My father brought the mail from Holland. My mother always cries when the mail comes from Holland. She is very homesick. As long as I can remember she has been homesick for Holland."

"Has she never gone back?" wondered Charity.

"No," he said. "My father's interests are here, and he prefers that she stay beside him. She has not been well of late. Annjanette sleeps in the dressing room to be near her in case she needs anything."

Now two people had told her that. Both most earnestly. Charity cocked an eye at him. "How long has Annjanette lived with you?" she asked.

"Two years," he said promptly. "I believe her father

wrote to my father and said that he was getting too old to care for her, and shipped her over here. Like you, she came upriver as a great surprise to us, for my father had told us nothing about her arrival in advance."

"Your father is full of surprises," said Charity dryly.

Pieter nodded soberly. "It is his way. He sees no need to take others into his confidence."

"A man met him at the dock to tell him some woman was weaving. Why is it forbidden to weave?"

"The looms of Holland are hungry for fibers," he said and smiled. "The Dutch West India Company established the law against weaving and here at Daarkenwyck we follow it."

"But . . . are you not English now?" asked Charity.

Her voice had carried a little farther than she had meant it to, and there was a sudden silence.

Into that silence Killian van Daarken's authoritative voice rose, informing her coldly that the Hudson Valley would still be Dutch but for the terrible events of 1663—first an earthquake, followed by a flood, then smallpox, and an Indian massacre—all of which, combined with poor fortifications due to bad management in the City of New Amsterdam, had weakened the Dutch settlers so that the arrival of the English fleet in 1664 had found them powerless to fight. However, aside from hurt pride, she got the impression that the Dutch did not mind English rule—indeed that they throve on it.

The van der Dooncks were staying overnight and the young people, led by a silent Annjanette—her spirits dampened by the gibe at dinner—retired early to their rooms. As Charity and Pieter followed them, Pieter took Charity's arm and his hand unnecessarily brushed her breast. She drew away instantly and from the hallway below came the stern voice of the patroon.

"Pieter—a word with you."

"Excuse me," Pieter said with a frown, and somewhat sulkily retraced his steps. From the stair landing Charity saw the scowling older man beckon his son toward the deserted library. He was going to chide

Pieter, she divined, for that slight transgression. She did not know whether to be glad or sorry.

In her room, Charity divested herself of her dress, letting it slide to the floor along with her petticoats and chemise, and stretched her firm young body before she got into her nightdress. She told herself that she would begin Pieter's language tutoring in earnest the next day in an attempt to pay for the clothes and her shelter at Daarkenwyck, and settled herself into the narrow bed to sleep dreamlessly.

She would not have slept so well if she had heard some of the heated remarks that were passing in the library below.

CHAPTER 13

Charity did not meet the patroon's wife, Clothilde, until dinner the second day. Clothilde was a pale wisp of a woman with dark circles under her eyes and a vague manner. Ineffectual, but graceful and a patrician like her son Pieter. She greeted Charity absently, and henceforth ignored her. She always looked sad.

Charity thought it a shame that Clothilde was not allowed to visit Holland, since she longed for it so much, and wondered if the woman's sleepwalking was a desire to reach a ship that would take her across the stormy Atlantic.

Neither the patroon nor his son paid much attention to Clothilde, and Charity saw pain in the woman's eyes, once, when she touched her son's arm and he ignored her. Clothilde drifted in and out during the days that followed and Charity continued to be puzzled by the family's attitude toward the lovely pathetic mother.

But Charity forgot all that in her interest in exploring the house. She learned that there were four major rooms on the first floor. Two were the large living rooms on either side of the entrance hall. Behind them extended respectively a library and the dining room. They too could be entered from the hall, which ran completely through the house. The big kitchen and pantries occupied the first floor of the rear wing. Upstairs there were five bedrooms in the main part, two of them occupied by the patroon and his wife, while Annjanette slept in the dressing room between them. One was occupied by Pieter, one by his grandmother, and the last reserved for guests who also sometimes overflowed into the wing where Charity had her small room. The attic was reserved for the servants, who—since there were so many of them—must have been crowded in like sardines, and who came down a back stairway that led into the big kitchen.

The patroon was right. Charity liked Daarkenwyck. She liked the deep-silled windows in the walls which were some three feet thick of solid stone. She liked the beautiful view of the river flowing past, the huge stone barn with its vast beams, the well-stocked cellar with its fruity smell from the bins of apples. And because she loved wildlife, she was charmed by the custom of nailing old hats to the kitchen windowsills, each with a small round hole in the crown to make a nest for the wrens. More surprising were the skeleton heads of horses and cattle mounted on poles that were also used as nesting places for the wrens—and much beloved by them.

She had learned that the *bouweries* produced corn, oats, wheat and hops for beer. The land was fertilized with rotted oyster shells from the old "kitchen middens" of past Indian feasts along the river banks. Oyster shells had been ground into mortar, too, and used in building the house at Daarkenwyck.

As Charity walked past the open door to the old lady's bedroom one day, she caught a glimpse of Pieter's grandmother. The obese, coarse-faced woman sat propped among many pillows in her big four-poster bed with its billowing feather mattress, her fat ringed hands lying idly on the damask counterpane, a large tray of cakes and sweetmeats ever at her side. That she ate heartily of fish and game and all else that graced the patroon's table could be attested to by the groaning trays that were carried up to her by the servants and the empty platters and broken bits that came downstairs again. The servants muttered that she got drunk on beer as well, but Charity was not certain. Although well served, Pieter's grandmother seemed pointedly ignored by the rest of the household.

Charity thought it a pity and suggested reading

to her, but Pieter said she would not welcome it. He added that his grandmother preferred a stolid life of eating and sleeping and would, when the occasion moved her, come down and join them at dinner, listening to the gossip and occasionally joining in it. He added that she never missed a ball that was held at Daarkenwyck.

One night Charity went downstairs, thinking to get a new candle from the kitchen pantry for her own was burning very low, and saw Annjanette in her nightdress slip out of the patroon's room and hurry down the stairs. Charity checked her advance and would have gone back, but Annjanette had already seen her. Her cheeks very red, Annjanette said defensively that Clothilde was "worse tonight" and that she was going down to get her some hot milk. Charity pretended to believe her. It was no business of hers where Annjanette slept or with whom.

In an odd way she was even grateful to the French girl, for she had the feeling that if Annjanette had left in a huff on Charity's arrival, she herself might have been summoned to tend "Cousin" Clothilde in the night—and in so doing would have been unpleasantly close to the patroon who ruled this manor as any other feudal lord ruled his demesne.

Although she would sometimes turn to find Killian van Daarken staring at her with something akin to dark greed in his small eyes, he made no move toward her. On the whole Charity found life at Daarkenwyck with its many servants very pleasant.

She rode horseback with Pieter to nearby portions of the estate and boated with him on the river. Often they were joined by Ryn and Cordelia as well, for the two young van der Dooncks were glad to leave their three younger sisters and brother at home and seek the more sophisticated company at Daarkenwyck.

Ryn made every effort to single her out, but Charity, sensing a competition in that regard between Ryn and Pieter, avoided being alone with Ryn. Her situation, she told herself grimly, her very livelihood, depended upon her spending long hours with Pieter. The

161

patroon might take a dim view of her spending too much time with happy-go-lucky Ryn.

And besides, there was something challenging and mocking in Ryn's eyes that told her he did not necessarily believe she was Killian's "cousin." Plain and open hostility was the only attitude Cordelia evinced toward her. The feeling was shared by the rest of the van der Doonck family, she knew. Once, when they went boating upriver as far as the van der Doonck's brick manor, they found it too late to go home and spent the night there. Charity was made aware all through dinner and afterward that her hostess despised her and felt affronted that she should be eating at the same table. And that night she was squeezed into the smallest, plainest room in the house—a servant's room tucked away under the eaves.

Ryn, ignoring his mother and sister, recklessly continued to pay court to Charity.

Pieter seemed not to notice, for which Charity was grateful. After that unpleasant stay at the van der Doonck's manor, she made an effort to steer Pieter in some other direction whenever he seemed to be heading his horse or the sailboat toward his neighbors to the north.

Still she was happy at Daarkenwyck, and could find nothing to criticize in the elegance of their life, which —except that they ate off pewter and silver rather than china—fully equaled Stéphanie's luxurious way of living in Bath. Their tumblers and teapots and tankards were of massive silver and very imposing. Even the lovely *ooma* or sifter for the cinnamon and sugar which was sprinkled over cakes and toast was of silver, and there were a few plates of fine delft. She enjoyed their well-laden table, with its pies and puddings and scrapple and sausage, headcheeses, milk cheeses and pickles and preserves. It surprised her that in a place where almost everything was dear to buy, both butter and beaver pelts were cheap.

But then beaver pelts were to the Dutch what the gold of Central and South America was to the Spanish, and fur pelts flowed out of this vast new continent by the hundreds of thousands.

With the patroon's family and servants, Charity attended services in the small stone *kerk* with its lofty pulpit. Services opened by a reading from the Bible by the clerk or *voorleser,* who stood in the baptistry below the pulpit and laid out his text. During this time Charity always watched the deacons who stood facing the pulpit, the alms bags in their hands. The deacons then collected the contributions of the congregation while the *domine* dwelt piously upon the necessities of the poor and invoked blessings on those who gave liberally. Charity watched with fascination the *kerk sacjes* of velvet which were suspended from the end of a long pole and thrust in front of each row of seats by the deacons. A bell was hung at the bottom of the bag which would call attention to niggardly gifts. Charity had a moment of deep mortification the first time she went to services when the bell rang for her. Having nothing to give, she had slipped into the velvet bag a handsome button from the blue velvet dress the patroon had given her. She estimated it to be of some value and something she could manage to do without. But her face reddened with shame as the entire congregation turned to stare at her. Killian van Daarken frowned, and the next morning she found beneath her pillow a small bag of copper coins which she understood to be "kerk money."

She did not enjoy the sermons, which were very long. As they began, the *voorsinger* would turn the hour-glass which marked their length. When the sermon was over, the *voorleser* would rise and with a long cleft rod hand to the *domine,* in the pulpit above, the requests for prayers or thanks from the members sitting solemnly below. The petitions were read aloud—the family of the patroon was prayed for frequently, their health and prosperity espoused—then another psalm was sung and everybody filed out in procession.

How different, she thought wistfully, from church services at home, and for a little time felt a homesickness for Devon, for the quaint little houses rising tier on tier in Torquay, with flowers spilling over their walls.

CHAPTER 14

As the days sped by, Charity learned more and more Dutch. She tested her proficiency on the maids, and found them quite willing to discuss the family with her. One of them, who had served the family for years, told her fondly that she remembered little Pieter when he was a wee one. He was always breaking or discarding his toys and getting new ones. A real little devil he was, she laughed. In those days it was toys. Now, of course, it was girls. Then she flushed scarlet as if she had said too much.

After that Charity began to notice the way the servant girls looked at Pieter. There was a certain archness in their manner toward him. Deviously, she asked the little maid who cleaned her room about Ryn and was told proudly that Mynheer Ryn had tried her, but she'd beaten him off. Indeed, she liked Mynheer Pieter's way much better! And then she too had blushed. In her confusion, she added that one of the servant girls had had a baby by Ryn.

Charity wondered if any of them had had a baby by Pieter. And what would happen to the mother and child if they had.

She could almost believe the event would go unnoticed, for delicate Clothilde hardly seemed to be aware of her surroundings.

Charity thought that a strange way for a grown woman to act, and warmed to Pieter, who was, she felt, saddled with an odd mother and a crude father and rather spiteful friends. Pieter responded eagerly to every encouragement she gave him. After that first night, however, he made no further effort to touch her intimately. She rather thought his father had laid down the law on the subject, and was glad.

But Pieter, young and fervent, still pursued her relentlessly. He was everywhere she was. He took her riding, he played cards with her, he taught her the game of bowles. He continued to teach her Dutch, which she learned readily, and conversed merrily with her in French or English—although he steadfastly refused to bother with Spanish, in spite of all her entreaties. But he was not leaving for Holland until spring and she hoped she could prevail on him to concentrate more earnestly on his studies before then.

The gift-giving season came early in December, Charity learned. St. Nicholas visited Dutch children December 6 instead of at Christmas. With it came the first really cold snap. A shallow pond near the house froze over and the clang of skates rang out across the smooth ice. Pieter offered to teach Charity to skate and she learned quickly. She soon was able to flash about the pond along with Pieter and the Dutch servants, all of whom skated. In fact, the younger ones took every available moment from their duties to hurry out into the crisp weather and glide about the pond.

By now she had come almost to think of herself as a member of the family, a lesser member, but indeed a cousin, and she faced the occasional insult of one of the neighboring ladies with cool unconcern.

She could almost forget her stormy arrival in New England, her cruel time in the jail, and her bittersweet romance with Tom Blade, as she found herself drifting along contentedly at Daarkenwyck. Pieter, she knew, yearned to possess her. Indeed he could hardly keep his hands to himself although he had never once so much as walked by her door at night. But when he set her skates to her shoes on the edge of the pond, his hands would close around her slender ankles and his suddenly upturned face would send her an unmistakable message: Pieter desired her.

Her skates made fast, Charity would give him a Mona Lisa smile and skate away until he caught her and they swooped together across the ice.

For Charity, these days passed in Pieter's company were unreal, a time of dreaming.

But the ice she skated on was thin and getting thinner. This was brought sharply to her attention the night of December 5, for that evening Pieter gave vent to what she had been reading in his face all along.

The younger children of the estate farmers had been invited to spend the festival of St. Nicholas at Daarkenwyck, as they were every year. Charity came downstairs that evening to find that the children had spread a white sheet on the floor of the living room and were singing verses enthusiastically imploring St. Nicholas to ride from Amsterdam to Spain, and promising to serve him always.

She smiled and met Pieter's eyes across the room. He stood a little behind the children, his hands clasped behind his back, waiting while the rest of the household gathered.

Suddenly the door burst open and a shower of candies and other goodies landed on the sheet, and St. Nicholas himself appeared. Charity recognized the enormous hulk of Big Jan, dressed up for the part. St. Nicholas was attended by his own servant who, Pieter explained, was the traditional Knech Ruprecht. Black Ruprecht, portrayed this night by one of the two black house servants of Daarkenwyck, carried a sack and threatened loudly to put all bad children in it. He gestured at a bundle of switches under his arm, at which they all pretended to cower. And all the while St. Nicholas was gravely handing out gifts from his sack.

To her surprise, Charity found that she was included in this gift-giving ceremony. Exclaiming with pleasure, she opened Killian's gift which was a handsome length of dark gold velvet, almost the color of her lashes. To this Clothilde graciously added a pair of gold satin slippers, while Annjanette shyly gave her some black satin ribbons. Charity was pleased and touched. Late in December there was to be a great ball at Daarkenwyck and she knew that all the ladies were to have new dresses for it, but she had not been certain that she would be included.

Pieter put his hand on her arm and murmured, "I have a gift for you too, but not here."

She followed him as he took a candle and led her into a pantry, which he insisted was practically the only place in the house with any privacy at the moment, since even the servants were all running about under the happy influence of jolly old St. Nick. Charity followed him past barrels of salt fish and sauerkraut and pickled pork, past stone jars of pickles, and cool butter in firkins, and kegs of soused pigs' feet.

Beside a bin of sweet-smelling apples he paused, put the candle down carefully and told her to close her eyes.

Charity did so warily, but peeking through her lashes, she saw that he was pulling a length of lovely creamy lace from his pocket. So, she promptly closed her eyes tightly and waited for the lace to be handed to her.

It was not.

A moment later she felt Pieter's hot hands at her breasts, his fingers pushing down beneath her clothing against the warm skin. Her eyes snapped open in shocked surprise.

"I—trying—" he said, "to fasten this lace around the top of your chemise where it belongs."

Charity gave him an affronted look as she reached up to push his hands away. To her surprise, he resisted her efforts, pushing the lace—and his fingers—down into the smooth valley between her breasts.

"Pieter!" she cried.

Suddenly, almost with a sob, he clutched both her breasts in his hands and buried his curly blond head in the valley between them, covering them with hot insistent kisses. As she jerked away from him, the material of her bodice ripped and one breast was exposed. The lace he had been pushing into her chemise pulled free and fell in a long wafting streamer to the floor as Charity jerked free and stood regarding him with blazing eyes.

Pieter stood a moment, undecided as to what to do. He took a step toward her, his expression wild, and she retreated.

"You must not misunderstand me," he cried beseechingly. "I swear I mean you no harm. It was touching you that maddened me. Oh, Charity, when you are near, my blood pounds in my head and throbs through my veins—oh, God, I can't stand it. Charity, I must have you—I must!"

She swayed away from that outburst, but his hands seized her shoulders, and Charity cried, "No!" violently.

In their concentration on each other, neither was aware that someone else had joined them. They both jumped when Annjanette's surprised voice cried, "Oh, I'm sorry. I didn't know there was anyone here!"

Charity, crimson faced, pulled at her clothing, tucking the material around her white breast to shield it from view.

"What are you doing here?" Pieter snarled.

"I—I only came for some candles," cried Annjanette, confused. "The servants were busy and—"

"Meddler!" cried Pieter. "Spy!" And before Annjanette could elude him, he delivered a stinging slap to her cheek that spun her around. She gave a short half-shriek as the blow struck her, then crouched white-faced for a moment staring at him before she turned and fled. Charity too stared at him for a moment in angry accusation before she hurried after Annjanette.

"I'm sorry," gasped Annjanette as they reached the first floor hall.

"Don't be!" snapped Charity. "I'm glad you came! I wasn't sure what was going to happen next. Is there anyone in the hall?"

"No," sniffed Annjanette.

"Would you walk in front of me? I—my bodice is ripped."

"I know," muttered Annjanette. "Pieter's always in a hurry."

Charity caught her breath. She stared at Annjanette.

Annjanette turned a tear-stained face to her as they hurried along the hall. "Pieter took me in the pantry too," she burst out, wiping her eyes with her hand. "Against that big apple bin. He slipped up behind me and whirled me around and bent me backwards. He tore my petticoats and he almost broke my back. I was sore for days."

"When was this?" demanded Charity, shocked.

"It was a month after I arrived. I didn't know then to watch out for him." She looked anxiously at Charity. "You won't say anything about it, will you? I mean, it's such a long time ago—"

"Well, surely you told the patroon?"

Annjanette hung her head. "I was afraid to," she muttered. "I was afraid he would say I had led Pieter on and deserved no better than I got." She bit her lips.

Annjanette looked about to say something else and thought better of it. "I—I must be going," she said hurriedly. "They will miss me and wonder where I am."

"You mean you aren't going back for the candles?" Charity said, sarcastically.

"No, I will ask that pretty new servant girl—Elyse. I will ask her to get them."

"But . . . Pieter may still be down there, raging about."

"I know." Annjanette did not meet her eyes. "That is why I will send Elyse." She moved nervously under Charity's shocked look. "It is better for all of us," she muttered. "I know that by interrupting I have made him very angry. Perhaps if I send Elyse that will appease him."

Charity forgot she was standing there in a torn dress. "You'll warn Elyse what she's walking into, won't you?" she demanded.

Annjanette shook her head. "Do not disturb yourself about it," she said in a colder voice. "I will take care of the matter."

She turned and walked rapidly away. Charity called, "Annjanette!" and started to run after her, and then remembered that her dress was torn, and hurried off to change it.

When she came back downstairs, Charity looked around for Elyse to warn her, but she was nowhere to be seen. Annjanette looked very subdued and promptly moved away when Charity approached. After a time Pieter rejoined them. He avoided Charity's eyes and retired early. No one noticed all this byplay in the general excitement of the gifts amid the dancing, shrieking children. Clothilde, looking very frail, watched the children, smiling sadly, and the patroon stood beside her, his face inscrutable.

When she went to bed that night, Charity paused by the attic stairs. She thought she heard someone sobbing. Elyse?

She was awakened by a scratching at her door. She padded to the door barefoot, checked the bolt, and whispered, "Who is it?"

"I couldn't sleep." Pieter's voice sounded subdued.

"Go away," she said harshly against the wood.

"Please," he pleaded. "Charity, you won't tell my father about this, will you? I—I got carried away."

"You did indeed," she said in a cold voice. "And whyever did you slap Annjanette? She had done nothing."

He hesitated. "I told Annjanette I was sorry," he said sulkily *"She* accepted my apology. Why can't you?"

"I accept your apology," she said coldly. "Now go away."

She heard his dejected footsteps slink down the hall and asked herself why she was so very angry with him? Not because of Elyse surely—she did not even know what had happened there. Nor because of Annjanette. No, she admitted to herself soberly, it was because Pieter had sprung on her like a low woman, his for the taking. She resented that bitterly.

The next morning when Charity woke she found the delicate lace had been slipped underneath her door. She picked up the fragile stuff and studied it with troubled eyes. She felt she was fast approaching a

171

crisis in her life at Daarkenwyck. But, like a leaf about to be swept over the brink of a roaring water-fall, she felt powerless to stay the irresistible tide that swept her along.

CHAPTER 15

Although Charity had last call on the resident seamstress, her length of dark gold velvet was made up into a gown in time for the great ball at Daarkenwyck. The ball was an annual event eagerly anticipated along the river.

Except for one prolonged cold spell, the weather had been unseasonably warm. Everyone blamed that unseasonable warmth for the colds that swept through the household, causing stuffed heads and runny noses. No matter, the late December ball would, she was told, be well attended. Two days before, the house began to fill up with guests, and soon they were overflowing. Others guests were staying at the estates that lay nearest Daarkenwyck. Guests had come upriver from New York and downriver from as far as Rensselaerwyck. For over a week the staff had been laboring with spices and picklings and cakes and other goodies. There would be dancing and all the ladies would wear their finest gowns.

Charity was delighted with hers. She had designed it herself from memory, recalling one of Stéphanie's. It was full-skirted, with a tight V-bodice. Its great sleeves were full and layered and tied with black satin ribbons. From the cuffs a great froth of creamy lace erupted—Pieter's gift. She had hesitated, but had decided, in view of his recent good behavior, to wear it after all.

On the night of the ball she was glad she had, for Pieter was confined to his room with a bad cold and under doctor's orders not to stir. Passing her in the hall, the patroon had murmured to Charity that her presence at the ball was required, which pleased her because she had had some fear that she would be expected to spend the evening discoursing with Pieter, who lay in his room coughing. He was a very bad patient, and plagued all the servants.

Dressed in the new gown, Charity whirled before the small mirror in her room, her eyes challenging her reflection. Around her neck, since she possessed no jewelry, she tied another black satin ribbon, and stuck a small patch of black court plaster low on her cheek where it contrasted coquettishly with the silky texture of her fair skin. She had done her pale gold hair up in great sweeps of curls. Even though she had had to eat dinner on a tray in her room, the dining room being so crowded with guests who had come from a distance that she could not have hoped to eat before the "third table" was served, she felt a wave of excitement sweep over her. Downstairs, the music struck up, and she drifted toward the wide staircase feeling as if she were to have, at last, the "London season" of which she had dreamed at Stéphanie's. Her lips twisted a little wryly. Not a London season perhaps, but a mid-Hudson season in the Colonies. . . . Below her in the hall, Ryn van der Doonck's upturned face and dancing eyes met hers and she did not care. What did it matter, the Hudson or London? There was music, the men were handsomely dressed, the women swirled about in beautiful clothes, she herself was wearing a lovely new gown. Why should she not believe for a little while that life would always treat her so kindly?

"You're late," Ryn said.

She smiled at him.

"But worth waiting for," he added, his eyes kindling, and led her through the lower hall toward the largest living room. Both front rooms had been cleared of major furniture for dancing. Only a few straight chairs had been left around the walls.

As they moved into the room they passed Pieter's grandmother, seated on a thronelike chair, observing the merriment. It was the first time Charity had seen her downstairs and she noticed that the old lady's

174

clothes were hopelessly out of date, but must have represented the latest style in her youth. Her long rich gown was of dark crimson silk, with ornate sleeves. A stiff white ruff edged in lace, starched and wired, encircled her massive neck and ran down into a fold of white lawn which was held in place by an enormous ruby brooch. Over all this she wore an overgarment of emerald colored wool, heavily trimmed in gold braid, fitted at the back and open in front to reveal her red dress, and held onto her shapeless figure by a gold satin ribbon. Its full open sleeves were tied at the elbow with other ribbons of the same bright gold. Her hair, which was quite sparse, was pulled into a knot at the back and was worn in short wavy locks in the front, with a little fringe of stiff curls marching across her forehead.

She looked formidable.

Charity heard Clothilde sigh to a friend. "I cannot dissuade her from dressing like that." Her voice was fretful. "Killian should speak to her. After all, she is *his* mother."

Charity's gaze slid past Clothilde, who seemed a fashionable silken mass of ruffles, and she looked at the old woman more closely. She had somehow assumed this fat old woman to be the patroon's mother-in-law, so little attention did he pay to her.

But now she observed the heavy look of strong peasant stock about her, noted the keen acquisitive little eyes hidden behind rolls of fat. So bulbous was her face that her expression had become a thing of the past, but those little eyes darting about were the same as the patroon's. Charity was suddenly repelled by them as they passed over her with a kind of derision.

Charity stiffened, but she reminded herself that she must be civil, and made a brief curtsy in the woman's direction.

The old woman pointedly ignored it.

Charity's color grew a little higher. She'd have bet her handsome gold satin slippers that this woman had begun life no better than her own mother. Possibly,

175

she had even struggled behind a plow. Or at a country loom. Or maybe scrubbing the floors of her betters at some inn.

Killian was a self-made man. He had bragged about it. And he had brought his mother up the social ladder with him. And now that old woman's gaze—Charity searched for a word; it was ribald! Her gaze insinuated that Charity was less than a lady. Upset, she turned away from the patroon's mother and gave Ryn a winsome smile. He led her out to dance the minuet.

Ryn liked to dance and danced well. After Ryn, there was a constant flow of partners with whom she danced lightly about the floor, imagining herself an heiress for whose hand some aristocratic titled lord would soon be suing.

Through the front windows, during a pause in the dancing, she saw new sails arrive at the boat landing and wondered if the boat brought more guests from the manors that lined the river! Wherever would Clothilde put them?

As Charity went out into the hall, intending to go upstairs and look in on Pieter, the front door was swung open and a late entry swept into the hall.

Charity stopped still and stared at him. She would always remember him as she saw him then, striding in out of the late December night, standing tall and formidable as his keen light eyes swept the room.

Instantly, the patroon hurried over toward the man, and the patroon's lady, looking confused, came to make him welcome as well.

Their broad-shouldered new guest, who seemed remarkably at his ease, was modishly dressed. His handsome coat was of the new cut that Charity had seen in England, collarless, shaped to fit the body, pleated and flaring toward the hem. It was of charcoal grey velvet and trimmed heavily with silver braid. The cuffs were enormous, perhaps eighteen inches deep, and handsomely decorated with silver braid. His tight-fitting knee breeches that hugged his lean muscular legs were of pale dove-gray satin, and his long waistcoat was of heavy white satin brocade. His strong calves were encased in white stockings, his feet in silver buckled square-toed shoes with red heels. Under one arm he carried a large plumed hat. His other hand rested negligently on a tall silver-headed cane. A jewel of size gleamed on the middle finger of the bronzed hand that rested on the cane.

But it was not his lordly demeanor, nor the striking figure he cut in his clothes that caused Charity to notice him. It was his face that arrested her. Dark and saturnine above the white froth of his neckpiece, that hawklike face held her attention. His eyes were strikingly light and keen and penetrating. They contrasted oddly with his great curled black periwig which spilled over his shoulders and gave him a massive leonine look as he gazed about him from his great height.

He looked a king, she thought whimsically. And from the wintry look in his hard gray eyes, he was a monarch with unruly subjects.

Every woman in the room had turned to look at him, Charity realized.

He seemed not to notice.

Staring at him like all the rest, she suddenly met his restless gaze. Cold and steely they were but there was a sudden humorous flicker in them, as if he appreciated the startling figure he cut.

She smiled back at him for a moment, her eyes sparkling in the candlelight, and then realized that glances were being cast at her. It was not considered maidenly to so forthrightly return a man's glance. She looked hastily away. But she lingered there, a golden woman in the candlelight. She decided not to go upstairs just yet.

The music had begun when she turned and suddenly discovered the tall stranger bowing or "making a leg" to her.

"Would you do me the honor of dancing this dance with me?" he inquired gravely.

Charity curtsyed silently, her color rising slightly, and he led her out onto the floor.

They made a striking couple at which envious looks were cast—a study in gold and silver; the lithe girl

177

whose shimmering pale gold hair was complemented by the dark gold of her velvet gown; the lean, arrogant silver-clad stranger with the watchful eyes and the handsome profile that lent itself to sinister imaginings.

Charity was well aware they were being watched. It heightened her color and made her feel reckless, as if the ball had been given expressly for her. She gave her partner a brilliant flirtatious smile—a smile that promised much, but which, like any coquette, she had no intention of fulfilling.

He was not an expert dancer—she had the feeling he seldom danced—but he moved with the light-footed step of natural grace.

"You are the center of all eyes, golden one," he said, as they danced. There was something tantalizingly familiar about his voice, something that throbbed in her memory. "Are you not afraid these she-wolves will set upon you with their fans and drive you away, in fear you'll turn their husbands' heads?"

"I do not fear them," she answered lightly.

"No?" he challenged. "But society is something to fear. Once the pack is baying at one's heels, one . . . changes."

There was a thoughtful look on his face when he said that, and she wondered suddenly if the pack had ever bayed at *his* heels.

"I believe *you* would be able to hold them off," she said with sincerity.

He looked startled for a moment and then laughed. "Oh, assuredly now I would. At least for a time. Our armaments change with the seasons."

"You are new to the Hudson?"

"I am new to nowhere," he answered, with a shrug. "All places are old to me. Some men wander ceaselessly. I am such a man."

"By . . . choice?" she asked, remembering Tom, that other wanderer.

He gave her an odd look. "Faith, ye've a penetrating mind," he observed. "It enables ye to see through velvet coats and such like, I take it?" He had mocking eyes.

178

"I have eyes that see the man behind the mask," she countered in a challenging voice.

"And what do you see behind *my* mask?" he asked smiling.

She looked into that dark sardonic face and decided the conversation had become too serious. "A man pursued by women," she said airily. As one of his eyebrows quirked upward, she added recklessly, "Though whether worthy of their attention has yet to be proved!"

His eyes kindled. "Such proof is easy wrought," he murmured. There was something in his voice that brought the color to her cheeks and made her miss a step. He seemed not to notice her slip. He was watching her, studying her intently as they danced, and seemed quite oblivious to all but the golden woman before him.

"We have a ball at this time every year," she said glibly, for all the world as if she were a daughter of the house. "Are we to expect you at the next one?"

"A year is the devil's own time away," he mused, his gaze passing over her flushed face and sparkling eyes and resting for a moment on the soft curve of her throat, the white sweep of her bosom above the gold velvet. "But yes, if I live, I shall find you and dance a dance with you this time next year."

"Of course—" she fluttered her lashes—"this time next year might find me married. . . ."

"It is a chance we all must take," he said.

She felt a little irritated by his light response.

"And is your suitor among this company?" he asked, looking about him with some curiosity.

"No. Unfortunately he lies abed upstairs with a deep cold. The doctors have forbidden him the pleasures of the evening." Why should she not claim the patroon's son as a suitor, she asked herself defiantly. Certainly he had pursued her.

"Upstairs?" His voice was questioning. "Then his malady came upon him suddenly?"

She shook her head. "The patroon's son."

"Ah, then you are not his daughter? The way you spoke, I thought——"

"No, I am his cousin."

"But you will become his daughter, I take it?"

"Perhaps."

His strange light eyes glinted in his dark face. "Then I envy the lad upstairs with the cold. He has a bright future to warm his heart."

She smiled in return for the compliment, and sought to turn the conversation. She did not want to talk about Pieter. She wanted to talk about *him*.

"You said, 'if you lived' you would come back to us. Do you then seek death?" she challenged.

"Death seeks me," he smiled. "But I am elusive."

"And that is why you move about?"

His smile deepened. "A moving target is harder to hit."

She looked up into those hard mocking eyes and felt somehow bested by him, even though his tone was courteous.

"I prefer men with secure futures," she said, in an attempt to strike back.

He shrugged. "Most women do."

She did not like being lumped with "most women."

"But only if the man is . . . outstanding," she amended.

"Outstanding?"

"Yes, in some way. A scholar perhaps or . . . a swordsman."

He laughed. "Faith, you've allowed some leeway there. How about politicians—or as they prefer to call themselves, 'statesmen'; do they also meet with your approval?"

She frowned, remembering suddenly the judge in Massachusetts who had sentenced her to death. "I do not like politicians," she said severely. "They are evil men."

He looked down at her with new interest. "You are indeed observant for one so young."

She felt patronized and her voice sharpened. "You can't be so terribly old yourself."

"Sure, I'm a deal older than you," he shrugged. "Several lifetimes, at least."

She was about to give him a hot reply when it occurred to her that this evening she *wanted* to be considered young and untried; it was part of her game tonight to taunt and tantalize, to flirt outrageously. She had never before attended a ball and she meant it to be memorable, an unparalleled success.

He was to be her first conquest in her new role.

"I suppose I haven't . . . lived," she said pensively.

He gave her a humorous look.

"Oh, there's plenty of time for that," he said. "The world will wait while you catch up with it."

Her big topaz eyes shone up at him. "Oh, but I wouldn't want the whole world to wait," she said innocently. "Just a—particular person."

"Indeed?" He seemed to be enjoying himself as he whirled her around. "It would be interesting to hear what you have in mind as a suitable choice."

"He must be handsome," said Charity. "And very wealthy—I have expensive tastes."

He threw back his head and laughed, ignoring some raised eyebrows around the room at the burst of merriment from the floor.

"And he should be well educated, a master of languages."

"I suppose you speak several?"

"Three," said Charity composedly. "And a little Dutch."

He greeted this statement with some respect.

"And he should be . . . amiable. And . . . fervent. He should love me passionately, of course."

"And with all of this, he should also possess great stamina," he suggested mockingly.

She ignored him. "And reputation," she added dreamily. "He must be a man of great reputation."

"Reputation," he mused. "Reputation, Mistress, has a way of recoiling on one. It is a two-edged blade. I would seek it not."

"Nevertheless," she said stubbornly. "He should be a man of reputation. For sternness. For valor."

181

He looked down on her with amusement. "Faith, I haven't heard such a refreshing bit of nonsense in a deal of a time. Mynheer van Daarken is lucky to own you his cousin."

She stiffened ever so slightly. The words "own you" had for a moment echoed in a sinister manner through her head.

When the music ended he led her gravely back toward the wall, but bypassed it suddenly and directed her adroitly out through the dancers to a hall where several groups of people stood talking. A servant offered champagne from a tray and they both accepted a glass.

Suddenly he looked down at her, smiling.

"You have not spoken for the space of five minutes," he said. "Surely that is unusual for a woman, Mistress Woodstock."

"I am an unusual woman," quipped Charity. "We were not introduced. How is it that you know my name?"

"I can well believe it," said he. "And I know your name because I inquired. My own is Roger Derwent."

She considered Roger Derwent through her lashes. She was still nagged by something hauntingly familiar about his voice. Deep and sardonic . . . stirring . . . she tried to remember where she had heard it.

When she made no comment, he said, "You have told me that you are the patroon's cousin, but your voice speaks of Devon."

"Torquay," she said, surprised. "Do you know it?"

"I have sailed to it many times," he said, and his eyes were shadowed as he looked out into the distance. "And I have made merry hell in its taverns."

"I would not know about those," she said carefully.

"No, I did not imagine so," he said.

"I was educated in Bath," she added, lamely presenting the one aristocratic credential she had to offer.

"I have been there," he said morosely.

"You are from that part of England then?"

He seemed to rouse himself. "No longer. But I

182

remember my childhood days in Devon . . . they were pleasant times."

"Mine also," she said pensively.

Together they strolled back into the ballroom, where the forceful and attractive Mr. Derwent continued to monopolize Charity's attention, whirling her about the floor in dance after dance. Ryn glowered; Charity tossed her blonde curls and ignored him. It amused her that Cordelia van der Doonck stared at her with vindictive jealousy, as if to say *first Pieter and now this new man everybody wants!*

Cordelia's glares brought out the devil in Charity. She redoubled her efforts to charm the gentleman who studied her so intently. She laughed coquettishly, and it irritated her when Mr. Derwent's gaze roved past her twice to the clock in the hall. But he turned back from the clock with a shrug. Charity swung round and curtsyed as the dance required, her great skirts sweeping out, the top of her round white breasts bare in her low-cut dress as she bent deeply before him, her pale gold curls spilling forward in a shimmering rain.

Neither Roger Derwent nor Charity noticed—or cared—that significant glances were being passed about at the remarkable devotion this strange gentleman showed to a young lady who common gossip said had been entirely monopolized heretofore by the patroon's son. The women's eyes behind their filagreed mirrored fans said plainly, *Out of sight, out of mind.* For did not the patroon's son lie upstairs ill, poor thing?

Heartlessly, Charity had forgotten Pieter, she so enjoyed swinging about in the arms of this tall lean stranger.

But once again Derwent's gray eyes strayed to the clock. And this time they also met the eyes of the patroon, who had also checked the clock—nervously. Roger Derwent frowned and regretfully relinquished Charity with a bow; she was claimed for a dance by one of the fat Vermeer brothers who had recently bought a small manor downriver.

Her new partner was most attentive, and tried to

capture her attention with all the wit he could muster. But Charity's gaze roamed impatiently over his shoulder, to follow Roger Derwent. He spoke to the patroon and nodded in Charity's direction and the patroon's eyes moved incredulously to Charity; then he laughed and said something in an offhand manner. Whereupon Mr. Derwent's head in its black periwig swung sharply round to look at Charity. Although his face did not register shock, there was a change in it— it had hardened perceptibly and his light gray eyes were more steely than ever.

He claimed her for the next dance, and this time, smiling at her in a more exuberant manner, danced her breathlessly right out the front door and continued for a few wild steps on the lawn. He looked very jaunty as he said, "Shall we take a turn about the lawn?" And gallantly offered her his arm.

Charity nodded blithely and took the proffered arm. With a light proud step, she walked along beside him toward a great tree on the lawn. "But you *must* promise to behave yourself," she said severely.

"I promise," he said, "that I will do nothing you would not expect of me."

Though the phrase had a sinister ring to it, she gave it no thought. She was thinking how very pleasant it was to be a lady, as they moved into the deeper shadows beneath the tree's overhanging branches.

He leaned back against the bole of the tree, and the hand on which his ring flashed lightly toyed with one of her curls, touched her ear with experimental fingers.

"I believe," he murmured, "we had some discussion as to whether I was worthy of a woman's attention. I am prepared to give proof."

Charity, warned now, turned to run, but he reached out and caught her wrist and spun her around and brought her flush against his velvet coat. Wrapped in his steely embrace, she opened her mouth to protest and his mouth covered hers with a kiss. The kiss did not ask, or suggest, it demanded. His lips moved deftly, expertly, over hers, and his tongue probed caressingly. Charity felt her head swim a bit and her senses come alive. She tried to move, to shrug him off, but he held her firm, and she could feel the strong resonant throb of his heart as her soft breasts were crushed against his chest.

For a moment she weakened, responding tremulously to that kiss, and he sensed it. His grip relaxed slightly, and one hand gently held her chin as his lips caressed hers, then that hand wandered tinglingly down the smooth skin of her throat, lingered a moment on her neck and moved gently across the white flesh of her bosom, leaving a trail of fire wherever he touched.

Charity felt her blood leap and her breath come fast. She seemed to hear a low chuckle as his questing fingers found the top of her low-cut velvet dress, toyed there idly, while she tried to control the sensations that were flashing through her like miniature lightning bolts.

She stiffened suddenly. He had somehow managed to undo the hooks at the top of her velvet bodice and had slipped his hand inside and was stroking her breast! He had no right! She had given him no such license! She tried desperately to jerk away, but still he held her firm, his lips so holding hers that breath was almost denied her and she seemed to beat in his arms like a frightened bird.

Now he had liberated her other breast from its velvet prison and was softly massaging it. She felt herself trembling, her own desire furiously awakened by his touch. She gasped and shivered and tried to wriggle free of those strong dexterous hands.

Worse, he knew she was trembling! He could sense the wild passions he was arousing. Panic rose in her along with small soft explosions of the senses, nerves that tingled and grew taut seemed to snap softly, like a satin garter against the skin, so that she quivered more violently.

He had taken her quivering response to him as consent! The thought went through her like a groan. His other hand was now slipping up under the folds of her velvet skirt and petticoats and her stomach muscles contracted violently as his hand moved deliberately, exploringly, across the smooth bare skin of her stomach, sending ripples of fire wherever it touched. Her knees seemed to be melting and she sagged against him.

But though her body had weakened, her mind had not.

As her body sagged against him, almost fainting in his arms, his mouth left hers and he buried his face in the column of her soft white throat. She gasped as his lips moved swiftly down to her breasts and nuzzled them. She felt her nipples grow hard and taut under his lips. When her eyes fluttered open, she commanded herself to speak—gaspingly, but with all the authority she could muster.

"If you do not release me at once, I will scream!" she cried.

He paused just long enough to plant a kiss on her quivering pink nipple, which flinched under this new assault. Then he rose to his full height, and as he towered above her, his voice was quite level and courteous but had an undertone of irony.

"Oh, and is that what you usually do on these occasions?"

The full weight of the insult bore in on her with stinging force, giving strength to her weakened limbs, and making her trembling backbone stiff again.

"You beast!" she cried in a low furious voice, and swinging back her slender arm brought it forward to strike his face with all her force.

He did not appear to have noticed. His head did not snap back as she had somehow expected. His slight, mocking smile did not waver. He stood quite impassively, and his hard gray eyes had in them something indefinable, something that might have been admiration.

She was never to know what it was, for in that moment a servant's voice she identified as Gerda's, called plaintively, "Mistress Charity! Mynheer Pieter is calling for you. He's sicker than he was. Mistress Charity, are you out here?"

"I believe you will find her here," Roger Derwent replied with a touch of contempt in his voice. "By all means, get you to Mynheer Pieter, who awaits your ministrations, Mistress Charity!"

Charity was so angry she would have struck him again, but her hands were occupied with trying to re-hook her bodice before Gerda arrived. As she hurried away from the shadows of the big tree, she hoped Gerda had not seen who she was with, and so would not report her lapse to the servants and make her the subject of gossip in the kitchen.

She left Roger Derwent standing in the darkness, leaning against the boll of the great tree and, lifting her skirts against the dampness of the grass fled across the lawn. Her blood still tingled angrily in her ears as she remembered his fiery touch—and her equally fiery response.

She was still thinking about Derwent when she arrived, breathless after a run up the back stairs, at Pieter's side. He did not look so bad, but his cheeks were flushed. He looked, if anything, resentful.

"So you went to the ball?" Pieter said bitterly. *Without me,* his tone implied.

She looked at him, dismayed, hoping he would not notice her dishevelement. "Your father told me I might go, Pieter."

His shrewd small blue eyes, so like the patroon's, took in her tumbled coiffure.

"I've been dancing," she said hastily. "It grew very warm."

"And running," he observed dryly. "You're gasping for breath."

"Yes, I ran all the way. I thought you were worse."

He appeared somewhat mollified, and hunched himself up, half sitting, half lying there almost covered by the enveloping featherbed.

"I should be down there dancing with you!" he said in a voice that accused doctors, fathers and the world in general with equal fury.

187

"No, you shouldn't," remonstrated Charity. "The doctor said you could develop pneumonia. You have a deep cold and fever."

As if to give proof to her remark, he sneezed and then began to cough. She waited sympathetically until the paroxysm had passed, and then handed him a white linen kerchief from a sack of the kerchiefs, each one embroidered with the crest of his mother's family, that lay upon a small rosewood bedside table.

"I'm supposed to sleep," he said fretfully. "But how can I be expected to sleep when there's all that music and laughter downstairs? All I can think of is that I should jump up out of bed and join them!"

"Why don't we close the door and play this music box instead?" she suggested.

He watched her glumly as she closed the door. Then a new thought occurred to him. "Why don't you lie here beside me?" he asked eagerly. "I think I might go to sleep then."

Charity stiffened and her voice was somewhat colder than it would have been before tonight's galling experience. "I will not lie down beside you, and if you persist in asking me, I will leave you here alone."

He accepted this rebuke and said in a subdued, rather bored tone, "Play the music box then."

Charity wound up the little music box, and as she listened to its delicate tinkle her mind kept slipping back to Roger Derwent, who had been so polite and then so inexplicably audacious—insulting even. What had happened to change him?

"Your color is very high tonight," commented Pieter sulkily, and added loudly, "Charity, I am speaking to you!"

Startled, Charity felt herself flush all over. She had been thinking of Roger Derwent's hands, as they had caressed first her breasts and then her stomach, and of Roger Derwent's lips, assaulting first her mouth and then her throat and breasts. She could still feel the tingling path of his lips as they moved smoothly down her throat and across her bosom and over the white mound of her breast to their final goal—the delicate sensitive skin of her pink nipple. An involuntary shiver went through her as she remembered that final kiss he had planted there.

"I was thinking of the tune on the music box," she faltered. "I—I remember it from my schooldays in Bath."

"You're sure you don't want to go back to the ball?"

The tumult in her had worn down now, and the fire that had burned so bright had left gray ashes behind it. What she remembered now was the fact that Roger Derwent, who had begun by treating her with the respect due an elegant young lady of fashion, had ended by treating her as a woman to be had for the asking. And yet she could not fault her own behavior for it; she had said nothing, done nothing, surely.

"No, Pieter," she said in a low tired voice. "I don't want to go back to the ball. I'd rather stay here with you."

And she sat there beside him, her hands clasped tightly in her lap, until he fell asleep, trying to forget that her first ball had not been a glorious success.

CHAPTER 16

Roger Derwent had departed when Charity came down the next morning, apparently having melted away the way he had come. Which was a pity because she had risen early, hoping to confront him before breakfast, eager for him to feel the sting of her tongue. For she had spent most of a sleepless night phrasing biting things to say to the insolent Mr. Derwent.

But the flyboat in which he had arrived was gone. Perhaps he had not come to spend the night, but to dance only a few dances. She inquired of the servants who were up and about, but no one seemed to remember the boat. That was natural enough, she told herself, with all the excitement of large parties and boats coming and going. Still it was a terrible disappointment and she felt quite let down.

She walked along the river bank, hoping forlornly for a last sight of it as it drifted downstream. But the river flowed by peacefully, an empty expanse of water, glistening in the morning sun.

She turned, cutting a diagonal path back to the house, and saw that the blockhouse to her left now sported a heavy chain on its door. She walked toward it curiously. Yesterday afternoon she had strolled down here on her way to watch some of the men playing at bowles on the lawn, and the blockhouse had been full of beaver pelts. Illegal? The door had been closed but not locked.

Yet today it was locked.

No one was about, so she strolled toward the blockhouse and peered in through the loopholes—those slender openings through which a musket could be thrust to snipe at the enemy. At first she could see nothing, and then through the weak light that filtered down through chinks in the roof, she saw that the beaver pelts were gone, and in their place was a small mountain of cloth. It appeared to be damasks, woolens, laces. And also some small kegs and barrels, and other objects whose shapes loomed up tantalizingly in the dimness.

And with the sight, like a rolling thunderclap down the Catskills, she remembered where she had heard Roger Derwent's voice. His was the voice that had so stirred her that first night on the patroon's sloop in New York!

Roger Derwent was the smuggler. He had come upriver to deliver his contraband in person and in darkness, and gone away with beaver pelts and no doubt gold in payment. Slipped away as he had come —silently like a thief. No wonder he had kept looking at the clock. He had been timing the unloading of the goods. And no wonder the patroon, too, had looked at the clock—nervously. He had been eager for his dangerous guest to be gone.

By now the smuggler was far downriver, perhaps keeping some other clandestine rendezvous before the weather closed down and the river froze again.

Charity's eyes narrowed as she stopped back from her surveillance of the interior of the blockhouse.

So Roger Derwent was the smuggler of whom Killian van Daarken had said, *Did you mark his rapier, Jan? It is said he has spitted more men with it than anyone since. . . .* and later, *He is a man of honor, Jan. But for his politics, he would be a force in his own country. But because of those politics, he cannot return home. So he makes his living as he can. Such men are to be pitied—and used.*

But there was no pity in Charity's heart for the unpleasant Mr. Derwent. He had spoiled her evening, robbed her of a few harmless dreams—and what was he? A damned smuggler.

Unable to resist questioning the servants, she was told the tall stranger had not stayed long after dancing with her. At least no one had seen him after that. Perhaps the house had been too crowded to give him a place to sleep and he was staying at a neighboring manor, Gerda suggested vaguely. Charity doubted it. She longed to retort that the aggravating Mr. Derwent probably never stayed in one place for long, lest the authorities catch up with him and end his career with hemp. But she stayed the angry rush of words to her lips because Roger Derwent's business was obviously with Killian van Daarken and she must be careful what she said to the servants.

She longed to say something nasty about the haughty Mr. Derwent to the patroon, but that would be to say she knew about their business together, and she felt that would not be wise.

Biting her lips, she went out to the kitchen and found herself a bite for breakfast. The big dining room was full to overflowing with invited guests and the staff completely distracted—it would probably have been another hour or two before anyone thought to bring her a tray.

Pieter mended rapidly, although his cough hung on, and Charity spent most of her time with him, talking to him by the fire. Sometimes they walked across the crisp lawn, once through the first skiff of a snowfall.

He seemed to tire more easily and was often irritable. Sometimes she waited for him and he did not come down at all, but slept late in his room.

One day she saw another less attractive side of life at Daarkenwyck: Pieter was supposed to take her riding, and she waited for him impatiently for some time at the stable, astride a dancing horse eager to be away. Finally, when Pieter did not appear she rode on without him, supposing he would catch up to her. In this way, she reached one of the small *bouweries,* as the farms belonging to the manor were called, where she came upon a man in his shirtsleeves and loose fitting leather knee breeches in the act of chopping wood.

He straightened up at her approach and eyed her curiously.

Just at that moment a woman carrying a bucket came around the corner of the house. She had big rolled-up sleeves, a laced bodice and full skirt of coarse dark cloth reaching to her ankles. Her frayed white collar was plain and swept to her shoulders and in long points to her waist, and her serviceable old apron had one big pocket across the front.

This was Charity's first time to have a chance to speak to any of the people on the *bouweries,* for Pieter always would have her nod and ride rapidly by. So, she smiled at them and they greeted her deferentially and warily, for although they did not know her, her clothes told them she came from the great manor house and was thus a subject for awe and some distrust.

Pleased to try out her knowledge of the Dutch language on these Hollanders, she admired everything and asked questions: how did they like the life here, was the game plentiful, had the crops been good?

The woman warmed to her and the man, with a smile, went back to his chopping. Invited into the small thatched log hut, Charity accepted a wooden mug of beer. As they talked, the woman grew confidential. Life was very expensive here, she said, not at all as she had expected when Jan Peter and she had set sail from Holland. Fortunately, the crops had been good this year—which was the patroon's good fortune as well, since one-tenth of all their produce went to the patroon. Charity was surprised, saying she had thought the patroon received his rent in money. That too, sighed the woman, a rent of 500 guilders each year they must pay for their *bouwerie.* In addition, her husband must give three days service with horse and wagon each year to the patroon, repair the buildings, keep up the roads and cut ten pieces of fir or oak and bring them to the waterside; as quit rent he must furnish the patroon with two bushels of wheat, twenty-five pounds of butter and two pairs of fowls—and Jan Peter must cut and split and bring to the water's side two fathoms of firewood—that was what he was doing now; he had no time to stop. She sighed.

"It is too bad you cannot supplement your income by weaving," murmured Charity, remembering many had done so in England.

"Yes," said the wife sadly, "it is too bad. On the patroon's land no man may traffic in furs and no woman may spin cloth. He keeps to the old ways." Her mouth trembled. "It is all so different from what Jan Peter and I expected."

Charity left them, sobered. What had seemed to her an idyllic life in Daarkenwyck loomed unprepossessingly hard outside its graceful tree-shaded lawns.

She returned to find Pieter very angry with her. She had strayed out alone, he told her fiercely. She could have been insulted by trappers who sometimes came through these lands, attacked by Indians, set upon by wild animals.

She smiled at him, her heart softening toward him. Pieter's storming meant just one thing to her; he was genuinely concerned for her safety.

He was more than concerned. Suddenly rough, he swept her into his arms and kissed her fiercely. Charity spun away from him breathless.

"You kiss others," he accused angrily.

"No, I do not!" she cried, thinking guiltily of the arrogant Mr. Derwent.

"You do," he flashed. "I saw you with Ryn van der Doonck in that clump of willows!"

So he did not know about Roger Derwent. . . . Still, Charity winced, remembering that during the brief time the pond was frozen, while dancing on the ice, Ryn had indeed spun her into the clump of willows and not only kissed her but had pinched her as well. She had slapped his face.

"You are mine!" cried Pieter in a jealous voice. "Ryn cannot have you."

Charity looked at him steadily.

"Oh, why do you not favor me, Charity?" he demanded. "Ryn does not love you—he and the rest

195

seek your favors only that they may brag of it, but I —I care for you, Charity."

Her eyes softened. "I know you do, Pieter."

He took a step forward and seized her around the waist again. They were standing in the big stable with its massive beams where she had brought her horse. The grooms had discreetly disappeared, seeing the patroon's son apparently wrestling with a lady. "Oh, Charity!" In a sudden abandoned gesture he drew her against him. "Will you not pity me, Charity? What am I to do?"

Charity pulled away, for the moment thinking bitterly of Roger Derwent, who had also seized her without asking. "I—I do not know, Pieter." Her voice hardened. "But this much is certain. You cannot have me here in the hay like a dairymaid!"

Charity straightened her dress and continued. "You must not treat me with disrespect as you might a servant girl," she said through her teeth. "You will never gain me that way."

He nodded in dumb misery, and to her horror sank down on his knees and threw his arms convulsively around her thighs, pulling her to him, his head pressed against her skirt.

"Name whatever price you want," he said urgently, his voice half smothered by the material of her skirt, "and it is yours."

Her lips twisted. *Name your price!* Roger Derwent's insolent handling of her had suggested that she had a price too.

She looked angrily down at Pieter's golden curls. She could feel the pressure of his head against her trembling thighs, feel the almost hysterical grip of his arms around the back of her knees, nearly causing her legs to buckle. "I am not to be had for gold," she gasped, shaken.

He looked up, and she saw that there were beads of perspiration on his brow. "I was not thinking of gold," he said. "I ask if your price is marriage."

For a long moment she stared at him as he gazed up at her pleadingly.

Marriage . . . to Pieter van Daarken . . . wife to the future patroon of Daarkenwyck.

It was a tempting offer.

Seeing the momentary indecision on her face, he followed up his advantage.

"Will you, Charity?" she heard him ask in a voice now wistful.

"I—I will think about it," she said brusquely, and flinched as his fingers touched her shoulder.

"I—am sorry I was so rough," he said. "It is that you are so beautiful and so desirable to me."

"I know how you feel." She turned and faced him. He had risen and was looking down at her with anxiety in his face. She spoke to him in a gentler tone. "I thank you for your offer of marriage, Pieter, but— I cannot give you your answer now, not here in a stable."

He looked taken aback. "I—I had not thought of it that way," he stammered in consternation.

"If you had asked Cordelia van der Doonck to marry you," said Charity bitterly, "you would have asked her on your knees beside the rosewood harpsichord. You would not have chosen a mound of hay as a setting for your courtship!"

"But I love you none the less, Charity."

"We will see the temper of your love," she replied. "When you have told your father of your proposal, and he has forbidden it—we will see how much you love me then!"

"Ah, but wait." He leaped forward to seize her hand and stay her going. "I would not tell my father of it yet."

She gave him a cynical look.

"Do not look at me so," he chided fiercely. "I *will* speak to him of it, but this is not the time."

"I see," she murmured. "This is not the time."

"My mother's father who lives in Holland is very wealthy," he surprised her by saying. "It was with her dowry that my father purchased Daarkenwyck."

Charity pricked up her ears.

"When I go to Holland," he said eagerly, "I will

197

ingratiate myself with him. He has no other grand-child and he is now old and feeble. I will find a way to get him to settle a large sum of money on me, and with that, when I return, we can live as man and wife! For I promise you, Charity—" his eyes glittered recklessly, but his voice held a ring of truth—"that when I return from Holland I shall be a rich man!"

Charity studied him. She did not love him but . . . he was a way up, a way to rise above the sneers of the Cordelia van der Dooncks and their kind. Was she not justified, she asked herself, in using men as they had used her? And was not here a man pleading on his knees to be used?

She lifted her chin and seemed to see beyond the confines of this stable and into the far distance. A great new world beckoned to those who were hard and purposeful and seized their opportunities.

She would be such a woman!

"I give you permission to try," she said. Hope sprang in his eyes and he would have seized her again had she not lifted a hand to push him away. "But not to use me in the meantime," she said wearily. "Would you take your future wife in a stable? Would you have your first child born out of wedlock while your father fumes and your doddering grandfather decides what he is to do with you? Ah, I see from your face that you had not considered these things. But you would do well to consider them, Pieter, for if we chose your course of romping in the hay, we would face them soon enough. You will wait and—we shall see how durable is this love you profess to bear me."

"But—you will have me, Charity? You are saying that you will?" His voice trembled with passion.

"In a marriage bed, Pieter—yes."

Very solicitously, Pieter bent to brush some hay from the hem of her skirt. He made no further attempt to touch her.

She told herself that she had tamed the wild boar in him and that he would turn a gentler face to her, in the future, now that she had promised to become his wife.

Somewhere in that decision—although she would not admit it, and closed the door of her mind hastily upon the whispering voices that told her it was so—was a smoldering resentment against Roger Derwent, who had treated her as something less than a lady.

She could not resist thinking how shocked Roger Derwent would be when he came back to Daarkenwyck—if ever he did—to find that she was mistress of the manor and could turn him out of the house at her pleasure.

She even went so far as to imagine a hangman's noose for him in her fancies, but hastily retreated from that—not, she told herself carefully, because a knife twisted in her bosom at the thought of his long attractive body dangling at the end of a rope—no, only because a living man feels taunts and scorn better than a dead one.

She hardly noticed Pieter, such a fiendish delight did she take in tormenting the memory of the hated Roger Derwent.

Damned smuggler that he was!

She turned absently to the man beside her. Pieter was speaking. She had no idea what he had said, but she bobbed her head earnestly and Pieter looked pleased.

His hot admiring glance followed Charity as she went into the house through the kitchen, but grew distracted when Elyse the maid came out and scowled at him, hands on hips.

Pieter's blood was up. He raked Elyse's young desirable body up and down with his hot gaze and she bridled under it. "Perhaps you've an errand that takes you to the barn, Elyse?" he asked slyly.

Through the small panes of her window above, as she sat in her room sewing a new hook on her bodice, Charity watched Elyse run from the kitchen to the barn. And, a little later, she saw Pieter saunter casually toward the barn, and stand gazing about him for a moment before he went into its dark interior.

Charity frowned. She told herself it did not matter. What mattered was not the fact that she did not love Pieter or that he would not be faithful to her.

What mattered was becoming the wife of a patroon. Rich. Powerful. Able to laugh scornfully in the faces of all the Roger Derwents of the world. In her anger she jabbed her finger with the needle. Tossing her sewing aside, she jumped up and paced restlessly about the room in her chemise.

Of course she was doing the right thing by marrying Pieter, she told herself.

But that night when she fell asleep it was not of Pieter she dreamed, nor yet of being a patroon's lady and commanding servants in a stately manor along the river. It was an arrogant and irritating stranger that she dreamed of, feeling his arms delightfully about her, feeling herself yielding happily, eagerly, vibrantly to his caresses, lifting her ardent mouth for his kisses, feeling his strong but gentle hands tingle down her body.

CHAPTER 17

Annjanette had not been present for meals the day before and when she sulkily flounced down for breakfast, the reason became apparent—she had a black eye.

Clothilde, whose face was a drawn white mask these days—the mail from Holland had arrived three days ago and she had been distracted ever since—looked at Annjanette without interest, perhaps without really seeing her.

Turning from the sight of Annjanette's bruised face, Charity could not help glancing at Killian van Daarken. The expression on his broad-jowled face was bland.

When Pieter asked Annjanette what had happened, she said she had fallen over a stool in the dark and struck the corner of the bed. And, with a sob, she jumped up and left the table.

Charity remembered, suddenly, that two nights ago someone had stood outside her room, breathing hard. She had clutched the covers around her and stared frightened at the latch, but whoever it was had gone away.

Had Killian struck Annjanette down and then . . . come up and stood by her door?

The thought made her uneasy.

Talk at breakfast centered on last night's high winds, probably presaging a change in the unseasonably warm weather the Hudson Valley had been enjoying. Charity did not take her part in the conversation. After breakfast she went upstairs and found herself drawn to Annjanette's small bedroom—that dressing room tucked between the patroon's bedroom and his wife's. Clothilde's door was standing open, so, she walked through the room and knocked on Annjanette's door.

"Annjanette," she called softly.

There was no answer and she turned away, but as she did she brushed a book from a table near the door to the floor. Bending over to pick it up, she saw that beneath it was a letter from Holland, addressed to Clothilde.

A letter from Holland . . . whenever the mail came from Holland, Clothilde spent the day in her room crying.

Charity held the letter uncertainly in her hand. She crossed to the window and looked out. As she had come upstairs, the patroon had spoken to Clothilde and she had listlessly accompanied him outside to look at a cherished shrub from Holland, badly broken by last night's wind. Her eyes swept the lawn. Yes, they were still there looking at the broken branches.

Though she did not read Dutch, but only spoke it Charity opened the letter.

To her surprise the letter was written in English—and tearstained. Clothilde's tears, Charity thought soberly.

It was a very tender letter, such a letter as a lover might write. It referred sadly to "our little M of loving memory" and wished Clothilde "all good things—and sweet memories ever," and added wistfully, "Would that I could come to you, but I am like to die soon. The old wound plagues me, but even were I not so crippled by it, I am so weak I could not walk the stairs. The monks here at the abbey care for me kindly as always and daily take me to the courtyard to spend a time in the sunshine. Do not cry, my dearest, for surely it is best for both of us that my death comes soon. You can then return to Holland and visit your kin without fear, and I will have earned only my just deserts for what I did so recklessly without regard to your welfare. I have your last dear letter before me as I write this and will hold your sweet words in my heart forever—nay, longer than that, a thousand forevers.

Farewell, my dearest heart." And it was signed, "Ever your devoted J."

A melancholy letter—perhaps the writer's last—and written to a Dutch lady in *English*.

That puzzled Charity.

Suddenly her eyes widened. The reason was obvious! It was written in English to cloak its contents from Killian van Daarken! Killian, for all that he spoke two languages, was not an educated man. He read and wrote Dutch, she knew. But English—no doubt Killian was unable to read English, while his better-educated wife did! There were some books in the library downstairs in English—and the patroon's lady seemed to be the only member of the family at Daarkenwyck who cared to read. Certainly Pieter and his father shunned books. So, by penning his message in English, the writer could manage a private correspondence with Clothilde even if Killian did open the letters.

Ah, but surely that would be a foolish ploy. Pieter read English passably well. Killian had only to hand these letters over to his son to have them translated.

Unless . . . there was something in the letters that he did not wish others to see.

But why then, would he allow them to be delivered to Clothilde? He certainly had the power to stop them, and if they were from a lover—even a lover of long ago—Killian would rage with jealousy to see those letters arriving in a tongue he could not understand.

Charity carefully replaced the letter where she had found it. She whirled around at a small sound.

Annjanette, with her black eye and sulky face, stood in the doorway surveying her.

"You have read it," the French girl said challengingly.

Charity bit her lip. It was not a good thing to admit.

"I came to see how you were, Annjanette," she evaded. "I knocked and called your name—"

"I know," interrupted Annjanette impatiently. "I heard you and tiptoed through Killian's room into the hall. I have been standing here watching you. Do not lie to me—I *saw* you reading the letter."

"Very well," agreed Charity coldly. "I read it." She started to brush by the French girl.

"Tell me what it said," entreated Annjanette, clutching her arm. "I cannot read English—indeed I can barely read French—but when Killian saw me with that letter in my hand—he *struck* me. I must know what it said!"

Charity thought of Clothilde's sad vacant eyes, and how she had stumbled about in a daze since this letter had arrived three days ago. She wanted to protect Clothilde. But Annjanette knew she had read the letter and could report that fact—and Annjanette's avid blue eyes were fixed on her, waiting.

"It was just a letter of pleasantries," Charity said in what she hoped was a casual voice.

Before Annjanette could press her further, they heard the front door open and close below, heard footsteps coming up the stairs.

"They are coming," whispered Annjanette. "They must not see us here. Quick, into my room."

She seized Charity by the wrist and almost dragged her into the small dressing room where she slept. A dainty embroidered nightdress had been tossed on a chair. It was savagely torn. Annjanette looked at it and for a moment she blanched. She put a finger to her lips, snatched the torn nightdress from the chair and motioned Charity to sit down.

They heard the patroon and his lady enter their separate rooms, heard them moving about.

Abruptly, the door that led from Annjanette's sleeping quarters into the patroon's room was jerked open and Killian van Daarken's square stolid form stood there.

His face darkened when he saw Charity, and Annjanette half rose as if in protest.

Charity felt that she must cover for the frightened French girl.

"I came up to see how Annjanette was," she said carelessly, rising. "Since she was ill at breakfast, I thought someone should look in on her. But I will take my leave now. I'll see you at dinner, Annjanette."

The patroon studied Charity. Though it was difficult under that heavy scrutiny, she gave him back an easy look. His face cleared a little. "Cousin Annjanette is very awkward," he observed. "She will have to change her ways if she is to avoid these unpleasant falls."

Annjanette paled.

Charity made her escape. She hurried along the hall and went downstairs. Pieter saw her and asked her why she was shivering. Was she cold? Why didn't she seek the warmth of the fire? Jochem had just built one in the library. They could put some more wood on it if it was not warm enough.

Charity insisted she wasn't cold but Pieter pulled her into the deserted library, sat her down before the hearth and chafed her hands. He smiled ingenuously into her eyes, for all the world like a lover.

Why should he not love her? she asked herself rebelliously. Just as long ago—no, it was not so long ago really; it just seemed light years away—she had asked herself at Stéphanie's school why she should not have what the other more fortunate girls had. Was she not just as pretty, just as bright? And now—why should Pieter not love her? And if he did love her, why should she not marry him? Why should she not some day replace Clothilde as the patroon's lady here at Daarkenwyck?

She stared at Pieter, so bent on pleasing her.

Pieter, she was convinced, did not love her any more than she loved him, but he wanted her—oh, how desperately he wanted her! And perhaps that was as much as she was going to get. Was she like Annjanette, that men would want her only for her pretty surface— and never really care how she felt about them, so long as she was warm in their arms?

Pieter was sitting beside her and now he moved his leg over so that it touched her leg. Letting go of her hand, he laid a careless hand on her thigh.

She stiffened.

205

"Why not?" he murmured. "After all, we are to be married, aren't we?"

"Your father would never permit it, Pieter. I—I have no dowry."

"But you said you would marry me if—"

"Yes, I said that. If you were allowed to do so. You will not be."

The word "yes" in her answer was all he seemed to comprehend. He pressed his advantage. "Why should we not live here at Daarkenwyck together?" he demanded in a low fiery voice. "This part of the river will be mine one day. I—and only I—will rule it. If I wish to marry you, who is to gainsay me?"

"Your father," she said ruefully again.

"He cannot live forever," muttered Pieter. He brightened. "He will come to it," he said. "When I have told him that I cannot live without you."

"Would you really do that, Pieter?" she asked soberly.

"Yes, of course I would do it. If I believed you loved me. . . ." His hands found her shoulders and he stroked them caressingly.

Charity sat very straight. "But you are going away. . . ."

"But I will return, Charity. And with money. You will see. It is only for a year. I will return and I promise you that we will be man and wife. Wait for me and we will live together here at Daarkenwyck." His young voice had a hypnotic quality, born of the intensity of his emotion. He toyed with a lock of her hair. "So why," he pleaded, "should we wait?"

Charity looked at him uncertainly. *I promise you,* he had said. Now his hands wandered over her back, her neck. He grasped the back of her head and bent his face down to kiss her, his other hand slipping nimbly into the top of her dress.

Charity pulled away from him. "No," she said, "I have listened to the soft words of men before. I do not believe you, Pieter—and I am not to be had without marriage."

His face darkened. He flung away from her and

went crashing out of the library, giving the door a hard swing that nearly tore it from its hinges. She knew she had made him furious, and at dinner he turned his back to her and held an animated conversation with a surprised Annjanette.

Charity sat silently picking at her lobster, her brooding topaz eyes fixed on her plate. But she hardly tasted her food. It was possible—just possible—that Pieter meant what he said. And she who had put aside the thought of love, believing it would not come to her, now saw dangled before her the bright future of a rich marriage . . . wife to the future patroon of Daarkenwyck.

After dinner Annjanette managed to get her aside, and asked her again what the letter contained. Charity answered morosely, "I have forgotten. Nothing important."

Annjanette pouted, then shrugged and turned away, smiling and fingering a new coral brooch.

Pieter made a great show of his displeasure. He ignored Charity so pointedly that the patroon smiled behind his hand. His wife, silent and downcast, her melancholy gaze fixed on the walls, appeared to notice nothing. Soon, with slow laboring footsteps, Clothilde went up to bed.

Charity said she was tired too and went upstairs, feeling Pieter's indignant gaze follow her.

That night she stood a long time and stared out through the small panes of her window at the land, stretching far away, the *bouweries* where men and women like Jan Peter and his wife labored long hours. She could still hear the woman's soft voice saying wistfully, *It was all so different from what we expected.*

So too had this new world been different from what Charity had expected. And it had treated her cruelly.

But now surely she was being offered a new chance, a new life. Pieter was spoiled. His parents had denied him nothing. Perhaps in the end they would not deny him the woman of his choice.

In which case, she would become mistress of Daarkenwyck, in fact if not in name, for shadowy Clothilde was no real mistress of this manor. It had no mistress, and Pieter's dynamic young wife would assume that role.

She stared into the darkness. Was it wrong? Would she regret it? Should she refuse this marriage which offered her so much that she had never had, merely because she did not love Pieter?

CHAPTER 18

When Charity woke the weather had changed overnight. An icy wind howled around the chimneys, bringing gusts down into the fireplace, and cold crept in around the window panes. Charity shivered and looked out into a gray sky. By midmorning snow had begun to fall, at first in light flakes and then hard-driving, pelting snow. It fell heavily all day and by the next morning it had drifted in great sugary piles around the house and its weight was bending down the branches of the trees.

That night was even colder and the bitter cold persisted. Ice crept out from the river bank and before the week was out the river had frozen from bank to bank and sleighs pulled by horses were charging merrily up and down it, while the crisp cold air rang with the clash of skates.

The cold spell with its winter sports sent Pieter off to a sleighing party at the van der Doonck's, and Charity, who refused to accompany him, was left to her own devices.

Growing restless one evening, she walked downstairs, intending to get a book. But at the library door she stopped. Clothilde sat inside rocking in misery, her face in her hands, an unopened book upon her lap. Charity stole away not wanting to intrude upon such grief.

On her way back upstairs, as she passed Clothilde's room, Charity saw that fat Gerda, the old Dutch servant who always made up the van Daarkens' rooms personally, was thumping Clothilde's pillows.

Charity went in. "I see that you got her to go downstairs," she said, shrewdly guessing that Gerda had insisted Clothilde get out of the room for a while. "It will do her good to try and forget her sorrows."

Gerda turned, still upset, and seeing sympathy in Charity's face, nodded. "It is that letter," she said simply.

"I know," said Charity, pretending to knowledge she did not have in an attempt to draw Gerda out. "It's very sad, isn't it?"

Gerda nodded gloomily, obviously assuming Charity to be in Clothilde's confidence.

Charity strolled around the spacious bedroom, examining the handsome furnishings imported from Holland, the windows richly hung in rose damask that looked out upon the broad lawns and the river. Clothilde's perfumes, her vanity articles, her silver comb, all lay daintily spread out upon her dressing table. Charity fingered the delicate coverlet on the tall carved fourposter bed. It was a mass of embroidery— a magnificent piece.

Charity sighed. How different from her own cramped little room! How wonderful it must be to live like this!

"How did it all start?" she asked with feigned indifference, sitting down on a rosewood chair and studying Gerda. "She never told me the whole story."

It was not exactly a lie, but could cause her trouble if exposed. She guessed, correctly, that Gerda was so worried that she would not stop to think, but would eagerly pour out the story to a sympathetic ear. Although Charity's newly acquired knowledge of the Dutch language sometimes caused her to miss a word or two, most of the time she understood Gerda very well.

"It started when Mistress Clothilde were but a fourteen-year-old," sighed Gerda. "Her Cousin Johannn, you see, were six year older than her, and he did quite turn her head. Johann he were tall and dark and thin with eyes that flashed like lightning, and he were a wild young man, always fighting duels or getting into scrapes with women." Gerda smiled fondly.

Charity had no difficulty imagining the type.

"She did plan to marry him when she were of age, but her father thought otherwise. I was with the family even before she were born, so I did try to tell her that he would never consent, but she would not listen. They were too close-related to marry, her father did say, but she would set her head and frown, and later she would write a note to Johannn and tell him all was well —which it were not." She shook her head sadly. "When Mistress Clothilde learned that her father had promised her to another, she did run off with Johann, but her father caught them two nights later at an inn. When he learned they had married against his will, they do say he killed Johann."

Charity flinched.

"I did think she would die of it," said old Gerda pensively, pausing in her work, remembering. "She were near out of her mind for a spell. Then the man her father had promised her to said he would have no wife who was not a virgin in his bed and did marry a girl from Austria. It was then Killian van Daarken spoke to her father and the marriage was arranged."

"Didn't she have anything to say about it?" asked Charity pityingly.

"La, no! A young girl such as her? Twas her father decided who she'd be marrying—and her already a widow. And he did choose Killian van Daarken, though all were surprised when he did it—and so sudden like. And after they married, they did travel to Brussels—I went with them even then—and it were there Mistress Maria was born."

"Maria? Oh—you mean the child who died?" Charity remembered now that Annjanette had mentioned a daughter who died.

"Miss Maria were her firstborn. Mynheer Pieter he were not born for a year after that."

"How did Maria die?" asked Charity. "Was she ill?"

"She did drown on the way to America. Fell overboard, she did, when that young nurse wasn't looking. I was watching over the baby, for he were so

211

little. And lucky it were he'd been born, for it did seem my poor lady would throw herself over the side of the ship to join her little Maria. She never left her cabin for the rest of the voyage and when we landed she were so weak they did have to carry her ashore."

Charity pondered that. "What did Maria look like?" she asked curiously.

"Oh, she were a tall, thin, dark-haired child with eyes that flashed and a terrible temper, but she were sweet too and her mother did so dote on her."

Tall, thin, dark-haired with eyes that flashed . . . not like the thickset peasant Clothilde had married, nor yet like short, graceful, small-boned Clothilde herself. Not Killian's daughter—*Johann's daughter*. Killian had recognized his opportunity and seized it, and for this hasty marriage of convenience he had been rewarded with a patroonship and the manor of Daarkenwyck.

But . . . the child had perished. For a moment Charity felt she heard the soft whirr of bats, flying around her head, brushing her with their dark wings.

She tried to shake off her fancies, to tell herself that the marriage had been one of convenience—surely common enough—that the child had died because of a nurse's inattention—that was all.

"Tis the letters from Mistress Joanna, Johann's sister, that break her heart," mused old Gerda. "I remember the first one, which came shortly after we had arrived here, and I remember how white her face went, and how she stayed in her room and cried all day. That evening when she came out, she told me that she had received a letter from Johann's sister, who would now be writing to her regularly, and that reading about Johann had made her sad. Then she went and stayed with little Pieter, had her bed moved into his room. And Mynheer Killian asked me why, and I told him truthful she'd had a letter from Johann's sister, Mistress Joanna."

And that was the beginning of the separate bedrooms, mused Charity. A letter from the grave. . . . How stunned poor Clothilde must have been to learn that Johann had not died. Charity surmised that he must have been dreadfully hurt but had survived the attack to live out his life as a cripple in a monastery under the care of the monks. From the monastery he wrote sad letters to the woman who had loved him too well, now an ocean away and married—bigamously, of course—to another man. And the woman wept when she received his letters, wept bitterly for a girlhood and a lover forever gone from her. For Charity realized Clothilde's problem. Maria was dead, and if Clothilde returned to Holland and claimed Johann as her legal husband, then Pieter would become illegitimate and perhaps would not even inherit his grandfather's wealth under Dutch law. Clothilde loved Johann—but she loved Pieter too and could not bring herself to destroy his future.

Charity was certain that Killian van Daarken had pushed little Maria overboard. He had rid himself forever of a "firstborn" who was not his own.

And in Holland, had the grandfather really cared?

Poor Clothilde, trapped forever. No wonder she had vacant eyes. No wonder her gaze passed over Annjanette as if she did not see her. What a small annoyance Annjanette must seem to her. Clothilde had scars so deep that Killian's dalliance must seem trivial indeed.

Charity wondered, did Clothilde suspect? Did she know in the dark reaches of her heart that Killian had killed Maria? Perhaps she did, because the letter had said "You can then return to Holland and visit your kin without fear." Pieter had said something about his father keeping Clothilde with him although she longed to visit Holland. Was Killian afraid that once in Holland, Clothilde would refuse to return? That she would run to the arms of her former lover, no matter in what condition she found him? And the bigamy thus be discovered? Charity knew Killian to be a shrewd man, and guessed that he would have made inquiries about a sister "Joanna"; perhaps there was no sister.

Charity pondered this.

Killian—not a man given to forbearance—had shown remarkable forbearance in this matter. Apparently he had made no move to intercept the letters though he knew their source.

Perhaps he feared to drive Clothilde too far. Perhaps, like the spider he was, he only sat and waited for Johann to die. And then there would be no one to challenge his son's legitimacy.

Charity got up. She had made a terrible discovery and no one must know she had made it.

"I will not tell her you told me," she said sympathetically, "but I am glad at last to understand." Her smile said, *It is our secret, that you have talked too much.*

Old Gerda, smoothing out the delicate coverlet, gave her a grateful look and Charity swiftly left the room, afraid to be found here talking so companionably to the old woman.

The matter concerned Pieter's future too, and Pieter's future might be *her* future.

The ringing skates from the river had ceased, the sleighs had started back upriver, and the winter cold lay around Daarkenwyck like a white blanket. Charity shivered and found a shawl to pull around her shoulders.

The world of Daarkenwyck was dark indeed.

CHAPTER 19

The extremely cold weather was winter's last gasp, and soon signs of spring began to appear everywhere on the estate. The warm days seemed to bring out a playfulness in Pieter, and he insisted that Charity spend her days riding out with him across the damp green earth as the land around the Hudson sprang to vibrant life.

Pieter was leaving very soon. His trunks were being packed for his year in Holland. But he did not seem terribly anxious to go. Rather, he became tense and worried as the time for his departure neared, and he clung to Charity, hardly leaving her side.

It seemed to Charity that the patroon, too, was acting strangely. His eyes were more and more inscrutable as he watched her with his son.

The ice had broken up and the river was navigable once again, though the weather was often damp and foggy and the nights were still quite sharp and cool. Annjanette had apparently been a good girl, for she now sported a coral necklace and dangling coral earrings hung on golden wires from her pierced ears. Poor Clothilde had withdrawn into herself even more dramatically. She had lost weight, refused to eat and no longer read. She lay in her great bed and stared at the ceiling, taking no interest even in Pieter, so soon to leave for the Holland for which she had longed. Gerda sighed and shook her head when Charity inquired about her. Charity guessed that Johann must have died and that Clothilde was pining. Wasting away, her death was only a matter of time.

And then Annjanette, the happy mistress, would

come into her own. . . . Charity watched Annjanette, who sometimes hummed as she walked about the big rooms, touching things acquisitively, waiting for Clothilde to die so they would become *her* things.

Did Annjanette really believe Killian would marry her? Charity wondered. It seemed far more likely that greedy Killian would marry a daughter of one of the rich river families—perhaps one of the older de Schmoot daughters, who were reputed to be very wealthy in their own right as a result of a legacy from a maiden aunt in Holland. Or perhaps he would try for the widow of Jacob van der Ruyden, whose great manor some said was now up for sale. It was not too far from Daarkenwyck—a joining of hands, a joining of fortunes. Charity thought wryly that Annjanette would have a few shocks in store for her if Clothilde died.

But mostly Charity's attention was concentrated on Pieter.

As the day before he was to leave came, he appeared absolutely distracted. He followed Charity mournfully about, and showed no interest whatever in the papers and letters and small gifts for people overseas, which family friends were pressing him to take for them.

Charity wondered what life at Daarkenwyck would be like without Pieter. Perhaps Killian would dismiss her. He had paid her no further attention since the night he had blacked Annjanette's eye. Perhaps he was too interested in selecting a new lady to rule the servants at Daarkenwyck when Clothilde died. At any rate, his diminished interest in her was very welcome, and left her free to think about Pieter.

The night before he was to leave they strolled about the cool spring-green lawns, getting their feet wet with the dew that sparkled on the grass, and Charity brought up the subject.

"I may be gone when you return, Pieter," she said soberly.

"What?" he cried. "You would not do it!"

She remembered again that she had given the patroon her promise that she would tell no one she was not a cousin. It prevented her from revealing to Pieter her true position in the household, from saying "Your father will have no use for my services now, and may well dismiss me."

She felt trapped, wanting to be truthful, hardly knowing what to say.

They had reached the deep shadow of some trees where the dew was very heavy. She shivered. "It's cold, Pieter. I must go in. I didn't bring my shawl with me."

He ignored that and seized her arm. "If I thought you would not be here——" he said hoarsely.

Charity saw no way out of her dilemma. "Of course, I'll be here," she said. "I only thought that your father. . . ." She let the words drift off.

"What has he to do with it?" burst out Pieter.

"I live here at his sufferance," Charity pointed out.

"But you are his cousin! He would not turn you out."

Charity sighed. "No, I suppose not."

Above them the moon was a pale sliver and the branches of the big trees swayed. His face shone in the darkness. She saw she had alarmed him.

"You have been cruel to me, Charity!" he accused. "You have denied me so much as a kiss!"

It was true; she felt suddenly shamed by her unrelenting attitude toward Pieter. He had poured out his love for her in a hundred ways, and she was holding out ruthlessly for the marriage vows.

"I know," she said, and lifted her lips for his kiss.

He crushed her to him fiercely, covering her face with kisses, then prying open her lips with his tongue, probing desperately. His hands were fumbling with her bodice. She felt her senses quicken, and managed to push him away.

"No," she said. "No, Pieter."

"I can't leave you," he panted. "I won't leave you. I won't!" His eyes were wild.

"Your father——" she began.

"Damn my father!" he cried. "Damn him to hell!" His words came out almost with physical pain. "Oh, Charity, a *year,* a whole year without you—I cannot stand it." He threw his arms about her with such violence that she could feel the breath leave her, and then his body was pressed against hers in what seemed a bitter rage.

"You *must* go," she said sensibly. "It's all arranged."

"Then I'll take you with me!" he cried.

"No . . . your father won't let you do that. He wants you to complete your education, remember? So you can follow in his footsteps and manage the large estates that will one day be yours. Oh, Pieter, a year is not a lifetime, not if . . ." she almost whispered the words, a gossamer shadow in the dusk—"not if you love me."

"I do love you!" His voice broke. "Oh, Charity, I do love you. I do. Charity, Charity, what am I to do? I am near crazy with wanting you. I cannot sleep, I cannot eat, I pound my pillow at night in anger that your head is not lying on it beside me. Charity, give me this one night—grant me that of your kindness, of your love for me. You do love me, don't you?" he asked anxiously.

"I . . . don't know, Pieter," she said ruefully. "I *want* to love you, but . . . I don't know."

"Then let me take you in my arms," he cried, grief-stricken. "Let me prove to you that for me there is no other! Ah, Charity, I cannot wed you before I leave, but when I come back we will be man and wife. Can you not find it in your heart to give me this one night to remember you by? To hold in my heart on restless nights? Else I will go mad without you! You could not be so cruel as to deny me!"

His arms tightened about her as he spoke, and tears overflowed his eyes. Confusion and pity swept over her, and a kind of wonder. *To remember her by . . .* there was a humbleness in his tone tonight as he asked her that, a humbleness that was new to him. She felt in that moment that Pieter truly loved her.

Held prisoner there in his arms, staring into the wild hungry depths of his eyes, his tear-streaked face, she hesitated—and was lost.

"You will!" he cried in a voice of rapture. "Ah, Charity, you will!"

218

Even as she opened her mouth to answer, his mouth clamped hungrily down over her own, effectively shutting off all speech.

She felt him tugging her dress down, tearing it in his hurry, and she struggled against him, but he seemed to take her struggles only as an eagerness to be in his arms. She could hear his breath rasping, feel his chest heave against her in his fury at the resistance of her garments until finally he had pulled her dress off her and next her petticoats and chemise, and fell with her upon the wet spring grass.

She felt the dew chill upon her naked back, and goose flesh trembled over her skin as the grass blades wet with dew probed and fingered up between her upper legs so that she writhed there—and Pieter mistook that too for desire.

For a moment he let her go as he opened his trousers, holding her body firmly to the ground by his weight, and in that moment she cried desperately, "No, Pieter! This is not the way. We are not—"

But his anguished voice cut into hers. "Oh, you would not change your mind now? You would not do it?"

And before she could struggle away he was on her again, his mouth cutting off her outcry, his hands pinioning her shoulders to the cold wet grass, his coat with its gold buttons cutting into the soft flesh of her breasts and stomach, his boots scratching the fine soft flesh of her legs—and his throbbing masculinity finding a swift entrance between her thrashing legs, driving home without regard to pain or pleasure.

Stunned by the suddenness of his assault, with the force of his taking, she quivered and stopped struggling. Though he had taken her against her will, she felt all her nerve ends quicken and over the pulsating beat of her heart, and over the rising fire in her veins floated his words: *A whole year without you—I cannot stand it*. They were sweet words, they had seemed wrested from the heart of him. And her heart responded to his words as her body did to his tempestuous embrace. Her own fires—kept banked these many months—now mounted to match his own so that she clung to him, almost weeping until, with a mighty surge, the volcano of their desire was surfeited and they fell apart spent upon the grass, cold and wet with the spring dew.

Her hair was soaked, she was shivering. She made to rise, but he turned over instantly, lying on his side beside her, and with a hand upon her stomach held her down.

"Ah, let me look at you." His voice thrilled. "You are mine! Mine at last!"

She lay back and stared at him, her eyes wide and dark as he feasted his eyes on her nakedness, her body pale and glistening with the dew in the dappled white moonlight as the branches overhead swayed.

"I am cold, Pieter," she whispered. "Cold and wet. I must go—"

"Not yet," he murmured sensuously. "Not yet." And he held her fast to the cold grass, his warm hands kneading her flesh, seeking every part of her, his lips following, tracing small patterns across her stomach, across her quivering breasts, setting his teeth gently into her thigh. She pushed at him weakly.

"I cannot let you go yet," he cried. "I must have you again!" And as she tried to edge away he rolled back upon her, lifting his body up a little so that she could still try to escape, turning this way and that beneath him, in an effort to get away from the wet, penetrating chill of the grass. But just as she would turn her body to the side so that her breasts brushed the grass blades and were wet with the dew, he would turn her over again toward him and his warm hands would fall upon them, warming them, and as her hips and thighs slid away from him over the slippery lawn, so he would turn her back toward the warmth of his own trouser legs again. At last fully aroused, he took her again, entering her this time with easy assurance, and plundered her secrets again until finally, he lay relaxed upon her cold, spent, half-crushed body, his face nestling in the bright tangled beauty of her hair, which was spread out like a golden fan upon the dew-washed grass.

Suddenly he rose, made a sweeping downward movement with his hands. Then adjusting his trousers and leaning over, he took her hands and pulled her to her feet.

"Let me look at you," he cried, pulling her out of the dappled shadows onto the bright moonlit lawn. "Here where I can see you."

Charity pulled back, protesting, "Please, Pieter. They can see us from the house."

"No matter," he said recklessly. "Let them see that you're mine! Mine!" And spun her around, holding her hand tightly above her head, in a wild dance upon the lawn as if in some Bacchanalian revel.

Charity sneezed and stumbled. "I will catch my death of cold." She reached down to snatch up her wet torn garments. "You, Pieter, are fully clothed. See, you have torn my dress so that I cannot wear it! You must give me your coat."

"Ah," he laughed exultantly, "I would rather lead you in as you are, stamped with the impress of my body, proving to the world that I have bedded you at last!"

She recoiled.

"You *couldn't* want to drag your future wife naked through the front door!" she gasped.

"We could go through the back," he said, his voice becoming sullen as if he had been stopped in the middle of some delightful game.

"And shame me before the servants?" she cried.

"The servants do not matter," he said sulkily, but he shrugged off his coat and slipped it around her as he marched her jauntily to a side door.

She shook him off with a reproachful look and, carrying her torn dress over one arm, said anxiously, "Look inside, Pieter. If there are servants there, send them away. I must get back to my room without being seen."

He left her shivering there, and in a moment was back to report there was no one inside, all had gone to bed. She slipped past him and hurried up to her room, he following fast on her heels. Under the pretext of retrieving his coat, he came inside and shut the door.

In silence Charity removed the coat and stood before him naked and used. Her wet hair streamed down her back and there were twigs caught up in it. Bits of grass still clung to her back and legs. She wanted nothing so much as a warm bath and to lie for hours and hours under a warm blanket on her narrow bed, oblivious to the world.

"I will dry you," he offered gaily, and seized a towel and began to rub her body vigorously.

Stiff with cold, her strength drained, Charity suffered him to do it.

Now he had reached her buttocks with the towel and he let the towel drop and squeezed her bottom so hard that she winced as he pulled her strongly toward him.

As he did so, her soft mouth hardened and some new cold core of her being she had not known existed counseled: *You have gone this far with him. Go now yet a little further and the world will be yours. Daarkenwyck will be yours.*

Charity wrenched herself free and stepped back and faced him. Her topaz eyes flung him a challenge and she stood very erect and unsubmissive, her chin high.

"And will you take me with you?" she challenged.

"Yes," he cried. "By God, if I cannot take you with me, I will not go! No man can make me!"

Charity sighed deeply. She had not meant it to come to this. A confrontation. She had hoped for some other course. But now his impetuosity had turned them down another road and he had had his way with her. He was young, excited, she did not know for sure how lasting his affection would be. But for the moment he was ablaze with desire for her. She must go with him now or he might be forever lost to her—Daarkenwyck might be forever lost to her.

She no longer protested as he tossed the blanket from her bed and pushed her down upon its soft surface. He spent the night in turbulent takings and leavings until with the dawn he slept.

But as Charity drifted off to exhausted slumber, something in her heart bled a little, and nameless whisperings echoed down the corridors of her mind, and those whisperings said to her, *You do not love him. You have sold yourself for gold.*

CHAPTER 20

When Charity woke, Pieter had left her room. His coat was gone. She stretched and smiled as she remembered the wild night just past.

Pieter was a spoiled young man who insisted on having his way. Just as he had had his way with her, so he would have his way with the heavy patroon, his father. And his listless mother, wasting away, would not deny him.

She rose, feeling tired and hard-used, but with a strange new hope in her wary heart.

She would go to Holland with Pieter, and even if she did not wed him here in America—for perhaps Killian would prevent that—they would be wed before they returned to these shores; she would see to that. She would return to the Hudson as wife to the future patroon of Daarkenwyck.

It was a golden future, and she would have it.

She lay back upon the bed, dreaming for a while. Then she got up and spent a long time mending her torn dress. It was stained by the grass and still slightly damp, but she wanted to wear it so that Pieter would see it, and seeing it remember last night.

She had thought him a boy but he had taken her with a man's passion.

Time sped by. Pieter was probably still sleeping. No one had brought her a tray. Perhaps the servants had guessed—or seen from the attic windows. . . . She flushed. Well, it was over and done. Now she had to make the most of it.

The afternoon sun had cast its light across the lawns when Charity at last made her way down the

225

front staircase, trailing down it elegantly, her hand lightly caressing the polished railing. A majestic stairway down which she would walk in innumerable lovely gowns to greet her guests at balls that were yet to be. Her hospitality would become a legend along the river. . . .

As she reached the bottom step she saw Killian van Daarken and hesitated. Had Pieter told him yet? Could she expect an explosion or a reluctant welcome as Pieter's betrothed? Would the elder van Daarken insist that Pieter take this trip alone before he married her? If they reached an impasse, she had no doubt Pieter would postpone his trip and that would give them time to talk about it, to work out something.

The man at the end of the hall stood patiently as if waiting for her.

She took a deep breath. She was no coward. If he wanted to try to talk her out of this marriage, she would face him now.

Briskly now, she walked down the hall and greeted him.

He gave her the smallest bow of acknowledgment, his tiny blue eyes alert. She wondered suddenly if Pieter would grow to look like that when he was old—heavy-jowled, gross. The thought repelled her.

The patroon made a slight gesture toward the library and with a little trepidation she preceded him into the room. After he closed the door, he stood looking at her, a faint smile upon his lips.

"May I sit down" she asked in a voice that was wooden with embarrassment.

"Please do." He indicated a chair and sat down himself, studying her in leisurely fashion.

"I—I suppose Pieter has told you," she said defensively, for she saw it in his eyes, a kind of knowledge of her as if Pieter had rushed to his father and blurted out everything.

"Yes." He did not elaborate.

She waited, growing desperate, her hands gripping the mahogany chair, tension building in her.

"Where—where is Pieter?" she asked at last.

"Pieter?" He raised his eyebrows. "But you knew he was leaving. Pieter is gone. By now he is far down-river—on his way to Holland."

Her breath left her. The world around her held very still. Only her senses reeled. Charity sat stiffly to absorb this shock.

"I don't believe you," she said, lifting her head. "Pieter wouldn't have left without telling me good-bye."

"Ah, but I thought he did," he said softly. "Last night. At least he told me he bade you a very fond goodbye. Very fond, indeed."

Charity stiffened at this further blow.

"Your face is a thundercloud," he remarked almost derisively. "It would seem you are not pleased with Pieter."

"How would you expect me to react" she asked hoarsely. "He lied to me, deceived me."

"Ah, I see." His fingers came together pontifically and he looked down his large nose at her, still in faint derision. "But you need not feel bereft. You are not alone."

Charity stared at him.

"I am here," he elaborated.

She felt something cold inside, a twist of a cold-bladed knife. His meaning could not have been more clear—or more sinister. She had been right about him when first she had looked into his eyes on the sloop coming upriver. He had desired her then—and now he meant to have her.

"I have had enough of the van Daarken men," she said in a voice that shook with anger.

"But it is wrong to feel so," he said, still speaking gently, as if to a recalcitrant child. "Pieter did no more than I expected him to do. I will not hold you lower in my esteem because my son held you in his arms before I did."

The bastard! Did he think she was something to be passed around like a warming pan to warm their beds for them? Her breath came faster, angrily.

"You will forget Pieter." His voice had acquired a

steely edge. "You will not mourn him, or grieve for him."

"Grieve for him?" Her contemptuous laugh was a mockery. "A man who says he loves me and does not even say goodbye?"

"But he told you goodbye rather thoroughly—he gave me an excellent account of it."

Charity writhed inwardly, but was too stunned to say anything further.

"Pieter did entreat me to let him take you with him as far as New York—it seems you have set a fire in his blood." His eyes dwelt thoughtfully on her rapidly rising and falling breasts beneath her mended bodice. "I advised against it, of course. Is it possible Pieter neglected to mention that he goes to Amsterdam to marry Margret van der Pol? She has a great dowry. He will return to us with his bride in one year's time."

Charity stared at him. Her world, which had been rocking, settled down and sank into bottomless depths.

"Since Pieter is irretrievably lost to you, had you not best set your face in the only direction possible?"

She hardly heard him. The landscape before her, stretching out endlessly in her mind, was a wasteland, empty and bleak.

The patroon's son, that golden boy, had used and flung away another toy.

A sob caught in her throat. And the landscape that she saw in her mind changed, and grew aslant. She seemed to be moving ever downward toward the edge of an abyss.

The patroon was speaking. Her attention came back to him slowly.

"No, I see from the set of your jaw that you are intractable," said he, "so I wish you to understand my reasoning in this matter."

Charity sat stonily, regarding him. Distant thunder grumbled in the hills.

His voice hardened. "As I have told you, I am a self-made man. My son will enter doors that have never been open to me. His future in the world at large will be dependent upon the good regard of men and

228

women. To the end that he may have the regard of men, I have taught him to shoot and to hunt, to play games well and to stand up for his rights. To the end that he may have the regard of women—and therefore not only the delights that brings, but also their cunning assistance with their husbands (here Charity stared at him in surprise), I wished him to learn the gentle art of seduction, and of disarming guile. He must be able to tell bald-faced lies to women that have the ring of truth. No, do not look so surprised. If he moves in court circles, as I fully intend that he should, it will be of great assistance to him if he can cozen his way into the beds of duchesses and countesses. But he could not seduce the daughters of my friends along the river. Another patroon would surely force him to marry any daughter he would seduce. So, his efforts thus far had been confined to scullery maids, with whom he has been quite successful."

Charity forbore saying, "And Annjanette." Perhaps the patroon did not know about that.

He continued. "It was in my mind that under my tutelage he should pursue some aristocratic young woman with whom he sat at table; a lady in satins and laces who would fend him off with pretty speeches and artfully evade him. I see your eyes widen in comprehension. That is well. You happened along at a time when I needed you, to fulfill this goal. You were destitute and hunted and willing to accept my largess. No need to redden. It is the truth and we both know it. I set you at my table, told all you were my cousin, bade them accept you as such, dressed you accordingly."

"And dangled me before him," choked Charity.

His voice was cool, his eyes even colder. "And made Pieter a wager that he could not seduce you before he embarked for Holland."

"A . . . wager?" she faltered.

"A wager. I wagered five hundred florins that Pieter could not bed you before he left for Holland."

"And mind you," he added, "the rules were to be those of good breeding and polite society. Pieter was

229

neither to take you by force nor to promise you marriage but to win you by wiles or lies—anything but force or betrothal."

"Then he cheated you," she said grimly. "For he not only repeatedly promised me marriage but used force to persuade me."

"The young puppy!" cried van Daarken. "I'll have his hide for that! He has my five hundred florins! And yet—" he sighed and cast a lingering eye over Charity's full round breasts—"I can understand the boy's being overcome, being maddened by your refusal after so long a siege. Yes, it is understandable. Nor did you shout to the world that he had ill-used you, so there must have been some measure of acquiescence, eh?"

"Some measure?" said Charity bitterly. "He had promised me honorable marriage and wept disconsolately over this year of separation. It seems I had more feeling for him than he had for me."

"Tears," murmured the patroon. "I would not have thought of that. Perhaps Pieter will have a talent for these matters after all."

Charity was sickened. She rose to leave.

"No, stay," he ordered. "This is not what I called you to hear."

She sank back down, hating him.

"I have long desired you, and it was only in deference to my son's education that I have held off so long. As you know, there is a small dressing room that lies between my room and my wife's."

Charity frowned. "That room is occupied by your Cousin Annjanette," she pointed out.

"True. Ostensibly she occupies it so that she may be near and answer any call of my wife's to assist her in any way. Actually that is not the case. There is a latch on the door between my wife's room and the dressing room, which Annjanette may close—but none which she may close toward me."

"So Annjanette is no more a cousin than I am," said Charity bitterly.

"Precisely," he said. "I have ordered your things

230

transferred to the dressing room. You are trading rooms with Annjanette."

"And what makes you think I will do this?" she demanded.

He sighed. "I had hoped you would be more tractable, but since you are not, I will tell you in no uncertain terms. My wife does not find me pleasing, nor do I find her pleasing. Annjanette is a pretty child, but she no longer amuses me. I find her dull. Beside my bed I keep a small bell—you will have observed it perhaps?"

"I have never been in your room, mynheer."

"No? Then I will tell you that it is there. At night you will keep the door latched between your small dressing room and my wife's bedroom."

"But what if she requires me?" she demanded ironically.

"She will not require you. It is I who will require you. If you hear one tinkle of the bell, you are to come into my room and see what it is that I desire. If you hear two tinkles of the bell, you are to disrobe and let your hair down—I prefer a woman's hair to hang loose about her naked body—and walk barefoot into my room and join me in my bed. My needs are—varied. I will perhaps have Annjanette instruct you in my preferences."

"And will not this interesting arrangement become known?" asked Charity sarcastically. "And so become a scandal?"

"No, because when I have finished with you, you will return quietly to your own room and behave as if you have passed the entire night there in your own bed."

"So I am to replace Annjanette," Charity said coldly, as if she were speaking of some third party and not of herself. "And what is to happen to her, pray?"

"Annjanette will continue in the household," he said smoothly. "She will have her uses."

Charity stared at him. "And what may they be?"

His voice sharpened. "They are no concern of yours, but since you are so curious, I occasionally have

231

guests who come from a distance to spend the night."

"Like Mr. Derwent," she whispered.

"Yes," he said shortly. "Like Mr. Derwent. And these guests from a distance have often traveled far without female companionship and would like their beds warmed for them. I will instruct Annjanette on these occasions to blunder prettily into their rooms as if she had lost her way, and allow herself to be seduced. In the morning my guest will discover that he has "ruined" my cousin. But I will not press any charge or demand satisfaction—I will indeed be most kindly disposed toward my alarmed guest who sees a great scandal brewing up around him. I will explain that I am a reasonable man and—my affairs should prosper, for under such circumstances a man will not quibble over who gets the better of a business deal."

A long roll of thunder almost drowned his words. Charity quivered at the sound, her very soul rocking with misery.

She gazed at the man before her, hating him. A light mist of cold perspiration lay on her forehead, but her hands were steady now in her lap, and her voice was strong and clear.

"Mynheer van Daarken," she said evenly, "you are not only a despoiler of trusting young women, you are a blackmailer."

Angry lights flickered in his eyes. He said coldly, as if to punish her for that, "In the future your presence will not be required at table. The servants will bring trays to your room or if you do not care for that, a place will be made for you in the kitchen." He smiled thinly. "Your presence at the table upsets my wife."

All her senses tingling under this last insult, Charity now rose to her full height and faced her tormentor with at least an outward calm. A terrible maturity had come to her in these last bitter moments. She felt her very soul had been hardened, melted and reshaped by the raging fires that had singed her spirit.

"You have been very frank with me, mynheer," she said, and though she trembled inwardly with rage, her voice was calm. "And now I will be as frank with you. I have no intention of staying here to become your mistress, and you may ring your bells in hell for all I care. The van Rensselaer sloop is due downriver this afternoon and I intend to be on it. I would rather walk the streets as a drab than wear silks as your trollop."

He laughed shortly. "The choice is not yours to make, but mine. You will remain here."

Charity paled a little.

"Do not think that I have not learned much while I have been here," she warned darkly. "Or that I will hesitate to expose you."

"Oh? And what have you learned?"

She took in a deep breath. "I heard your arrangements that night in New York with Mr. Derwent—that same Mr. Derwent who came upriver ostensibly for a ball, but who actually came to transact his smuggling business with you, mynheer—an offense against the laws of this Colony. He brought with him silks and other goods and departed with beaver skins." He watched her as she lifted her chin and added, "And if you try to prevent me from leaving *in any way,* I will tell the authorities what I know."

He laughed wryly. "And you think that I will be upset by this childish threat? On the contrary, it will enliven my reputation, which has been a bit dull of late. Not that you can prove anything. Derwent is gone back to—God knows where. No, you will have to do better than that."

Charity glowered at him. "Then I will tell all who will listen of your disreputable sleeping arrangements —of Annjanette, of your loathsome proposals to me, of your base wager and your son's treachery!"

His eyes narrowed and there was anger in them, but his voice remained cool. "Such threats will not dissuade me in my purpose. If you carry them out, they will bring only punishment. You will find your nice new clothes taken away; you will labor as a scullery maid instead of being served as a member of the family. But—the sleeping arrangements will remain 'disreputable' as you call them."

Charity threw back her head confidently and took a deep breath. Now she would play her trump card.

"I have nothing to fear from you," she stated with a courage she did not entirely feel, and to his lifted eyebrows, "You would do well to let me get downriver as fast as possible. For I will reveal that you murdered your wife's first-born, Maria, who was lost overboard so fortuitously on her way to America."

"That is a ridiculous accusation," he cried scornfully. "You cannot prove I killed Maria."

"I have seen a letter that will prove she was not your daughter but conceived before your marriage— your *bigamous* marriage. *That*, mynheer, gives you a motive and makes Pieter a bastard."

His heavy face suffused with color. He leaned forward. "*You* a convicted witch, dare to confront me thus? Sentence has already been passed upon you! I have but to return you to Massachusetts whence you came for it to be carried out."

"We will hang together," said Charity with a calm she was far from feeling.

He ripped out an oath and his voice rose to a roar. "By God, you will not dictate to me here in my own house!" He looked into her blazing topaz eyes. "You will find the tongue torn from your mouth if you but utter a word about Maria or 'bigamous' marriages."

Too late Charity realized her error. She had pushed him too far; she could not now escape his vengeance.

"You can buy my silence by letting me go," she cried in a last desperate effort. "What are matters at Daarkenwyck to me if I am far away?"

He sneered and her heart sank. "You have become dangerous to me." Outside the thunder rolled again, but to her it seemed scarcely louder than his thunderous voice as he roared, "Jan! Jochem! Come to me!"

Charity heard heavy footsteps and turned to run. She rushed from the library into the hall, out the back door and fled from the house. She had run a hundred paces across the lawn before they caught her—Big

Jan and Jochem, coming from opposite directions—and dragged her back to the house.

"Do not think that you will bed me, Mynheer van Daarken!" cried Charity, struggling in their arms. "For that you will never do!"

"The rats may bed you for all I care," he growled, his whole expression lowering. "Take her to the blockhouse—there." He indicated the one to the left of the landing. "Chain her to the wall and leave her."

Charity's eyes widened in horror. Those deserted blockhouses—they harbored spiders and vermin and rats and—possibly snakes. "No," she screamed, "you would not do that!"

"There you will stay until you have come to your senses," he sneered. "And if you grovel on your knees to me, it may be that I will reconsider your case. If not, consider that you will live the remainder of your life chained in a dark room. Take her away, Jan!"

CHAPTER 21

Charity found herself being dragged roughly along, across the spongy spring grass, by expressionless captors who thrust her summarily into the log blockhouse. It was dark inside. The only light came from the slits for sniping and chinks in the roof which needed repair.

"We have no leg irons," muttered Jochem, holding onto Charity with one hand while his other ran down her back and crept along her buttocks. "How should we secure her?"

He lurched as Charity kicked at him.

"Hold there!" cried Jan, giving Charity a rough jerk. "We could put leg irons on her at the forge."

"Ah, but we might injure her ankles and the patroon would not like that," said Jochem, speaking with slow deliberation as his hand again began its quest about her lower hips. Charity struggled and gave him a venomous look. He spat and added, "Suppose the patroon has a change of heart? He would not then want her to be marked. She's a fine-looking wench and may yet come to her senses and obey him."

"What then?" demanded Jan impatiently.

"I know a better way," said Jochem.

He passed a heavy chain around Charity's neck, ran it over to the wall and secured one end to a great iron ring. Then he took the other end of the chain, now looped lightly around Charity's neck, and ran it through a ring in the opposite wall. "Will you fasten this for me, Jan, when I say it's tight enough?" he asked, returning to Charity, who stood stiff and tense. "Now sit you down on the floor," he said, pushing her down ignominiously. Working the chain around her neck, he pulled it sufficiently taut so that if she tried to maneuver her head to free herself she cut off her breathing entirely. She knew she would not be able to stand or to lie down, because the chain became unbearably tight if she moved. She could but sit on the earthen floor, feeling the weight of the heavy chain around her neck press down wearingly into her soft flesh.

"Tight enough?" growled Jan.

"Almost." Jochem bent over her, ostensibly to adjust the chain, but actually to keep it so taut that she could not speak. While her hands tugged at it in agony, he explored her breasts, pawing, pinching. Charity writhed, feeling her senses begin to leave her as the chain tightened. Finally, Jochem loosened it a little and said, "There, that'll do." She began to cough and still could not speak when they left her. As she heard the sound of a heavy key turning in the lock, she gave a sob and tried to move. Instantly the chain bit into her throat. She realized that she must stay awake to live. If her head sagged too far her breath would be cut off and she would surely suffocate.

She swallowed and coughed again—this time not from being half strangled but because she had caught cold lying on the damp ground while Pieter had his way with her. Soon her body was wracked with coughing, and every cough sent a pain through her throat as the chain constricted around it and threatened to strangle her.

When the paroxysm was over she sat weakly blinking and gulping in air. A roll of thunder startled her and she jumped and groaned as the chain tightened punishingly around her white throat.

There was going to be a storm. . . . She looked up at the light showing through the chinks in the roof overhead. When the rain broke, she would be drenched, sitting there immobilized on the damp ground. She began to shiver. But after a while she stopped shivering and started to feel hot. She wiped her face with the skirt of her dress and tried holding the heavy chains in both hands so that they would not choke her when the paroxysms of coughing came.

Time passed. Sometimes she heard voices outside but no one came near her. Through the roof chinks the murky gray from the overcast sky deepened as night came. They were going to leave her here . . . all night.

She shivered again. She was very cold. They had not left her a blanket or a shawl. She presumed that was part of the patroon's punishment—no food, no warmth, no comfort. Just to sit here on the cold floor through the night—a floor that would soon be wet when the rain began coming in through the roof—and contemplate submission to him.

She was damned if she would submit! Better to die!

She moved against the chain with violence and the resultant pain drew a moan from her inflamed and aching throat.

The thunder boomed again. And then again.

The long rolls of thunder that resounded from hill to hill made the blockhouse seem to be under cannonade, and the small scurrying noises that might be rats sent a black fear through her. During that time of rage and terror, her will hardened and Charity became a woman of stone, a woman with a dark hatred of men and all their works.

If she got out of there, she promised herself vengefully between groaning and coughing, if she got out alive, she would use men as evilly as they had used her! She would exact her own payment from the world of men, if she were ever released from this foul prison.

She fought to keep from fainting, for to faint was to die. If she sagged against those chains in her weariness, her rasping breath would be instantly cut off.

She managed to straighten up once again. Doubtless Killian was sitting comfortably at dinner now, beside a submissive Annjanette, while his wife lay listlessly upstairs. Doubtless he was enjoying his food, his wine, contemplating her plight alone in the blockhouse with grim amusement.

And Pieter, who had pretended to love her so desperately, and who was now proceeding happily down-river on his way to his betrothed in Amsterdam, had left her to this!

Indignation warmed her for the moment, and her back straightened in fury so that she did not sag so painfully against the chains.

As the hours wore on and darkness came, the chinks in the roof were hardly lighter than the dark interior of the blockhouse. Strange noises floated in and out of the blackness surrounding her. Then she heard something strike the door, and she shrank back in terror. The wind again, throwing a branch against it, she told herself. A token of the coming storm. No, this time there were voices, too, and the scrape of metal.

One voice she recognized as Annjanette's saying furiously, "I tell you it *is* the key. I took it from the patroon's room myself!" Then, "If you implicate me in this, Jochem, I will drag you down with me!" And an answer she could not catch.

As the door swung wide, Charity stared wild-eyed at the dark shapes of her rescuers.

Annjanette stumbled toward her. "Do not think I do this for love of you, Charity," she said in a hard voice. "I do it only to get you gone. Killian looks at you too . . . often."

"No matter why you do it, Annjanette, I thank you," croaked Charity. "But—what about this chain?"

"Jochem will strike it off," said Annjanette coldly. "Then you may make your way upriver or down—to the devil, for all I care. Hurry, Jochem, before I am missed."

Jochem, who had brushed by Charity, hammer in hand, now stood by the wall. "I am waiting for the next thunderclap," he said impassively. "Then the noise will not be marked from the house."

Charity closed her eyes and tried to swallow. Jochem was holding the chain against the wall too tightly for that. Dizzily, she prayed for thunder and in a moment her prayers were answered when a flash of blue lightning illuminated the scene. Then Jochem brought his hammer down upon the ring to set her free. Chari-

240

ty rubbed her bruised throat, unable for the moment to speak.

"I have only this advice for you," said Annjanette threateningly, as she pulled Charity to her feet. "And that is, get you gone. If you return to Daarkenwyck, Killian will wring the truth from you, and we will both die."

Charity nodded dumbly.

"Out now," said Annjanette. "I must lock this door before I leave. How you escaped will remain a mystery—they will say you were a witch."

"Where will I go?" Charity croaked. "I have no money, no—"

"That is Jochem's affair. He has a boat hidden." Annjanette pushed them both out the door and struggled to lock it, but Jochem had to help her. Numb and weak, Charity leaned against the log wall for support.

"Why are you doing this, Jochem?" Charity asked, confused, when Annjanette had gone. "The patroon may kill you for it!"

"He'll not be findin' out," he crowed, "because Mistress Annjanette had the chance to get the key which I had not—so he'll not be lookin' in my direction. Nor will he miss me tomorrow while I take you downriver, for he thinks I am off to check the *bouweries*. The patroon, he would not have let me have a boat. He would have me workin' instead on repairin' the buildings and things what nets me no money. So I made a boat that he does not know of. And while he looks for you with dogs and men, beatin' the brush for you, we'll be floatin' down the river in my boat. I have it hid now under yon clump of willows." He nodded.

A paroxysm of coughing wracked Charity.

"And what is your price for all this, Jochem?" she gasped, when she could speak again.

His eyes gleamed. "Ah, that I lay with you just like Pieter did—I saw you out here dancin' naked on the grass!"

Charity flinched.

"My price is that ye lay with me this night and before dawn I'll push us off in my boat, headin' downstream and we'll be gone from here before the sun is up."

But her escape might be discovered before then. The patroon might drop in to see how she was enduring her confinement and find her gone. Then dogs and men would beat the bushes . . . and they would find them. She shivered.

"It's cold and damp on the grass," she objected.

"The blockhouse?" he suggested.

Charity shuddered. "I'm afraid to stay here lest I be discovered. Couldn't we lie in your boat?"

He shrugged. "One place is as good as another."

"Then let us go there," said Charity. "It's going to rain any minute and we'll be drenched out here."

He saw the logic of that. "There is a piece of canvas in the boat," he said eagerly. "We could lie in the boat and pull that over us—twould keep out the rain."

She nodded, coughing again. "Hurry then." She took a step and had to put a hand on his arm for support. "The next lightning bolt will show us plainly to anyone who is looking out the windows."

He looked apprehensively up toward the great house. "That's true," he muttered, and hurried her along the murky darkness until they reached the clump of willows by the bank. She was running, choking back a coughing fit, and when he stopped she bumped into him. He smiled at the contact of her soft body against him and reached out to fondle her. But she brushed him off irritably, saying the storm might break any minute, they had best get in the boat.

As if to underscore her words, there was another jagged flash of lightning, a long peal of thunder and the rain began. They were somewhat protected under the willows, but Jochem reached quickly for the rope that held the rowboat, tossed back the canvas that lay in it and gestured her inside.

Charity's eyes lit on what she had been hoping for —an oar. She reached down and picked it up. "I can't lie on this thing," she cried fretfully. "It will break my back. Let's leave it here on shore." She turned as if to toss the oar away and brought it up hard against the side of the Dutchman's head. All the hatred she felt for the patroon and his lying son, all the indignation that rose in her at what she had suffered at the hands of men, were focused in that sudden hard swing of the oar. As Jochem staggered, she swung it again, striking him in the forehead.

He went down like a stone on the muddy bank.

Charity collapsed, in a paroxysm of coughing, into the boat. After a while she got her breath and, struggling up weakly, she regarded the fallen man. In that fierce moment, she did not care if he was alive or dead. Her experiences at Daarkenwyck had hardened her. She remembered how cruelly tight Jochem had drawn the chain around her throat. No, she did not mind cheating Jochem of his evil sport with her. Doubtless the cold pelting rain would soon bring him around. She looked up at Daarkenwyck, whose lights she could see through the moving branches of the willows, and for an evil moment she hoped she had killed him, and only wished it had been the patroon instead.

With difficulty she untied the rope that held the boat and let it fall into the bottom. On the bank, Jochem groaned slightly. She did not look at him. She shoved at the bank and then at an overhanging branch with the oar, and the boat moved sluggishly out into the rain-pelted river. Between fits of coughing, she paddled until the current caught her. Then she huddled, stiff with cold, beneath the bit of canvas and let the current sweep her along.

Except for her earlier experience in the blockhouse, she had never felt so physically miserable as she did huddled there, wet and cramped and half frozen by the cold rain. She slept a little part of the night, and woke at dawn with a raging fever. The rain had stopped, but her boat had become entangled in some overhanging branches and was now firmly moored by them to the shore.

With trembling hands she worked frantically to free the boat from the entangling branches, stopping sometimes to wait for coughing fits that left her weak and dizzy to pass. How long had she slept there,

243

trapped thus? she wondered uneasily. At last she was free of the branches and paddled weakly out into the mainstream again. Shivering in her wet clothes, she tossed the oar into the bottom of the boat, pushed back her long wet hair with weary fingers and tried to dry out the bit of canvas she had huddled under, against the dampness of the coming night.

For hours she drifted, sometimes sleeping in the bottom of the boat, sometimes using the paddle to bring the boat more centrally into the river. But mainly she slumped down and let the current sweep her along.

It was dangerous, she knew, traveling by daylight. But she also knew that her chills and fever were becoming worse, that there was a pain knifing through her chest when she coughed. She must get far away from Daarkenwyck as fast as she could, so she huddled beneath the canvas whenever she passed anything that looked like a human habitation and hoped anyone seeing the boat from shore would think it only a drifting rowboat that had come loose from its moorings.

The sun came out and dried her hair and her clothes —but she was hot with fever and parched with thirst. Reaching stiff fingers over the edge of the boat, she cupped her hand to bring up the clear cold river water. It revived her a little. She fell back and looked up at the hard bright sky.

Dizzily she sat up.

That odd configuration of trees over there, surely she had seen it before. Had she dreamed it? Now as she looked at that bit of shoreline it seemed to drift past her toward the south.

Toward the south! She was moving upstream! Back toward Daarkenwyck and its dread patroon!

In her fever and fright she had forgotten that this was the river the Algonquins called "the water that flows two ways." The river current had been carrying her south, but now the tidal current was sweeping her back toward the north!

She glanced behind her, upriver. She could see

something, just coming around the bend. Was it the patroon's river sloop? It was, it was! It seemed pale gold in the distance behind her, but it had sails, while she had only oars to pit against this tide that drove her back upriver.

Perhaps they had not yet seen her. She must be a mere speck on the river compared to the big yellow sloop with its billowing white sails. She seized the oar and, dizzy and weak, paddled as hard as she could toward the western shore, which happened to be the nearest. Reaching it, she slid her boat beneath the overhanging branches of an enormous oak that grew close to the water's edge. The vegetation was heavy there, and she was able to maneuver the rowboat out of the water, sliding it along the ground to wedge it firmly, with the last of her strength, between some young saplings. Well concealed by the leafy cover, she crouched down to watch the approach of the menacing yellow sloop.

Her heart pounded fiercely as it came nearer, but it stayed, she noted, near the opposite shore, sailing along quite briskly. She remembered vaguely Killian mentioning that the currents were uneven on different sides of the river. At least they had not seen her, for the sloop went on past, to disappear downstream.

Now she had another problem. If she moved on downstream, she might be running into Killian's hands. If she reached New York, he might be waiting for her there, with big Jan scanning the river to greet her as she arrived. Or, at any time, the long yellow sloop might turn around and she would run into it coming back upstream.

She had not eaten for a long time, and saw nothing edible nearby. She realized that she was very weak and wracked by fever, yet she dared not try her luck upriver. Surely Killian van Daarken would have put the word out that his demented cousin had wandered away and must be returned to him. Men would consider it a good deed to return her to Daarkenwyck!

She shivered.

And heard a sound in the underbrush behind her.

The blood seemed to freeze in her veins. There were black bears in these woods, she knew, and wolves and mountain lions, as well as smaller deadly things—timber rattlesnakes and copperheads. She forced herself not to panic. Instead, she stood up to see what caused the noise.

It was a horse! Saddleless and bridleless, it was not too prepossessing an animal. It looked at her gravely and continued chewing some succulent grasses it had found at the river's edge.

She looked about her. A horse! The perfect answer. She would ride him downriver, hiding whenever she saw boats. There must be berries and other things to eat along the way that would sustain her until she reached civilization.

She edged toward the horse, being careful not to frighten him, and spoke soothingly. He was quite tame and willing to let her approach. She came up and patted his head and he nuzzled her hand. Now she leaned against him weakly, gathering her strength.

Without protest, the horse let her pull herself up on his back and at her urging walked obediently downstream for a few yards. After that he veered off into the trees. She tried to turn him, but he would not turn. Stubbornly, he continued his jogging gait into the trees. She realized then that he was walking down one of the tiny paths that led through the forest—some Indian trail probably, winding through tamaracks and elms and flowering dogwood. She hoped desperately she would not end up in an Indian village and considered sliding off his back and going back to where she had hidden the boat.

But she had made her decision too late. They had crossed several other paths and she had got her directions confused. She might not be able to tell which path led to the river. Far better to be lost on horseback than afoot!

Besides, although the sight of the horse seemed to buoy her for a little while and give her renewed vitality, her strength was ebbing fast. Ahead of her, through butternuts and red maples, she could see the forest growing even more dense. The ground was rising. She gave up trying to influence the horse's direction and lay along his neck, only half conscious, letting him find his own way. She could only hope he knew where he was going.

Low branches tore at her hair, struck at her legs, ran twiggy fingers down her back, but she remained aboard him, her body sagging, her fingers twined into the horse's mane. She was tired, so tired. Even coughing seemed too much effort. When she opened her eyes, the world began to waver, so she closed them again with a groan.

Only one thought sustained her: At least she was not at Daarkenwyck in the hands of the patroon!

CHAPTER 22

Lying limp and almost lifeless across the horse's back, Charity must have dozed, but she came to with a cry. She was falling off the horse—no, being lifted off! Instinctively she raised her hands and struck at the arms that were holding her. At her outburst, a masculine voice, with a reassuringly surprised note in it, said, "There now! Wilt thou strike at a man who was but catching thee as thou fell to the ground?" Charity looked up into a pair of honest brown eyes set in a square sunburned face only inches from her own.

"I . . . didn't steal the horse," she said faintly and keeled over.

She did not know that he held her carefully in his arms, looking down at her, perplexed. She did not know anything at all for days. She moaned in delirium on a narrow bed. Sometimes she thought her mother came to her, and she wept brokenly. And at other times the patroon or Jochem—and her terrified screams rent the air. Sometimes she was so hot she thought she was tied to a tall pole looking down through a pillar of black smoke into an inferno, feeling her own flesh burning while the crowd below laughed and jeered. She was so frightened she coughed incessantly and could not stop. Always she seemed to be on fire, suffocating.

It was days before the fever broke and Charity lay, damp and sane and awake at last, and looked about her.

She could not imagine where she was.

Overhead were rough timbers and a coating of bark. Around her were crude walls covered with bark. There was one small window and a rough-hewn wooden door. Across the room sat a crude table and two benches, and two large leather-bound chests with rounded tops stood against the opposite wall.

The door opened, letting in bright sunlight, and a man came in. Charity tried to sit up, but fell back weakly. She gazed at him.

She saw that he was of medium height, square-jawed, tanned. He wore a wide-brimmed hat of coarse, dark felt; his hair was brown and rather short. He sported a shirt with rolled-up sleeves and no coat, loose-fitting leather knee breeches, coarse woven stockings and blocky-looking shoes. He looked strong and clean and he gazed back at her steadily.

"Ah, I see thou art awake," he said softly.

Charity nodded. "Who are you?" she whispered.

"I am Ben Goode," he said gravely. "And thou?"

"Charity Woodstock," murmured Charity weakly. She felt very tired. The exertion of speaking was too much. A great enveloping fatigue seemed to be sweeping over her.

"Rest," he said. "Later we will talk."

Charity's eyes closed. She slept.

Later Ben brought her hot broth. He sat on the edge of the narrow bed and fed it to her with a wooden spoon. By now she was aware that she was wearing a strange nightdress of rough cotton. Her chemise, neatly laundered, was hanging from a nail driven into the wall some distance away, and beside it her dress and petticoats. She stared at them, fascinated.

"Is there—a woman here?" she asked.

An expression of pain passed over his face and was quickly gone. For a moment the spoon in his hand quivered. "No," he said quietly. "Only myself."

Then *he* had undressed her and laundered her chemise. Charity cast another quick glance at the chemise and a hot blush flooded her face.

"Eat," Ben commanded gently. "I did hear thy story in bits and pieces as thou didst toss in delirium. Here thou art safe from harm."

His jaw hardened as he said that and Charity looked up at him with curiosity. Meekly, she swallowed another spoonful of hot soup.

250

"How didst thou find this place, Mistress Woodstock?"

"The horse brought me," said Charity absently.

"I am aware the horse brought thee," he said, a tinge of irony in his voice. "Tis my horse."

Charity's head swung around to look at him. She caught her breath. Stealing horses was a punishable offense. "I didn't steal the horse," she protested quickly. "I—I was much in need of transportation and—and he was there. I do not remember the ride."

He nodded gravely. "And so thou didst bring him home to me. A good deed, surely, for otherwise I would needs have gone to fetch him. Were others with thee?"

"No, I was alone."

In the corner of the room she heard a baby crying and Charity looked at him in surprise.

"Tis mine," he said proudly. "Tis my little Letty."

Before Charity could question him further, he rose and went to tend the baby, who lay, wrapped in soft linen, in a small wooden crib. She looked awfully tiny. He cradled the baby in his arms, spoke to her soothingly, but when he turned to face Charity again his face was wracked with pain. Without a word he turned and plunged from the cabin.

The next day, when Charity was well enough to rise feebly and sit at dinner with him at the crude wooden table, Ben told her his story. It was a simple one, but shocking. They were Quakers, he and his Rachel. They had saved their money thriftily in England before they were wed, doing without all but the necessities, and had come here to the Colonies where, he told her proudly, he had bought this "holding." He had built this cabin for his Rachel, who then had a child on the way. His voice rang with pride and Charity looked around her, again. The cabin was actually quite cozy in its crude way.

Ben continued his story. A few weeks ago there had been some friction with the Indians. He had not known about it, for he was out of touch with his neighbors, none of whom lived close. But while he was out hewing

251

logs near the house, Rachel had gone searching for herbs in the forest. He had warned her not to go far, but she had not listened. He knew this because he and three others had followed the trail of her soft moccasins—moccasins bought from the Indians—over the soft spring earth wet from recent rains. They had found a number of footprints—Indian footprints, possibly a war party. They had seen where Rachel's footprints turned and ran, and a few yards later where those other footprints had caught up with her. There must have been a struggle, for small pieces of her dress were left on the brambles, along with her basket and scattered herbs. Then they had found her smaller footprints mingled with those of the Indians', heading toward the northwest. By a stream they had lost the prints, so the Indians must have gone on by canoe. Ben's friends had followed the course of the stream a long way northward, but Ben himself had had to return home lest the baby starve. His three friends had returned saying they had lost Rachel's trail, but that they suspected she was being taken to the big Indian slave market situated near a great northern lake. All Ben could do was to send word to the trappers who frequented the area to watch for her,—and that he would pay a good ransom to get her back.

Charity could see that he was filled with terror that his Rachel was dead and lost to him. She remembered with horror the trappers' conversation in New York about the many white women captured and dragged to the Indians' northern slave market. Her sympathy went out to Ben, who was held fast to his cabin by a tiny baby, frantic with worry about his young wife, unable to leave even to go look for her.

Charity felt her eyes mist over with tears. *She* would look after the baby, she offered. She had no friends, nowhere to go. Ben brightened. Would she do that?

But, Charity admitted sadly, she had no experience of life in the wilds. She would try to learn—if he would teach her.

He did. Life with Ben was a perpetual wonder to her. He was very courteous and grave and patient with her at all times. The first night that she was strong enough to be up, he escorted her to her new sleeping quarters in the tiny dark attic beneath the thatched roof, reached by a rude ladder through a hole in the attic floor. He would willingly sleep up there himself, he explained, but it was best he be downstairs in case of attack by Indians or wild beasts.

Charity was very glad to let Ben have the downstairs room. She had no desire to contend with either Indians or wild beasts.

Under Ben's tutelage, Charity learned to make butter, to milk a cow and to skin game. She learned to dip candles and make the coarse brown bread of Indian meal. She tended the baby—and those were the happiest times, for Letty was a sweet affectionate child who soon won her completely. She also fed the sow and her litter with scraps from the table, and carried water endlessly in a wooden bucket from the nearby stream.

She worked from dawn to after dark.

And was happy.

She knew that Ben was not. Often he would walk to the edge of the clearing at night and stand dejectedly and stare into the dark woods—and she knew he was inwardly willing his Rachel to return to him. At other times he stared down at little Letty with such a woebegone face that Charity winced, realizing how deeply Ben missed his young wife for whom hope was fast fading.

Charity sometimes pondered Rachel's fate, shuddering, as she imagined the young woman pulled along by the Indian braves, made to endure forced marches, to cook for them—and no doubt sleep with them. And then to come stumbling, after her long terrible journey, into the Indian-run slave market and find herself sold to the highest bidder—it was a fate that made Charity blanch.

She could see that the thought of it ate at Ben too, and that he yearned to be off seeking his Rachel. But Charity was still not well enough acquainted with life in the wilds to be self-reliant. She could manage with

Ben there to guide her, but she knew, from the thoughtful searching look he sometimes gave her, that he did not consider her ready to meet frontier life alone.

Ben was always polite and courteous. Sometimes their bodies brushed inadvertently as he taught her some new skill, and always he moved nimbly away from her as if he had been stung by the contact. Once at dusk, she heard a crashing amid the tamaracks at the edge of the clearing and turned instinctively to seek reassurance by clutching his arm. She felt his muscles respond spasmodically to her touch, though he flinched away from her. Another time, when she was trying to carry her pillow down the ladder from the attic, she stumbled and he leaped forward to steady her. She fell against his chest and, for a moment, lingered there before she could right herself. Ben seemed quite shaken by the incident and avoided her eyes for several days.

Charity, who had not felt any great electrical surge as their bodies met, looked on Ben with great warmth and respect. She was grateful that he had not asked her many questions, but had accepted at its face value her lie that she had come downriver from Albany on a boat which had capsized, drowning all the other passengers. She had been seeking shelter, she explained, when she found his horse and let it bring her to him.

It was, she supposed, as good a story as any other. And it did not involve her with the patroon. Nor would Ben be implicated in her escape if the patroon found her. To Charity that was very important; she felt her own life was a shambles, but she had no wish to involve those who were kind enough to help her in her troubles. She discounted Ben's remark that he knew her story from her disjointed fever ravings since he never mentioned it again.

Though her hatred for the patroon still held, with a kind of bitter clarity here in Ben's simple cabin in the forest, Charity could now view her life at Daarkenwyck and her relationship with Pieter almost in the abstract—as if it had happened to some other girl.

I got no more than I deserved, she told herself fiercely. *I did not love Pieter. I would have learned to hate him. For his grossness, his disregard of others, his insensitivity . . . so many things. If I had married him, I would indeed have been selling myself for gold.*

Before, she had been obsessed with the thought of marriage, intending to save herself only for a marriage bed, now her view shifted subtly.

I will let no man hold me in his arms for his own purposes, she vowed. *I will not suffer any man to touch me intimately unless I wish it. And I must love him.*

Then she frowned to herself and thought, *If need be, I will dissemble, I will flirt and entice—and so gain my own ends. But I will give myself only for love—and never for gold.*

So the bright days of early summer passed, and Charity's emotional wounds gradually mended and she was made whole again in the simple woodland surroundings.

As time went by, Charity realized that Ben was torn by great conflicting emotions: he still loved Rachel but in his heart he knew he had lost her, and Charity was young and lovely and within his grasp. She was aware that his eyes followed her with yearning, although he tried never to let her see it, and she carefully looked away at those times when his face might reveal too much.

Her fondness for Ben deepened. She saw him as clean and bright against the darkness she had known. In her mind Tom, the light-hearted highwayman, had faded, grown dim, obscured by the harsh realities and intrigue of Daarkenwyck with its resident spider. And Roger Derwent . . . her feelings about him were confused, for he was a man to whom she might, recklessly, have given her heart. She tried never to think about Roger Derwent. Ben filled her life now, Ben and Letty, and she was happy in a sweet fulfilled way that had no passion in it. She supposed it was not really a full existence, that she was not a whole woman never lying in a man's arms, never feeling his warm body pressed against hers, but Daarkenwyck had left such a coldness in her heart that she sometimes shivered and thought never to be really warm again. And now Ben, with his kindness, his simple goodness, was melting that coldness so that she had become a woman again, a creature of feelings and passions and vulnerability.

So she drifted through the summer days, content to be in this leafy shelter away from the torments that had plagued her in this wild raw land.

She knew of course, in a vague sort of way, that some word might eventually reach them about Rachel.

But it was a shock to see who brought it.

CHAPTER 23

Charity had been out searching for berries that grew near the clearing in the forest. She returned carrying a small basket, sufficient for their supper and tomorrow's breakfast. As she paused in the doorway, to accustom her eyes to the darkened cabin, she was conscious that there was another man in the room with Ben. The other man had his back to her.

"Charity," said Ben, "this is Bart Symonds. Mistress Woodstock."

And as Charity stood stiff with shock, basket in hand, Bart turned and gave a smirk. "I think we've met," said he.

"Ah, then ye be from Albany?" said Ben.

"Near enough," shrugged Bart, his eyes devouring Charity. He grinned and his tongue passed over his lips as if savouring a feast he would soon be enjoying. Charity shrank away from him.

"He comes from the Indian slave market by the great northern lake," explained Ben, and Charity noticed how drawn Ben's face was.

"Nay," Bart was swift to correct Ben. "I never reached the slave market, but I had word from French trappers who did reach there that none had seen a woman by the name or description of your wife."

"I thank thee for thy kindness in bringing me these sad tidings," said Ben, his head sinking to his breast. He roused himself. "Wilt thou not take supper with us and spend the night? Tis late for a traveler to venture out into these woods."

Bart gave Charity a sly look. "I'd be much beholden for some good food and a place to lay my head."

With compressed lips, Charity laid out the supper. Before serving the fresh berries, she brought in a pitcher of clotted cream that had been poured from a crock wedged in by rocks in the cold running stream near the house. As she watched Bart devour the food with the silent devotion of a starving animal, she was appalled by his crudeness. How could Tom ever have liked him, she wondered.

"Have you—heard from Tom?"

Bart paused in mid-bite, while wolfing down a joint of wild turkey Ben had shot. "No," he said. "Have you?"

She shook her head, and to Ben's questioning glance, she said, "Tom is a mutual friend."

Those were the only words she spoke at supper. Ben sat, crushed and sad, half-heartedly trying to eat. Charity picked at her food uneasily. She was afraid of Bart, and suddenly she realized that she was afraid of him not only for herself but for Ben. She thought it quite likely that Bart would try to pick a fight with Ben, kill him deliberately, and make off with her leaving the baby to starve. Her hands grew cold, thinking of it.

After dinner as she cleared the dishes, Bart asked Ben if he had anything to drink.

"Only water and milk," responded Ben. "I do not drink spirits."

Bart settled back sulkily and tried a new tack. He challenged Ben to a contest of strength. Charity bit her lip, watching the two men lock hands. Ben's solid woodsman's strength was unavailing. Powerful Bart easily bore Ben's hand down upon the table, and crowed of his victory, demanding as a forfeit from Ben for losing—a kiss from Charity.

"That is for Mistress Charity to say," said Ben stiffly. "She has the giving of her own kisses."

"Oh, that's the way it is, is it?" said Bart with a nasty laugh. Charity gave him a venomous look and began to prepare snap beans for next day's dinner in the farthest corner of the room.

When Bart left the room for a moment, she set down the bowl and rushed to Ben's side.

"Bart is a dangerous man," she whispered. "He will most likely kill you if you turn your back on him."

"Why?" murmured Ben in surprise. "Why should he kill me? I have not harmed him."

"Because he wants *me*," said Charity in exasperation. "Last year in New York he tried to sell me to some trappers, but I escaped him. Oh, be careful, Ben."

"Go to bed," he instructed. "And pull the ladder up after thee. I will guard through the night."

Charity climbed the ladder and had pulled it up before Bart came back. She realized that this was the first time it had ever occurred to either of them that she should pull the ladder up. She had slept up here from the first, completely unafraid of Ben; she had had no fear that he would climb that ladder unasked.

She lay there tensely, listening to Bart ask about her and then grow surly when Ben said she had gone to bed since she always rose early in the morning. Charity realized with a sinking feeling that her stay on this little isolated farm in the wilds must now come to an end. If Bart heard she had escaped from the patroon, he would scent a reward and make his way to Daarkenwyck—even as he had made his way to this small cabin for a reward. Charity had little doubt but that the patroon would pay a good price to get her back, even if only to humiliate her.

To her surprise and unease she heard Bart say that since the weather was so comfortable he would sleep in the lean-to beside the cabin on the hay, rather than "crowd the cabin." She hoped Ben would latch the door securely before going to bed, but she could not be sure he did. At every sound she tensed, expecting to hear sounds of fighting erupt from below.

Somehow the night passed.

Morning found her heavy-eyed and not anxious to rise. Ben had taken care of the baby through the night and she felt she must get up at last. When finally she did, she could smell meat cooking and realized Ben was getting breakfast. Contrite that she had left him to do her chores, she hurried down and saw Bart sitting calmly at the rude wooden table considering her.

Ben was nowhere to be seen.

"Where is Ben?" she gasped, and Bart laughed.

"Ben's getting water," he said. "It gives us a chance to talk."

"We have nothing to talk about," said Charity, edging toward the door.

"I say we have," said Bart, his face clouding. "You were angry that I was going to take money from the trappers for you, weren't you? Didn't you know it was only a ruse? Twould have been only for a night or two I'd have left you with them. I meant to trick them and we'd have been long gone on some river boat or schooner before they found out."

"I want nothing from you, Bart," she said in a cold voice, "except never to see your face again."

His eyes narrowed, and she could see his mouth turn down through his heavy unkempt black beard. She noted with distaste his buckskin clothes.

"Ah, now that's no way to talk to me, Charity," he wheedled. "After all, didn't I save you and bring you to New York on a wagon?"

"You were saving your own skin as well," she corrected him. "And having a woman on the wagon beside you made you safer—everyone we passed assumed I was your wife going in with you to market."

"I see you've grown wiser," he said in a nasty tone. "You'll be sorry you spoke that way to old Bart!"

Angrily, Charity flounced away from him as Ben entered the room carrying two buckets of water. He set the buckets down and spoke to Charity. "Breakfast is ready."

"I'm—not hungry," said Charity, hating to sit down with Bart.

"Come, thou must eat or wilt lose thy strength and be of no help to me," remonstrated Ben.

Meekly Charity sat down and the three of them ate a silent breakfast, listening to a noisy jay outside perched on a limb of the big sycamore that overshadowed the cabin.

After breakfast Bart announced he must leave and Ben, thanking him again for bringing that sad message about Rachel, pressed on him a florin.

Charity hated to see him do it. Bart might decide that Ben had money hidden away—which she was sure he had not—and come back someday and bushwhack him. She said as much to Ben after Bart had gone whistling off.

Charity had planned to pick some more berries for their dinner. "Wait a bit," advised Ben, showing no interest in going out to chop wood or clear away trees today.

After a while, he instructed her to, "Stay in the house and keep the door and window shutters barred," and went away. She wondered what he was going to do. But just then Letty started crying and she took the child in her arms and soothed her gently. Poor little Letty, all hope of her mother's return now seemed gone. She must grow up motherless in a wild raw world.

Ben returned shortly, and she unbarred the door to let him in.

"Our guest is gone," he reported. "I followed his tracks a long way and they did not falter. He is heading toward the river."

Charity breathed a sigh of relief. Tracks! Of course, why hadn't she thought of that? A man's tracks told where he had been, and pointed the direction he was going. But she was still uneasy that Bart might ask questions along the river and perhaps learn that the patroon was searching for her. She knew she could not stay here too much longer. Going outside, she looked about her at the little space in the mighty virgin woodlands, hacked out at such great effort by the hand of one determined man, and she realized how fond of it she had become.

Red squirrels gamboled in the big oak that marked a corner of the clearing. Birds sang sweetly in the great sycamore that shaded the cabin and the air was fresh and clean. Even the thunderstorms that resounded through the Catskills seemed more hushed through the green protective walls of these giant trees.

She would miss it. And she would miss good gentle Ben and dear little Letty.

Feeling sad, she headed for the clearing to pick more berries for their dinner. Bart's advent had left them with none for dinner and they were at their ripest; she had seen many more ripe ones than she had picked. She told Ben what she was going to do and sauntered off through the trees, intending to fill her basket and come right back.

She had picked only a few when she heard a crashing in the undergrowth behind her and, fearing bears, turned in fright.

What she saw frightened her even more.

Bart, a nasty smile on his face, was walking toward her.

She turned in panic, spilling the berries to the ground, and began to run. Bart caught her easily and she screamed once before he slapped his hand over her mouth and bore her to the ground.

"I doubled back," he said. "Did you think I'd leave you here?"

She made an inarticulate protest against his hand.

"Now are you going to come with me nice? Or is it going to be some other way?" he asked grimly. "Because either way, you're coming along, Charity. You and me together. I'll set us up in some inn near the waterfront, and you can entertain a couple of sailors during the evening—I'll find 'em for you—and then you and me'll go to bed just like married folks. You'll see how easy it is!"

For answer she struck him in the face.

The change in his expression terrified her. His face took on a dark ugly hue and his big hand pressed down over her throat and stopped her breathing. "Still high and mighty?" he said. And brought his other hand down in a heavy slap along the side of her face that made her head ring. Above her, the trees seemed to sway crazily as she felt herself slipping toward unconsciousness.

But he moved his hand from her throat so that she

could again take a gasping breath and looked down at her. In terror she looked away from those dark evil eyes so close to her own, and a scream rose in her throat.

"Look at me when I'm talking to you!" he said, and slapped her again. This time her head lolled and she made no attempt to scream, but only looked up at him, blinded by pain.

"That's better," he growled. "You're going to act respectful toward me, Charity. You're going to do what I say. And don't think you can be calling for Ben. He's nowhere near. I saw him take his musket and head out in the other direction after you left—I was watching the cabin and saw him go." He looked down at her, lying on the ground and said, "You're a tasty wench, Charity, I've half a mind to enjoy you right now."

She moaned.

A twig snapped and Ben's voice said, "Let her go, and be gone thyself."

Bart jumped up, and Charity lifted her head to see Ben standing a few feet away, armed with his musket. His square honest face was pale under its tan and he had the musket pointed right at Bart.

Bart sneered. "She's mine," he said. "She was mine before. Even though she's living with you now. And I mean to take her back with me."

"It's not true," croaked Charity. "I was never his."

"Get you gone," said Ben, his voice shaking. "And do not speak her name again."

Bart was edging toward his own gun, which lay on the ground nearby. "You're a Quaker," he cried tauntingly. "Your faith won't let you take a life!"

Oh, God, that was true! Charity sat up, her head now a little clearer.

"Tempt me not too far," cried Ben. Then sharply, "Thou'lt go without thy musket!"

Heedless, Bart made a sudden grab for his musket and Ben's long gun spoke. With a startled cry, Bart fell to the ground clutching his chest and lay on his back, holding the wound, blood gushing from between his fingers. As they both watched, transfixed, his head lolled suddenly and his wide staring eyes took on a glaze.

Ben groaned. "I have killed him," he said in horror. "I have taken a life."

Charity scrambled up, alarmed at the torment on his face. "You couldn't help it, Ben," she cried. "He'd have killed you if he'd been able to reach his gun."

"Nay," he cried wildly. "I meant to kill him! Why did I not shoot him in the arm? Or the leg? I had started off hunting, meaning to find us a fat turkey for our dinner, but I heard thee scream—faintly, in the distance. I hurried toward the sound and when I saw thee lying on the ground—no, no, I meant to kill him!"

He flung away in such anguish that Charity hurried after him in alarm, but he outdistanced her. When she reached the cabin she found him bent over the table, his head in his arms—and he was not to be comforted.

"I must tell the authorities," he said in a tired voice, looking up at her at last. "I have murdered a man."

"And leave your child and me here alone?" cried Charity, aghast.

Horror filled his eyes as that sank in on him.

"Oh, God!" he cried, and his head fell back upon the table and his shoulders shook.

Charity considered him silently. Bart had been an evil man, and his death—no matter who had contrived it—should not be allowed to drag this good man down. Suddenly an idea came to her. Taking the bucket as if she were going for water, she left the cabin. When she reached the shelter of the trees, she picked up her skirts and ran as fast as she could back to the berrying place where Bart's body lay.

She stopped as she reached his side. He lay very still, his glazed eyes staring up unblinkingly at a sun that he would never see again.

Gritting her teeth, she picked up his musket and wedged it under his belt. Then, seizing his boots, she dragged him along over the rocky ground. She remembered a tiny cave she had found while berrying. It was hardly more than a deep crevice in the rocks, but she dragged Bart's body there.

As she pulled him along she thought of the florin. Ben needed his florins. With a shudder she felt for Bart's money pouch, found it, fastened by a rawhide thong to his belt, and put it into a pocket of her apron. Removing his boots, she pushed Bart's body into the crevice, and rolled heavy rocks to cover the entrance. Then, she piled brush up around it. Having done that, she obliterated the signs of dragging as well as she could, and went back to the dried pool of blood that was now attracting flies. There, she put on Bart's boots, which were huge and awkward for her, picked up as heavy a stone as she could carry so that the footprints would be impressed heavier into the soft earth, and made her way down to the stream that ran nearby. Taking her own shoes from her apron pockets, she sat down by the stream to put them on again. On her way back to the cabin she threw Bart's boots into a deep thicket.

When she got back, carrying her bucket of water, Ben roused himself wearily.

"I have been waiting for thee," he said in a dull voice. "What took thee so long?"

"I had much to think on," said Charity wearily. "I sat by the stream and realized that I have brought all this upon you. If I had not come here—"

He gave her a long sad look. "Nay, thou must not feel so, Charity. Thou hast lightened my life. Were it not for thee, I would not have found these last weeks bearable, knowing my Rachel gone." He rose. "I must go to bury the man I have killed. Since I cannot leave thee and the baby alone here to die, I must carry this black deed forever on my conscience."

"I'll go with you," offered Charity, rising.

"No, do thou stay. I can do it readily without thee."

"You will need help," she insisted and accompanied him as they retraced their steps through the forest to the place where the berries grew.

"He is gone!" she cried when they reached the spot.

265

"Some animal has dragged his body away," Ben muttered. "I should have come back sooner."

"No," pointed out Charity excitedly. "Look—here are his footprints. You did not kill him after all!"

"Impossible," objected Ben. "Thou didst see him. The man was dead."

"Maybe he was able to get up and staggered a little way. We should try to find him, Ben. Perhaps we will be able to save his life."

Ben brightened. He began to follow the footprints until they reached the little stream. He frowned and followed the banks of the stream up and down on both sides for a while. "There are no other footprints," he reported. "Yet he was grievously hurt."

"But not so grievously hurt that he did not get up and walk away," Charity retorted grimly. "Do you not see, Ben? Bart feared that you would follow him and kill him! It is what *he* would have done in your place. So, he is probably finding his way back to the river now. He has even taken his musket."

"That is so," agreed Ben thoughtfully. "The musket is gone."

"We must get back," she said hastily. "We have left the baby and it is growing dark. I am afraid to be in the cabin alone after dark. There is no point lingering here, Ben. The man is gone. And although he is dangerous, I think that you have managed to frighten him away so that he will not be back to trouble us."

Ben gave her a confused look. She knew he was thinking that he had not actually bent over and inspected Bart's body. But he had seen that look of death spreading over his face and known it for what it was—and turned, sickened by his deed, and strode off toward the house. Now he was unsure. He told himself that his bullet must have struck lower. Or higher. That Bart had not been so badly hurt after all if he could get up and stagger away.

"He must have gone a long way sloshing down the stream, Ben, afraid you would track him and catch up to him," she added anxiously.

"Yes," said Ben, his taut face clearing a bit. "That must be the way of it."

Together, in silence, they walked among the great boles of the trees back to the house, and Charity looked up at the leafy roof above their heads and knew that she had done the right thing. Now Ben would not go flying off to the law to be punished for murder. He would soon forget that he had ever lifted his hand against one of his fellows.

She smiled at him, and touched his arm comfortingly. He sighed and then gave her a grave slow smile.

Yes, she told herself, she had done the right thing.

As Charity prepared dinner, she could see Ben through the window standing at the edge of the clearing peering into the trees. She knew he was brooding over the loss of Rachel.

He was very silent at dinner and she soon went up to bed, thinking not to disturb him in his grief.

She awoke to the sound of the baby giving a little cry, and crept down to see that his bed was empty. As she cradled Letty, soothing her, lulling her to sleep, she could see Ben kneeling in the clearing in the moonlight, clad only in his nightshirt, his body rocking, his head in his hands.

Such grief moved her. She put the baby gently back into the crib and tiptoed out onto the moonlit patch of ground Ben had cleared with such back-breaking effort. He was kneeling almost in the shadow of the huge old sycamore that shaded the cabin.

"Ben," she said softly, "do not grieve so."

He started at the sound of her voice, and shivered at the touch of her fingers as she patted his shoulder.

"She will not come back," he muttered brokenly. "I had held onto hope all these weeks, but now—they have not seen her at the Indian slave market in the north. It was my last hope. She will never come back. I will never see her again."

Charity knew it was true. The chances of life for a white woman on forced marches with the Indians were slim at best; a few were bought back at the market and some even returned to their homes by way of the French trappers—they were the lucky ones. Ben's Rachel had not been so lucky.

"Ben," she whispered, stroking his hair. "What good will it do to mourn? Rachel wouldn't wish that."

He turned a tortured face toward her. "No, she wouldn't. But how can I do anything else knowing my Rachel's bones bleach somewhere beside a trail where the savages scalped her and left her to die?" Sobs shook him.

"Oh, Ben, Ben." Charity sank down beside him on the ground and put her arms around him and cradled his face against her own. She had never felt so sorry for anyone as she felt for Ben at that moment. He had killed a man to save her, even though it went strongly against his beliefs, and now he was torn by a frenzy of grief. "Ben," she soothed, stroking his hair.

He moved against her with a shuddering sigh, and she pressed his head wordlessly against her breast, stroking his cheek, feeling his face digging into her soft rounded breasts as she soothed him with little broken endearments much as she had soothed the baby a short while before.

"Ah, Charity, Charity!" It was a wild cry of grief, and Ben's arms went round her and he held her fiercely. She looked tenderly down at that head, pressed against her breasts, and was filled with a wild sweet aching desire to comfort him. He had suffered so much—and part of it for her. And with that thought she loosened the ribbon that held her gown about the neck and moved a little, letting the gown slip down so that his cheek brushed against the softness of her naked breast.

He started violently and moved back, casting a sudden almost fearful look up at her.

"It's all right, Ben," she said brokenly, her head bent over his as she let down her pale gold hair, letting it cascade down over his shoulders and tenderly stroked the back of his neck. She was nearly crying herself. "It's all right."

He buried his head between her white breasts, his lips moving along them as if for succor, and she strained against him, hoping to relieve some of the agony that coursed through him, and feeling within her a quiver of mounting desire as his lips pressed softly at her neck, as his hands sought her waist and below them her hips, and he groaned. She relaxed against him, melted into his arms in complete submission and he lifted his head again and gave her a look of wonder—and of hunger.

Suddenly, he pulled away and gave her a look of terrible consternation. "What have I done?" he cried in such a wild voice that Charity sat up, bewildered, and reached out a hand to touch him.

"No!" He leaped up and ran toward the house, and Charity rose and shook back her tumbled hair and followed, frowning uneasily. Ben was already in his bed when she came in, lying with his back turned toward her. So, she bolted the door and closed the shutters and barred them, and made her way tiredly up the ladder to her straw mattress, pondering on the puzzling ways of men.

CHAPTER 24

At breakfast Ben kept his head turned away from her and could not meet her eyes.

"I am sorry," he burst out at last. "I am not a free man that I could stand up before the meeting and take thee to wife. I have wronged thee—and I have wronged Rachel."

Charity considered him soberly.

"Ben," she said gently, "we both know Rachel is dead."

The words lingered in the air. He gave a great sob. "I know it," he said in a voice of anguish. "In my mind I know it. But in my heart she still lives."

The words went through Charity with a bittersweet pain. Last night Ben had held her most tenderly in his arms, but in his heart he still cradled the young wife who had come with him to work this land and had had his child alone in this wilderness, and then had been so cruelly wrested from him.

"It's right you should love her, Ben," she said softly, and turned away with blurred eyes.

And why should her treacherous fancy summon up at that moment not the good man who had held her the night before, but the wicked arms of sardonic Roger Derwent, who had held her body contemptuously yet made heat lightning race through it at his very touch?

Impatiently, she brushed back a lock of gold hair that kept falling into her eyes. Hers was an unruly heart that refused to follow the road down which her head would fling it. But she would master these wild deep yearnings, she would become wise and calm if not—her lip curled a little—if not virtuous as the world viewed virtue.

She sighed and began her morning's chores, leaving Ben brooding at the table. Finally he went outside, where she could hear his axe savagely biting into the wood of a tall pine tree which he had felled yesterday.

The baby cried and Charity picked her up to feed her. Such a lovely child was little Letty, so pink cheeked, with big trusting eyes. Rachel was lucky to have—the smile died on her face. Rachel was *not* lucky. Rachel's luck had run out. Rachel had had all the world—a place of her own, a man who loved her, a child smiling up into her face—but Rachel's perfect world had been rent asunder . . . Rachel was dead.

With these dark thoughts Charity went to the window and pensively watched Ben as, axe in hand, he cleared his land. She looked at his straining body, his strong limbs, and wondered if he would ever allow himself to do more than want her.

A whole week went by that way, with Ben obviously warring with his troubled conscience at the "injury" he had done Charity, and the sad disrespect to Rachel's memory. Then, one evening his mood changed.

Charity had spent the day churning butter in a wooden churn, making beeswax candles, and roasting to a succulent turn a brace of heath hens which Ben had brought in and silently laid on the wooden table. After the cleaning up was done and the baby rocked to sleep in her cradle, Charity climbed wearily up to bed and sank down with a groan upon her straw mattress and lay there drowsily, sinking slowly into sleep.

There was a sudden creaking of the wooden ladder. Charity's eyes flew open. Ben had been watching her all through dinner, almost covertly, but she had paid no attention. Now, she saw his head come through the opening in the attic floor.

She lay quietly, waiting, her heartbeat quickening. "Charity," he said hoarsely, "I would thee wouldst

272

come down and share my bed below. I would deem it a great privilege."

So humbly spoken were his words that Charity was touched. She sat up, leaning on an elbow, her head almost bumping the low slanting roof above her head.

"Are you . . . sure you want me, Ben?" she asked hesitantly. Her voice was wistful. Poor Ben had tortured himself enough and—yes, she had unintentionally had a hand in that torture. She had meant only to console him, but he had turned his recriminations against himself.

"Yes," he cried, his whole body now thrusting through the opening in the floor as, bending over, he made for her straw mattress, knelt there beside her.

"I know that I have no right to ask thee," he said humbly, kneeling there. "But thou hast done so much for me and for the child. I do think I would have gone mad with grief without thee, Charity. Thou didst come into my life like an angel to make me whole again."

"No, Ben, no." Tears spilled over her lashes as she touched his cheek with a gentle hand. "Not an angel—and it was the other way around. I was lost and bitter when I came here, and you have helped me see my way again. It is I who should be grateful to you."

He bent over her, kissing her hands, and she felt his own hot tears fall on her hands. He was doing what for him was a very great thing, she knew, a momentous thing. He was casting out the ghost of Rachel, his lovely lost young wife, and asking her to supplant Rachel, to share with him Rachel's bed, in which Rachel's child had been born.

Charity's heart throbbed so painfully she felt that it would burst.

"I will do as you ask, Ben," she said, smoothing back his thick brown hair that fell over her hands as he bent over them. "But not tonight. Tomorrow . . . tomorrow I will come downstairs and I will sleep in your bed."

"Thou dost know that I cannot offer thee marriage?" he cried in an anguished voice. "For I have no proof Rachel is dead."

"Yes, I know that, Ben." She caressed his head with her hands.

"But to me it will be a marriage, Charity," he added fiercely. "For I will hew to you even as I hewed to Rachel, and strive to make thee happy always." His voice broke.

Charity closed her eyes and swallowed.

"Hush, Ben," she said at last and kissed him lovingly.

After a few moments, he stood up and said in a strong voice, more confident than she had ever heard him, "I will go down now; it is best that I be downstairs the better to guard thee and the child." And before his head disappeared through the hole in the attic flooring, he added gravely, "And tomorrow, Charity, thou wilt become my wife in my sight and I will take thee before God here in this home that I have built with my hands—although we may never be man and wife in the sight of man."

And he disappeared from view.

She awoke to the full blaze of the late morning sun and sat up with a guilty start. How had she slept so late? The baby! The poor little thing must be hungry!

"Ben," she called, reaching out for her clothes. There was no answer. She saw that her worn, torn dress was gone. Replacing it, neatly folded on the floor near the top of the ladder, was another dress, one she had seen before when she had been searching through Rachel's wooden chest looking for a ribbon to tie the baby's bonnet. It was a dress of russet linen with collar and cuffs of fine white cambric. She felt a lump rise in her throat.

Ben had searched the chest for a wedding dress for her—and had found one, for this was obviously Rachel's "go-to-meeting" dress. She put it on. It was a little tight about the bust, for Rachel had been not quite so rounded as she, and yet a little loose about the waist, for her own waist cut in more deeply than had Rachel's. But the length was all right and the buttons could be set over later. Careful not to dirty the

274

cuffs, she turned up the sleeves and, holding up the skirt carefully, started down the ladder, calling once again, "Ben."

"I let thee sleep," his voice called happily from below. "And I have milked the cow and fed little Letty and brought the water from the stream and cooked our breakfast."

"Ben, you shouldn't have," she said contritely. As she climbed down the ladder in haste, Ben was just setting down the two buckets of water he had brought from the stream. "These things are woman's work and you have so much to do—so many heavy things that I cannot even attempt."

"But this is thy wedding day." He smiled at her. "Tonight this room becomes a bridal chamber."

He looked so happy when he said that, that Charity smiled back at him, trying to reflect his joy. She felt a hurt in her heart that she could not love him more, that she could not be in all ways the wife he desired. In a way she *did* love him, she told herself fiercely. She admired Ben, she was grateful to him, and if her divided heart was still unruly and would not be stilled, that too would change in time.

She went toward him and kissed him and felt him tremble at her touch. Then his arms went round her and he said hoarsely, "Charity, Charity, I do not deserve thee." She thought his mind toyed with doing something more than merely hold her, but he thrust her away from him suddenly as if the thought were unworthy, with a merry, "But thou hast had no breakfast and I have prepared for us a wedding feast!" He led her toward the crude trestle table he had fashioned from a fallen beech tree, and she smiled to see the wooden trenchers piled high with the bread she had made yesterday and some trout he must have caught this morning.

She watched him fondly as he ate with a healthy morning appetite. Then he rose from the table and announced that he would this day tackle "yon great tree that has defied my axe." She knew he meant the grand old sycamore that threw its shade about the cabin like a cool umbrella.

"No—not the sycamore, Ben," she said, touching his arm. "It is such a lovely tree beneath which to rest in the shade. And besides, beneath its branches was where you first held me in your arms. We should keep the tree and hope that our life together will grow as strong and as upright."

He looked at her as if she had said something profound, and nodded.

"Thou art right," he agreed. "We should keep the tree. I will work at the eastward edge of the clearing where there is much red pine."

Charity sang a little snatch of song as she cleared the breakfast leavings and took them out to feed the great sow whose litter of little pigs would soon be fattening on the chestnuts that abounded in the forest. Her heart had lightened now that she had decided upon her course of action.

She had "looked up," as her mother would have wished her to, at Daarkenwyck—and she had come to grief. Now she had "looked down," as her mother would have viewed it, and had found the arms of a plain and simple man, but one deserving of her love, one she felt would always cherish and protect her.

She had found security.

Still feeling light-hearted and happy, she took a bucket of washwater and moved out into the little planted "patch" that surrounded the house on three sides and served them for a yard. She intended to dump the washwater on some bean plants, when she came to a sudden halt, the bucket held forgotten in her arms.

Out of the trees staggered a figure, a living scarecrow. And when the scarecrow saw Ben, axe in hand, at the far side of the clearing, it broke into a run.

Charity stared, speechless.

The scarecrow had a woman's face. Tangles of light brown hair flew about the head, and a few scraps of a fabric that had once been a dress of service-

276

able gray-green holland, flapped about her ragged petticoat and scrawny shanks.

"Ben!" cried the figure brokenly, and rapture transformed her face with its hollowed cheeks as the woman stumbled forward across the uneven ground.

No one had to tell Charity that this was Rachel.

Rachel, returned from the dead, Rachel come back from hell itself to claim her husband and her child.

CHAPTER 25

Ben stood frozen, as if he had no power to move, his mouth open, his eyes fixed on the figure that staggered toward him. Then, "Rachel!" The cry was ripped from his lips and he sped toward her, flinging away the axe, and enfolded her with his arms as she collapsed in tears against him.

"Oh, Ben, Ben, all that sustained me on the trail was the thought of thee," sobbed Rachel. "Many's the time I would sink down and think to die, but each time I would hear thy voice urging me on and somehow manage to go another weary mile." She lifted her head, her face anxious, and pushed him away. "The baby, what of the baby, Ben?" she cried.

"Letty's fine, Rachel," he said, his gruff voice full of tears, and Rachel sank back against him with a grateful sob. He nestled her thin body against him and buried his face in her emaciated neck. "Ah, Rachel, I went to find thee, I searched the woods for thee, and others searched also, but we lost thy trail among the rocks by the waterside. And I sent word to the French trappers who frequent the great Indian slave market by the northern lake to buy thee, that I would repay them—but word came back to me that you had never reached the slave market."

"Nor did I, Ben, My captors fell out among themselves, and while they fought I slipped away and sloshed down a little stream and hid in a small cave. I heard them go by as they searched for me, but then they gave up and went away. Night had fallen, but I started out anyway, so wild was I to return—and that, that is where I made my mistake, Ben. For I must have turned the wrong way in the dark and I became lost and I have wandered from that day to this, living only on berries and nuts and the water from the streams. Twice I saw Indians, but always I hid and they went by without seeing me. Ah, sometimes I thought I'd never find my way to thee, Ben, that I would leave my bones bleaching with the winter snows, or that some wild animal would eat me, but God has given me his grace, Ben, and brought me home to thee."

Charity's throat closed at this recital of Rachel's sufferings.

As she continued, Rachel's voice caught raggedly. "I did fear, Ben, that the Indians who took me—or some others of their group—had attacked our home and had killed thee and and my little Letty." Her voice quavered, and Ben, almost crying himself, said, "Letty is fine, Rachel. She's just fine. Come see for yourself."

Gently, he disengaged those wasted clawlike hands and, with one arm about Rachel's thin shoulders, led her toward the cabin. As they walked, her eyes fell on something she had not up to this time observed—Charity—and flew full open.

In shock and fear, Rachel's face, which had been so happy, now fell apart.

"Who's—who's this, Ben?" she asked in a trembling voice, and in that moment Charity saw herself as Rachel must see her: young and strong and well-fed, a woman with pink cheeks and sunshiny hair and bright challenging eyes—the kind of woman a man would wish to make his own.

Standing in *her* yard before *her* cabin and wearing *her* best go-to-meeting dress!

Beside Rachel, Ben—who in the intensity of the moment of Rachel's return had forgotten her too—now gazed at Charity in silent anguish. His brown eyes begged her to be kind, not to hurt more this pitiful shadow of a woman whom life had already used so cruelly.

Charity, her eyes brighter than usual with unshed tears, took a deep breath and said in a steady voice, "I am Charity Woodstock. I was living in Albany and was on my way downriver to take ship in New York for Virginia, where my betrothed awaits me. But our boat capsized and all were lost. I swam ashore and tried to find my way through the forest, but I became lost. Your husband found me and saved my life and in gratitude I have tended your child for you until you should be found and returned to him."

Gradually a little of the fear left Rachel's white face. "Is this the truth, Ben?" She turned to him, her face upturned anxiously.

For a moment Charity feared Ben's straight-laced conscience. She wanted to shout at him, *Tell her it's true!*

But she need not have worried. As Ben looked down into that sweet exhausted white face he so loved, he could never have destroyed the anxious hope that shone in her tired eyes.

"Did she not tell thee?" he asked gently. "Dost she look to be a liar, Rachel?" His voice was ever so lightly chiding and Rachel looked confused.

"No, of course she does not," Rachel said hastily. "I am sorry, Mistress Woodstock. It was—the shock of seeing thee standing there clad in my best gown."

"I'll go take it off," said Charity abruptly.

"No, no." This walking skeleton raised its hand. "I give it to thee freely. It is little enough for caring for my little Letty and for my Ben. It is hard for a man in the wilderness alone—and impossible with a small baby."

Charity inclined her head gravely. Then she carried the bucket of washwater over to the bean plants and watered them more carefully than beans had ever been watered before. From the cabin she could hear Rachel's happy cry and her gentle sobbing as she murmured over and over again. "Oh, Letty, Letty, my little Letty. I had thought never to see thee again!"

Charity, looking for some other task—for she could not bear to go into the cabin just now—stumbled toward the stream with the bucket. She would fill the bucket with water before she returned.

But having filled the bucket, she still could not bring herself to carry it back in. How could she intrude upon this homecoming that should have in it nothing but joy?

She sat with her chin in her hands staring into the thicket of tamarack and red mulberry and black willow that lay on the other side of the stream. She felt drained of all emotion.

Rachel's return had rent her own world apart. It was a long time before she realized that Ben had come up and was standing silently behind her.

"Charity," he ventured in a timid voice. And when she did not respond, more urgently he said, "Charity, turn thou and look at me."

With a sigh, Charity rose and faced him.

"I am glad for you, Ben," she said simply. "And I am glad for Rachel too. Her child will grow up knowing its own mother, and you will grow old with your real wife beside you. You are a man of conscience, Ben, and I—I might have trod on it." She thought of Bart's body hidden in the cave and heaped with stones.

"I—I have wronged thee," he said thickly.

"No." She patted his arm. "You never wronged me, Ben. It is best what happened. You must see that." She smiled up at him a little bleakly. "You could never have forgotten Rachel in your heart anyway, Ben."

"That is true," he muttered. "I thought it a miracle when I didst see her across the clearing. I could not believe it."

Charity watched him with a little sad smile. Finally she fetched a sigh. "I will go now and return Rachel's dress, which is the finest she owns and to which I have no right."

"Nay," he said thickly. "Rachel bids thee keep the dress."

"No," said Charity firmly. *Not the dress, nor the man,* she told herself fiercely, *although both had been hers for a season.*

She faced him with determination. "I must go now, Ben," she said in a sober voice. "Can't you see I must leave? It isn't right that I should be here to . . . to spoil things for her, to make her wonder . . . about us. Don't you see, this is her homecoming. She's dreamed of it so long, during all the terrible days and nights she's been through—it wouldn't be right to rob her of a second of it."

Ben looked upset. "But what of thee, Charity? Whither wilt thou go? Canst wait but a day or two until I can take thee to the river and see thee safely on a boat? Rachel is too weak to make a further journey and I—I cannnot leave her here by herself."

"Of course you can't, Ben," said Charity briskly, keeping her voice firm. "And it's high time I started before my—my lover in Virginia finds another woman."

Ben looked at her doubtfully. "Thou didst not tell me before of any lover."

Charity sighed. "Ah, but I am fickle, Ben. I was not so sure then that I loved him. But he waits for me and I must go to him."

He looked down. "Then . . . thou will forgive me for not being able to offer you more?"

She touched his arm gently and her voice grew husky. "Ben, you saved my life—twice. First from the fever and then from a man I detested."

He looked sharply up at that. "But he may be out there!" he cried. "I did not think of that! His wounds may have mended!" He frowned. "Nay, I cannot let thee go alone, Charity."

"Bart will be long gone by now, Ben," she said impatiently. "He'll have found someone else by now. I told you I'd hid a boat there at the river. But I'll need some food for my journey."

"And a horse. Thou mayst leave him at the river. Turn him back upon the path, give him a slap on the flank and he will find his own way home where there is food waiting."

"I'll do that." Having made her decision, Charity was anxious to be gone. She wanted to get away before the light faded—and before her own spirits failed and she crept back to the safety of that small rude attic where she had known peace and a wistful unselfish love.

"Thou'lt start at dawn," decided Ben. "I'll not have thee riding by night more than is necessary. Nay." He held up his hand at her protest. "I'll brook no more argument. That's my last word on the subject."

So Charity spent one more night in the tiny attic, hearing soft murmured endearments from the room below as Rachel was enfolded in her husbands arms. Covering her head with her pillow, Charity pressed her hands to her mouth to keep from sobbing.

She had come to love this tiny farm in the wilderness, and in a peaceful way to love the honest, forthright young Quaker who had carved it from the wilds. . . .

And now it was lost to her.

In the first light of false dawn she got up and crept down the rude ladder that led to the dirt floor below, pausing for a moment to look at the pair who lay, their legs entwined, beneath a bit of thin coverlet. Her heart wrenched at the sight of Rachel's thin face, ravaged from her terrible journey, lying exhausted in the crook of Ben's arm.

Charity smiled sadly at them, lying thus . . . so *right* for each other. She stood for a moment beside the crib and smiled wistfully down at Rachel's little Letty—the baby that she had, for a little while, pretended was her own—just as she had pretended for a little while that Rachel's strong young husband was her own. Then she found a piece of hard brown bread and a bit of smoked venison and put them in a small reed basket Ben had woven for her.

Making her way softly into the lean-to that formed a stable against the house, she climbed bareback upon the horse, patted his head and stroked his mane and walked him over the soft sod into the vast expanse of trees beyond the clearing. Charity rode down the trail toward the river, ducking to keep low branches from brushing her off her horse's back, lifting her legs warily to avoid brambles, trying to discern the vague trail that lay ahead.

Sometimes she gently touched the little reed basket that Ben had given her, and which she had affixed to a ribbon around her slender waist. It was in its way a keepsake, a token of the—not love perhaps—but affection that he had borne her.

Charity rode for a long time, her horse willing enough to follow this path he knew led toward the succulent riverside grasses. But her heart was heavy in her chest as she thought of her situation—without friends, with not even a change of clothes—although she did have Bart's pouch of gold coins in her pocket —sought, perhaps, by the angry patroon who would find a way to bring her back to a life of shame and fury at Daarkenwyck.

What had she done to deserve all this trouble? It wasn't fair! Two tears fell on her hand as she leaned forward, jogging along. She did not know what would become of her.

Her tears were falling thick and fast, as she stopped to water her horse at a small stream that wound through the forest, a place of mossy rocks and cool air and rustling leaves from giant trees that rose straight and true amid girdles and ruffs of dogwood. She got off and drank the icy cold water from a clear little pool between big dark rocks where tiny silvery trout darted. And washed her hot face and streaming eyes. But she could not stop weeping.

She covered her wet face with her hands and rocked with misery. There was no future for her. She was accursed!

A tiny sound roused her and she dropped her hands from her face.

She was looking into the dark-golden eyes of a full-grown mountain lioness not three feet from her. Charity sat frozen, staring at that great tawny head, those wicked-looking dark gold eyes so near her own. Her horse, upwind from the lioness, continued to drink the cold water greedily, unaware of the big cat's existence as Charity stared into the face of death.

For a long time neither the lioness nor Charity moved, the girl held spellbound by that hypnotic gaze. Then the lioness made a light growling sound in her throat and plunged away into the underbrush. The horse snorted in fear and Charity sprang up, trembling, to stroke his mane and try, in a shaky voice, to calm him.

She had thought the big cats killers all, but now she knew better. Unlike man, they did not kill senselessly, and now she knew why the lioness had come up to look her in the face, for in the underbrush Charity had glimpsed two pretty young cubs, rolling over each other playfully. From the noise of breaking twigs, she knew that the lioness was moving her precious little ones to a less threatening environment, one unpeopled by crying women and agitated horses.

The golden-eyed lioness had only been trying to defend her lair and her cubs.

Unbidden in Charity's mind rose the sight of Rachel, her thin face streaming tears, hurling her emaciated frame across the little "patch" and staggering into Ben's waiting arms.

She saw them again, embracing, holding each other as if all the world had stopped and time stood still while they were reunited.

Charity's throat ached, remembering. She swallowed.

She had done the right thing.

Resolutely she climbed back on her nervous horse and guided him down toward the Hudson.

When she reached the river bank, she had not long to wait. One of the flyboats that plied the river trade, bringing goods from the ships for sale to the upriver people, came by on its way downstream and Charity hailed it. She had little doubt that it would stop for her, for she had loosened her long gold hair so that it glistened in the sun and had thrown her skirts back with studied carelessness so that one long white leg was exposed to view.

They sighted her and stopped and a rowboat came over to pick her up.

Charity smoothed down her skirts, gave the horse's head a last affectionate pat and a brisk slap on the flank. With a goodbye whinny, he trotted away from her, back down the path that led toward home and grain. Charity studied the men in the small boat who had come to pick her up.

They were most admiring as they took her aboard the flyboat, where an even more admiring middle-aged Dutch captain said they'd be glad to give the lady passage downriver.

Then a woman came up on deck and glared at Charity.

She was middle-aged, like her captain husband, and somewhat frowzily dressed. After a moment's staring at Charity she looked puzzled. Charity calmly passed herself off as "a daughter of Sebastian Eelkens of New York, who'd been visiting her sister upriver and was now returning early and alone due to a disagreement over some ribbons." No one questioned it.

But later that night, when they thought her asleep curled up on deck, she heard a low-voiced argument in the cabin below and crept closer to listen. She had not liked the way that woman had looked at her earlier.

The captain and his wife were speaking vehemently in Dutch.

"I tell you she is the same," insisted the woman. "I saw her once on the lawn at Daarkenwyck. She's dressed different today and wears her hair different, but it's the same woman. And Mynheer van Daarken will pay a good price for her return! He has offered a reward for any knowledge as to her whereabouts."

"It may be, but we cannot be sure."

"We should turn this boat around and take her upriver to him."

Charity's heart sank. She pressed forward, listening.

"No," demurred the captain, "that I will not do. Suppose we are wrong? She would have a good case against us. This man, this Sebastian Eelkens she claims is her father, may have some influence in New York and might charge us with kidnapping his daughter."

"Bah! Hast ever heard of a Sebastian Eelkens in New York?"

"Nay, but there might well be such a one. New

people arrive every week. I'll not turn the boat around. When we reach New York, we'll make inquiries."

"Ask yourself, does she sound like a Dutch girl? No. We should not let her disembark—we should keep her aboard."

"Nay, she has no trunk, no baggage. Odds are she'll have no money either. We'll inquire if there's a Sebastian Eelkens in New York, and if there is none, we'll send word to the patroon upriver by the next flyboat that we've found his missing cousin, and claim the reward."

"She'll escape you," warned his wife sourly.

"Tis not such a large place that we can't find her again," he said comfortably.

Charity crept back and huddled into her place, but sleep was now impossible. That sharp-eyed woman remembered her. And would send word upriver to Killian.

Her days in New York were surely numbered.

By morning she was still undecided as to what to do.

As they passed the palisades, Charity, leaning on the rail deep in thought, hardly noticed the awesome sight. Then, she noticed that the little basket, which had been affixed to the ribbon tied round her waist, had come loose and, as she made a grasp for it, it fell into the water. She watched as it floated away and finally, caught in a swirling eddy, sank from view. She gazed back at the spot where it had disappeared with a bittersweet pang. The little basket, like the part of her life it had represented, was gone.

When they docked in New York, amid a great bustle and din, for several ships were loading and unloading, and fishwives and others were hawking their wares, Charity made a great show of winsomely thanking the flyboat captain for conveying her here. She promised that her father, Sebastian Eelkens, who had not been very well, would come down in person either today or tomorrow with a gift for the captain's wife. Explaining that she wished to purchase some fruit for her ailing father, she waved another goodbye and was off briskly along the dock.

Standing once again with the sea breeze blowing her fair hair and surveying the ships riding at anchor in New York harbor, Charity looked around her at a mass of scurrying humanity, hoping an opportunity would present itself.

Near her a man was selling oranges, fresh from the Indies, and people were crowded around to buy the ripe orange fruit. While Charity mingled with that crowd, her sharp eyes noted a gaunt rat-faced urchin surreptitiously stealing oranges and edging out of the crowd to stuff them into a small leather casket shoved against some barrels and then returning for some more. He looked dock-wise enough for her purposes.

Charity approached the lad.

"You look a bright boy," she said in Dutch. "Canst tell me, is there a ship sailing out of the harbor this day?"

"Aye," he said, regarding her warily. "The *Marybella*. Bound for Charles Town."

"And where is that?"

"Tis in a place called Carolina far to the south."

Carolina . . . she had heard of it. "When do they cast off?" she asked.

"With the tide," he said. "In about an hour, thereabouts."

She pulled out a shilling from the pouch she had taken from Bart and gave it to the lad. "Sell me yon little leathern casket," she said, "and take me to the captain of the *Marybella,* and there's a gold piece in it for you."

His eyes widened, and before the hour was out her small guide had indeed led her to the captain, where she had prettily explained that she was a maid-servant sent to bring home some luggage left behind by "one of the Merriweather sisters of Charles Town." She paid for her passage with the rest of the gold from Bart's pouch, and conspicuously exhibited the little leather casket as she was welcomed aboard.

The tall ship rode out with the tide, and Charity stared back at the receding yellow brick houses with their step gables and red tiled roofs. Along about this time, the flyboat's captain and his long-memoried wife would have completed their inquiries and learned that New York had no Sebastian Eelkens—at least none with a daughter fitting Charity's description—and would be excitedly sending their message upriver to the patroon.

She cast a last look at the low retreating skyline of the port. Killian van Daarken would be disappointed of his prey. . . . She stood and watched until the land had faded from view and night closed down.

Whatever lay ahead of her, she told herself resolutely, it could be no worse than the difficulties she had encountered in these northern Colonies. And although she was not much older in age, she was infinitely older in experience.

She would try her luck in the south.

BOOK III

Charles Towne 1687

CHAPTER 26

To Charity's surprise, the *Marybella* was crowded with passengers on their way to Carolina. She found herself stuffed into a tiny cabin, hardly more than a broom closet for size, with a big yellow-haired woman named Helga, who might have stepped out of a Titian canvas. Helga seemed irritated—Charity guessed that was because she had expected to occupy the cabin alone in comfort all the way to Carolina. But after a few minutes Helga, who had a rollicking personality beneath her flounces and ruffles, warmed to her cabin mate. She confided that she was a tavern maid who'd "got into a mite of trouble" in New York and was on her way to Carolina where none knew her and she could, she added with a roaring laugh, "start out her life afresh as a virgin"!

Charity liked Helga, and they spent some time together walking about the ship. As they strolled Helga passed along her observations about the male passengers: That one was too old—well past it, if she was any judge. Another was chasing all the women aboard but had no money—look out for the likes of him. Now *there*—her eyes narrowed—was exactly the right man if Charity could but nab him. See that tall blue-eyed man in the blond periwig over there? Yes, the one in the blue coat with silver braid and silver buttons. He'd taken a whole cabin to himself—the best on the *Marybella*. His luggage was expensive, too, and look at the rich lace of his cuffs! That ring he was wearing was an emerald, she'd be bound. Even the buckles of his shoes were a fine chased silver—see, they'd a different sheen from pewter, couldn't Charity see it?

Charity hardly listened. Instead her gaze was riveted on the face of the handsome passenger who occupied the *Marybella*'s best cabin. It was a calm face, rather broad, with chiseled features like the Roman statuary Charity had admired in Bath. He was very fair with rosy cheeks and an almost pink and white complexion. For a big man he had a leisurely way of moving, as if nothing in his life caused him any immediate hurry. His clothes, she saw, were of the latest cut and Helga was right when she said they were expensive. His brocade waistcoat of palest blue matched his knee breeches and stockings, complementing the deeper blue of his fitted, flaring coat with its silver trimmings. Even here on shipboard, where many of the land amenities were forgotten, he carried his hat—a broad hat with yellow plumes—correctly under his arm as he walked about and placed it upon his head when he sat down, exactly as the court dandies did.

Charity wished she could meet him, but there was always a crowd about him. A planter from Tidewater, Virginia, and his family were aboard. They were returning from a visit with New York relatives, and the planter's wife and well-dressed daughters were always interfering with Charity's view of that silver-trimmed blue coat. These fortunate women swept about him in their big skirts, flirting their fans. Sometimes he was merrily allowed to catch them as they "lost their footing" from the roll of the ship, and giggling, lingered a moment too long in his arresting arms.

On inquiry Charity learned that the blue-clad gentleman was a wealthy planter from Carolina named Alan Bellingham. The name had a pleasant ring. To her disappointment, she learned that he and the Virginians took their meals in the captain's cabin while the rest of the passengers ate in a common room.

"He's married," Helga told her slyly, when she caught Charity gazing at the man she had pointed out earlier. "But then ain't all the best ones married?" She nudged Charity with her elbow and Charity turned away from Helga's coarse laugh. Whether he was married or single, it wasn't likely she'd meet the handsome Mr. Bellingham.

All through dinner that night Helga flirted aggressively with a little balding fellow whose wife was too seasick to come to table. Charity felt rather depressed watching Helga move her big breasts and shoulders expressively under her bright Turkey-red shawl. Across from her the wispy little man in his dapper clothes could hardly keep his eyes from Helga's breasts. Beside Charity, a nervous young fellow with a tic tittered at the sight and edged closer, pressing his leg against Charity's.

Charity stiffened and drew away. She might not be good enough for the captain's cabin, but she was certainly better than the present assemblage.

Feeling somewhat affronted, she went up on deck and strolled about for a while, enjoying the night air until it became too cool, for she did not own a shawl. When she returned to her cabin, however, she put her hand on the door and stopped.

From within came a woman's low giggling laughter, a man's mumbled words. Helga was entertaining.

Charity frowned and hesitated. It was cold on deck and she had nowhere to go, but if what was going on inside the cabin was what she thought was going on there, she had no desire to open the door. Back upstairs she went, to spend two shivering hours pacing about the windy deck. When she came down again, Helga was alone and apparently asleep. The next morning Helga slept late, but woke as Charity rose and said in a sleepy voice, "Take my red shawl if you're going on deck. It's breezy there."

Assuming that the offer was Helga's way of saying "thank you" for not being interrupted last night, Charity wrapped the red shawl around her and went up on deck. A lowering day it was, too, with gray skies clouding up for a squall and the sea air damp and cutting. There were a number of passengers about and she spied Alan Bellingham surrounded by the planter's family, at one end of the ship. Deliberately, she chose the other end of the vessel for her stroll—not so very great a distance since the *Marybella* was not a large ship.

She was standing by the rail, thinking rather gloomily of Ben and of Rachel, when she heard behind her a bellow of rage.

"You there! You with your yellow hair and red shawl!"

So fierce was the tone that Charity whirled about. Bearing down on her with a rolling gait was a large woman dressed in a flounced tan cambric dress. Her eyes were dark and mean. Every hair on her head seemed to quiver with anger. "Don't look so innocent," roared the woman. "I heard all about you, I did!"

With horror Charity saw that a long leather strap swung in the woman's big hand. As Charity backed away, she came up sharply against the rail.

In her surge forward, the big woman never faltered. "You've been with my husband, you trollop!" she boomed. "And I aim to stripe your pretty hide for you!"

"Your husband?" cried Charity, finding her voice. "I don't even *know* your husband!"

"Not with his clothes on perhaps, but without 'em you're well acquainted!" the woman snarled, and reached out and snatched the red shawl from Charity's shoulders.

"You're mad," gasped Charity, making a grab for the shawl which, after all, didn't belong to her. "Your husband will tell you he doesn't know me. Ask him!"

"He's a liar," said the big woman imperturbably and raised her arm. "Doesn't tell nothing but lies." She brought her arm down and the leather strap struck Charity hard across her shoulder, almost bringing her to her knees. As she reeled against the ship's rail, she realized that, across the deck, a horrified knot of people were riveted, watching. The woman's arm raised again, and Charity saw a man in a blue coat detach himself from the group to run toward her. She screamed and tried to dodge the next blow but the strap struck her savagely full across her back just as

296

the ship rolled. She felt a lashing pain, heard a ripping sound and plummeted to her face on the deck.

"Dirty hussy!" screamed the big woman in fury. "I'll teach you to lie with *my* husband!"

Charity moaned and felt the heavy strap graze her back again, before the man who had run forward was able to grab her assailant's arm. For a moment they struggled there—the big woman in tan flounces and the big man in the blue coat. Then the strap was in the man's possession and the woman fell back against the rail, almost sobbing with rage.

"Ye've got naught to do with this, Mr. Bellingham!" she cried, her face convulsed with fury. "Tis between me and this yellow-haired chit here, who lured my husband to her bed, she did!"

By now the rest of the passengers had reached them and they were surrounded by curious eager faces. Charity looked around her, shamed, feeling the marks of the strap like fire across her slender back and shoulders. She struggled to a sitting position.

"Let's hear what the lady has to say about it," Alan Bellingham said, leaning down and offering Charity his hand.

"*Lady!*" The big woman's voice rose to a howl. "You call *that* a lady?"

Alan Bellingham looked down into Charity's flushed, rebellious face, her wild bright hair blowing, one white shoulder showing through a sleeve torn from her fall.

"Yes," he said softly. "I do so call her."

Charity took the proffered hand and looked up wonderingly into that grave, handsomely sculptured face, that broad calm brow below the curled ash-blond periwig, the wide mouth that smiled in repose and the slate-blue eyes that looked so steadily into her own—and felt her senses reel.

"Twas a yellow-haired wench in a red shawl," bellowed the woman. "I was told twas her!"

"She's mistaken me for somebody else," explained Charity painfully.

"Begone," said Alan Bellingham curtly over his

shoulder to Charity's attacker. "And if ye bother this lady again, I'll see ye flogged for your day's work."

Sputtering, the woman departed and Alan retrieved the shawl, spread it over Charity's shoulders and asked in a solicitous voice if he might help her to her cabin. Still wincing from the pain of the attack and afraid the strap had torn the material of her only dress, Charity nodded, hardly noticing in her misery the furious faces of the Virginia planter's family. Leaning on Mr. Bellingham's strong arm, Charity made her way to her cabin—to find the door ajar and her little leather casket, which she had so carefully tied with thongs, sitting open on her bed. At the sight, she cried out in dismay and Alan Bellingham said sharply, "Is that empty casket yours then?"

Dismally, Charity nodded.

"What is this, a ship of thieves?" he demanded, furious. "Surely you have been stripped of your possessions, mistress, whilst that woman attacked you on the deck! Was she then a decoy to occupy your attention so you would not note you were being robbed?"

"Oh, no." Charity flung the red shawl down upon the bunk. "She but mistook me for Helga with whom I share this cabin. Tis Helga's shawl and doubtless twas Helga with her husband last night!"

He frowned. "Helga's morals are no concern of mine. But if the cabins of this ship are being pilfered, I'll bring the culprits to justice, that I will! Someone will swing for it!"

In horror Charity realized to what a pass her pretense that the little casket was valuable had brought her. Helga had eyed it curiously from the first. Doubtless she had opened it and finding it empty, left it open in contempt. Now Charity wondered what kind of "trouble" Helga had got into in New York.

The enraged Mister Bellingham was about to swing away when Charity caught his arm. "No, wait," she cried. "I—I must tell you the casket was empty. It was empty when I brought it aboard."

"What? You're teling me you travel with empty baggage? Who is it you're shielding, mistress?"

"No one," admitted Charity sadly. "I—it's a long story. . . ." Pain and the reaction to the unprovoked attack on her made her reel light-headedly for a moment against the wall. Instantly contrite, Alan was by her side again.

"S'death," he cried. "Here you're like. to faint and I'm crashing about. There's wine in my cabin to restore you. That is—if you'll accompany me there?" He cast a worried look at her. "The back's near gone from your dress, mistress. Wouldst change it first?"

"I . . . have no other," said Charity miserably.

He looked shocked, but he put his coat about her and helped her to his cabin. She winced as the coat rubbed against the sore places on her back and shoulders. It was with relief that she sank down on a chair in his cabin and watched him pour wine into a silver flagon. Over the wine he introduced himself.

"I am Alan Bellingham," he said.

"I am Charity Woodstock," said Charity. "Late of Torquay." She shifted her smarting shoulders.

He noted that. "Sit you here, mistress, and recover yourself. I will return shortly."

She watched him go and then looked around the cabin. Helga had been right: his luggage was indeed handsome. Some silver toilet articles were scattered about as well as a pale green coat as fine as the blue one he was wearing.

Bellingham returned with a dress flung over his arm.

"Mistress Amalie is about your size," he said gravely. And, to Charity's surprised look, added: "She is Mr. Wigstrom's eldest daughter." Charity guessed he meant the Virginia planter whose family had hovered over him during the voyage.

"I—have no money to pay for it," she said, with a yearning look at the dress.

"That I have already done," he said curtly. "So there will be no need for you to do so. I will stand outside to see that you are not disturbed while you dress." He frowned. "But first, the blows that foul woman rained upon you—I have with me some ointment. Could I call this Helga with whom you share a cabin?"

Charity had no desire to lay eyes on Helga again. She had taken a beating for Helga already, and enough was enough.

"Tis only where the lash struck my back that I think the skin is broken," she said wistfully. "Do you think you could put a bit of salve on it? I'd be most beholden. It shames me for word to be put about the ship of my plight," she added.

He looked startled, but at the plaintive note of her last words he opened a small leather chest and looked about until he found the ointment he sought. With gentle fingers he felt through the rip of the back of Charity's dress and reported that the skin there was broken "but not very much." Nevertheless she flinched as his fingers—trembling a little—touched the raw place on her back.

"My shoulders too," she murmured. "Perhaps just a bit of the salve?" And she undid the top of her bodice and shrugged her dress and chemise down about her white shoulders. "Not too much," she added anxiously. "It might stain my dress. Perhaps you'd best rub a bit off."

Although only the very tops of her breasts and her smooth rounded shoulders were exposed, she saw his face flame and heard his quick indrawn breath. He touched her very carefully, with great courtesy. He was so *nice,* she thought. He was also handsome and wealthy and a gentleman.

And married.

That thought stiffened her spine. She had had one adventure with a married man in which she had come off with a badly bruised heart; she could ill afford another.

"Thank you," she said, and turning, smiled up into his eyes.

The color in his face deepened and he stepped quickly away from her. As if, she thought grimly, she might be a hot stove that would burn him if he stayed.

300

With a look of relief, he left the cabin and closed the door behind him.

Being careful not to drag the material against her hurt back and shoulders any more than necessary, Charity eased off her dress and put on the one he had brought.

It fit her perfectly!

She stood up, hardly believing her good luck. It had been worth a few stripes to arrive in Charles Town in a dress in which she might seek genteel employment—instead of a worn, mended garment in which she would look fit only to empty chamber pots.

The petticoats were of delicate green lawn, with an overskirt and fitted bodice of sprigged white and green cambric with billowing sleeves. It was as cool as mint and suited the sunshine of her hair as the summer sun suited the shimmering green of the leaves. After she had combed her hair with Alan's silver comb, arranging it carefully and modishly, she opened the door. With a heart bursting with gratitude, she curtsied to Alan Bellingham. who looked quite startled at this instant transformation from serving wench to lady.

"It becomes you well," he said. "May I see you to your cabin?"

"The sun is coming out," observed Charity. "I would rather chance the deck—if there are no more madwomen about bent on flogging the nearest stranger."

"I will assure that there are none," he said gravely. "For I will be glad to accompany you on your stroll."

Her topaz eyes shining, Charity swept to the deck and paced up and down it on the arm of the fashionable Mr. Bellingham, noting with satisfaction the fury in the eyes of the Virginia planter's family. She gave them a sweet smile as she passed. After all, one of them—probably the one with the pretty figure and the angry face—had furnished this lovely dress she was wearing. She felt a kind of ironic gratitude toward her detractor, whose spiteful low-voiced comments she could hear as they passed.

Beside her Alan Bellingham heard too, frowned and marched her to the far end of the ship. Pausing by the rail, he asked her if this was her first visit to America. Warily, Charity admitted that it was, adding a vague bit about having come to Boston to live with relatives who had turned her out because their daughter's betrothed had unfortunately preferred Charity and had begun to pay her court. When Alan nodded understandingly, she added that she "could not bear to talk about them, they had used her so wickedly," and hoped she would not have to elaborate further on her experiences here in the Colonies. To her surprise, her remark about Boston struck quite another chord.

"I have been to Boston," he said, "I went last year."

She caught her breath in fear. Perhaps he had heard about the escaped witch who had fled a burning in Dynestown. . . .

"I stayed but briefly," he added in a moody voice. "'Twas a sad errand brought me there—one which ended badly."

Charity looked sympathetic but he did not elaborate. He began, instead, telling her about his plantation near Charles Towne where he had first raised indigo and, now, had gone heavily into rice. Rice, he assured her with enthusiasm, was the "crop of the future" for the swampy land was ideally suited for its culture. For a long time they talked and when at last he left—barely in time for his dinner in the captain's cabin—Charity watched him go wistfully. How she would have liked to accompany him. . . .

Soberly she went down to eat with the less illustrious passengers in the common room, where Helga looked flustered at the sight of her. Charity gave her a grim look and retired to the cabin immediately after dinner. Let Helga entertain her "gentlemen friends" on deck for all she cared! As Charity prepared for bed, Helga came in and stood, for a moment, frowning and uncertain, then angrily got into bed herself without even putting on her nightgown. For the remainder of the voyage, they did not speak.

Charity could not have cared less what Helga did, for she spent most of her daytime hours with Alan Bellingham. All the way to Carolina she strolled about the deck with him, ignoring the whisperings and stares of the Virginia planter's family. Together they leaned on the ship's rail and he told her about himself and about his wife. For Charity, it was a respite from thinking about whatever lay ahead. Glad to be standing there, glad to hear his rich, charming, masculine voice, she listened.

Although Bellingham himself had been born in the Colonies—his father had been a planter on the James, who had succumbed to yellow fever and died—his wife was from Devon. Three years ago on a visit to England he had married Marie and brought her to her new home in Carolina—but this new land charmed her not. She was wistful for England and the comforts of life there. Then, too, her health was a problem. He sighed deeply and Charity began to wonder if Marie was consumptive. She knew what it was like to watch someone you loved waste away. She had watched her own mother die—so slowly. Her heart went out to Alan, looking so pensive and so handsome with the sea wind blowing his ash-blond hair.

When he asked her about her future plans, she admitted she hoped to become a governess. Would she consider a position as a scribe? he wondered. There was need for such a one at his plantation, for his factor, though a good manager, wrote so poorly that none could read his scrawl, and penmanship was sorely needed for the bills and accounts.

Charity caught her breath. To work for Alan! And not as a chambermaid, but as a scribe! Instantly she agreed, hardly listening as he soberly told her the terms of her employment, adding morosely that there was "not overmuch work" and he'd "be much obliged if she could assist his wife in other duties" as might be required." Eagerly, Charity promised to assist his wife, and she looked out upon the blue ocean with a glowing hope for the future. At least she would be beside Alan!

"My wife is devoted to her family," he explained. "Her sister in Barbadoes falls ill frequently and she must needs go there and be at her side. And her brother—ah, there is a situation that causes her many sleepless nights and takes the bloom from her cheeks." Seeing Charity's puzzled look, he explained, "Twas on her brother's account that I made this trip to New York—and at a time when the plantation sorely needed my attention. But she did so plead with me. . . . My wife has not seen her brother in some five years. Not since before she left England. It is known only that he ran away to sea . . . many boys perish that way and their fate is never known. But my wife has never given up hope that her brother might have reached America and, after she came here, she got the idea that we should advertise for him in several newspapers."

"And did you receive an answer?"

He looked gloomy. "No less than three answers—at different times. The last was from New York and said that a man of her brother's description had but recently arrived there, was ill and delirious and without funds, and requested us to come and get him—he owed then a large bill at an inn." He sighed. "My wife, as I told you, is in indifferent health. Even though she desired it most ardently, she had not the strength to come with me to New York."

"So you went alone?"

"Yes, to please her. And now I return empty-handed. No one had seen him; there was no bill at an inn—the earth seemed to have swallowed him up." He sighed. "I can hardly bear to return and tell her this was yet another wild goose chase. It will break her heart. She wept piteously the last time."

"The . . . last time?"

"I have been to both Williamsburg and Boston at different times seeking him," Alan admitted. "These elusive letters arrive and they give us each time a fresh scent, but always when I arrive his trail is cold —nay, everyone, with truth ringing sincere in their voices—insists that they have not seen him nor yet heard of him."

"Could you have enemies?" puzzled Charity. "People who would write such things to plague you?"

He sighed. "I have thought of that. But for myself, I know of no enemies nor ever did, for I have set my hand against no man. And my wife is of such a lovable disposition that she could not have an enemy in the world."

Charity hoped so, if she was going to live in the woman's household, for she had become cynical and hardly dared to hope that she could find peace of mind in another's house.

Beside her, Alan Bellingham mused, "Perhaps we will find him yet. . . ."

She smiled pensively at him. He was a generous man, she thought. Generous of his time. Open and generous in his dealings. Sad to think of him saddled with a delicate wife who was always running off to Barbadoes or pining for a lost brother. A wife who kept him chasing through the Colonies on luckless errands. He was a kind man and unfortunate. And oh, so startlingly good to look upon. When she was not with him she brooded about him.

Long before they reached Carolina, Charity realized that she was hopelessly in love with Alan Bellingham.

She told herself, of course, that such a love could come to nothing. Her head told her that. Her heart responded fiercely that such was not the case, that life had not given her much, but this one thing she would have—Alan's love. His wife she might never be, but his mistress—ah, that was possible.

CHAPTER 27

With the little leather casket, now containing her torn "other dress," clutched in her arms, Charity viewed the Carolina coastline with a different expression from that with which she had viewed other shores. The New England coastline she had regarded with hope, the New York coast with fear—but this Carolina coastline she considered with narrowed eyes.

There would be a future for her here. With Alan Bellingham. She would see to that.

She would forget all the men who had loved—and used—her. She would begin her life anew.

When they landed, she looked around and saw before her a relatively new town, about four squares long and three squares wide. The first street fronted on a stream she was told was the Cooper River, and wharves projected from the river front. A number of vessels rode the blue water of the harbor, and there was a brisk coming and going as furs and lumber and turpentine, pitch and tar were loaded onto the incoming ships—and practically everything else unloaded for the use of the settlers. She was glad that she already had a job at Alan's plantation, for the town was disturbingly small and she realized, with a sinking feeling, how slim would have been her chance of finding suitable employment.

After they disembarked, Alan took charge of her small leather casket, which he piled peremptorily on his other luggage and left in the custody of a young black boy in colorful shirt and trousers, whose wide grin cut a slash across his dark face. Announcing he had "business" to attend to, Alan suggested she might "look about the town" and meet him back here on the docks in about an hour.

Charity watched with interest a disembarking shipload of French Huguenots who had fled from the Terror following the Revocation of the Edict of Nantes in France. Some of them were tearfully telling the people who met them that they had been "dragooned." As she strolled about, Charity noticed that all sorts of seafood—the tiny delicious native shrimp as well as turtles and oysters and crabs—were being sold on the docks, and gulls and black skimmers and brown pelicans and other seabirds wheeled overhead and swooped low over the baskets, adding their raucous calls to the general din. Beaver skins and other furs were piled high beside kegs and barrels, dugout canoes shuttled back and forth. And on the river great logs of cedar floated by for transshipment to England.

Charity stopped to sniff some spices and someone jostled her and apologized. She found herself wedged between piles of coconuts and oranges brought in from the isles of the Caribbees and listened, fascinated, to the conversation behind her: These damn pirates were getting bolder! At first they had preyed upon only the Spanish and the buccaneers had been right welcome in Charles Towne, they had! But things were changing. Three English merchant ships that had sailed from the harbor had been attacked and taken, and just yesterday the crew of a fourth had rowed in, in a longboat. Twas rumored the buccaneer Captain Court was behind it. Not that his ship the *Sea Witch* had been in the engagement, but twas well known he was an organizer of these freebooters. Called him their admiral, the rogues did! Well, he'd soon have a price on his head, he would. And those rogues had better keep to their base in Tortuga or else sally out against Spain—if twas English ships they were after, England would send her Navy, that she would, and Charles Towne would be the first to request it!

With a pang, Charity remembered the pirate ship that had taken Tom away from her in the north. She hoped he hadn't become a buccaneer, for such men ended their lives dangling on hemp or buried in wet and restless graves between the high water mark and the low.

Brushing aside these dark thoughts, she moved on through the chattering throng and into a street which, like the dock, teemed with activity. As she strolled through town in the sultry late afternoon air, she was surprised to hear a great deal of French spoken as well as English. A number of black slaves brushed by her, bustling about on numerous errands, including one dressed as a coachman in a velvet coat.

At a waterfront tavern her progress was halted by a cursing sailor who staggered out the open door, propelled by a boot, while inside a shrill voice cried, "Ye don't pinch *me* without ye pay for my ale!" From within there was a ripple of bawdy laughter. Charity glanced at the dark interior, realizing grimly that but for Alan she might well have ended up there, serving tankards of ale and rum, and fending off the rough caresses of the seafaring men who frequented it. With a frown she strolled on, observing buildings of black cypress built on brick foundations, and others built of a kind of concrete called "tappy," made from the oyster shells piled in heaps along the river from the Indians' "kitchen middens" and mixed with lime to become as hard as stone.

In a butcher's shop—through whose door Charity had retreated hastily to avoid a big cart carrying lumber and tar—she learned mutton was scarce because wolves preyed on the lambs. But she saw plenty of pork. The hogs could take care of themselves and they grew fat on the acorns that were strewed on the ground below the mighty oaks.

At a baker's shop she cast a wistful glance at the large fresh-baked breadloaves, but said hastily she had "forgotten to bring her money." The proprietor, a twinkling-eyed Scot, pressed a sweet cake on her "to sample my wares, lassie, so ye'll be coming back." And as Charity munched it, he told her that this land was ruled by the Lords Proprietors and that there was a landed gentry here—but that titles could be bought for gold as well as inherited. Charity listened, fascinated, as he told her land might be bought for a penny an acre, and if one bought 12,000 acres, one became a baron; with 24,000 acres one became a cassique, while 48,000 acres made one a landgrave. Were there many such? she inquired.

Oh, no, he assured her. Not many baronies, as the great estates were called. But there were a few—for instance, Landgrave Bellingham's great estate "Magnolia Barony" was some four miles from here and could be reached by cart track or by pirogue up the Cooper River.

Charity felt a swell of pride and noted the respect in his eyes as she told him she was to be a scribe at Magnolia Barony. Then, thanking him for the sweet cake and the information, she hurried back to the dock to find Alan waiting impatiently beside a carriage. Somewhat dazzled, as it had been some time since she had traveled in a carriage, Charity climbed in beside him. They started off, followed by a cart, driven by a large black man in a pink turban, with their luggage.

Charity was conscious of a change in Alan, a tension, an eagerness, and a squaring of the shoulders. There was pride in his voice when he told her that they were now riding over his own land. *He loves this land,* she thought, and jealously tried to distract him. She leaned forward to push aside a branch from the great overarching trees that shaded the cart track, and managed to brush Alan with her shoulder. Then, turning toward him with a tantalizing smile, she settled her lissome figure so that it was more fetchingly displayed.

But Alan was looking about him anxiously. "It was bad for me to be away," he muttered. "McNabb has too much to attend to."

"McNabb?"

"The factor who manages the plantation when I'm gone. You'll be working with him."

She felt a little disappointed. She'd hoped to work directly with Alan, where she could see him, brush

310

against him with a careless arm, remind him she was there. No matter, she'd make the best of things. *And* manage to ensnare Alan.

For that first tender gloss was gone. Charity was a woman now and she knew what she wanted: Alan Bellingham. Someway, somehow, he would be hers. She settled back on the seat beside him, determined, listening to the rhythmic clipclop of hooves that were taking her to Magnolia Barony.

On through the overarching liveoaks and hickories and magnolias they plodded. Sometimes thick palmetto clumps pressed in like green walls about them. Dogwood branches reached out to brush them and long festoons of gray beardlike Spanish moss hung down to trail over their heads. In low spots rose pond pines and tall cypresses, and everywhere there was a tangled growth of smilax and sweet bay and jessamine. Sometimes through the trees they glimpsed the river, the dark water sparkling. It was hot in the thick green forest but Charity remained alert. Once she saw a white-tailed deer, and twice rabbits scurried out of their paths—a cottontail and a darker one which Alan told her absently was a short-eared marsh rabbit. When the horses shied and reared up at a snake coiled in the road, Alan flicked at it with his whip and the snake retreated. He turned and called back a warning to the turbaned fellow who drove the luggage cart behind them.

She did not know what to expect, but the green tangle of woods about them hardly prepared her for the beauty of the house itself. They came out into a little clearing as the sun sank low in the sky, a red ball that turned the river—now seen clearly through the big boles of the live oaks—to flame. At the end of a dusky avenue of trees stood a white-pillared house made of the same stone-like "tappy" she had seen in town, a house the setting sun turned into a pink temple against a dark background of magnolias and old moss-hung oaks.

"It's beautiful," she murmured, and turned to Alan. But he was not looking at her. He had shaken the reins and the horses speeded their pace so that they drew up smartly before the row of rosy columns. His face was aglow as he turned to Charity, and she thought *he has discovered me!*

The thought died. He was looking past her to the trees beside the house where a rider had appeared, galloping toward them on a black horse.

The rider was Alan's wife, Marie, and she was everything Charity had expected her not to be. Marie was tall and lithe, with a full figure. She rode side-saddle, and her slender back was straight and arrogant. With great skirts billowing and the plumes on her hat blowing, Marie Bellingham came to a fast stop before them. Her horse reared up and she laughed exultantly, handling the reins with practiced ease.

"Alan!" she cried, and slid off the horse into his arms. Charity winced at the warmth of his embrace.

After a moment Marie pushed him away and took off her plumed hat with a lazy gesture. Charity saw that her ash-blonde hair—identical in color to Alan's periwig—was swept up and fell into soft shining curls to frame a lovely face.

"Did you learn anything . . . about my brother?" she inquired in a tremulous voice.

"No," said Alan sadly. "No one had heard of him there. It's as if someone is deliberately tormenting us, leading us on with false hopes."

At his first words, Marie had turned away. Now she covered her face with her hands as if she could not bear it. "We must—hope," she declared hoarsely. "We must not give up! We must not, Alan!"

"I know, I know." Gently he took his wife by the shoulders, turned her around. "I have brought someone with me. Will you not greet her?"

Marie's wide violet eyes were a deeper color than her sweeping lavender riding dress. Now those wide eyes frosted as they looked Charity over.

"And who indeed have you brought?" she inquired coldly.

Alan hastened to explain Charity's position as scribe to McNabb and "helper" to Marie. Marie shrugged

312

and, with a gesture of dismissal, turned to a stalwart gray-haired Irish woman who had come silently out of the house.

"Give—Charity, is it—the room Flossie had," instructed Marie. "She will eat with you and McNabb."

Alan opened his mouth—perhaps to protest—but closed it again.

As Marie locked an arm companionably in Alan's, Charity realized bitterly that she had made a mistake. Alan was not up for the taking. She would have to fight for him.

Charity followed the big Irish woman, who turned congenially as they entered the wide hall and said, "My name's Megan O'Reilly. I'm housekeeper here."

"Charity Woodstock," smiled Charity, and followed Megan up the delicate, curving wainscoted stairway to the second floor and down a hall toward the rear.

"Backstairs is there—next to m'lady's bedroom." Megan nodded. "You'll be using that." She gave Charity a conspiratorial look and opened a paneled door. Ahead lay the winding attic stairs. "You and me'll be the only ones up here. M'lady did dismiss her maid Flossie, and it's her room you'll be after taking."

Charity balked. She'd promised to assist Alan's wife in "other duties as might be required." Would ladies' maid be one of them? She hoped not.

Ahead of her Megan missed a step on the narrow stair and swore. "May the Lord forgive me," she said. "'Tis a troubling place, as you'll soon be learning."

Charity forbore to ask why, for they had reached the top and had just passed a cheerful little room with a big window that looked out over the grounds. She realized now that the house wasn't all that large, but its vast pillars made it look imposing.

"Don't waste your time looking at that room," advised Megan, turning to discover Charity eyeing it. "It's over m'lady's head and she won't allow no one to occupy it—won't allow no one in the rooms on this side of the attic at all. Says they tramp about over the floor and wake her up. She's a light sleeper and has

313

headaches." Megan emphasized the word and again gave Charity a jaundiced glance. "So you'll be stuck over on t'other side same as me." She sighed. "The rooms are smaller. Less light. You'd best keep your windows open at night. Bats or other birds may fly in, but tis better than suffocatin'!"

As Megan showed Charity into a small mean room, about half the size of the one she had admired, Charity looked around her in some discouragement.

"Supper's in the kitchen, same time as the master and mistress eat theirs in the dining room. Get yourself settled. I'll send you up some water."

Megan departed cheerfully and Charity, sinking down on the hard narrow bed, stared in disappointment at the tiny battered washstand with its cracked ironstone bowl and pitcher, the single wooden chair. Somehow she had expected better.

After she had washed her face with water brought to her by a little black girl, Charity went downstairs. From the back of the hall Megan beckoned her to the kitchen. As she passed the dining room she paused for a moment. Sitting at the gleaming mahogany table were Alan and Marie, who sipped from silver goblets. The table, lit by tall straight tapers of a clean transparent green, was lavishly set. How Charity longed to join them in that elegant dining room! Over Alan's shoulder she caught Marie's mocking glance. *Never, never,* was what that glance told her. Charity stiffened and moved on toward the kitchen to sit at a plain wooden table with a preoccupied whitehaired McNabb and Megan, the housekeeper. Since Megan kept jumping up to supervise the black servants who manned the big swinging pots over the fire and carried hot dishes and laden trenchers into the dining room, and McNabb never spoke as he shoveled food into his mouth, it was a silent meal. Charity kept looking at the dining room door, which opened as the servants moved through it, to reveal its glittering interior.

In a salty moment, Charity's mother had once told her that the road from the kitchen to the dining room led by way of the bedroom. The bedroom. . . . From the dining room as the door swung open, Charity could hear Marie's distinctive light tantalizing laugh. A vision in gray brocade and silver lace, Marie was looking across that candlelit table, her sparkling violet eyes smiling into Alan's. Once again Charity was reminded that the distance between the kitchen and the dining room was the longest distance of all.

"Twill be all right. You'll get used to it here," Megan said placatingly as Charity left to go upstairs to bed, and Charity replied, "Yes, I'm sure I will."

In the attic, she paused wistfully beside the small pretty room that was directly over Marie's bedroom, and then trudged down the hall to her own unattractive one. Taking off everything but her chemise, she crawled into bed.

Tomorrow she would start her new duties here—whatever they might be. As she turned restlessly—for the little room was very hot and airless—she thought of Marie, casually emptying the rooms above her on the cool side of the house, consigning Charity and Megan to tiny cramped quarters. McNabb apparently slept elsewhere, perhaps in a little building Charity had glimpsed some distance away. The black house servants lived in slave "quarters" behind the house which, she was sure, were cooler than this room! With a rebellious palm, Charity gave her hard pillow a thump.

She turned over miserably, remembering how Alan's face had lit up at sight of Marie.

That woman! That lovely haughty scented scornful woman whose violet eyes had raked her and dismissed her as not worth trifling with—at this very moment Alan was holding that scornful woman in his arms! And Charity could not sleep for thinking of it.

The next day dawned hot and Charity rose early and went downstairs to find McNabb. But he had gone to check the sluices and floodgates of the rice fields with Landgrave Bellingham, she was told, so she wandered down to the river. As she approached it, she was startled to see an alligator slither into the water. She retreated to the boat landing and watched a long pirogue glide by carrying indigo.

Remembering she needed a candle for her room, hers having guttered out in the night, she returned to the house to find one. She discovered a small stack of the clear green ones she had seen on the dining room table the night before and asked Megan if she could have one of them.

"Indeed no," reproved Megan. "Them's for m'lady. Them's made of bayberry wax—they don't melt in summer and don't smoke and they smell good when they're snuffed. We make sealing wax from the bayberries too. Here—take one of these." She thrust a stubby candle into Charity's hand.

"Tallow?" wondered Charity.

"La, no! Too many wolves for sheep to do well. Tis deer suet this be made of. Farther inland they use bear grease too."

As Charity took the candle, she recalled that Ben had told her some of his candles were made of moose fat. It seemed strange to a girl bred in England and used to tallow.

In the afternoon, McNabb returned to show her the books and ledgers. She'd been right; his "office" was located in the small square building she'd glimpsed near the house and he slept in a loft above. Charity climbed onto a high wooden stool and copied off several sheets of figures with a turkey-quill pen and tallied them up. When she had finished, she began leafing idly through the ledgers. The financial condition of Magnolia Barony was not nearly so good as the luxury about her had led her to expect. Frowning, she put down the quill pen and gazed through the small-paned window at the squirrels running about the lawn. If she'd read these figures aright, Alan was deep in debt to English merchants and needed a good rice crop to get him through. No wonder he had seemed so worried.

The next day as she passed Marie's door, Marie called to her sharply. Her color somewhat heightened by Marie's commanding tone, Charity walked into the bedroom. From its embroidered mauve satin coverlet on the feather bed to its gilt-framed mirrors and sheer blowing curtains, the room was the essence of luxury. It could have been Stéphanie's bedroom in Bath, she thought.

"I want you to hold these dolls up and turn them slowly so that I can see them at a distance," explained Marie.

At once Charity realized what Marie was doing. A row of little dolls, all dressed in the latest fashions, lay on the bed. It was customary for the English dressmakers to send small dolls garbed in the latest creations across the ocean to the Colonies. These clothes might then be copied or ordered. Charity was familiar with the custom, for Parisian fashions had reached England in the same manner. She picked up a doll wearing a sweeping purple velvet gown with big sleeves, held it at arm's length and turned it slowly about.

Fanning herself with a long-handled silk fan, Marie surveyed the doll critically. "It makes her look fat," she complained.

"The waist is too high," pointed out Charity, "and the sleeves are ungainly. With a lowered waist and smaller sleeves it would be very *chic.*"

"God's life!" cried Marie. "Do not tell me you sew as well as keep accounts? You are indeed a paragon of all the virtues!"

Before that mocking expression, Charity's pride flared. "I do not sew," she snapped. "But I am familiar with fine clothes, because I have worn them."

"And what is your opinion about this one? The green satin?"

"It will turn your eyes a murky color if you wear it," said Charity shortly. "That shade of green does not suit you."

"Nonsense," sniffed Marie. "Green has always been my lucky color."

Charity was not aware that Alan had approached

silently and was listening. She was amazed at the sudden change in Marie's expression.

"Your protégée has been giving me lessons in fashion," Marie said lightly.

"Beware she does not give you lessons in deportment, my love," smiled Alan with an indulgent look at his wife. "Methinks you could use them!"

Marie laughed, but her violet eyes narrowed. She studied Charity's hair. "You're right, Alan," she murmured. "Charity *does* wear her hair as a lady of fashion. Alan, do you think she could do mine?" She turned her head lazily so that he could view her shining tresses.

"I have no doubt she could—and will," said Alan, smiling at Charity. "Wouldst do it? We seem to be lacking a lady's maid."

Charity bit her lip. "Of course," she said in a muffled voice. "I'd be happy to."

And fled.

After that she found herself combing out Marie's long lustrous ash-blonde hair every day, arranging it into graceful curls, staring bitterly at the woman's beautiful face in the mirror as Marie criticized her every move.

Marie's, she admitted, was a face not easily forgotten. Her large eyes had a perpetually startled expression, and her hair was so light as to appear almost white—in the moonlight it would be silver. In the daylight, Marie was the most pastel and fragile of blondes. Like Alan her complexion was pink and white, and she had a low seductive laugh. Taller than Charity, her walk was a long-stemmed sway that was at once enticing and regal. That there was sometimes a frost in her violet eyes was not to be denied, for Marie came of the landed gentry; she had been brought up to command and considered it her God-given right. She was extravagant, and sometimes sulky and childish, but when she smiled her whole face broke into sunshine, with a surpassing sweetness.

Her husband, the landgrave, adored her.

Marie considered herself a member of a titled nobility. It was a Colonial nobility, but that did not matter to her at all. Her husband was a landgrave, and she was a landgrave's lady. All must bow.

Charity formed a violent dislike for the woman. Sometimes her hand holding the silver comb trembled and she yearned to slap Marie's lovely face. She was afraid this dislike would show in her eyes and cause Marie to dismiss her, so she kept her eyes downcast whenever possible in Marie's presence. Once, Marie met her gaze full on and murmured "Insolent," almost abstractedly, as if she were speaking of someone beneath notice.

One afternoon when old Dr. Cavendish and several other guests arrived unexpectedly from upriver, Charity, who was caught in their midst on the lawn, overheard a woman say, "Aren't they fabulous together, Alan and Marie? They look so alike—the same coloring and so handsome! Like a pair of Dresden figurines . . . so right for each other."

Charity's cheeks were stained an indignant red as she hurried back to McNabb's hot little office. Right for each other indeed!

And yet, although she told herself he wanted to, Alan never sought her out. Sometimes if their bodies brushed in passing through a door, he might look at her in confusion. And at those times she hoped for something, some sign. But always he turned away.

That evening she listened to the field slaves singing as they returned home from the rice fields. Their melodious voices had a mournful note that touched Charity deeply. Like her, they were far, far from home.

She pressed her hot face into her pillow and tried to sleep.

CHAPTER 28

Life at Magnolia Barony was painful for Charity, though it had two sides: dark and light. The brighter times were those days when she had some contact with Alan, when he came into McNabb's office and made some pleasantry. On those occasions she would turn on her high stool and favor him with a brilliant smile, her eyes glowing. Once, coming out of the office after a rain, she slipped on some wet leaves and fell heavily, turning her ankle. Alan picked her up and carried her to the house. It was a memorable trip for her—being held in his arms, her soft hip pressing against his hard stomach. With a moan that was less from pain than from desire, she turned so that her left breast was thrust against his chest and clung to him, arms around his neck. Obviously very shaken when he put her down, he called hoarsely to Megan for assistance and fled.

She loved him for his loyalty, Charity told herself staunchly. Even if that loyalty was to another woman. It meant that he would be just as loyal to her, once she had won him.

But the days passed and winning him seemed a long way off. Marie's grip was firm, her hand on the reins steady. Even her eyes challenged Charity. *Alan is mine,* they said. *He will always be mine.*

Nights were the worst. In her stuffy little attic room, Charity imagined them going to bed downstairs, pictured him holding Marie in his arms, fondling her . . . she could almost hear Marie's low seductive laugh as Alan took her.

At other times Charity writhed upon her bed in a

frenzy of grief because Alan had not noticed her, or he had passed her by with only a brusque word, or there had been no answering light in his blue eyes to some sally of hers.

He rubbed her feelings raw and did not know it.

The torment that she endured was bitter—but it was sweet. Sometimes on hot magnolia-scented nights with the singing of the slaves drifting up to her, she would lie on her back and imagine him above her, his big handsome body descending onto hers. Imagine she felt his gentle fingers easing her chemise down about her shoulders until her breasts were bare and palpitating under his gaze, then down around her hips until finally she lay naked and willing before him, filled with desire. Restless, she would turn in her torment and stare at the door. If only he would forget Marie and turn to her. . . .

By the end of a month, after studying the accounts closely, she was certain. Alan's financial situation was indeed precarious. When McNabb handed her still another sheet of his illegible figures and she copied them off in her precise handwriting, she was certain she had found her opportunity to seek out the land-grave of Magnolia Barony.

She found Alan giving instructions to the groom who was currying his big roan horse. Courteously he gave her his attention.

"I am worried about the figures," she began. "Can they possibly be right? I mean, do you really owe so much?"

He sighed. "I do indeed," he said. "Like most of the planters around here, I am up to my ears in debt to merchants on the other side of the water."

"Then why," she ventured, "don't you cut down on this order I just copied off? Do you really need a service for fifty? All these dishes? So many bolts of linen and lace?"

"They're for Marie," he admitted. "She's used to a better way of life than the rude shelter I can give her here. It's to ease her circumstances that I buy them."

Charity choked back the angry words that rose up.

322

Reminding herself that Marie was Alan's wife and she was not, she said in a voice half-smothered, "You'll need a good crop to pay for them."

"Aye," he agreed. "It looks like twill be a good crop too, in spite of my being away at crucial times. But I'll be shaking in my boots when it leaves the docks." At her questioning look, he explained, "The buccaneers! They were once very popular here in Charles Towne. They sailed in, brought their goods, sold it, drank and departed. Twas Spanish shipping they preyed on then. But lately all that's changed. Four times this year English ships leaving this port have been set upon by buccaneers and relieved of their cargo."

"And the passengers? The crew?"

"Spirited away to Tortuga, some of them. Ransomed or sold, I suppose, in some damned pirates' auction. They say it's a buccaneer named Court that's behind it. The fellow's got the devil's own gall; like as not he's the one."

"Oh? Do you know him then?"

Alan shook his head. "Court's never been to Charles Towne. He'd have had a hero's welcome after his raid on Maracaibo, but he didn't come."

"Why? Why would a man like that have a hero's welcome?"

"Maracaibo's a Spanish town," Alan explained. "And here on these shores we're in a constant undeclared war against Spain. They contest our right to sail these waters. They claim this very land we're standing on. The Spanish and the Portuguese divided the New World between them and fought to keep us from colonizing. When they catch an English ship, they torture and kill the crew. It's all done in the name of the Inquisition, but whether you're burned as a heretic or hanged as an Englishman the result is the same—you're dead. And we're uncomfortably near them here. Castillo de San Marcos at St. Augustine is Spanish. It gives me an uneasy feeling, to know that the Spanish might sail up here in force any day and burn us out. They've done it to other settlements. *And*

323

tried to colonize as far north as the Chesapeake. So anything that weakens the power of Spain in this part of the world is welcome, including the buccaneers."

"I see," she said in a small voice. "You mean these men we call buccaneers are really privateers."

· "Well, they were," he said with a twisted smile. "Most of them sail on letters of marque, privateering commissions, against the Spanish. But now that they've turned their guns on *us*. . . ."

"Four ships you say?"

"Four so far. We're all uneasy now. These fellows lie off the coast or sail the seas in fast vessels with the gunports disguised. They're desperate men and they'll blow a ship out of the water or board it, swinging cutlasses, if the captain doesn't heave to when they fire a shot across the bows."

Charity felt a little shiver go through her as she looked out through the magnolias to the east.

Beyond the trees, beyond her vision, a sluggish river flowed slowly toward the sea. And on that sea, lean dark ships bellied their sails and ran before the wind in pursuit of the rich merchantmen and golden galleons that warily plied these waters. Among the sapphire Caribbean's pearl-white beaches and coral reefs and emerald islands rising from the foam lay another, a darker world: The world of the buccaneers.

CHAPTER 29

An itinerant candlemaker had arrived and all the house servants were busy under his supervision, melting what looked like tallow but was perhaps deer suet, in big kettles and filling the large candle-molds he carried with him. Charity, who had helped Ben make beeswax tapers by pressing bits of heated wax around a wick, had never made candles this way. She watched, fascinated, as they poured the hot tallow carefully down into the molds.

Reminding herself there was work to do, she walked back toward the house. Alan passed her, lost in thought, and did not return her greeting. Charity turned to glare after him and went off in search of the industrious Megan. In the back yard, on a long line of hemp drawn between two live oaks, Megan was hanging out the wash.

"This stuff will mildew if it's left overnight and those girls are slow as molasses working with the candlemaker," Megan grumbled. "They're all thumbs."

"Here, let me help you," offered Charity. "Why didn't you ask Lally to help? I didn't see her making candles."

"What? Lally? Sure, m'lady's new maid takes on airs. Thinks she's too good to hang out clothes!"

Charity smiled as she tossed a wet sheet over the line. She'd been glad to see Lally, a slender, pert French Huguenot girl, arrive. The only flaw was that Lally could not "do" hair as well as Charity, and Marie still demanded Charity's services on a daily basis. But perhaps Lally would learn.

Swinging a heavy coverlet over the line with a grunt,

Megan turned to Charity. "D'you think all men are daft?" she asked conversationally. "Or is it just that they won't see what's plain before them?"

"Both," said Charity, still smarting at Alan's walking past without apparently seeing her. "Why?"

Megan waved at the bed linens, blowing in the breeze. "I was just thinking about how the mistress only lets the master into her bedroom one week a month—she tells him she 'can't' the rest of the time."

Charity was intrigued. At the moment she felt spiteful toward Alan and was glad his insufferable wife locked him out. "Why do you think she lies to him?" she wondered.

Megan looked around as if the trees might denounce her, rolled her eyes and mouthed the words, *"Other men!"*

Charity was taken aback. Marie was much admired, she knew, but where were other men who could equal Alan? His stalwart strength, his charming manners, his bluff good humor? That Alan's wife might not view him in the same exalted light did not at the moment occur to her. "It can't be true," she said slowly.

"Can't it now?" Megan's voice was tart. "Well, just you come out and sit in the garden o' nights and you'll be after seein' who slips out the side door with a hood over her head and walks down the road where, I'm told, a coach picks her up! So now you know why she locks the master out! Tells him she has a bleedin' migraine! And with her pretty face, I guess he'll believe anything she tells him, eh?" She shook her head and went on hanging up the clothes.

Charity thought about that. Two nights ago, rebelling against the insufferable heat, she had slipped into the attractive room that was right over Marie's head. Carefully she had spread a sheet over the bed, replaced the pillow with her own, and then stretched out with a sigh of relief to enjoy the cooler room.

She had heard footsteps moving about below and had been surprised. Marie up at this hour? No, she told herself—more likely the new maid, Lally, scurrying around at Marie's bidding, for Marie had absolutely no regard for the servants and called them at all hours if she wanted the least thing. The night was so warm that Charity was afraid she would perspire through the sheet and dampen the coverlet. Getting up, she stood in the window to let the rising breeze cool her, and saw below her a hooded figure run from the house, fly like a wraith across the lawn and into the shadow of the trees.

So swiftly did the figure appear and disappear that she could almost believe she had not seen it. Charity waited but it did not return. With a shrug she went back to bed, telling herself the hooded figure was Lally gone to meet some swain. But that figure could easily have been Marie.

"Why do they have separate bedrooms anyway?" She asked Megan. "I'd have thought—"

"You'd have thought being brought out here as a bride, and him buildin' this house for her, that she'd at least sleep with him, wouldn't you?" Wearily Megan straightened up and pushed back a strand of gray hair that kept falling into her eyes. "Well, she did— at first. Then she told him he snored and kept her awake. Tell me, when you've walked past his room, have you ever heard him snore? No more have I. Then she took to having sick headaches—"

"Marie must be mad," Charity said slowly. "Alan Bellingham is all that a man should be."

Megan gave her a sharp look. "Don't tell me you too are smitten by the landgrave? Twas why m'lady sent her last maid Flossie away—couldn't stand her mooning over her husband."

Charity flushed. "Of course I'm not," she protested staunchly. "I just think he's too good for her, that's all."

"They all think that," said Megan, giving the sheet in her hands a vicious slap. They were silent, working rapidly. Then Megan added in a confidential tone, "I'm thinking that's why she goes to Barbadoes so much."

"You mean—to get away from him?"

Megan nodded. "She's got a sister married to a rich planter there. They've three little children and one or the other is always sick—especially the sister. M'lady gets letters from her and it's off to Barbadoes she goes and stays a long time. Twice in the past year she's gone. And I'm thinkin' the reason she goes is not so much her sister's problems as that her husband's sniffing around her bedroom door more than she likes. You mark it, when he starts getting restless and too attentive, she'll get a letter from Barbadoes that says her sister needs her. Easy for her to say—her sister writes all the time. M'lady reads the letters aloud and then burns them. Hates clutter, she says." Megan snorted.

Charity's gaze grew somber. Let Marie go to Barbadoes! She adored Alan as his wife never had, and if he came into *her* bedroom, *she* would never put him out!

Last night she had dreamed that dream again, and now she told herself that the face was—must be—Alan's. But stubbornly her unconscious self dreamed as it pleased. And when in that oft-recurring dream she walked naked into her lover's arms, his face was still hidden from her.

Perhaps, she told herself honestly, that face deserved to be Tom Blade's. Or Ben's. But somehow she knew that it was not. No, it had to be Alan, whom she was sure she loved with all her heart.

The long oppressive summer days drifted by. In September, Marie went to Barbadoes. She had received a letter from her sister saying the youngest daughter had fallen ill, and Marie went about the house looking quite distrait. Charity decided she had been wrong—selfish Marie did love her family. It was only her husband she did not love.

Alan drove Marie in the carriage to Charles Towne where she embarked. With sparkling eyes Charity watched the carriage and the baggage cart disappear down the rutted track, and that night did her hair with especial care. She managed to be in the hallway when Alan came in to dinner. He saw her standing there bright-eyed in her newly-ironed green calico dress and, after a moment's hesitation, smiled and suggested she dine with him. Happily Charity preceded him into the handsome dining room, feeling every inch the lady of the manor. Firmly she seated herself in Marie's chair. And, across the clear green bayberry tapers that burned so smokelessly in their silver holders, she smiled into Alan's eyes and they talked about plantation matters.

Through the kitchen door, when it opened for the servants to bring in the big silver trenchers of meat, Charity saw Megan's skeptical face, an eyebrow cocked at her. She returned a demure smile and turned once more to bask in Alan's attention.

Marie was gone a month. It was a month of bittersweet happiness for Charity, spent adoringly at Alan's side—she only wished it could have been a year.

For Charity was young, though thrust by hard circumstance into maturity. And in her heart still lurked a dreaming child who sought a lover—pure, unsullied, lofty, the White Knight of her childhood, a man half father, half lover, strong yet gentle. In Alan, she felt she had found that man, and all her girlish dreams rushed up unbidden to make her body tremble and her eyes be cast down suddenly in shyness.

Had she but thought about it, she would have cursed her folly. Who should know better than she not to trust a man—men had taught her that much, hadn't they?

But as the days wore on in his company and he did nothing to destroy the illusion she had first had of him, her first willful attraction deepened into devotion, so that she began to regard him almost as divine, a creature above human fears and doubts, a rock to lean against and turn to.

Had Alan come to her room in the night, she would have suffered him to do so, but the dream she carried of him in her heart would have been broken, because she began to view him in a rather pure virginal way as being without stain—a man who would not stoop to offer her less than marriage, and who was unable to do that in honor. Her feeling for Alan had definitely suffered a sea change. Like the sultry weather, it had blown hot all summer, but now with the coming of September it was lightened by cool breezes, a floating feeling. She had come to realize in Marie's absence how she really felt about him. He was to her an almost godlike being. In fact, she loved him now because he was unattainable.

A rather simple man of steady proven tastes, Alan would have been astonished to know that he had inspired this reaction in the tempestuous beauty he had rescued from the deck of the *Marybella*.

Charity's eyes dreamed more now, and Megan watched her narrowly. Charity walked along humming pensively, and when the slaves sang at night she stopped to listen, and once she found her cheeks were wet with tears at the sadness in their mellow voices. On those sultry September nights their songs reached out to her . . . songs that spoke to her of the lost, of worlds forgotten.

At those moments, Charity wondered sadly if Alan would ever be hers.

Marie returned with an ever so slight dusting of tan deepening the pink of her cheeks and emphasizing the brilliance of her amethyst eyes. Her sister's child was recovered now, she said; she had stayed until the crisis was over. When Alan asked point-blank what had been the matter with the infant, Marie shrugged helplessly and said, "One of those terrible tropical fevers—who knows why they strike? But she's well now." She put both hands on Alan's shoulders and looked up into his face. "It's all right now, darling," she murmured, stroking the back of his neck. "I'm back."

That day Charity returned to eating in the kitchen with Megan and the dour McNabb. Through the dining room door, as it swung open for the dishes to be carried away, Charity heard Marie's low seductive laugh, heard her indolent voice say, "I know it's early, Alan, but . . . could we retire early tonight?" and his enthusiastic reply.

Jealousy struck like a knife turning in her heart. And now she knew it had been lurking there all the time, waiting for Marie to return—like a tooth that had stopped aching for a while. She had had a respite—a dreaming respite—with Marie in Barbadoes, but now Marie was back and her life was blasted apart.

Lally, who had been abruptly dismissed by Marie just before her departure ("That girl has stolen my best chemise—I'm sure of it!") had not been replaced and Charity found herself spending more and more time dressing and combing Marie and less and less time sitting on the high stool working on the books and accounts. Alan, Charity realized bitterly, was putty in his wife's hands. Though he saw Charity's distress, he turned away. When she complained that the accounts were getting behind, he mumbled something about Marie needing her. It was as if their wonderful September had never been. She was back where she started—little better than a ladies' maid to arrogant Marie.

CHAPTER 30

In mid-November Marie suddenly decided to give a huge ball at Magnolia Barony. It would be held at the end of the month and everyone who was anyone would come. The servants sighed, Megan cursed under her breath. Alan, as expected, acquiesced and slaves were dispatched with invitations to upriver planters, some of whom would glide down to the party on pirogues, while the others would stay as houseguests at Magnolia Barony or go on into Charles Towne and stay with friends there.

Still deeply in love with Alan, Charity felt resentful at this further squandering of his money in view of his precarious financial situation. She watched as the meats were brought in—great hams and sides of beef and venison, turkeys and other wild game. At Magnolia Barony, like so many of the other plantations, an Indian servant was kept whose sole duty it was to hunt and bring back game for the plantation table. Their Indian was overworked these days. In the plantation kitchen, Megan and the house slaves toiled to concoct delicacies for the impending event.

Remembering the great ball at Daarkenwyck—and with a wild thrill the insolent Roger Derwent—Charity wondered if she would be invited to this one. Just in case, she went in to Charles Towne and with her small wages purchased ribbons and new white lace for her chemise sleeves and neck, and a length of pumpkin-colored cotton satin. She would have preferred a length of rich gold brocade but could not afford it, since she had but recently bought new shoes and a chemise. Borrowing a needle and thread from Megan, who helped pin her up, she managed—with many pin prickings and stabbed fingers—to complete the dress two days before the ball. The dress was copied from one of the little fashion dolls that had been sent over from London. Megan, who liked Charity, contributed a gay yellow silk embroidered petticoat and made bawdy comments about the low-cut neckline that displayed the top of Charity's white breasts. But when the left sleeve didn't quite match the right, Megan said, "Here, let me," and corrected it. Charity thanked Megan gratefully. If she was ever to catch Alan's eye, surely this ball would be the place to do it.

It was a blow to learn the following day that she was not to come downstairs for the dancing, but was to "help the ladies arrange their hair and put on their ball gowns above stairs, and remain on call with smelling salts and so on." This decree of Marie's was handed down casually in front of Alan, who never turned a hair but continued his preoccupied study of some papers. Charity forgave him for not seeing her disappointment and taking her part. She told herself that a ball to Alan was a thing beneath his notice, and went back to her room and rocked with misery. She could hardly bear to look at her new dress, for she would not be wearing it.

The day of the ball Marie still had not decided which of several handsome new dresses she would wear. At teatime, she told Charity in a peremptory voice that she would require her help while she tried on the dresses and studied her reflection in the mirror to decide which gown was most becoming. Still smarting from the fact that she would not be in attendance at the dance, Charity made her way silently upstairs after breakfast and stood looking out the window of her room. Clear and sunny. Lucky Marie had been blessed with perfect weather for her party. Although Marie had not specified a time for her "trying on," Charity decided bitterly that she had better get it over with. Soon guests would be arriving and she would have other work to do.

In her soft house slippers, which she had fashioned

from a piece of old velvet in order to save her new shoes, she walked downstairs not making a sound on the thick oak flooring. The door of Marie's bedroom stood slightly ajar and, without bothering to knock, she pushed it open.

Across the room from her Marie was studying her jewels and the sight of them took Charity's breath away. A lower drawer of a tall cherry chest stood open and Marie was bent over a handsomely carved coffer that sparkled with diamonds and rubies and emeralds. As Charity watched, Marie lifted a diamond necklace lovingly, letting it flow like sparkling water through her fingers. Charity assumed that Marie was trying to decide which pieces to wear. But when she became aware of Charity's interested gaze, Marie swung around and, for a moment, looked trapped.

"You did not knock!" Marie accused.

"The door was ajar," protested the bewildered Charity.

Marie flung the jewels back into the coffer, slammed shut the lid and almost hurled it into the lower drawer which she kicked shut with her foot. "Insolent!" she cried. "Always insolent! I don't know why I put up with such insolence!"

Charity, her own nerves rubbed raw, was about to tell Marie there'd be no need to put up with it any longer, she was leaving, when Alan came in and she bit back the words.

Suddenly Marie changed her tack. "I have a terrible headache," she moaned. "Oh, Alan—all these people coming and I have to have a headache." She sank down, pressing her fingers against her temple. Charity watched as Alan, moving toward Marie, asked in a solicitous voice if he could do anything to help. Marie was already acting out a little charade which would end up with a sick headache that night, Charity assumed, and gave Marie a scornful glance.

Still meek, Marie said, "Alan, I have decided to wear my amethysts. And the chemise trimmed in silver lace. It should look well spilling out of the sleeves of the mauve brocade with silver threads, don't you think? I

335

really have not the strength to try on more than one dress."

"Charity will help you," soothed Alan, and at his beseeching glance, Charity came forward, unable to do otherwise under the circumstances. In silence she went to the big wardrobe, took out the mauve brocade and brought it to Marie. She helped her dress and skillfully arranged her hair. Marie's beautiful face pouted at her. "It isn't right," she said fretfully. "Comb it out and do it again."

With difficulty Charity controlled her rage and redid Marie's hair, then left silently and went upstairs to her room. Once again she had been reminded how far she sat below the salt. For a moment she cursed her clever fingers that could arrange other women's hair, then realized that her skill could be even better employed on herself and with shaking fingers arranged her own coiffure, enjoying the reflection in the mirror of her sweet rebellious mouth and snapping topaz eyes.

Though she was not going to the dance, Charity decided she would wear her new dress anyway. She had just finished dressing as the first guests were beginning to arrive. She looked out to see them strolling across the lawns from their pirogues, alighting from carriages; the women's big-skirted dresses bright splashes of color like huge tropical flowers swaying on the lawn, the men almost as colorful with their gold and silver braid and glittering satins and brocades. As Charity went downstairs, she met Marie coming out of the dining room after making a last inspection of the silver before she went to greet her guests. At sight of Charity, Marie paused and frowned.

"That dress is hardly suitable for a servant," she muttered. "It's cut much too low."

Charity's low-cut bodice rose and fell with rage. She was well aware that whenever an attractive man appeared, Marie had always sent her on some errand away from the house. It was clear to her that Marie intended to occupy the center of the stage—always. Without competition.

Squarely Charity faced her tormentor. "It's too late

336

to do anything about it," she said with studied insolence. "Unless you'd prefer me not to help the ladies
with their dressing. My other clothes are badly
worn."

Marie bit her lip. "Then you must assist as you are,"
she snapped. "But for God's sake, pull up that bodice.
You're near coming out!"

Pretending to pull up the bodice, Charity sailed
past her toward the door.

"Upstairs," ordered Marie brusquely. "You can help
the guests who have already arrived to unpack."

"I feel faint." Charity paused and gave Marie a
studied look. "I must get a breath of air first."

Having thus crossed swords with her employer's
wife, Charity went on out the front door and strolled
pensively about the long verandah, watching the
guests arrive. She was happily aware of Marie's mur-
derous glance as the eyes of the approaching gentlemen wandered alertly to the girl whose pale gold hair
was highlighted by her yellow silk petticoat and pumpkin gown.

A girl to whom they would not be introduced, Charity thought bitterly. A girl in a pumpkin-colored dress
who would be gone like Cinderella before the musicians struck a note. A girl with whom they would
never dance a measure or exchange a pleasantry.

Chastened by her situation, she went back indoors
and trudged upstairs to "help the ladies."

Upstairs was a madhouse. Many of the upriver
planters' wives and daughters, who had arrived with
their dresses in trunks, had brought their own maids
to attend them. The maids giggled, they chattered, they
got underfoot. Some of the maids were penniless
French Huguenot girls, lucky to have made their escape from the Terror in France; others were round-
eyed black women in bright flounced cottons who
had done this many times before and looked forward
to the occasion as an opportunity to see their friends
and relatives from other plantations.

With what composure she could muster, Charity
took control. She learned that Megan had assigned the

337

rooms. The "ladies" would be sleeping packed two and three to a bed in the big second floor bedrooms. The younger ones were assigned to trundle beds which would be pulled out at night. But the maids were to be crammed into the attic, some of them on mattresses on the floor. The "gentlemen" were to be quartered downstairs in makeshift beds after the frivolities ended—and the overflow would go back in a covey of carriages to Charles Towne.

Caught up in a sea of swirling petticoats, with maids running about trying to unpack amid angry cries as hurrying ladies barked their shins against hastily opened trunks set on the floor, Charity tried to make order out of the madness. She combed hair—on heads that would not stay still as they turned from side to side to gossip. She pinned on ribbons and helped pull petticoats over too-large bosoms and fiercely tightened sashes around protesting waistlines. By the time the music struck up she was exhausted and sank down grimly to await the arrival of the first lady who—her circulation impaired by her tight waist—would succumb to heat and require the smelling salts.

But Charity's hair clung damply to her neck and her new dress stuck to her so, that she decided to risk Marie's displeasure again by taking a turn around the dark lawn. Leaving the churning group of maids—who would surely be able to deal with whatever rent gowns or attacks of the vapors might arise—she made her way downstairs.

At the foot of the stairs stood a little knot of people. Marie, a vision in silvery lace and mauve brocade, was among them, but she had her back to Charity and so could not immediately banish her upstairs. They were talking animatedly and drinking champagne from the tall crystal goblets that had arrived with the last shipment of goods the extravagant Marie had ordered from England. The champagne had doubtless been smuggled in from France, Charity decided.

An oldish gentleman Charity recognized as Dr. Cavendish was talking to Marie as Charity reached them. His legs were encased—as they always were—

in voluminous old-fashioned "rhinegrave" trousers, but he had vast estates upriver so everybody overlooked his eccentricities.

"The lights of London will shine ne'er so bright as the candles of Magnolia Barony," he was saying gallantly, as Charity reached them.

"Then nothing will dissuade you from taking the *Gull* and leaving us?" cried Marie on a note of mock despair. "How will we pass the winter without your company?"

"As I told ye last April, I'll be taking the *Gull* when she sails, and that's Saturday with the tide. But the ten thousand pounds I was taking has dwindled to five."

"Oh, and how is that?"

Charity paused to listen.

"'Tis for a friend upriver I'm carrying the money to pay off his son's gaming debts in London. But the lad writes he's had a bit of luck lately and won some back. So I'll be taking five thousand pounds to buy the lad out of trouble—and bringing him back with me."

"You'd better be careful, carrying so much money," laughed Marie, "that these cursed pirates don't take it from you!"

"They'll not, they'll not. As I told you, twill be in the false bottom of a most disreputable wooden chest—no respectable pirate would be wanting it!"

"Unless they sink you and the disreputable chest goes to the bottom!" Marie continued to tease him.

"Ah, that's why I'm sailing on the *Gull,* even though she's going first to Barbadoes, which is not a place I want to visit," said Dr. Cavendish triumphantly. "But the *Gull*'s captain is a friend of mine and a sensible fellow. If he sees the Jolly Roger hoisted and they fire a shot across his bows, he'll stop. And as all know, these pirates are out for gain, not blood— they'll let us go quietly."

At this there was a storm of protest, but Charity moved on. Dr. Cavendish and his dangerous excursion into pirate-infested waters held no interest for her.

All the doors and windows had been opened to

their widest extent to admit the breezes, and Charity, slipping out one, walked disconsolately down the lawn toward the river.

She turned as she heard a step behind her suddenly. One of the gentlemen had followed her from the house.

His elegant clothes were of pink satin of a shade Charity preferred on women. His periwig was large and correct and very tightly curled. She was sure he must wax his mustache to give it such a stiff pointed appearance. But his face was what interested her most. Long and slightly sallow in complexion, with heavy lids that drooped over dark brown eyes. Watchful eyes, and a slightly sneering mouth.

"Ah," he said. "In the moonlight here under the trees, I thought you were someone else."

His narrowed eyes and half smile told her that he would willingly accept her as a substitute. She glared at him. His name was René du Bois, and she had seen him on several occasions when he had come with groups to the plantation. But she had never liked his face or the calculating way he had of stripping women with his eyes.

"I am myself," she said quietly, "and no one else." And started back toward the house.

Idly she wondered for whom he waited, lingering out there under the trees. On impulse she decided to find out, and instead of returning, made her way into a tangle of shrubbery where she could see him standing in the fitful moonlight by the river bank, a wiry arrogant figure, foppishly well dressed.

As the moon went behind a bank of clouds, she cursed the darkness for there was a swift swish of running footsteps across the lawn and she heard René's whispered, "Here, chérie, under these branches where we will not be discovered!"

At that moment, Charity regretted her decision to stay, for the couple were coming in her direction. They halted only a few feet from her and, in the darkness, she heard René's low laugh, heard him say, "Ah, these hooks on the bodice—they are hard to undo!"

Charity's face reddened. She had not intended to be a Peeping Tom—only from idle curiosity to identify the woman who would creep into the darkness to meet René. And yet she dared not leave or she would surely be discovered.

Now, from under its cloud cover, the white moon appeared again and through the sheltering bushes Charity could see them plainly.

It was Marie! Skirts up, bodice undone, she lay on her back looking up at the thin dark Frenchman resting on his arms above her.

"Ah, René, René," she sighed. "If only I could be with you more. . . ."

"Ah, but you could, *chérie*." With a supple motion his body closed with hers and he pressed his lips against her ear, her throat. Lazily she pushed him away, turned on her side, staring moodily toward the bushes and causing Charity hastily to move back, lest she be seen.

"No, René, it is not possible," Marie said moodily.

"There is always your long-lost brother," he said.

"I cannot send Alan on another wild goose chase," she protested, and Charity's pulse quickened. Wild goose chase? She bent closer, more afraid she would not catch the next words than she was of being discovered.

René looked surprised. "You have used this ploy before?"

"Twice before. Once I told him I had a letter from Williamsburg. Another time from Boston."

"Ah," he said. "Then you have had other lovers before me?"

She twisted away from him impatiently. "Of course. Many. Did you think you were the first?"

He caught her wrist in such a painful grip that she winced. "No, *chérie,* I did not. I had only hoped I would be the last."

"Of course you are the last, René. What do you take me for?" Again she tried to twist away from him. "You're hurting me," she said sharply.

He gave a low laugh but kept his cruel hold on her wrist.

"I have never taken you for anything but what you are," he said. "Completely desirable, completely irresistible." He kissed her again, then his head came up, his eyes glittering. "But tell me, the flame must have burned bright with these other lovers that you would go to—shall we say 'equal lengths'—to rid yourself of your burdensome husband for a time so that you might linger on the grass with them?"

"I should never have told you," she said pettishly. "Now you will give me no peace!"

"Ah, but I would know, Marie." He twisted her arm so that she gave a low cry. "Who were they?"

"One was a—a planter who lived near here," she gasped. "He has since died. The Indians killed him. So, you have no need to be jealous of him."

"And the other?"

"Please, René, you are hurting me!"

He kept his grip. "And the other?"

"My groom!" she gasped. "The boy who took care of my horse."

He gave a sneering laugh. "So you would stoop to the servants?"

"He was not born a servant, René. He was of good blood and bound to my husband by his father in England for a period of three years—to pay his passage and give him a start in this new land and some education."

"And you supplied him with this education." His voice was heavy with irony as he let her go.

Her hand lashed across his face. "How dare you speak to me like that?" she cried. "He was handsome and homesick and I was lonely for England. Alan was busy—he neglected me."

"Yes," he said. "I begin to understand." His hands stroked her throat, wandered down to her breasts, found their way under her skirts. "You are a woman of hot blood, Marie. You cannot be packed away like winter clothing in a trunk to be taken out when needed. So, you looked about and your eyes lit on this

342

young stalwart fresh from England and you took him to your bed. Tell me, what happened to him? Is he still about?"

"No, he ran away. Before my husband returned from Boston."

"Ah, I see. This groom was a man of honor. He could not face what he had done. And do you hear from him?"

"No, never. Oh, have done with this talk, René!" she cried impatiently. "There is no one but you—no one else, ever."

"Not even your husband?" he laughed, as he lowered his body once again to hers.

"No one," she murmured brokenly, almost with grief in her voice. "No one. You have destroyed all men for me, René. There can never be another."

They were silent then, their bodies straining against each other in desperate passion, and the only sound was the wind sighing through the trees and an occasional moan almost of pain from the lovers on the grass.

Charity was staggered by what she had heard. White-faced and wrathful, she turned away from what she had seen.

Marie—the lying cheat! She had duped her husband, told him lies, sent him on wild goose chases, had a succession of lovers. Wild with rage, Charity waited until René rolled over on his side and Marie sat up, hurriedly fastening the hooks of her bodice.

"Do not go," René said lazily.

"Oh, René," she whispered. "I told Alan I felt faint and would lie down for a while upstairs. But if I am gone too long he will go up to see what is wrong. Please, René, I must get back to my guests. To stay is to court discovery."

Reluctantly, he let her go and she hurried back through the trees toward the kitchen door, while he sauntered back toward the front door. Charity waited impatiently and then followed. When she reached the house she saw René standing in the front door smiling at her with narrowed eyes. Her face reddened as she brushed past him and went upstairs.

There the bedrooms were as busy as coach stops, with big-skirted women jostling each other and maids colliding as corsets were loosened for a "breath of air" and needles were swiftly applied to burst seams and torn stepped-on hems. But the cyclone of skirts and petticoats swirling about her seemed unimportant now. As did the fact that she had not been invited to the ball.

She had seen René and Marie, and René knew that she had seen them. Would he tell Marie?

The next day, when Charity combed out Marie's hair, she was sure that he had. Silently Charity wielded the silver comb, and when she had finished, the scented woman in the lace combing jacket turned and considered her with a look of cool hard resentment.

"The other ladies will need your services," Marie said. "Be about it." Not all the guests had departed; many still lingered to enjoy Alan Bellingham's lavish hospitality.

In silent fury, Charity left to see to the other ladies.

She had no doubt that Marie knew and would take appropriate measures. What those measures would be she could not even guess, but if Marie thought that Charity would inform on her to Alan, she would stop at nothing to get rid of her.

Three days later Charity finally learned what it could mean to threaten the beautiful Marie.

All the guests had departed by then and Alan had gone in to Charles Towne by pirogue. When he returned, in the midst of a drenching storm, he brought with him the mail from Barbadoes.

Alan rushed into the house dripping rainwater and, taking off his periwig, he shook it out quickly. Charity smiled. She much preferred his own hair, which was the same ash-blond shade as his wig. With a light-hearted greeting she walked past him and made a swift run across the wet lawn to McNabb's office.

She had just climbed on the high stool near Mc-

Nabb's desk to begin working on the accounts when there was a noise at the door.

She looked up as a little black face peered in the door and a piping voice said she was wanted at the big house.

Arriving wet and panting after her second run across the lawn, Charity shook out her wet skirts like a spaniel shaking itself. She found Marie and Alan in the long double living room. Both of the great fireplaces were lit and the room was cozy and bright. Soaked almost to the skin, Charity sneezed, destroying the dignity of her entrance.

"You wanted me?" she asked, noting that Marie was regarding her with a wolfish smile.

Alan frowned. "Yes, we do." He looked very handsome today, even though the rain had streaked his velvet coat. "My wife heard from her sister in Barbadoes."

Charity waited, thinking: *And now she'll go running off to Barbadoes again, but how does that concern me?*

"The children's governess has eloped," said Marie. "It is a difficult situation since there is no one to replace her."

Alan cleared his throat. "We hoped you would be willing to go out there and replace the governess until—"

"Until a more suitable governess can be sent out from England," said Marie flatly.

Alan looked unhappy. "Of course, if you feel you don't—"

"Nonsense," Marie cut in crisply. "Charity would enjoy the change. Barbadoes is lovely this time of year. I only wish I could go myself but—" she sighed —"I've been away so much this year." Her gaze on Charity was expectant.

Charity looked at Alan. "Don't you need me here?"

"Oh, we can make do," he assured her, "until you return. It cannot be for long. Four or five months at the outside."

An eternity without him! Charity looked stricken.

Her gaze flew to Marie. No help could be expected there. Marie was looking at her with steady unreadable eyes.

"We'd be awfully grateful," said Alan in a humble tone.

Charity melted. "I'll be glad to do it," she said. "Shall I write to you when their new governess arrives?"

"My sister will keep us advised," said Marie lightly. "But you can write and keep us informed of the children's well-being. I am very attached to them, you know."

Charity knew. More attached to her sister's children than to her own husband apparently.

"When am I to leave?"

"On Saturday," said Marie promptly. "You will sail on the *Gull*."

"Isn't that rather soon?" protested Alan. "I'd like her to go over the accounts with McNabb first."

"No, Dr. Cavendish is sailing on the *Gull*," insisted Marie. "He can look after Charity and make sure she reaches my sister safely. I'll send word to him today—I'm sure he'll be glad to do this small favor for me. You must arrange for her passage, Alan."

All the way to Barbadoes in the company of a man in his seventies. A delightful prospect for a twenty-year-old girl. Charity gave Marie a sour look and went off to her room. As she climbed the stairs, she looked back to see Alan squaring his shoulders in an effort to express his unconcern.

The next day, the weather turned perfect with clear sunny skies. The magnolia leaves were a dark shiny green and the lawn had never seemed more lush. Heartbroken at being sent away, Charity walked about during the two days she had left, moving idly across the lawns, strolling through the rose garden. At the landing she lingered, wistfully watching an occasional pirogue glide by on the sluggish river.

Magnolia Barony had never seemed so beautiful as it did now that she was leaving it.

On Friday night, with tightly compressed lips,

Charity packed her pitifully few belongings—the old mended dress and chemise, the brave new pumpkin-colored dress and stockings and ribbons she had bought with her earnings.

On Saturday morning with her head held high and her expression unconcerned, in case Marie should be watching, Charity sauntered down the stairs with everything she owned in the little casket. She wore new shoes and chemise, but her dress was the same one in which she had arrived—the green cotton Alan had bought for her on board the *Marybella*. She was leaving as she had come—with practically nothing. At the doorway, Megan gave her a hug and pressed on her the shawl Charity had so often borrowed. "You might be cold," she whispered, and Charity felt her throat constrict.

Marie slept late and did not wish her goodbye, for which she was grateful.

Riding into Charles Towne in the carriage beside Alan, Charity was sad and silent and resentful. Alan had not spoken up for her. He had let Marie push her into this journey—indeed he had abetted it. Well, once arrived in Barbadoes she would stay there! She'd show him! She'd find another job—perhaps as governess to some other planter's children—and forget him. No, she couldn't do that. She knew she'd never forget him. . . .

Tears trembled on her dark gold lashes, and she turned her head quickly so Alan wouldn't see them. On both sides the green clumps of palmettos were closing in. Just as life had closed in on her. Forcing her out, and onward . . . ever onward.

Beside her, Alan sat keeping his steady blue eyes solely on the driver of the carriage. He was outfitted in lavender silk, his shoulders broad in his fitted coat, his knee breeches very tight and modish, his lavender silk-stockinged legs almost brushing her own.

Months . . . *months* without him. She could hardly bear to think about it. But she knew that wherever she went she would always carry him in her heart.

At the docks Alan commended her to Dr. Cavendish's care and bade her a friendly goodbye—almost as if he were an elder brother who didn't know her very well.

Her heart bled.

Then he was gone and she was aboard the *Gull*. It was a good thing her eyes had been wide open when she sailed into Charles Towne harbor or she would never have seen it, for her eyes were filled with tears that misted her view of it as she left.

On the *Gull* she found herself sharing a decent cabin with a stocky little red-haired English girl named Polly Dawes. Polly's hands were red and workworn, but her smile was bright and her manner sprightly. Like Dr. Cavendish, she was going to England by way of Barbadoes—not because it was the shortest route but because the *Gull*'s captain had often dined with her former employer and she preferred to sail with him. Charity liked Polly and was sorry Polly wouldn't be staying in Barbadoes. Cheering up was what she needed and Polly's open ingenuous face and infectious laugh were good for her.

The third morning out brought disaster.

As Charity went out on deck she realized at once that something was wrong. A grim-faced captain was issuing orders to his crew, a desperate note in his voice. Everything was hurry and confusion. Looking aloft, she saw above her the enormous billowing shrouds and her eyes widened. Surely they would capsize, carrying so much canvas!

Dr. Cavendish stood by the rail. She hurried over and asked him what was wrong.

"That ship," he said, pointing. "We know not whether she's merchantman or pirate but tis plain she's overtaking us."

Even as he pointed, Charity saw the lean yellow ship, her great sails billowing too.

"Can ye see what flag she's flying?" he asked. "My old eyes are none so good."

"French, I think—no, wait, they've hoisted another. It's black."

"Plain black?"

"No, there's some kind of white streak on it."

Cavendish groaned. "A white oar on a black ground. Tis Captain Court's flag then. We're for it, I'm afraid."

Polly had joined them and heard his last remark. "Pirates!" she gasped. "Oh, lord ha' mercy! We'll be taken!"

"Maybe we can outrun them," said Charity, eyeing the billowing shrouds above.

"No, she's closing," said Cavendish regretfully. "You ladies had better get below."

"Why?" demanded Charity. "I heard you say yourself the captain of this ship would have the common sense to stop if he met a pirate!"

Cavendish looked upset. "Ah, so I did, so I did. But one never knows when a—" He paused as a warning shot came across the bows. "They're telling us to stop," he said unhappily.

Everyone turned to look silently at the captain. For a moment he wavered. Charity could see from his face that he wanted to fight for his ship. Then his gaze passed over the two women and the elderly doctor and, sighing, he gave the order to heave to.

Charity and Polly stayed on deck as the grappling hooks came over and their ship was boarded by what seemed a disreputable pack of scoundrels. The men carried cutlasses and pistols and spoke a medley of tongues. All were bronzed by the sun, and their yellow-hulled ship looked as if it had seen action recently for part of its poop was shattered. Methodically, the pirates went about breaking into barrels and boxes and chests, transferring what they wanted to the yellow vessel.

One of the men, carrying a heavy box, barged into Polly and as she fell another caught her in his arms. She looked up into that wild bearded face and fainted. With a shrug, the fellow pushed her toward Charity, muttering something in a language Charity did not understand. Carefully she eased Polly to the deck and looked up in time to see Dr. Cavendish's horrified expression as one of the pirates broke open his "disreputable little wooden chest." At the direction of his captain, the man knocked through its false bottom and revealed the five thousand pounds the doctor had thought so skillfully hidden.

The pirate captain, who was French and ill-tempered, looked at the money and said in heavily accented English, "A man who carries so much wealth with him must have more at home. You can ransom yourself for a like sum, monsieur."

The doctor quailed.

"As can you, mademoiselle," he added ironically to Charity.

"But we—we have no money, Polly and I," faltered Charity.

The Frenchman gave a nasty laugh. "Still you will be worth something. We will sell you to the highest bidder in Tortuga."

Like the doctor, Charity fell silent. Polly regained consciousness and Charity helped her up. Along with the doctor, the two women were transferred to the yellow ship. There they watched from the rail as the crew of the *Gull* was loaded into longboats and forced to row themselves toward the mainland. As they left, the pirate captain waved a cutlass at them and shouted in his strong French accent, "Tell Charles Towne that Captain Court sends them greetings!" Then he threw back his big head and laughed.

Beside him, nearly in tears, the old doctor was plucking at the captain's sleeve and crying, "You must let the women go with the crew, Captain Court! God's life, man, would you harm the women?"

The tall pirate turned on him with contempt. "Take your hand from my sleeve," he said in French, "or I will cut off your arm. I am not Captain Court—I am Captain St. Clair."

The doctor did not speak French. Hastily Charity translated and he let go of Captain St. Clair's sleeve and fell silent, his face ashen.

A moment later there was a wail from the longboats—the pirates had tossed several flaming torches into the *Gull*'s shrouds. As the rakish yellow ship sped away from her, those shrouds burst into flame and soon the whole tall ship became a pillar of fire against the hard brilliant blue of the sky. Charity watched this wanton destruction with horror and fascination, until the *Gull* was only a bright smudge in the distance, soon to dip below the level of the water.

Polly asked hoarsely, "What are they going to do with us?"

"They're going to sell us," Charity said, amazed that her voice could sound so calm. "In Tortuga."

BOOK IV

The Caribbean 1687–1688

CHAPTER 31

Unceremoniously the two women were thrust into a cabin, and kept cooped up there the whole of the way to Tortuga. The pirate captain obviously did not trust such valuable cargo among his men. Gloomy and afraid, they huddled together to keep their mind off the fate that awaited them. They talked. Soon Charity knew Polly Dawes's whole life story, and felt she had known Polly all her life.

While working as a chambermaid in London, Polly had been unfairly accused of theft at a bakeshop. The real culprit had escaped, and there was no one to speak up for Polly. She had languished in gaol for a while and then been deported to the Colonies. Of her seven years' indenture she had served but three when her employer, a kindly old Scot, died. In his will, he set all his servants and slaves, both black and white, free and left them each a small sum of money. Polly's inheritance was just enough to buy her passage back to the little town in the west of England where she was born and where, she confidently believed, her Jack would still be waiting. He'd had a widowed mother and six little sisters to look after, and they'd agreed that Polly would go to London and save her money until they had enough to marry.

Charity's eyes grew damp at this recital, for with every creak of the ship that carried them into tropical waters she felt sure that neither she nor Polly would ever see England again.

Nor would she ever see Alan again. That was what hurt most of all.

When at last they anchored in Cayona Bay, the two

355

women were brought, blinking, up into the sunlight of the deck. Before them lay the island of Tortuga baking in the sun. All at once, Polly swayed on her feet, her cheeks flushed and her eyes unnaturally bright, as she clung to Charity.

"This woman needs a doctor," cried Charity, but she was ignored. The two women were helped over the side into the longboat, and they settled down together as strong backs bent to row them to the shore. Neither Charity nor Polly observed the rugged upthrust rocks of the island's natural citadel. Looming above them over the sprawling town, the massive gray bulk of the Mountain Fort with its fixed guns pointed toward the sea made no impression at all. Nor did they really notice the crowded quay with its fishy smell, its piles of fruit and merchandise, its many-tongued babble of swarming humanity as Dutch, French, and English traders rubbed elbows with golden-skinned Caribs and black Africans and swarthy cutlass-sporting buccaneers of every country. Above them the tropical sun burned down—but they hardly felt it.

On a bouncing cart, the two women were carried through the town amid catcalls and cheers and an occasional sympathetic look. Dr. Cavendish had disappeared before they left the ship. Polly was near fainting, and Charity felt like a felon indeed on that humiliating journey. Face hot with shame, she refused to look at those who mocked, but kept her head high. Her eyes lifted to observe the Spanish style buildings, built with heavy iron grillwork—to keep the thieves out as well as in, she thought with a certain amount of irony.

At last the cart jolted to a halt on the rough cobbles before a small building with wooden shutters. Ushered —rather, pushed into the dark stuffy interior, they passed a number of disconsolate Spaniards sitting on the floor, and made their way up a rickety stair to a room where the shutters were open and they could look out and view the sunny harbor studded with ships.

A crone with straggly gray hair came in with a pitcher of water and they drank thirstily. Charity

356

thought the old woman had a kind face and spoke to her. The crone answered readily enough, saying she was the woman who "tended" the female prisoners, emptied the slops and brought them food and water until they could be sold. Charity had no intention of staying to be sold, and having drunk, was making for the door when she noticed the burly guard standing at ease outside. His eyes moved over her body lustfully and she drew back.

"E won't hurt you, dearie," soothed the crone in a sing-song voice. "E's here more to keep *them* out than *you* in!" She cackled at her own joke. "After all, where's to go if ye did escape this room? Tis an island, dearie, and evil Spanish ships be all about once you leave the harbor." She added that it was too bad Captain Court's *Sea Witch* was not in harbor, for he'd buy her sure—he always bought the captive English women. In a hoarse whisper she confided that most of the English women had been rescued from Spanish ships and "weren't worth much," having been ill-used. Still, were he here he'd surely have saved Charity and Polly from those who'd bid heavy to put them in the brothels.

Charity winced. "And the Spanish women," she asked, "what happened to them, if Captain Court didn't buy them?"

The crone, her eyes gleaming suddenly evil, said that Spanish women were another matter. Of course Captain Court—and other buccaneers, too, for that matter—had in his Articles with his men that he was the sole judge of which captives to hold for ransom, which to sell and which to release. He'd never brought in but one Spanish woman—all the rest he'd sent in longboats to the nearest Spanish port.

"And that one?" asked Charity.

"Ah, she were a willing prisoner." The old woman laughed. "She did lean toward him as she walked; she seduced him with her black eyes. Tis said Captain Court was happy the whilst he had her—which wasn't very long."

"What happened to her?"

The old woman frowned. "None rightly know, except that Captain Court's housekeeper did say that he got a letter and sat a long time thinking, and then went into the Spanish woman's bedroom. She could hear them shouting, and then Court gave a yell and the woman did run out looking scared—she'd taken a knife to Court and stabbed him. He did lay near death for two weeks, but being strong as leather he mended good as new."

"And the woman?"

Her informant shrugged. "She disappeared. Naught was heard from her after that. Perhaps he had her thrown to the barracuda, or perhaps one of his men slit her gullet for her." She spat. "Spanish filth, not to appreciate a man like Captain Court!"

Charity shivered. The prospect of being saved by "a man like Captain Court" seemed vastly unappealing. Nor did her chances appear much better from the men who swaggered by in the narrow street below, some with a single gold earring dangling from one ear. All were heavily armed, with swords and cutlasses banging against their thighs as they walked, and wicked-looking knives and pistols thrust into belts and wide sashes. Many of them bore deep scars, some were one-legged or limping or had an arm bound up or a head bandaged. Often as not, her informant told her, these wounds were received in tavern brawls instead of in their nefarious activities upon the seas.

It was announced that the auction would not be held until the next afternoon. Charity, leaning on the window sill, brooded about who would buy her. She was roused by the sound of chattering teeth. In a corner Polly huddled, shaking with cold in the tropical heat. Minutes later she was burning up with fever.

When the crone brought their next meal, Charity asked if there wasn't a doctor around. Tomorrow, the crone said. There'd be a ship's doctor or two coming around to the auction. She looked at Polly with interest. Everyone had fevers here, she shrugged. These islands were full of plagues. She'd had fever herself more than once; the girl would probably get over it all alone. And there were worse things than fevers, she added darkly. For, some like that Captain St. Clair, the pirate who'd captured Polly and Charity, had never felt anything for any woman; only the length of his blade piercing human flesh ever thrilled *him*. St. Clair was unpopular and he knew it, and his crew had grumbled because they'd not been allowed this pretty duo for their playthings, the old woman told Charity. It was rumored that St. Clair had bragged in a tavern that he was going to buy Polly and Charity as gifts for his fine crew! The crone added that she hoped the story wasn't true for the last time this was done, the unfortunate young woman had survived but two weeks, having been torn to pieces in a bloody fight in the forecastle over whose "turn" it was to rape her.

Charity's knees went weak with horror. After all she'd been through, to come to this!

"No call to worry yet," soothed the stringy-haired crone. The brothel keepers would most likely outbid St. Clair, she explained. For St. Clair, along with his other vices, was known to be tight.

When the woman left, Polly asked weakly what they'd been muttering about and Charity hadn't the heart to tell her. Charity was unable to eat her supper, and spent a sleepless night lying on a pallet on the floor. The next morning the crone rushed in joyfully, almost spilling the gruel she carried.

"Ah, ye're in luck," she crowed. "Look—tis the *Sea Witch!* Captain Court's sailing in!"

Through the window Charity could see a fast tall ship with gray sails and a black hull. It looked at first like a ghost ship, and Charity recalling that its captain's mistress had "disappeared," shuddered.

About noon another group of captives arrived; from the window Charity could see them marched in. All were Spaniards; several dejected looking men, some wounded, and three women in whom she took more interest. Two were obviously serving wenches. One had a roguish eye for every man on the street, while the other, who was very fat, plodded along dumbly. But the third was a lady of quality who held her head high and gazed about her scornfully. Her arrogant aquiline features and dark eyes spoke of centuries of Spanish nobility. She resisted furiously when they brought her in. Her mantilla was torn in the struggle and her high-backed Spanish comb fell to the floor and was crushed under a boot. She reeled backward as the door slammed. Charity, feeling pity for this arrogant daughter of Spain, tried to speak to her, but she turned her head contemptuously away and sat down in a corner alone. Charity shrugged. This one was no better than she; they would all be sold this day like so many cattle.

Charity's apprehension mounted as she saw a knot of men gathering below the window. They were a fierce-looking lot. Among them was the swaggering Captain St. Clair. Just before the guards hustled the women out, the crone hurried up to her and pointed into the crowd. "See that big man?" she asked. "That's John Ravenal, Captain Court's man—Court must've sent him to buy you." Charity saw a veritable giant standing almost a head above the crowd, a wolfish grin on his dark face. She swallowed and looked away. The guards had to help Polly to walk. Near fainting herself, Charity tried to maintain a haughty mein and face down the crowd as she was marched outside. The Spanish lady, who stalked along scowling, muttered imprecations in Spanish.

In the blazing sun the prisoners were stood one by one upon a block from which, Charity suspected, on other days black slaves from Africa were sold. Today the offerings were all white—and all Spanish save for herself and Polly.

"They ought not to be selling English women," muttered one young ruffian. "It shames me to see it."

"'Tis only St. Clair and one or two others that do it," rejoined another glumly. "Captains like Court release any English prisoners they find on Spanish ships —anyone who isn't Spanish, for that mattter. And return their women to them."

Trying not to shake, Charity watched a frowning Spaniard with a bandaged arm sold. He was a stonemason, the crowd was earnestly informed by the auctioneer—a good man to have about if you wanted to build a house.

"Is that man being sold for life?" she asked a guard.

"Nay, tis but for three years—like any other articles of indenture," she was told with a shrug. "Tis a form of ranson, y'see, for those without money."

Three years, she thought. Three years in a brothel or . . . perhaps even worse . . . "given" to that raffish pack aboard St. Clair's vessel for their enjoyment. She felt her hands tremble and clenched them to hide their weakness.

The sale dragged on. The virtues of each prisoner were extolled, but none of them brought a very high price. Plainly, human flesh was not at a premium in Tortuga.

At one point the auctioneer held up a Spanish prisoner's burly arm and pinched the muscles. "See that brawn?" he cried. "That's strength to lift!" He touched the prisoner's calf with the toe of his shoe. "And strong legs to pull and carry for you!"

"La," muttered Polly in a shaky voice. "What will they be doin' with us? Raisin' our skirts to see if we've legs under them?"

Charity didn't answer. She wanted to tell Polly it would be all right, but the words stuck in her throat. It wasn't going to be all right. How could it?

Of the women, the Spanish lady was sold first. A fresh-faced young fellow who looked for all the world like the seamen Charity remembered in Torquay, had been studying her with open admiration. Rather old-fashioned in dress, he wore no coat, a clean white ruffled shirt, a wide sash and big floppy boots. He stepped forward promptly and made the first bid.

The Spanish woman eyed him with contempt. His honest gray eyes smiled back at her. Charity thought he looked the best of the bunch, and watched as he bid eagerly—once even raising his own bid. He's bound to have her, she thought, as the auctioneer brought down his palm with a thump on the block. "Sold to Timothy Hobbs," he said, adding under his breath, "I wish you joy of her, Tim. They have long claws, those Spanish wenches."

Haughtily, Timothy Hobbs's purchase stepped down from the block and stared with loathing at her buyer. He was taken aback. With a shrug she turned her back on him, folded her arms and tapped her foot. He looked worried and stood beside her indecisively, not knowing what course to take.

Charity was propelled to the block next. She stood above the crowd in the brilliant sunlight, her bright hair—long ago having come loose from its pins— blowing in the trade winds. Her dress was untidy, her eyes dark from sleepless nights, but there was a defiance in her gaze and she held herself proudly.

Damned pirates, the lot of them—they wouldn't make *her* crawl!

The bidders went wild. Captain St. Clair, bidding for her as a "gift" to his men, was soon left out, and the brothel owners, their eyes kindling at such a boon to their trade, snapped out bids against each other so fast the auctioneer could not keep up. Two hundred pounds—three. Five hundred. Seven. Nine. At this unprecedented bidding, the crowd pressed forward. Hoping her pounding heart would not burst through her chest, Charity kept her chin lifted and looked out toward the harbor.

"One thousand!" roared a big voice.

"Ravenal bids one thousand," intoned the auctioneer. "Come on, my hearties, are you going to let Court have this fair bit of England washed up on our shores?"

"Twelve hundred!" howled a red-faced brothel owner.

There was a momentary pause. Charity swallowed.

"Captain Court bids fifteen hundred!" roared the big voice.

The brothel owner turned to glare at him. Then he looked up at Charity, standing cool and beautiful above him, and moistened his lips with his tongue. "Seventeen hundred!" he screeched and his voice cracked.

Alertly the auctioneer looked toward the big booming voice..

"Too rich for your blood, Ravenal?" he demanded.

"Eighteen," boomed the reply.

"Nineteen hundred!" screamed the brothel owner.

"Two thousand."

There was a dead stillness. The brothel man turned white and stumbled away through the crowd.

"Sold to Captain Court for two thousand pounds," said the auctioneer, slapping his palm down upon the block. "Come and pay up, Ravenal."

"I've one more yet to buy," roared the big voice.

Glad of the arm that reached out to help her from the block, Charity descended a little shakily. She had escaped the brothels and the horrors of St. Clair's ship but she had yet to face the pirate Court.

Polly's turn was next.

To her shame, Charity had forgotten all about asking for a doctor. Now she wasn't sure Polly was going to be able to stand upright on the block. Her face deeply flushed, eyes glazed, Polly swayed under the blazing tropical sun. She looked very sick and the men gazed at her uneasily. Bidding was not brisk. She was quickly knocked down to the big voice.

"Sold to Ravenal," cried the auctioneer.

"Not to Ravenal," announced the big voice. "Sold to Captain Court."

"I stand corrected," laughed the auctioneer. "Come collect your property, Ravenal. I think she's going to fall down."

"This woman is sick," cried Charity in indignation, as Polly wavered. "You surely aren't going to—"

Polly righted herself. "It's a fever," she gasped. "I did feel it coming over me on shipboard."

The big voice boomed, "Leeds, you're a doctor. Have a look at her."

A slender wiry man eased through the throng and bowed deferentially before Charity and Polly. "My name is Kirby. I'm a doctor."

Polly gave him a doubtful look.

"Even though I'm a buccaneer," he grinned, and

there was something in his sharp face to inspire confidence, "sure and I'm still a doctor." With a practiced hand, he touched Polly's forehead. "You're very hot," he muttered. "It might be best you come with me, mistress. I've got a room or two in my house that serve as an infirmary for my friends when they get themselves sliced up. I could take care of you there; there's a Frenchwoman who helps me—you'll like her." As he spoke, he was leading a doubtful Polly, who looked quite dizzy and glassy-eyed, away with him. Charity watched her go half in approval, half in dread.

"Tell Court I've taken this one to my house, John," Leeds Kirby called through that confusing hubbub of voices, the clank and clash of scabbards and sword hilts banging against each other as they jostled. Then a heavy hand fell on Charity's shoulder and she looked up and up—for the man was a giant—into that big smiling face that had looked so wolfish at a distance. Up close it seemed only a weathered English face with honest blue eyes. This man could not have looked more unlike a pirate if he had tried. Charity felt he must have but recently escaped from some woodpile, where he had been earnestly chopping wood for a buxom wife and six children.

"I'm John Ravenal, mistress," he said in that voice that matched his frame. And then more gently, "You've nothing to worry about, mistress. Tis Jeremy Court that's bought you and he's a real gentleman."

Charity found that hard to believe.

At a cry from behind her, she turned. Timothy Hobbs, the young fellow who had bought the Spanish lady, was finding he'd got a little more than he'd bargained for. He must have tired of waiting and taken her arm, for now she had scratched his face—a wicked-looking scratch that had drawn blood.

Charity held her breath. Would this fresh-faced young fellow punish his new-bought slave for that small attack? She stared at him, noting how upset he looked. His was a good English face, she thought,

364

such a face as she had often seen in Devon, on the thin side and with resolute eyes and chin.

"I but asked her would she take my arm," he cried, upset.

"She speaks only Spanish," said Charity sharply, adding in that tongue, "He only wanted to take your arm, senorita."

The Spanish lady sniffed, but Charity asked her name and learned that it was Dona Isabel de Cordoba y Hernandez. She conveyed this information to Dona Isabel's owner.

"Wouldst tell her that I intend her no mischief, m'lady?" implored the slender young buccaneer with the scratched face. "I but wish to convey her to my lodgings and set before her a good dinner."

Charity supposed that was the most either of them could hope for. She translated to Dona Isabel, who cried fiercely, "I will go with him, but if he so much as lays a hand upon my person, I will run him through with this hatpin which I carry in my bosom."

"He seems a decent fellow," cautioned Charity. "You might end up in worse hands. I wouldn't be in a hurry to run him through with a hatpin."

From Dona Isabel's cold eyes flashed a look that said in Spain honor was measured by loftier standards. But she accepted the arm proffered her, and Timothy gave Charity a brilliant smile as they departed.

Now Charity realized her giant was waiting patiently. "I will see you safe through the streets of the town," he explained. "'Tis a rough town and Captain Court would not wish you to be hurt or insulted on the way."

She was astonished. Somehow she had believed all pirates, when ashore, spent their time guzzling in filthy taverns with half-naked women, whom they bedded beneath the dirty tables.

The buccaneers of Tortuga, she was told, were not all low criminal types.

"We are the Brethren of the Coast, mistress," Ravenal explained gravely as they wound their way through the narrow twisting streets lined with Spanish style houses.

"And what does that mean?" asked Charity, still tense from the galling experience of being publicly sold like a horse or a cow.

"Why, it means we abide by rules, mistress, that we do not attack ships flying our own country's flag. We are not such as your Barbary corsairs stabbing out at all of Christendom. We are men of honor."

Although she considered this statement ludicrous in the light of his being by his own admission a buccaneer, his honest face glowed so with righteousness that she held her tongue and tried to keep up with his long stride as they made their way over the cobbles. Overhead the sun beat down fiercely. She could feel her green dress sticking to her, and the men who passed them—many of them were such as to strike terror into the heart of any honest citizen—stripped her boldly with their eyes, although she observed that they gave a wide berth to her stalwart companion. Obviously, Captain Court had given his new purchase a more than adequate escort.

There was some consolation in that, but her heart was still beating wildly when they reached a house that stood higher than the others and looked out over the harbor. The big square Spanish house was two stories tall and built of stone. Its first floor windows were protected by heavy iron grille as well as shutters, and the upper casements reached the floor behind iron lacework balconies.

At any other time she would have appreciated the beauty of the house. Today she did not.

Ravenal knocked, and a servant appeared. With trepidation, Charity accompanied the blond giant through a heavily carved nail-studded door and into a cool high-ceilinged hall that seemed dark after the brilliant sunlight. Following the clomp of Ravenal's heavy boots into a beautiful inner courtyard in which a pinkish stone fountain tinkled, she blinked as the bright sunlight, shafting down through the waving palms of the patio, struck her eyes.

"I will leave you now, mistress," Ravenal said

gravely. "Captain Court's servants will attend to your needs."

"Is he not here?" she asked, bewildered.

"Nay, he has business elsewhere. I doubt you'll see him tonight, but if you do twill no doubt be late. I wouldn't wait to dine with him."

Charity gave him a look of complete amazement. She had been bought in a pirate's market and by now she had expected to be fighting off her purchaser tooth and nail. Instead, she was being treated as if she were the honored guest of a Colonial planter.

She told herself suspiciously it was too good to last, and when the gentle-looking young servant girl reappeared again—no doubt to escort her to some dark room that could be securely locked from the outside —Charity waved her imperiously away. The girl went, looking bewildered. Still nervous, Charity paced about the courtyard, which was paved with beautiful tiles— stolen, she guessed, from a ship conveying them to the Colonies. Curiously she looked about her at her new prison. Two-tiered collonaded galleries encircled the courtyard, and an outside stone stairway led upward to the second floor. The pillars were of uniform round stone—booty also, she guessed, being brought to New Spain, as was the handsome iron grillwork balustrade that connected the pillars.

In some ways, the house rivaled Magnolia Barony. It was not so rawly new, for one thing. The doors, for instance, must have been seized in the sack of some Spanish Colonial town; they were richly ornate, and might have been torn from the dwelling of a rich merchant or even a Colonial governor, to grace the home of a swaggering buccaneer.

That Court was a swaggering buccaneer, Charity had no doubt. He would arrive shortly to claim her as his prize. The thought made her leap up from the stone bench where she had rested for the moment, and pace about again.

She considered the possibilities. Running away would be difficult. This was an island surrounded by a deceptively beautiful sea—she could not walk

367

away from her jailer on land as she had done in Dynestown. Nor was there a laughing Tom Blade to come to her rescue. Her heart hurt a little at the thought of him. The *Gull* had been taking her to Barbadoes; she had assented to the journey partly hoping to see him again—if he was still alive. He had been after all her first love.

She returned to her situation. If she slipped out and made her way back into the heart of the town and tried to find employment as a barmaid and dyed her hair—no, she shrank from a dash into the town. Remembering the rough evil bearded faces that had passed her in the street, the lecherous bawdy laughter of the few women she had seen, she knew the town held no answer.

She must think of something else. Suddenly the answer came to her. There was some sort of government here, a French governor, she thought she had heard. She would appeal to him. Although he might not be able to keep order along the wild waterfront, he surely would not countenance an English woman being sold in the market like a head of livestock. She would go to him now.

She jumped up and started across the courtyard when she heard the heavy front doors thrust open and the sound of boots. A number of booted feet. Quickly, she shrank back and hid behind a cabbage palm that flung itself riotously upward, clambering over the ironwork. Men strode through the courtyard, three of them, their boots clattering over the stones, and disappeared into a room at the other side. She waited, afraid to move lest she be discovered—and waited too long.

The three of them tramped back again, carrying a long roll that looked like a map—she could not really see them through the leaves in the gathering dusk. They settled themselves, she guessed from the scraping of chairs, in the big room beside the front door.

She had lost her chance to leave.

Perhaps there was a back entrance. She looked uneasily upward. Night fell fast in the tropics, and it was

368

falling fast here. Already the sky was a darker blue and the shadows had deepened around the palms in the courtyard. She moved back through the courtyard and found her way to the kitchen.

It was occupied by a broad-beamed, muscular cook who wore big skirts and wide gold loops hanging from her ears, and by the little servant girl who had admitted them. Although the cook scowled fiercely at sight of Charity, the slender little servant girl leaped up and smiled reassuringly. She moved toward Charity, light-footed, dark braids swinging, the light from the fireplace playing over her gold bracelets.

There was no passing the cook to go through that small heavy wooden door at the back of the kitchen, for as Charity moved toward it, the big woman stepped forward belligerently and barred her way.

Charity glanced toward the meat roasting on a spit in the fireplace. It smelled delicious. She was very hungry and felt herself weakening in her resolve to leave at once. The servant girl, her dark eyes anxiously studying Charity, noted that glance and gestured toward the heavy wooden trestle in the center of the room. The fragile little maid ran to the cook and made signs. Charity began to understand. The girl was a mute. She came back and took Charity's wrist in her slender hand and led her to a wooden bench before the table.

Her resolve now entirely weakened by the delicious aroma wafting from the meat revolving over the fire, Charity sat and allowed a heavy silver trencher to be set before her and a chased flagon, also of heavy silver, filled with wine. Fresh bread was brought and a dish of beans and some vegetables Charity could not identify. The girl watched anxiously to see if she was pleased.

Charity smiled and beckoned her to sit down. Looking delighted, the girl did so. The cook spoke sharply, and the girl bounced up again and began piling bread on a silver charger while the cook cut great hunks of the freshly roasted meat, savory and dripping, onto another even more massive charger. The girl trundled

away with the first charger into the now dark courtyard her bare feet making no sound on the smooth
stones.

Charity ate slowly, watching the girl return and
stagger away under the weight of the second charger
piled high with hot meat. The bread was coarse but it
was good. When the girl returned, she brought Charity
a hunk of the delicious meat, which Charity washed
down with fine Madeira. Two tall flagons she drank
to bolster her for what lay ahead. Escape tonight was
now impossible. Even if she could find the governor's
house in the darkness—and she would never make it
through these evil streets, she would surely be dragged
down and ill-used before she ever reached it—it was
unlikely that his servants would open the door at
night to a stranger.

No, she must face things out here. Perhaps the
group across the courtyard would get so drunk they
would pass out and forget her. In the meantime she
felt safer in the kitchen with the evil-visaged cook
and the friendly mute girl.

Time passed. The cook cleaned up and began shell-
ing beans, presumably for the next day's meal. The
mute girl helped, her nimble fingers breaking the pods
deftly, spilling their contents into a great pottery bowl
decorated with Indian designs, that she held upon her
lap.

Charity, having now finished her third flagon of
wine, was feeling pleasantly drowsy, when she was
snapped awake by the sound of chairs scraping in the
room across the courtyard, voices growing louder,
the clash of cutlasses being buckled on, heavy footsteps, a noisy wrench as the front door opened and
closed amid goodnights.

Hands clapped. Almost spilling the contents of the
pottery bowl, the mute girl leapt up and ran across
the courtyard in answer to that signal.

Charity grew rigid.

When the girl came back she smiled and gestured
to Charity to accompany her.

Her knees feeling like butter, Charity got up and

370

followed cautiously. She found herself wishing she had brought along the knife she had used to cut her meat. To her surprise, the mute girl did not lead her to the big front room but to a room at the side with a handsome door. Swinging it wide, she gestured Charity inside, and left her.

Charity, who like her mother had never lacked for courage, took a deep breath, lifted her chin defiantly and stepped inside. So surprised was she, she hardly heard the door close softly behind her.

She might have been in an English manor house in Devon.

About her the walls were richly paneled in dark wood; there was a handsome fireplace with huge brass andirons and fender. Portraits in baroque gold-leaf frames adorned the walls. Underfoot was a large deep Turkish carpet. The shutters were open so that the deep blue wonder of the tropic night poured in through the black lacework of the iron grille.

Her tall host had his back to her and was standing in semi-darkness. As the yellow glow flared up, showing his broad back in silhouette, Charity saw that he was lighting a row of candles. When the candlelight flickered about the room, she realized that she had been in part mistaken. The furniture had a heavy carved Spanish look to it, and the portraits were not of Englishmen but of Spanish dons and their dark-eyed ladies. The table that graced the center of the room held a huge silver bowl of exotic tropical fruit.

The man swung around. He was of good height, with an arresting span of shoulder. His dark straight hair, which hung to his shoulders, looked as if it had been hacked off with a knife. He had removed his coat and he was wearing a fine white linen shirt with ruffled cuffs that came down over his strong sun-browned hands. Tight-fitting black knee breeches of a material she took to be heavy silk, and silk stockings, encased his legs. The coat, which he had obviously just flung onto a chair, was black and trimmed with a quantity of gold braid. About his lean torso was a waistcoat of black silk shot with gold threads, and spilling down over that a white shirt ruffle. A wide black leather belt with a gold buckle held a very serviceable-looking brass hilted rapier in a chased silver scabbard. Instead of shoes he wore black boots with turned-over cuffs, not of the latest style, but perhaps suited to the life in Tortuga.

His whole mein was arresting. As he turned toward her, his dark face was lit by the branched silver candelabra he had been lighting when she entered. But it was not that which caused her to stand there stunned in the candlelight, her face at first registering shock and then fury.

The man who stood before her, considering her with narrowed eyes from a saturnine hawklike face was the man who had ruined her first ball at Daarkenwyck, and whose face and impudent hands she had never quite been able to forget.

The man who stood before her, tall and sinister in the candlelight, was Roger Derwent.

CHAPTER 32

"*You* are Captain Court?" she cried on a rising note, unable to believe it.

"The same. At your service, mistress," he said gravely, and gestured toward a chair. "Will you sit and take a glass of wine with me?"

"Then you are also someone else," she accused. "For surely you are Roger Derwent!"

"A name I use when convenient," he admitted. "I thought you might remember me," he added. "You called me a beast at our last meeting, if I remember correctly."

"And now I'll call you something else you are—a sea robber and a pirate!'" cried Charity angrily.

"Ah, there's no need for heat," he murmured. "I admit I may have been under some misapprehension about you when last we met."

"Misapprehension? Your intent was obvious! You were tearing my clothes off."

"Hardly that," he said coolly, "for you left me quite fully attired as I remember. But I'd taken you for a green girl who'd never been kissed. Then the patroon told me, when I asked if it was your first ball, that you were an escaped felon, that both he and his son had known you, and that in fact they shared you for their pleasure."

"That's a lie!" flashed Charity. "I never shared a bed with Killian van Daarken—not even though he chained me in that cold dark blockhouse with the rats!"

"Ah, he did that, did he?" His face grew bleak. "I must have a word with him when next we meet." He

373

was silent for a moment and then added, as if impelled by a curiosity too great to be denied, "And the son?"

Charity caught her breath. Lies did not come easily to her. "Not—not at the time of the ball," she muttered. "It was afterward. He'd promised to marry me!" she cried defensively. "And he was leaving, and he cried and—oh, damn, what business is it of yours anyway?"

"Yes," he echoed moodily, "what business is it of mine?" He turned away from her and stared out the window at the tropical night that had settled its dark wings over the town. "And before the patroon's son there were no others?" he shot at her.

"I did not say that," said Charity stiffly, sticking out her lower lip truculently. She wasn't going to tell him about Tom, not even if he caned her!

"No, you did not say that," he said in a weary voice, and turned to her with a suddenly courtly gesture. "In any case, I owe you an apology, Mistress Charity, that is long overdue. My only defense is that I felt that I, a man of some experience with women, had been fooled by a slip of a girl into thinking her more virtuous than she was, and it galled me. Indeed, I was punishing you for being a tease. I behaved very badly, I am afraid."

She bit her lip, still angry, and gave him a dark look. "I accept your apology," she muttered.

"But not too willingly, I see," he said gravely. "Perhaps after you have supped—"

"I'm not hungry," she interrupted. No need for him to know she'd eaten already in the kitchen!

"Come then, shall we tuck old enmities away into their proper places with other lost things, and share a bottle of wine together like new-found friends?"

She gave him a sulky look, and nodded stiffly as he held one of the high-backed chairs for her. Sitting bolt upright, she accepted a tall golden goblet of wine that he had poured and handed to her with an easy grace.

"This is an excellent Madeira. It was part of a shipment I intercepted on the way to the governor of Cartagena." He lifted his glass in a smiling toast. "If *you*,

Mistress Woodstock, are an escaped felon," he observed, "we should all haunt the jails."

"It is true that I am," sighed Charity, feeling the wine warm her as it went down.

He did her the courtesy of looking astonished. "What was your crime?" he asked. "A crime of passion? You slew your lover?"

Charity hesitated. The memory of that bleak New England courtroom and even bleaker jail was so harsh that she could hardly bear to recall it. "Witchcraft," she muttered, and his face cleared.

"Witchcraft is not a crime," he said with a shrug. "It is a diversion."

"In my case it was a charge that covered up a crime," said Charity grimly, draining her goblet and allowing it to be refilled. Warmed with wine, she yearned suddenly to tell someone all about it, all the wrongs she had suffered. Why should she not speak? she asked herself recklessly. Court was behaving civilly toward her now, however outrageous his behavior at Daarkenwyck had been. Why not tell him her story? Had she not been assured that he sent all the English women he bought back to England? And if he was going to send her home, she would never see him again. So it could not matter to her if he knew.

"I had come to Massachusetts to receive an inheritance under—under a misapprehension," she said, careful not to bring her mother's name into anything she said. "The fortune was not rightfully mine, but my aunt's. I told her I would forswear it, but she did not believe me. She ordered me to marry her son, and when I refused she locked us in a room together and he raped me. When I would have brought charges, my aunt swiftly brought her own charge of witchcraft. She and my cousins testified against me and I was sentenced to be burned as a witch."

Court's jaw hardened. A shadow that might have been pity passed over his hard watchful face.

"There was a highwayman who bribed his way out of the jail, and he took me with him when he left. I—I lived with him until—until he was shot." Charity paused for a moment, as she recalled Tom with both joy and sadness in her heart. Then she took a deep breath and went on. "His partner took me into New York and tried to sell me to some trappers. But I escaped and hid from them on a river boat. It was there I first heard your voice. You were making arrangements with Killian van Daarken to sell him some goods."

Court looked astonished. "We were as close as that in the dark, were we?"

"I could not see you," she admitted. "I was afraid to lift my head to peer out from behind the great coil of rope for fear I'd be seen and returned to shore. At Daarkenwyck I remembered your voice but could not recall where I had heard it—not until later." She shivered and took another quick drink of wine. "When I remembered, I threatened the patroon with exposure."

"Did you now?" He looked amused. "That took some courage. And what did the patroon say?"

"He laughed and said it would enliven his reputation. He had just told me that he had wagered with his son that he could not seduce me before his departure for Holland and—" her voice lowered—"that his son had collected the wager just before his departure." And, thus, obliquely, Charity managed to tell Court that her relationship with Pieter was not a long one.

"Ah, yes," he said dryly. "You said he wept."

"Yes." Her voice grew sad. "I regard it as my one sin; all else that has happened was not my fault."

"What was your sin?" he asked curiously.

"Promising to marry a man I did not love," she said savagely. "I had confused him with the life he led, his background, his wealth, his fine clothes and fine manners, the servants who pattered about after him doing his bidding, the heritage that would one day be his. I told myself that I loved him, but I did not. It was pity and—and avarice, I admit it—that led me to his bed." There was grief in her voice as she accused herself of these things.

Court stared at her in surprise. "Faith, tis a wonder you can admit it," he murmured. "Most of us cannot face what we are. We lie to ourselves most of all."

"Yes, I had lied to myself," she said, dashing an angry tear from her eye. "And when the patroon told me of the wager, he also told me that Pieter had been betrothed all the time. Pieter was off to Amsterdam to marry an heiress whom he would bring back to Daarkenwyck as his bride. It was then old Killian offered me his own bed. He seemed to think I would find it as good as any other."

Court nodded, still watching her intently. "A consolation prize."

"An ultimatum. I said I would leave; he said I would not. I ran but his servants caught me and put me in the blockhouse. They chained me to the floor."

"And how did you escape?" he asked curiously. "I might have the sinews to break a chain, but assuredly you have not."

Shaking her head, Charity accepted another glass of wine, and continued her narration. She told Court of striking down the patroon's man with an oar, and how she had escaped downriver to be found by Ben.

"Why did you not stay with this good man?" Court asked, when she finished telling him of her life with Ben.

Staring into her now empty glass, Charity explained that Rachel, Ben's wife, had returned to him at last. "Then I managed to buy passage on a ship bound for Carolina," she added. "On board, I was mistaken for someone else by a mad woman who attacked me. But I was rescued from her by the finest man in all the world."

Court lifted his head.

"His name is Alan Bellingham. He is a planter in Charles Towne." Having finished her glass, Charity held it out to be refilled. She was crying openly at this point and did not notice the sudden change in Court's expression. "I was being sent to Barbadoes to his wife's sister's to be governess to her children until one could be brought from England when that damn pirate ship attacked us and Polly and I were brought here to Tortuga and sold." Her voice slurred.

Court watched her drain her glass and rose quickly to catch her as she slumped from her chair. As he picked her limp body up in his arms, there was a mixture of tenderness and hardness in the pirate's expression that would have puzzled an observer. Thoughtfully he stared down at his enticing burden with conflicting emotions playing across his face. Then, with a dark scowl on his face, he carried her across the courtyard and upstairs to the room that had been prepared for her. He put her down carefully upon the great fourposter bed and stood contemplating her.

The moon moved fitfully in and out behind the clouds and fell softly on the girl's beautiful body, shimmered on her pale hair spread out on the pillow. As that same moonlight bathed Court's dark saturnine face in light, an onlooker, had there been one, would have said that his visage was threatening, and there were moments when his expression was evil indeed.

CHAPTER 33

Charity awoke, huddling down deliciously between clean sheets, faintly perfumed. She looked around in confusion at the richly appointed room, breathing the faint perfume of the linens. For a moment she thought she was back in Stéphanie's house in Bath.

As she stretched, the sheets pleasantly abraded her bare skin. Her eyes widened and she felt herself quickly. Naked! Stark naked! Had he slept with her last night? She sat bolt upright and turned her head sharply to look at the pillow beside her.

Turning her head brought an agonizing pain to her temples and she fell back again. She closed her eyes, trying to think. Was that the impress of a male head on the pillow beside her, or had she merely rolled over in her sleep?

Last night she had been talking with Jeremy Court, whom she'd known at Daarkenwyck as Roger Derwent, talking—yes, and drinking wine with him. She had been telling him about her experiences in America, talking far too much—drinking far too much, obviously, for she had no memory of how the evening had ended.

Her eyes flew open again. Had he undressed her? She winced. How else had she arrived in this unclothed condition? No memory of having undressed herself came to her and, as she tried with a groan to get out of bed, she suspected that she had been incapable of undressing herself.

Wincing, she sat up again and saw what she had not noticed before. At the foot of the bed lay a thin white silk dress with gold embroidery tracing a hand-

379

some design across the tight bodice and the full skirt. She got out of bed gingerly, picked up the dress and stared at it in wonder. It appeared to be her size.

She looked about for her chemise and petticoats. They, and her green dress, were nowhere to be seen.

She wrapped the white dress about her and stumbled to the door. Holding her head, she peered out. Below her in the courtyard she could see the mute girl, sitting on a bench cutting up some kind of fruit. At the sound of the door opening, the girl raised her head, stopped what she was doing and moved toward the stairway. Charity, her head splitting, retreated into the room and closed the door.

A discreet knock sounded.

"Come in," Charity called. The girl brought in her bath water and poured it into a metal tub. "My clothes!" Charity asked, climbing into the tub. "What has happened to them?"

The girl smiled, made washing motions with her hands, and went out. When she returned to towel Charity dry, she carried a pretty little shawl. Charity stared at it. She hoped she wasn't supposed to wear only a shawl and a thin silk dress.

At the girl's urging, Charity wrapped the shawl around her and followed her down the empty gallery and into another room, which contained a number of trunks. As the girl opened the lid of one, Charity's eyes widened.

There reposed before her a trunkload of women's clothes. Stunned, she began pulling them out. They were stiff and handsome—obviously meant for some Spanish girl, perhaps in Cartagena or Maracaibo. With some excitement, she pulled out several petticoats and chose one of heavy white silk—it would do nicely with the dress that she had found on her bed. Beside her the mute girl was rummaging, too, and offered an assortment of chemises, a big square silk shawl of pale sea-green heavily embroidered in the same color, and deeply fringed in gleaming silk, and a high-backed Spanish comb of tortoiseshell. A pair of white satin slippers edged in gold leather completed her costume.

When she had dressed, Charity felt able to meet the world again. At least she did not look poor and downtrodden in the way she had yesterday. She looked like a woman of refinement, which she was—and of wealth, which she was not.

Telling herself that whatever had happened could not be helped, she went down to breakfast, her thin white skirts trailing behind her.

She would have gone into the kitchen, but the mute girl shook her head and escorted her to a handsome dining room, furnished in the Spanish manner in somber dark carved woods. The high-backed chairs had rich red tapestry coverings. The walls were hung with tapestries depicting—ironically, since they graced the home of the buccaneer who had taken them by force —the glory of Spain. There was also a quantity of gold and silver plate, and massive candlesticks.

Charity sat down to breakfast somewhat awed by the amount of loot that resided in the house. Obviously Court's reputation as a scourge of the seas was not to be taken lightly. Here before her was the proof of his success.

Perched on one of the tall chairs, Charity sat back and let the little mute girl serve her. She picked at the fruit and thin cakes of cooked meal that were put before her, ignoring the heavier fare, the cold meats and heavy meat pudding. Her head was still throbbing and, in spite of her fine clothes, she felt disconsolate and ill-used.

She was halfway through her breakfast when Jeremy Court came in. He was dressed as she had not seen him, in serviceable leather boucan-hunter breeches and thick heavy boots, wet, with grains of sand still stuck to them. He wore a wide black belt with a big iron buckle and his serviceable brass-hilted rapier clattered beside him. Only his white shirt, of fine linen, reminded her of the genteel clothing he had worn the night before—and even it had the sleeves rolled up displaying the hard sinews of his bronzed forearms,

381

while it gaped open to the waist, displaying a light dusting of dark hair on his powerful chest. His thick dark hair hung lank to his shoulders—and looked a little shorter, as if he might have hacked at it again with his knife.

Charity stared at him. Last night to look at him one would not have thought him a buccaneer. Today he was the very picture of one. Even his face had changed. His eyes were pale agates set against his bronzed hawklike countenance and his mouth was an unsmiling gash across that face.

"I see you have risen," he observed unnecessarily.

"I—I found someone had undressed me last night," she stammered.

For a moment there was a flicker in his eyes. "And you are wondering who it might have been?"

"Yes."

He considered her coldly. "And you are thinking that because I am, as you have termed me, a sea-robber and a pirate—"

She looked hastily away, her fingers clenching and unclenching nervously.

"Yes," she whispered. "I—"

There was no glimmer of amusement in the harsh smile he flashed at her suddenly; it was instead a wolfish gleam of white teeth. He leaned his knuckles upon the table and bent toward her. "Ask yourself what your pure planter would have done under similar circumstances."

Stung, Charity lifted her head. "He would not have touched me," she cried. "He would have called a maidservant to put me to bed properly!"

"Even so," he said coldly, and turned on his heel and strode from the room.

Charity pushed away her plate. She had had her answer, but somehow it brought her no comfort. Though handsomely housed, well fed and dressed like a pampered daughter, she was still his prisoner, and the dark perfumed tropic night would fall again. . . .

Some time later, from her room she heard the heavy outer door open and a man's boots cross the tiles of the courtyard. Going to the balustrade, she peered over. Below her the ship's doctor, Leeds Kirby, was striding across the patio. Hoping for news of Polly, Charity picked up her skirts and dashed down the stairs.

She arrived breathless in the courtyard. "Dr. Kirby, a word with you!" she cried.

He turned and paused at sight of her, an appreciative smile lighting his face. Charity had hardly looked at him before, but now she saw that he was very narrowly built, of an exceptional leanness, tall and with sun-streaked sandy hair which fell carelessly onto his shoulders. His brilliant green eyes took in the sumptuousness of her appearance—so different from yesterday's disheveled state.

"Mistress Woodstock." He acknowledged her greeting with a formal bow.

"How is Polly?" She was almost afraid to ask.

"Her condition is grave," he said. "That is why I stayed and did not accompany the *Sea Witch* when she left port this day."

"She . . . left port?" faltered Charity.

"With the tide, mistress."

"Then Captain Court is not—is not now in Tortuga?"

Kirby grinned. "When the *Sea Witch* is out prowling? Nay, Jeremy's not in Tortuga."

She pondered that. "Will you not have a glass of wine with me?"

He looked pleased and accepted, as Charity said, "The little mute girl will bring it. I have not been able to learn her name."

"Her name is Ella," supplied Kirby promptly. "That much about her we know, but little else. We took her from a Spanish ship where she was held captive, foully chained. She was terrified and she could not speak. Since I can find nothing wrong with her vocal chords, I assume it was fright that lost her the power of speech. Court brought her home with him and has treated her very tenderly, hoping she would regain her voice. She could have lived here as a daughter of the house, but she chose to help out in the kitchen—a role she seems to understand. Perhaps she was a maidservant at some time."

"She is a dear little thing," said Charity. "What do you think the Spaniards did to her?"

Leeds Kirby frowned. "Whatever it was frightened her so deeply that she cannot voice it. Perhaps some day. . . ." Ella approached them with a wine bottle and goblets, and he was silent while she poured the wine and departed.

They were silent for a space. Then the doctor raised his goblet, studying the color. "A fine Malaga," he murmured, adding that he had actually come here to see her on delicate business. Young Timothy Hobbs, it seemed, was having a devil of a time with the Spanish lady he had bought. Charity stiffened and Kirby quickly explained that young Hobbs had shown the lady the greatest of courtesy, but she refused to eat and when he had but offered her some wine, she had again scratched his face. Charity hid a smile. She had guessed Dona Isabel to be a woman of spirit.

"Tim does wish to pay court to the lady," Kirby added with a raised eyebrow. "In true old-fashioned style, he would sue for her hand. So, to put her mind at ease, he wonders if you would be so kind as to keep her here and let him call on her formally as he tries to learn her language. He hopes that you will be interpreter for these unlikely meetings until such time as he can take over and throw himself properly at her feet."

Charity was touched. In spite of herself, her heart warmed to Timothy Hobbs, so humbly dedicated to the pursuit of a woman who despised him.

"I will try," she said doubtfully, "but this is Captain Court's house."

"Of that I am aware. But I think it likely Jeremy will approve any decision you might make in this matter."

"Oh? And why do you think that, pray?"

He shrugged, his green eyes veiled, and countered with a question. "Is that not the wedding gown of a Spanish lady you are wearing?"

Charity blushed furiously. It had indeed looked like a bridal gown to her but . . . now she wondered angrily if Court had left it on her bed in mockery.

"I did not know that," she mumbled. "It is just a dress he left—" she started to say "on my bed" but caught herself in time. "Stop looking at me that way," she added wrathfully. "I loathe Court and all he stands for."

"So, that's the way of it, is it? And on such short acquaintance, too. . . ."

"We've met before," snapped Charity before she thought.

"Ah," he said softly. "That explains it."

"It explains nothing!" she flashed. "Stop implying he's my lover—no, don't protest, your eyes said it!"

"My eyes are bold fellows, always prying about where they've no legitimate right," he admitted, his green gaze deliberately roving over her round young breasts, her slender waist and hips. "But then, like me, they're rovers and take what's offered."

"Nothing's being offered," said Charity, setting down her glass rather hard. "Not to you and not to Court."

"Disappointing," he said. "But not surprising. I thought he'd have difficulty breaking you to hand."

Charity leaned forward. "Is that what he did to that poor Spanish girl? Break her to his hand? Did *she* wear this dress? What happened to her? Oh, don't look so innocent, Dr. Kirby. I heard all about his Spanish mistress, the one who disappeared! Did he—did he kill her?"

"Kill her?" Leeds Kirby looked startled; then he threw back his head and laughed. "Oh, nothing so melodramatic. And poor she was not. Court merely sent her to Havana via a Spanish ship he stopped for that very purpose. From there she could take ship for Spain where she'd been headed when we interrupted her journey." His eyes twinkled. "I can tell you she had no wish to leave him."

So he had sent away the discarded mistress.

"I thought he hated the Spaniards."

"Ah, but this was a lady. A most elegant lady, well

385

versed in the ways of love. She had had two husbands, had Dona Elena. And I understand she had killed them both with the intensity of her affections. You could understand that a man like Court, hearing this, might be fascinated?"

Her face grew hot. "And how long did he live with this—with her?"

"A month. He had no desire to sully her reputation —he would have been content with less. But she had to be returned forcibly. It seemed she preferred the easy life in Tortuga to the grimmer ways of Spain, where her next husband had already been chosen for her. An old man, I understand—if not, he soon will be."

"Are you never serious?" she demanded, suspicious he might be baiting her.

"Rarely. It doesn't go well with the heat down here." He fanned himself with his hat. "It's better to take things as they come—as you will learn."

"Learn?" She drew herself up. "I'm not staying!"

"Are you not?" he murmured. "Well, that's between you and Jeremy."

"Court has nothing to do with it—it is my decision."

He shrugged. "If you should chance to change your mind and find time hangs heavy, I'd be glad to while away the hours with you when I'm in port."

She smiled scornfully. "And suppose Court catches us . . . whiling away the hours? What then?"

"Why, then we'll learn which is the better blade, won't we?" he said. "Faith, it's a chance worth taking for such a face as yours. I'd have bought you myself, mistress, but I'd gambled away all my ready gold—a condition that's usual to me. But you're right to count the danger. Court's a very durable opponent. He's crossed swords with the best and cut them down." His face turned grim for a moment. "Twould seem he enjoys doing it."

She shivered. *And women,* she wanted to ask. *Does he enjoy cutting them down too?*

"In any event, I'll be leaving Tortuga shortly," she said, as if to reassure herself by repetition. "But in the meantime, I'd be delighted to act as translator for Timothy and his lady—and please bring me news of Polly, Dr. Kirby."

"Every day," he promised smoothly. His green eyes seemed to heat up like burning copper as they played over her desirable flesh.

When he left, Charity went back upstairs to pace around in fury in her wedding finery. The dress represented Court's way of mocking her, she realized. For now she remembered that under the spell of the wine, believing herself speaking to a man who might the very next morning set her upon an outbound ship, she had talked too much. She clenched her hands, remembering she had told him about the patroon and Pieter—and that she had been a highwayman's mistress.

And so he had cruelly left a wedding dress upon her bed, and taken himself off to sea.

Looking out the open casements toward the ocean, she frowned. Not even to Alan Bellingham had she told the whole truth about herself. But her tongue had rushed to give a buccaneer all those details that must surely damn her in a man's eyes.

She leaned against the lacy iron grill of the balcony and studied the sea's hard blue shimmer, reflecting in the distance the diamond brilliance of the sky over Cayona Bay. And she asked herself, *Why had she told all this to Jeremy Court, and no other?*

In the afternoon Timothy Hobbs brought his reluctant captive over and Charity was struck again with his fresh face and honest gray eyes. Just looking at him made her homesick for England. Gravely he stood by while Charity introduced herself to Dona Isabel again, and explained the situation.

Dona Isabel looked startled. She turned and gave Timothy Hobbs a long slow critical look. His face and neck turned fiery red under her inspection and he waited eagerly.

"Ridiculous," she said in Spanish, with a toss of her

387

head. "That I would marry a pirate? And an English pirate at that? Ridiculous! Tell him never."

Charity explained to Dona Isabel that she had no choice but to endure this courtship, and turned back to Timothy. "Dona Isabel said she won't marry you." He looked so crestfallen that she added in spite of herself, "Perhaps she'll change her mind after she knows you better." At that he took heart and gave Charity a flashing smile. She knew she had made a friend.

Timothy was persuaded to let Isabel get settled before he continued his suit. He went out to the courtyard and waved goodbye as Charity showed the proud black-haired woman to a bedroom down the hall from her own. She noted that Isabel was wearing a new lace mantilla and an even handsomer Spanish comb than the one her captors had crushed underfoot. Her dress was different, too, from the one in which she had been sold. This one was a stiff maroon brocade, perhaps unsuitable for the climate, but very handsome. Earlier, a small trunk had been brought in on Ravenal's broad shoulders. Plainly Timothy was treating his captive well.

Dona Isabel looked around her at the spacious room with its handsome carved furniture. *"Madre de Dios,* these pirates live well," she muttered. "We had nothing so fine in my father's house in Spain."

That surprised Charity. Somehow she had assumed Dona Isabel to be wealthy, and had wondered why she had not been ransomed rather than sold.

"My home had nothing so fine either," she told her Spanish guest frankly. "Although I attended a fine school, and it was my mother's hope that I would make a good marriage."

Isabel looked at her sharply, as if recognizing in Charity a fellow-sufferer. After a while, Isabel poured out her own story, striding around the room as she did so, dark eyes flashing. She was unfortunate, she cried. Before God, she was! Her family in Castile, impoverished but aristocratic, had sacrificed everything to raise a suitable dowry for her, their only daughter. She had been on her way to Porto Bello to marry Don Jaime Alvarez, a wealthy young man whom she had never seen, when these damned English dogs—pardon, senorita, French dogs—had attacked. She would take her own life, yes, gladly, before she would submit to any of them.

Charity interposed that she doubted Tim would push her to such lengths, and left to give orders to the servants for Isabel's comfort. Charity had expected difficulty from the cook, but to her surprise that big fierce woman accepted her meekly enough as mistress of the house. At least in Court's absence, she would rule here.

Except in one thing: The cook blocked all efforts to leave by the back door, and John Ravenal, who slept in a tiny room at the front of the house, guarded the front door. Charity never saw him without his cutlass and a wicked-looking pistol thrust into his belt. With his giant size and meek expression that could turn wolfish and formidable in a flash, Ravenal was a wise choice for her guard, she decided.

Yet it chafed her. Though she was mistress here, she was a prisoner also.

Well-treated, well-fed, well-clothed, she and Dona Isabel were not allowed to leave.

The next weeks were perhaps the oddest Charity had ever spent. Day after day by a tinkling fountain amid spilling exotic flowers, she sat in the tropical courtyard as a *duenna* and watched while Timothy, dressed in his best—a rather strange best, for he had no sense of style—paid court to his aristocratic captive. Gravely Charity translated for Dona Isabel's edification the story of Tim's life, a story which touched Charity deeply for Tim had been born in a seafaring town much like Torquay. One of fourteen children, there had been little for him to eat and less to wear. As soon as he was big enough, young Tim had signed on as a cabin boy and had sailed the seas ever since. Smart and hard-working, he had learned all he could, but times were hard and promotion didn't come easy. Several days out of Plymouth on a merchantman bound for Barbadoes, his ship had been set upon by a Spanish warship. Although they'd given a good account of themselves, they'd been outgunned from the first and taken captive. Tim had been wounded in the engagement and he had known what lay ahead—the Inquisition, torture and a painful death.

Charity looked at Dona Isabel, whose dark eyes were inscrutable as she studied her English captor.

But his luck had not yet run out, Tim told them proudly. On the way to Cartegena with the English prisoners, the Spanish warship had chanced upon the *Sea Witch*, Court's vessel, and had promptly fired upon the celebrated English buccaneer.

The Spaniards had had reason to regret it. Outmanned, outgunned, still Court had, with reckless daring, crippled his adversary. Court had released the captives, after he boarded the ship, which was laden with fine wines and other good things. Timothy was among those who decided to stay with Court. Since his shipmaster had been killed in the engagement, Court had given battered young Timothy the job.

Timothy's voice rang with pride when he spoke of the pirate. Charity could see he counted Court his friend. It did not jibe with her opinion of the man.

As the days passed, Ella became very friendly, often seeking Charity out, and Charity had begun to understand Ella's sign language. She tried to get Ella to eat in the dining room with Isabel and herself, but the girl hung back. Bright fear blazed up in her eyes when Charity tried to make her sit in one of the high-backed chairs. It was the same when Charity tried to persuade her to move from her little room beside the kitchen into one of the large bedrooms: Ella gasped and broke away from her. There were terrible things in Ella's past, Charity realized, things she'd best leave alone. And they had to do with sitting at a fine table and sleeping in a fine bed. . . .

As he had promised, Leeds Kirby dropped by daily to report on Polly's condition. These reports were delivered over wine, served in the courtyard. For it amused Charity to play at being mistress of this hand-

390

some house. And it was very restoring to her damaged self-esteem to sip her wine, aware of Kirby's hot bold gaze roving over her, to smile at him seductively and let the trade winds blow her fair hair. She did not admit, even to herself, that part of her reason for enticing the doctor was to spite Court.

"Like Jeremy, I've developed a taste for fine Spanish wines," he told her, staring into his glass.

"Stolen wines," she amended.

"Like other forbidden fruits, they taste the better," he agreed, smiling. "But this particular wine, if I'm not mistaken, was lifted by the Spanish from a French ship—and Jeremy merely lifted it from them."

"At gunpoint, of course."

"Of course. Twenty guns—all pointed at the galleon's golden side."

She sniffed. "Since you're his apologist, what about my white dress? Didn't you say it was some Spanish girl's bridal gown? So Court robbed her!"

"I spoke a bit out of turn there," he admitted. "But Jeremy didn't rob her of the gown. She'd had it made and merely refused to take it with her when she left."

So, it had belonged to his Spanish mistress. No doubt she had meant to wear it at her wedding to Court.

To shield her confusion she asked Kirby again what had happened to Dr. Cavendish, who had been captured with her and taken aboard the *Gull*. Kirby reported that the old doctor was all right. But St. Clair was holding him for five thousand pounds' ransom.

Charity wanted to send him a message but Kirby vetoed it. St. Clair was an evil man, he explained, and one who hated Court. It might go hard with a prisoner of his who received a message from Court's house.

She shuddered, seeing the thrust of his words. And was reminded that she too was a prisoner. Well, she'd not endure it! She'd see the governor forthwith and obtain her release!

When Kirby rose to leave, she said casually, "I think I'll accompany you as far as the quay. The weather's so fine, I'd enjoy a stroll."

On his way to the door, he came to a full stop and

swung toward her. From the keen gaze he focused on her, the smile that played around his reckless mouth, she knew he had divined her meaning.

"Mistress Charity," he said softly, "I think you are like to get me killed."

She flushed. "How so?"

"If you'll notice, Ravenal guards the door, and Jeremy's left him orders to slice in half the man who takes you through it."

She paled. "I—I did not know."

He gave her a light-hearted look. "Of course, I might be persuaded to chance it," he murmured. "With the right bait. . . ."

With Court away, she told herself she had no immediate need to see the governor. "I've lost my taste for strolling," she said hastily. "I—I think it may rain." Changing the subject, she asked him how long he thought Court would be gone.

Kirby shrugged. "Who knows? Another week or so if he runs into luck and a good prize strays into his path. Hardly longer; he wasn't provisioned for a long voyage. Of course," he grinned, "in our profession he may not be coming back. Don't forget, all the dons of Spain are gunning for him."

"And half of Charles Towne," she said grimly.

"Ah? I hadn't heard that."

"They say he's behind the attacks on English shipping—that he masterminds them, even though it isn't his ship that carries out the actual attack."

Kirby laughed. "Don't believe all you hear. Gossip's not very reliable. If Court really wanted Charles Towne he'd set sail for Carolina and sack the town."

Her eyes widened. "He would not be so bold!" she gasped.

"Have you not heard of the raid on Maracaibo? Made us all rich."

She had heard . . . vaguely. It had not interested her then. A Spanish town. . . .

"It's where he got the material for that blue dress you're wearing," he added wickedly. "He had it made

392

for a lady who departed before it was finished. And since it fits, ye know her dimensions!"

The Spanish mistress again! Kirby plainly enjoyed baiting her. She bade him goodbye, abruptly, and was almost glad to return to her stiff-spined Castilian guest.

Dona Isabel and Charity were united in one thing: their fierce desire to escape. It brought them together. For long hours they talked about it—return to England, return to Castile. Charity noted that Dona Isabel's waspishness toward Timothy had grown milder and finally seemed to disappear altogether.

"I have made a discovery," she told Charity one day, her expression sly and rather pleased. "Our cook speaks Spanish."

Since Charity had never heard the cook do more than growl or mutter, she waited for some revelation. It was not long in coming.

"Your Captain Court," said Dona Isabel in a leisurely voice, "has a mistress. She comes to see him from time to time and stays for upwards of a week."

Her words stung Charity. "He is not *my* Captain Court," she responded sharply. And driven by curiosity, "Who is she?"

Dona Isabel shrugged her expressive shoulders. "The cook said only that she always wears a heavy black lace mantilla over her head. No one has ever seen her face. They call her 'the lady in the mantilla.'" She laughed. "Perhaps she is married."

His Spanish mistress, thought Charity, eyes widening. The one who had had to be removed forcibly. Did she return for visits? Undoubtedly she had married again. This would be her . . . let's see, third husband? This woman who had killed two already with excessive affection. Charity's cheeks burned. Isabel took a dainty bite of avocado flavored with fresh limes and laughed softly.

That afternoon Dona Isabel surprised Timothy by graciously offering him her hand when he came to call. He reddened joyfully as he took it and sat down on the edge of a stone bench, earnestly trying to converse with her in his halting Spanish. Charity knew he was spending all his waking hours trying to learn Spanish, that he had acquired a tutor from among the Spanish captives on the island. Several times Dona Isabel hesitatingly corrected something Timothy said and he repeated the words correctly and gave her an adoring look.

Charity realized that Dona Isabel had abandoned talking about Porto Bello and the waiting Don Jaime. She mentioned this to Leeds Kirby, who quirked an eyebrow at her. "Tim's softening her up," he said. "She'll smile on him yet, you'll see. Women are attracted to the man who is there. Absence brings . . . forgetfulness."

Under that hot green gaze, Charity flushed. The implication was obvious: Kirby was the man who was *here.* From that first moment she'd never doubted that he wanted her. She smiled at him. "You're a cynic, Leeds." For they'd been on a first-name basis for some time.

He nodded. "That I am and life has made me so. Look at me. Irish and trained as a doctor and yet, could I make a living in my chosen profession? I could not. It would seem I did not inspire trust. Men did not want me tending their wives and daughters —thought I showed too much interest in them already. For that same reason these gentlemen wouldn't let me tend *them.* They feared I'd hurry them to their graves and be off after the widows and the beautiful orphans!" He laughed and Charity was caught up by the gaiety of his mood.

"Is that why you became a buccaneer?"

"No, that's why I signed up with Monmouth when he invaded England thinking to be its king. Devil did I care for Monmouth; twas good pay and advancement I was seeking." He grinned. "And the thought did cross my mind that if he won—slight as his chances were—I might end up the king's physician, a somewhat favored post."

"The west country favored Monmouth."

"Aye. We landed at Lyme. We were met by singing schoolgirls and flowers; it all seemed a great lark.

On to Taunton with five thousand men. What cared we that Parliament had condemned our leader to death? We hailed him as king. But the tide turned and we fell back on Bridgwater. . . ." He sighed. "Our poor raw recruits were cut to pieces. And those that weren't were hanged forthwith or tried by the Bloody Assizes."

"Were you taken?"

"Aye. With Jeremy. We made our escape by separate routes."

She was surprised. "Was Court with Monmouth then?"

Kirby laughed. "No, he was there on personal business and got caught up in it."

"Personal business?"

"A lady," said Kirby, but he would elucidate no further.

It came as no surprise to Charity when Dona Isabel announced that she had decided to reconsider Timothy Hobbs's proposal. Isabel added bitterly that she would have no dowry since the jewelry and plate and fine linens she had been bringing to her affianced Don Jaime had all been stolen by—she started to say "pirates" and softened the word to "buccaneers."

Later, Timothy arrived with a cart that contained her entire dowry, and Isabel nearly fainted with delight. Charity thought it must have cost the young man a packet to run about and buy it all back, but she could see from his blissful expression that it was worth it. He even offered recklessly to kidnap a priest of her choice for the nuptials. At this, Dona Isabel paled and said rather severely that enough kidnapping had been done already, adding vaguely that she would like to be married somewhere that had the flavor of Spain.

Two days later a prize crew of buccaneers brought into port a Spanish galleon that had struck its colors because it had already been disabled by a storm, and Timothy learned there was a priest aboard. He had them all rowed out in a longboat—Dona Isabel,

Charity, Ravenal—and Leeds Kirby, who gave the bride away.

The marriage was performed on the galleon's swaying deck, beneath the frowning guns of a buccaneer citadel. In the stiff white brocade gown and white mantilla in which she would have wed Don Jaime, Dona Isabel took her vows beside the proud young Englishman. The group toasted the bride's health with stolen Spanish wine, and fired a broadside from the disabled galleon to announce the event. Bells rang in Tortuga in answer. Everyone was rowed ashore again, where a roaring crowd of buccaneers greeted them. Pistols were fired into the air, and a laughing Timothy —for he was very popular in the port—carried his bride away to his house.

Wistfully, Charity watched them go. Gentle Ella was a mute, cook only growled, and Ravenal seldom spoke. It was going to be a silent household without Dona Isabel.

Beside her Leeds Kirby said, "I think your friend Polly's well enough to be moved. It would do her good to have someone to talk to. Why don't I bring her over?"

With a grateful smile, Charity turned to him. "That would be wonderful, Leeds. When can you do it?"

"I will go and get her now, if you like."

So Charity and Polly were reunited and spent long hours together as Polly regained her strength. She was very thin and her hair came out in handsful when she combed it, which made her cry. Charity comforted her, saying it would all grow back and she'd soon be returning to England. What would she care then how she'd looked in Tortuga?

Polly smiled at that and consented to sit in a big chair before the open casements on the second floor "taking the sun." Outside lay a sparkling tropical world, the world of the Caribbean where treasure-laden ships made a dangerous passage.

Charity heard the front door open. "That'll be Leeds," she told Polly. "He'll be coming up to see how you are. I'd better tell him we're up here."

Polly put a detaining hand on her arm. "Tis a friend to me you've been, Charity," she said hesitantly, "but I do think you should know that Dr. Kirby has his eye on you."

Charity laughed. "I'm well aware of that."

"I did ask him why he hadn't gone with Captain Court—I was none so sick the Frenchwoman who serves him as a nurse could not have tended me. And he said that there was greater booty in Jeremy Court's house in Tortuga than any Court might take on the seas—a woman with hair of gold."

Charity's senses quickened. "Leeds," she called, "we're up here."

"And he did say, too, a man could have any woman if he waited long enough, but that usually he found they weren't worth waiting for."

"Did he now?" said Charity carelessly. "Well, Leeds Kirby will wait many a long day before he has me!"

Leaning against the railing of the iron grillwork balcony, Charity looked out through the crystal air toward piles of big white clouds that drifted with the trade winds, then at the frowning gray Mountain Fort and the red-roofed town below. For Court's house enjoyed a view of both the town and Cayona Bay. Into that bay, flying before the rising wind, swooped a fast rakish ship, tall-masted, fleet, with a dark hull and billowing gray sails.

Behind her, Leeds Kirby said softly, "That's the *Sea Witch*. Jeremy is back."

CHAPTER 34

All Tortuga was aware that the daring Captain Court was back in harbor, and that he'd captured the richest prizes of the season—not one but two heavily laden Spanish merchantmen. On shore most of his crew of buccaneers swaggered and spent their gold in grog houses and taverns and brothels. From her conversations with Leeds, Charity knew that within a week or two most of them would be penniless and eager to put to sea again to fill their pockets.

"Do not judge these men too harshly," Leeds had said. "Most of them were once peaceful boucan hunters on Hispaniola, where great herds abounded. They hunted and smoked the meat."

"They were wanted men?"

"Not necessarily for crimes—political mistakes, let us say. They lived quietly enough on Hispaniola until the Spaniards drove them off. When they returned to their island anyway—faith, they had nowhere else to go—the Spaniards destroyed the herds. So they took to the sea in little boats and used those to take bigger ones, sailing right in under the guns and killing the gunners with small arms. The island of Tortuga was unoccupied, so the buccaneers took it and fortified it. Those are stolen Spanish guns that command the harbor. The men formed a confederation, that of the Brethren of the Coast. And here they eke out a living the only way they know—by plundering Spanish ships that pass through these waters on the way to greedy Spain. You must not blame them too much. Desperate men seek desperate bargains."

"And you?" She gave him a level look. "You and Jeremy Court were peaceful boucan hunters?"

He burst out laughing. *"Touché!"* he cried. "No, indeed we were not. But both of us," he grew sober, "have our own grievances against Spain. Court was aboard a peaceful English vessel the Spaniards seized; he was sentenced to death, and that sentence commuted to life imprisonment in the galleys. For two years he rowed, a naked galley slave; it is a living death."

"How did he escape?" she asked, shuddering.

"The ship broke apart in a storm off the Irish coast. A spar snapped the chain that bound him and he made it ashore clinging to some wreckage and staggered down the coast to freedom."

"And you?" she asked. "Were you a galley slave that you hate Spain so much?"

His lean face grew very set. "I have personal reasons for hating Spain. I was betrothed to a young lady from Somerset. I had fled the Monmouth debacle unscathed, had settled on Barbadoes and had written her to join me. The ship she came out on was attacked by the Spaniards." His jaw turned to stone. "She was never seen or heard from again. I could never find out what happened to her. At that point I joined the Brethren of the Coast—which suits me admirably," he added, regaining his jauntiness. "So you see, Jeremy and I have a score to settle with Spain, and we exact a toll from Spanish ships when they pass through our waters!"

Now Court had exacted from Spain yet another toll and he was back. Nervously, Charity waited for him to arrive.

He came in like a great wave breaking green across the deck, sweeping all before him, his serviceable rapier clanking beside him. Behind him came a straggling line of husky men: the first carrying the back and breast of steel and the Spanish headpiece that he wore in battle; the second and third staggering under large sea chests, and four others carrying kegs of what appeared to be wine. In long strides Court crossed the distance to the courtyard and indicated to Ravenal that the big man should supervise carrying the sea chests and battle gear upstairs, while he saw that the kegs were hefted out to the kitchen and storerooms.

Halfway across the courtyard stood Charity, wearing —on a reckless impulse—the white and gold bridal gown she had found lying across the foot of her bed the first morning she had waked in this house. Her pale gold hair shimmered down her shoulders and she stood as erect as he and faced him boldly.

She felt that she was armed with knowledge for a change—she knew much more about Court now. Kirby had told her enough so that she saw Court more clearly. The fires of hell had tempered this man. The cruel forge of fate had shaped him and the sharp files of loss had honed him and sharpened him into a dangerous weapon. His heart, she felt, was a stone, his morals, nonexistent. He had become a scourge of the seas, a killer of men—and he looked the part.

Gone was the scintillating gentleman she had met at Daarkenwyck. Gone was the great periwig that had somehow softened that hard face. Gone were the satins and velvets that bespoke the dandy. Gone were the affectations of tall silver-headed cane and jeweled snuff box, the decorous courtly pace.

Here was a man who took stairs three at a time, a man whose straight hair fell dark and gleaming to his shoulders and swung as his tanned hawkface turned, keen light eyes appraising each new circumstance. His was not the body of a dandy, but of a warrior; lean and bred for stamina and strength. That arm that she remembered in its deep cuffed velvet coat was a mighty arm to swing a mighty sword and carve his enemies in half.

He stopped and regarded her with his dark unsmiling visage, his strange light eyes gleaming like steel. His voice was the voice she remembered, a little colder, a little more embittered perhaps, but the same stirring voice she had first heard on the patroon's boat in New York.

"I think there is something you did not tell me, mistress," Court said in a hard voice.

Charity's pulse quickened. She considered the great strapping buccaneer with a thrill of alarm. "And what might that be?"

"You did not tell me that the captain of the ship that took you pretended to be under orders from me!"

Her eyes widened innocently. "And was he not?"

"You have my word that he was not. Now tell me, what flag did St. Clair fly under?"

"French, I think—until they hoisted another. A black one, with some kind of white streak. Dr. Cavendish thought it might be an oar."

Court's head lowered a little, like a bull before it charges. "Are you sure?" he growled.

"It might have been an oar," she said. "but I am not sure now."

"Not sure?" he echoed, looking at her with contempt.

"It did not interest me!" she flashed. "I was more interested in what they might do to us than what flag they flew!" And then, because she hoped to anger him, she added, "I do remember that Captain St. Clair called after the *Gull's* crew in the longboats, 'Tell Charles Towne Captain Court sends them greetings'."

He ripped out an oath. "And you did not tell me that!"

"Why should I?" she cried. "And how could it possibly matter? Don't you take ships too?"

"Not English ones," he said grimly. "I'm a buccaneer, not a pirate. There's a deal of a difference as Captain St. Clair will soon be learning."

With that he swung on his heel and made a gesture to the men who had brought in his goods. They trooped out after him, grinning. John Ravenal, watching them, smiled grimly.

"Where are they going?" Charity asked, bewildered. "He just got here. Why is he running out like that?"

"He'll be looking for Captain St. Clair," Ravenal said. "And from the look on his face, he'll most certainly be finding him. I would not wish to be St. Clair at this moment."

"Why? In God's name, *why,* John?"

"'Tis proof he has now of what before was only a suspicion," explained Ravenal. "There's a price on the captain's head in Charles Towne now, ye know that, don't ye? And on Kirby's as well."

She shook her head.

"Well, there is. And the reason is that English ships are being taken by French pirates, yet somehow the blame is being thrown on Captain Court. He must have got wind of how they were doing it—and now ye've told him what St. Clair said. Captain Court's not a man who cares to hang for another's doing. He'll be carving Captain St. Clair's vitals for it, I'll be bound."

Charity shuddered.

Polly was asleep upstairs and Charity had half a mind to go up and wake her, but decided against it. Restlessly she paced the courtyard, listening for every sound from the street. Finally she went to stare out the barred front windows. Cook had dinner ready and it was growing late. Darkness had fallen before Charity, who sat slumped in a chair by then, heard the heavy front door open. She started up as Ravenal's voice boomed, "Did ye find him?" Court's deep resonant voice answered, "Aye, but I bungled it. He'll live, Leeds tells me."

The man would live and Court said he'd *bungled* it! Charity waited speechless, half expecting to see him come in with his arm in a sling or a bloody bandage tied around his head.

What greeted her was the same stern-faced man as before, who stopped short at sight of her. "Have ye supped?" he inquired.

She shook her head. "I waited."

"Then sup with me. I haven't eaten since dawn." He strode into the dining room, letting her trail after, unfastened his swordbelt and let his rapier fall with a clatter onto a chair.

Charity ate little, but watched with fascination as he demolished a huge cut of beef and drank numerous flagons of wine. "You are very silent," he remarked, when he had finished. "Well, since you choose not to talk, I'll say something. You cost me a packet, but in that dress I'm thinking you're worth it."

She flushed—and not entirely with pleasure. Something in his voice said *I own you and will take you in my own good time*.

"I was thinking of the man you injured and my part in it," she said stiffly.

He looked astonished. "Oh, so that's what's bothering you, is it? I'd remind you that that same St. Clair, whom I carved but a little, plucked you off your ship and would, I'm told, have bought you as a gift for his crew. I'd not waste time grieving over him, were I you, mistress."

Charity shivered. In this safe comfortable house, in these fine silken garments, she had somehow forgotten that. But now a cold wind brought it back to her.

"Will ye take wine?" he asked.

She nodded soberly and he filled a flagon for her. She sipped it, wishing she could understand him.

"You were with Monmouth, were you?" she asked suddenly.

He looked at her sharply. "What has Kirby told you?"

"That you were in England on personal business and got caught up in the uprising. You were captured together and escaped."

"That is true," he said. "I had sought shelter in a friendly house when the soldiers came. I had other things to do that seemed more pressing, so instead of hiding I tried to fight my way out. It was a mistake; there were too many of them. When they searched the house, they found Kirby too. I hadn't known he was there, hadn't met him till then. Later, when our captors broke into our host's wine cellar and were the worse for drink, we managed to make our escape."

"He said you were there because of . . . a lady."

His eyes grew keener. "So you wish to hear about that?"

404

She waited in silence.

"'Tis the story of my life you're asking for," he said slowly. "Well, there's no reason you should not hear it —and from me, rather than in bits and pieces, dragged out of Kirby."

She flushed, but he had got up and was pacing about the room, head lowered, hands behind his back.

"Mine was a seafaring family in Plymouth," he said. "My father owned two tall ships. My betrothed did not like the sea—she was of the landed gentry though her father had fallen on hard times—and so I made shift to leave it. I sailed away on one of my father's ships as second in command to its captain, intending to establish myself as a merchant in the Colonies. I never reached the Colonies. We were attacked by a Spanish warship and taken as prisoners to Spain, where the files were ransacked and much was found against our good captain—piracy and I know not what else. He was sentenced to death. As was I and the rest of the crew."

"Why?"

"For keeping bad company, I suppose. Because of my strength, my sentence was commuted to life in the galleys and I served two years chained to an oar."

She shivered. "At Daarkenwyck they chained me."

He gave her an inscrutable look. "So we both remember chains. . . ." He returned to his pacing. "A storm broke the galleon apart off the Irish coast and by good fortune my chains were broken. Others were not so lucky. It seems I was meant to live and not to die. I clawed my way ashore, nearly drowned, and made my way in rags to England—where I arrived unfortunately at the height of the Monmouth Rebellion. My mind was not on rebellions but on my betrothed, who believed me dead. I was too late. Her father had insisted that she would not spend her life waiting for a dead man, and forcibly married her off to a "better catch." When I discovered that she was lost to me, I struck out for Plymouth—but was caught as a Monmouth supporter and would have been hanged had I not managed to escape. When I reached Plymouth I

405

found that my father and brother were both dead, our fortune gone."

Raging from his treatment at the hands of the king's men, his very soul blackened to frenzy by the loss of the girl he loved, he had signed on incognito for Barbadoes. There, with a picked band of cutthroats, he had taken a ship and roared into the Caribbean with so much hell in his heart that, as Charity knew, his very name had become a legend and ballads were sung of him in the taverns of Tortuga and the dens of Port Royal.

He had sacked Spanish towns, Court told Charity, his voice level and cold. His brass-hilted rapier had drunk deep of Spanish blood; he had caught more than one rich treasure galleon by surprise and sent a warning shot across her bows; he had boarded Spanish merchantmen and taken their rich cargoes, sold their men into slavery—even as had been done to him—sent his gold to French banks, to Dutch banks, anywhere but England. He was now a rich man with a handsome house in Tortuga, several ships in addition to the *Sea Witch,* and many shares of stock in the Dutch East India Company.

But, she realized, he is still a renegade, a man with a price on his head. He can never go home to England.

And the woman he had yearned for in the long hard months when he had strained naked at the oars, burned by the sun, lashed by the whip, dreaming of vengeance . . . that woman now belonged to another. She would never father his sons or walk beside him at eventide in the fair English countryside.

No wonder his eyes grew cruel at times, Charity thought. He wanted to make the world pay for his ruined life.

CHAPTER 35

Polly was very upset when she learned that Court had arrived and that she had been allowed to sleep through dinner. "He'll be thinkin' me ungrateful," she cried. "Not to greet him after what he saved me from!"

"Maybe we'd better wait and see what he's saved us *for*," said Charity tartly, and Polly looked bewildered.

"He's a fine gentleman," she insisted. "Dr. Kirby did tell me all about him."

Not quite, thought Charity grimly. But she kept silent for she thought it not too wise to upset Polly, who was still weak. "Leeds said we weren't to disturb you when you were sleeping," she said. "He wants you to regain your strength."

As she left Polly's room, Charity met Court.

"It is December 23rd," he said gravely. "Tonight I shall expect you downstairs, dressed for dancing."

She stared at him. Was he making some joke?

"Ah, I see your memory is even shorter than your temper," he said whimsically. "On a night in December last year, I made you a promise that if I lived, I should find you and dance a dance with you on the anniversary of our meeting."

She was startled. He had remembered her foolish words, so lightly spoken!

"I ended hating you that night," she said.

"I am aware of that." He bowed slightly. "But now that we have exchanged the story of our lives, is it too much to hope that we could begin again?"

"I . . . will be there," murmured Charity, as he strode past her and was gone for the day.

In the afternoon Kirby dropped in for his usual glass of wine.

"How is St. Clair?" she asked him.

Kirby shrugged. "As good as may be. He'll lie abed for a few months, but he'll recover."

"Isabel and Timothy?"

He laughed. "Happy as turtle doves. Tim and his Spanish bride haven't even left the house—though I presume he will now that Jeremy's back. Twas the first voyage Tim's missed since he signed on. Love does evil things to a man!"

Charity was still thinking about that remark, later in the evening, as she dressed for dancing. Polly—also dressed in her best—joined her and they went down the gallery stairs to supper. Both wore shawls clutched about them, for it had begun to rain and the air was damp and cold. Gloomily Charity surveyed the dripping palms and wet hibiscus, streaming water. It was hard for her to believe that tomorrow would be Christmas Eve.

For the occasion, Court had dressed in the Spanish style. Tall and stern he looked, dressed in his coat of heavy lustrous black silk trimmed with silver, black silk knee breeches and stockings, and a silver brocade waistcoat. He stood at ease, as the court gentlemen did, with his plumed hat under one arm.

Charity introduced Polly and, as if they were duchesses, he made a leg to them both. "There is a fire in the dining room, ladies," he said and escorted them there, gravely taking their shawls and depositing them on a chair while they warmed themselves at the fire.

Charity was first to turn to him. She wore a sweeping copper-velvet dress, full-skirted, tiny-waisted, its color deepening to flame in the glow from the hearth. The reflection of the flames seemed to race down her sumptuous velvet-clad figure and along her white throat to caress the tops of her breasts, turning her skin to iridescent peach and gold. Firelight deepened

408

her pale hair to shimmering gold and danced in her topaz eyes.

"All Tortuga would be dazzled could they see you now," Court said gravely, and Charity thanked him with a deep curtsy. His eyes flickered for a moment as they rested on Charity's neckline. Inclining his head, Court said, "I have brought gifts for you both and I will not wait till Christmas Day for I may have business that takes me away. Ella and cook already have theirs. Mistress Polly, I will give you yours now, and Mistress Charity's after we have danced a turn."

On the table lay two identical carved wooden boxes. Court picked one up and opened it, took out a letter sealed with sealing wax.

"The *Swallow* sails for England ten days hence, weather permitting," he told her. "Dr. Kirby says you will be well enough to travel so I have arranged for your passage." He handed her the letter. "When you arrive in Plymouth, Mistress Polly, take this letter to George Cotter at the address given here. Give it to no one but him. Should he be out, wait for him at a decent inn. He will arrange for your return home and see that you have enough money to be able to marry the man who is waiting for you there."

"My Jack?" gasped Polly. "But how do you know about him, sir?"

"Kirby told me. Merry Christmas, Mistress Polly."

She burst into tears and, dropping to the floor, hugged him about the knees. "Oh, sir," she sobbed. "Nobody's ever been so kind to me ever. I'll say my prayers for you always, that I will. And my Jack will too!"

"Faith, I may need them," he muttered, leaning down and gently disengaging her arms. "Drink deep of English air for me, Mistress Polly," he added on a somber note. "For tis a draught I've missed of late."

Her eyes abrim with tears, Polly nodded.

Charity felt her own throat constrict at Polly's happiness. Her eyes met Court's and she gave him a gentle

409

smile. He turned swiftly away as if he could not bear it and poured them both some wine.

"Your health, Mistress Polly. And yours, Mistress Charity." He drained his glass.

Polly, silent and happy at dinner, had a withdrawn air about her, as if she was already back in England with her Jack in a little cottage all their own. Charity picked at her roast goose. In a way she envied Polly, whose problems could so easily be resolved with a little largess.

The other gift box lay unopened on the table, piquing her curiosity. She supposed it, too, contained passage money, that would send her back on the *Swallow* with Polly. Court's mood was mellow. He drank and talked of Christmas in Devon, and she recalled Christmas in Torquay and in Bath. Lifetimes ago . . . a world of mistletoe and holly. She remembered the twelve days of Christmas she had spent visiting Priscilla Walsingford in Hampshire, and the boy from Oxford who had proposed and whose guardian had taken him away because she wasn't good enough for him. In England at Christmas Yule logs were burned and carolers made their rounds through falling snow.

Here in Tortuga it was raining, the hard-pelting rain of the tropics, gushing out of the skies like a million tears. Already the courtyard was soaked and rain beat against the windows. It was not really cold but the excessive dampness in the air made it seem so. Under the battering sheets of water, the palms in the courtyard swayed and bent.

So much had happened to her here. . . . It would seem strange to go back to England—for she did not think that Court would send her to Barbadoes. He was not a man, she thought ruefully, to do anything halfway. To England she would go. She felt a certain disappointment about leaving, and told herself that was because Alan Bellingham would be far away across the water, even more unreachable than he was from Tortuga.

Sadly she realized that in spite of all the terrible

things that had happened to her here, she would miss the New World.

After they had eaten, Polly, who had been tired by the events of the evening, asked to be excused. Dr. Kirby had told her to retire early to ensure her recovery.

Charity and Court were left alone in the firelight.

She started as she heard the front door open, the scrape of boots. He watched her.

"Ravenal's let them into the hall," he said. "Musicians. To play for us."

She was touched. All this time he had remembered his promise to dance a measure with her. From the hall drifted in the plaintive sound of guitars.

Court rose and bowed. "Mistress Charity, will you do me the honor?"

She rose and took his hand and whirled with him light-footedly across the floor. As the music throbbed, she found she was far too aware of Jeremy Court, of his touch, of his pale intent gaze. After a while, in an effort to shake off the sheer physical pressure of his nearness, she closed her eyes and imagined they were dancing at a great ball at Magnolia Barony. The raindrops pattered a steady accompaniment to the guitars.

"I think you are not with me," he murmured. "Your mind is elsewhere."

She opened her eyes and smiled dreamily. "I was imagining we were dancing at Magnolia Barony," she said. "They gave a great ball there, but I was not allowed to attend."

Something changed in his face. Now his light eyes flickered with malice. "Perhaps the mistress of the manor felt you would distract her husband," he suggested.

"Oh, no," objected Charity. "He adores her. In Charles Towne they are called 'the perfect couple'." She was thinking of Marie's perfidy, of her many lovers, but said no more.

"You have mentioned this perfect planter before," he said coldly. "What is it that so ennobles him to women? His wealth?"

411

She felt indignant. "His selflessness! His consideration! His generosity! His—his—I am tired of dancing, Captain Court."

"Then perhaps it is time for me to give you your gift." He opened the second small box. "Turn around," he instructed.

She did so, bewildered, and felt the cold stones of a necklace go around her neck. "Topaz and diamonds, like your eyes," he said. As he adjusted the necklace his fingers brushed her bare bosom and—just as they had at Daarkenwyck—left a trail of fire in their wake. With slow deliberation his hands left the necklace and moved about her bare throat, down to her velvet bodice's low-cut top. Charity's senses whirled.

"Is this necklace your gift to me?" she cried.

"Not the only one. I have others." He laughed low in his throat and his fingers quested farther into the cleft between her breasts, probing the soft flesh there. Suddenly his head bent and he spun her around so that his lips met hers, closed over them with a soft sudden pressure as his hands explored farther. She was held to him tightly, feeling the hard pressure of his thighs through her velvet dress, his hard chest pressed against her own. Her every sense quickened and came alive. As he lifted his head and stared down at her, she, with a swift cry of shame wrenched away from him.

"You cannot buy me with a necklace," she said in a shaking voice.

"Ah, was I buying you?" he said softly. "Perhaps I was." His face turned moody. "The necklace is yours, Mistress Charity. I bid you good evening."

Before she had time to frame a reply, he had reached the door and passed through it. She heard him talking to the musicians in the hall, heard the jingle of coins, heard the front door open. She waited but he did not return.

After a while, she went upstairs to her room. Gazing into the mirror, she studied the topaz and diamond necklace, then took it off and flung it down. Outside the rain continued to beat down. Later, she tossed and

412

turned in bed, scolding herself. Had she but waited a little longer and held her tongue, he would have told her to ready herself for passage on the *Swallow* like Polly—and perhaps given her an envelope to a banking gentleman as well.

With an angry gesture, she pulled the covers over her head and managed at last to go to sleep—to dream of dark-faced buccaneers and the clash of cutlasses and dead men underfoot. In the morning it occurred to her that since her arrival in Tortuga she had not dreamed once her old dream of walking naked into her lover's arms.

CHAPTER 36

Of course Court would send her back! Did he not always return the English women he bought to England? Charity was still telling herself that the next morning when Polly asked her anxiously if she had begun to pack. Charity bit her lip and turned away, ashamed to admit that Court had not yet told her when she could leave.

"What did he give you?" asked Polly innocently.

"A necklace," said Charity in a strangled voice. "Topaz and diamonds."

Polly's jaw dropped. Before she could pounce on that and ask her a barrage of questions, Charity fled. Downstairs, she was told that Court had already left.

They spent Christmas Eve together, Polly and Charity. And were joined by Kirby, who'd been drinking rum and roguishly kissed them both under a sprig of what he insisted was mistletoe but looked more like some exotic tropical plant to her.

Christmas Day dawned and Court still had not returned. Charity suspected that he had sailed away to deliver goods to some dark mynheer, for he did not return until the day before the *Swallow* was to sail.

By now Charity had determined to sail on the *Swallow*, with or without his permission. The necklace would pay for her passage! But when she saw the *Sea Witch* race into the bay—and she saw it at once for she had kept watch—some perverse spirit made her change from her silken finery to the green dress Alan Bellingham had bought for her aboard the *Marybella*. The dress seemed worn and tired looking although it still fit prettily. She stared at herself in the mirror. *Do I want him to pity me?* she asked herself.

Swiftly, before the *Sea Witch* could dock, she changed into the pumpkin dress she had made at Magnolia Barony. The mirror told her that was better but . . . it needed something. Her eyes strayed toward the topaz and diamond necklace. As she heard the front door open, she hurriedly put it on.

When Court came into the courtyard, she was on her way down the stairs.

At sight of him, she came to a full stop and regarded him closely. His was an arresting figure such as might make the heart of a . . . a lesser woman leap, she told herself. A woman without scruples. She was not interested in him, of course, but she admitted that others might be.

He stood, boots planted well apart, dressed once again in rakish Spanish fashion, and watched her descend the stairs. With a low ironic bow he greeted her. Something about his manner irritated her. She returned his greeting and observed, "I see for all you profess to hate the Spanish, you prefer their fashions."

"On the contrary. Spain took her toll of me—now I take my toll of her. In my war with Spain, I take my recompense any way I can. It amuses me to don my enemies' clothes—as I see it amuses you to wear their jewels."

"Supper is not yet ready," she said menacingly. "I would change my gown before I dine."

His eyebrow had a sardonic quirk. "As you wish," he said and strode past her, upstairs toward the room she thought of as his treasure room.

With fingers that trembled—she did not know why his every word and gesture should upset her so—she removed the necklace and the pumpkin dress and changed once again to the worn green dress that Alan had given her. Her fingers brushed the material lovingly. Its very touch reminded her of Alan. Her eyes flashed. She would make this buccaneer return her to Charles Towne, that she would!

When she was ready to dine, she went looking for

Polly and found her in her room, half-dressed and very upset. "My stockings," Polly wailed. "I can't find those good ones you gave me!"

"Cook had water boiling a while ago. Perhaps Ella thought it was a good chance to wash them and took them down."

"Oh, but if she washes my stockings now," gasped Polly, "they'll be wet and I won't be able to take them with me—I can't go on board carrying wet stockings! Can't you stop her?"

"I'll try," promised Charity and dashed from the room. In the hallway she collided with Court. He caught her and for a moment their bodies, flung together, were locked in a warm embrace. She felt little thrills fan out like ripples in the water wherever he touched her. For a moment her blood sang and the world seemed aslant as he stared down at her.

Then another expression, something indefinable, came over his face and with firmness he set her away from him and moved on. He moved with determination as if his will had for a moment weakened and he would now make up for it.

Shaken, she stared after him, damning her treacherous body because it was so sensitive to this man's touch. Her eyes were dark as she watched him go. And not till he had disappeared did she start downstairs to prevent Ella from washing Polly's stockings. She returned with the stockings and gave them to Polly absently. Then she squared her shoulders and again started downstairs. Polly followed in her wake, looking alarmed.

In the dining room Court greeted them with a bow.

"Ah, I see we are now drenched in modesty," he commented, eyeing Charity's worn green dress.

"It was given to me by the finest man in all the world," Charity said loftily. "I wear it in remembrance of him."

He studied it. "A fitting memorial—prim of cut, somewhat worn, a little faded."

She glared at him. All through dinner she fumed. Across the table Polly looked scared and made haste

417

to excuse herself and scurry away as soon as the near-silent meal had ended.

Still Charity sat at table, brooding on Jeremy Court's remarks about the gown she was wearing. Across from her, the buccaneer sat at his ease, richly attired in garments he had taken at gunpoint, while he cast snide remarks at the kindly gifts of a man of character like Alan Bellingham! Her temper rose fiercely. How dared he criticize her? He, a sea-going robber, a bloody pirate! And he was playing with her cruelly, leaving her dangling, for he had not told her when she was to depart. In the intensity of her emotion she leaned forward. "I was brought to my present situation by men like you," she said. "Betrayers of trust!"

"Oh, am I that?" His voice was bored, his gaze flicked over her contemptuously.

"Yes," she cried, her fists clenching. "And those who deal with you!" In her wild excitement, she had entirely lost sight of the fact that her problems had been brought on by her mother's avarice, her aunt's avarice, and a fierce religious group who had eagerly condemned her to death—all that had come after was merely consequence.

"Well," he said lightly, "those who deal with such as I are less than perfect, I'll admit. Sure, you must have seen a deal of injustice in your day."

"That I have!" she flashed. "And been the butt of much of it!"

"Having lived so long," he added with an ironic tone.

Charity flushed. "I have lived a lifetime since I arrived in these Colonies."

When he stared at her, her flush deepened. Obviously he thought she meant something else, that she had been held in the arms of many men. There had been after all not so many!

"I am not what you think!" she snapped.

"Oh?" For the first time that day amusement gleamed in his wintry eyes. "And pray what do I think you to be?"

"A whore," she said flatly.

"Ah, now that I don't. Were you that, you'd be easily dealt with. No, I think you're one of life's unfortunates, like myself, washed up on these shores to paddle about as best we can. Will you have a glass of wine with me, or is your blood up so much you can't swallow it?"

He was making fun of her! She seethed inwardly. "I would enjoy a glass of wine," she answered in a voice that shook.

He smiled. She was not sure it was a nice smile. His was a face the rages of hell had blown across. There was death in his eyes too; many men had seen it there. For a moment the image reached her, but it was gone as his competent hands poured out the wine.

"If you must entice me with your low-cut dresses and your long fluttering lashes, you must take the consequences," he said lazily, proffering her a glass. "I'm a man used to taking."

Rebellious color stained her face as she remembered the deep decolletage of the velvet gown she had worn before he left. "I but wore the dress you gave me!"

"No, you wore your own *choice* of those dresses I gave you. Not all of them are so revealing."

"You said to come down dressed for dancing!"

"That I did. And that you did. But it seems you were dancing with someone else. I liked not your choice of dancing partners."

"When am I to be released?" she demanded.

He studied her, his light eyes mocking her. "Oh? Are you to be released?"

"But—but . . ." stammered Charity. "They told me you always release the English women that you buy."

"Not all," he said, turning away to pick up a pipe. "For example, I have no intention of releasing you."

Charity stared at him. His back was to her as he lit his pipe and he cut a haughty figure in his lean Spanish silks.

"But you *can't* keep me here!" she burst out.

"Can I not? Faith, it cost me a packet to buy you.

Why should I not keep you for the full three years, mistress?"

"Because I will not let you!" she said through clenched teeth and ran from the room.

His mocking laughter followed her up the stairs.

The *Swallow* sailed on schedule. From the quay, Charity waved farewell to Polly and grew wistful as the tall-masted ship fled the harbor, white sails billowing against the brilliant blue sea. Polly, she thought, lucky Polly, was going home. . . .

Around her all was confusion. A popular pirate captain had just put into port with a considerable haul. Dangling cutlasses and swords clinked against each other in the jostling crowd and bright-eyed women moved among them, pairing up with the disembarking buccaneers and taking them off to rum shops and brothels.

One of the women, wearing a wild striped dress, caught Ravenal's eye. When he turned to gaze at her admiringly, Charity saw her opportunity and she seized it. Quickly, slipping behind a big black island woman selling oranges, she edged through the crowd of vendors and harlots and buccaneers and traders and began to run. She ran toward the governor's mansion.

She knew where it was because Kirby had told her. She could even see it from the dockside. A big stone house with a walled courtyard which, like Court's, commanded a view of the harbor. "We've a governor of sorts," Kirby had said in answer to her inquiry. "He's French—name of d'Ogeron." She had tucked away the name and the information for future reference, and now she would make use of it.

Skirts flying, she ran. Behind her, she heard Ravenal's deep-voiced shout, heard him knocking his way through the crowd, scattering buccaneers and vendors alike as he pounded after her. But Charity was fleet and she had a head start. Like an arrow, she flew straight for that big stone house, whose courtyard gate lay open before her. Through that gate she plunged, slamming and bolting it in Ravenal's face as he thundered up.

"Tis no use doing this, mistress," he pleaded. "The governor—"

But Charity had already pushed past an astonished servant who was carrying out the slops and had flung herself into the cool elegant hall of the governor's mansion.

Two startled women saw her arrive and fled in opposite directions, disappearing behind closed doors, to be immediately replaced by a man with a naked cutlass who stared at her for a moment, then sheathed his blade. He was big and fierce-looking and he limped on a leg that ended in a wooden peg. In dockside French he asked Charity what she required.

She stated that she required an immediate audience with the governor, that she was beset by rogues who had imprisoned her.

Peg-leg considered this, chewing it over as he might a tough cut of meat. Then he sighed and beckoned her to follow him. Still panting from her wild flight, Charity walked across the stone floor and was brought up before a handsome door on which Peg-leg knocked discreetly.

Bade to enter, he swung open the door and Charity had her first look at the governor of Tortuga. Monsieur d'Ogeron was middle-aged, slightly built and dapper and dressed in the latest styles of France. His lace-cuffed hand was at that moment handing a paper to a square-cut fellow in leathern breeches, who sported a wide gold earring in one ear.

"Thankee kindly for the letters of marque," said Gold Earring, and brushed past Charity on his way out.

With a deprecatory smile the governor thrust some gold coins that were lying on his desk into a drawer and rose.

"Mademoiselle," he said in French with a courtly bow, "please to sit down. In what way may I assist you?"

"You are the governor here?"

"I have that honor." He inclined his head gravely.

"Then I wish to seek asylum here in your house." Charity sank into a chair.

His eyebrows elevated. "Asylum, mademoiselle?"

"I was seized from the *Gull* and brought to Tortuga against my will."

He sat down behind his desk. "And who did this thing?" he inquired.

"Captain St. Clair. He had me sold at the slave auction with the Spanish prisoners. Captain Court bought me and detains me in his house. I wish to leave your island, Monsieur d'Ogeron, by the next ship. Although I am expected in Barbadoes, I would be glad to return to Charles Towne—or failing that, to England."

The governor's fingers drummed on the polished desk. "You say Captain Court detains you in his house?"

She nodded. "He has refused to release me."

"I see. Captain Court detains you and you have come to me." He was thoughtful. "Will you have a glass of wine with me, mademoiselle?"

Charity blinked. "I—I would be delighted, monsieur."

Over the wine, which was an excellent Bordeaux, the governor murmured, "I am surprised that Captain Court keeps an unwilling woman in his house. Somehow I would not have thought it of him."

"I can assure you that it is true."

"And you have come through the streets of Tortuga to me . . . these are dangerous streets, mademoiselle. Buccaneers are turbulent men."

"I well believe it," said Charity. She set down her glass, turned her big topaz eyes full upon him. "Can you help me, Governor d'Ogeron?" she asked appealingly.

The face of the middle-aged governor appeared somewhat dazzled. "For one of such beauty to ask and be refused would be to dishonor the fair name of France," he said gallantly. "I will help you to the saf-

422

est place in Tortuga, mademoiselle. Far safer than my own poor establishment."

She would have asked where that was, but d'Ogeron turned and snapped his fingers. When a servant appeared, the governor muttered something she could not catch. The servant excused himself and, after a moment, Peg-leg reappeared with two others.

"My men will escort you," d'Ogeron told Charity and waved them all away. As Charity moved toward the door, the governor sat down and mopped the perspiration from his forehead with a lace kerchief.

Flanked on either side by these two stalwarts, Charity walked back down the hall, through the pleasant tropical courtyard with its spicy smells and once again ventured into the street. Ravenal, she saw, had gone—scared away, no doubt, by the governor's outreaching authority. He would doubtless be telling Court about her escape at this very moment. She smiled at the idea.

Charity expected her escorts to take her to the quay and row her out to a ship—a French ship perhaps, one undoubtedly inviolate to those who would live under a French governor. But they did not. As they walked her briskly along, suddenly, fear overcame her. They were going back the way she had come. They were leading her back to—

"Oh, no!" she moaned. "I won't go back there!"

She turned to run, but the men seized her, and she realized they must have been expecting her to bolt. With both arms held firmly by the governor's lackeys, Charity waited as they knocked on Captain Court's nail-studded door. It opened and she was thrust forward at Ravenal.

"A gift from the governor," one said laconically.

"Mistress," John Ravenal, looking reproachful, scolded her, "ye could have been assaulted there on the street. Or snatched into one of the houses. Ye should not have run from me."

"Where is Court?" she asked tonelessly.

"He's in the chart room with Kirby and Timothy Hobbs."

She flounced past Ravenal and threw open the door to the chart room. Three pairs of eyes swung toward her, startled, as the heavy door banged against the wall. Directly in front of her stood Court, looking even more formidable than usual, his long body bent over a large map which he had been studying intently. On either side of him stood Timothy Hobbs and Leeds Kirby. She stopped and glared at them all impartially.

Court considered her, eyes narrowed. "Ah, I see you are back," he said lightly.

"You filthy pirate," she choked. "You have bought the governor!"

Timothy Hobbs looked amazed at this outburst and Leeds Kirby hid a grin.

"Filthy pirate I may be," said Court, "but there is certainly no need to buy the governor of Tortuga. He had already been paid for many times. In gold."

She was panting. "I will not stay here! Do you hear me? *I will not!*"

For a moment he regarded her. "Then shut the door quietly as you leave," he said, a warning note invading his silky tone.

For answer she flung out of the room, slamming the door with all her force.

She had not reached the stairs before he overtook her, gripped her shoulders and swung her around to face him. "Faith, your behavior needs a deal of mending," he said grimly. "Do not force me to mend it for you."

She was acutely aware of his strong hands gripping her shoulders. Of his nearness. Of the dark visage that bent over her own.

"You will not bend me to your will!" she shouted.

"You will bend or you will break," he retorted savagely. "I have no time for women's moods and tempests!"

He let her go so suddenly that she fell against the newel post for support. "Now hear me well," he said slowly, "for I will say this but once. You will keep a civil tongue in your head, Charity, or you will regret it." He turned to go and then paused. "In truth I have not used you so badly," he murmured.

Clutching the newel post in fury, Charity watched his long legs stride back to the chart room, his boots ringing on the tiles. Anger and disappointment so overwhelmed her that she felt she could not make the stairs. She went into the courtyard and sank into a chair. After a while she heard the chart room door open, heard the men saying their goodbyes. Timothy went on out, but Leeds saw her in the courtyard and came to speak to her.

"So you ran away?" he said.

"Yes. To that filthy governor!"

"D'Ogeron's not so bad," said Kirby. "Remember, the buccaneers are the owners in fact of this island. The governor's here on our sufferance. He gives us letters of marque—privateering commissions—to go against the Spanish, and it gives a color of legality to our doings which helps us in non-Spanish ports. The Spanish of course don't give a damn for his letters of marque—they hang us with the letters of marque around our necks."

"Then there's no government here at all?"

"Well," he mused, "I guess Jeremy's as near lord mayor of our city as any. He's well liked, he's dangerous—the best man with rapier or cutlass I've ever seen, and a dead shot. Few would cross him."

"I see," she said bitterly. "My cause is hopeless."

His green eyes regarded her, smiling. "I wouldn't say that," he murmured. "There are divertissements to be had, even in Tortuga."

"Divertissements!" She almost spat the word. "I've seen none. Court comes in with loot and goes out with it again, God knows where. He keeps me penned up here—for what purpose? I don't understand him."

"You mean he doesn't—"

"No!" said Charity, turning red.

"Faith," said Kirby in astonishment, "I'd never thought him a fool. Still . . ." he mused, "I suppose in Jeremy's case it's understandable."

"And what is that supposed to mean?" she flashed at him.

"Oh, he has his moods, has our Jeremy," said Kirby. She shot him a questioning glance.

"Bide your time and maybe you'll meet the cause of them," he said and bowed. And with that puzzling remark he left her, unsatisfied and staring after him.

CHAPTER 37

After her forcible return from the governor's house, Charity had kept a wary eye on Court, but he seemed to bear her no ill will for her attempt to escape. If anything, he ignored her. His days were spent either on business in the town or at his ship, which was being careened and refitted. His evenings were spent studying maps and charts with his shipmaster, Timothy Hobbs. She saw him only at meals, and not always then.

The weather continued to be pleasant: glorious days, and soft tropical nights in which the moon rode gleaming in the black skies and palm trees swayed on scented winds. Beguiling nights when Charity tossed and turned in her bed, wondering what would become of her. It seemed that Court did not desire her body. Perhaps, he kept her because of some whim—the desire to have an Englishwoman to breakfast with, to hear an accent whose sounds he remembered from his boyhood. Occasionally, her thoughts grew darker and she wondered if he might not be saving her for some worse fate. After all, he had reminded her that he had "paid a packet" for her. Perhaps he intended to turn a profit. . . .

To take her mind off such things, Charity spent her afternoons improving her Spanish with Dona Isabel, who seemed completely happy in her new house and new life. When Isabel confided that she was expecting a baby, Charity envied her.

For a while, Kirby's visits, which had made life more bearable, stopped. There was an epidemic of fever in the town and he was kept busy day and night.

Finally, the epidemic abated and Kirby did come by to tell her that old Dr. Cavendish, whose ransom had been paid, had departed in his outmoded rhine-grave trousers for his Carolina plantation. Charity smiled at that, and breathed a sigh of genuine relief when Kirby told her that St. Clair's men had scattered, signed on with other captains. St. Clair himself was making a slow recovery, and was a warning to others who might try to sail under Jeremy Court's colors. For the white oar on a black ground had a special meaning to Court: Spain had bent his proud back to the oar and now that oar was flung at them in challenge as the former galley slave brought their proudest ships to heel.

Lonely, Charity pressed Kirby to stay and talk to her. He was considered the island's best doctor and was much sought after. So, she asked him about his cases. Today—two stab wounds, a severed ear, one gunshot wound in the shoulder and a case of manzanilla poisoning, he told her.

"Manzanilla?" she asked.

"Swift and deadly," he elaborated. "Tis made from the fruit of the manchineel tree—the apples of death. Tis native to these islands. One of the Spaniards poisoned the food of the Dutch buccaneer captain who bought him. Twas a horrible death. The captain went raving mad and was threshing about on the floor."

"And the Spanish prisoner?"

He looked away. "Ye'll not like to be hearing what happened to him," he said grimly. "Let's just say he's no longer with us."

Charity shivered. Outside the thick walls of this house vile deeds were being committed every day in the dens and byways of Tortuga. She supposed she should be grateful for these thick walls, but she was not. Her anger at Court for keeping her here with an uncertain future increased daily and caused her to needle him.

"Were I old and ugly," she asked one day as they sat eating ripe golden oranges after dinner, "would you keep me here?"

His eyes narrowed. "I think you put too much value on your desirable flesh. There are many women in the world who tempt men. You are but one of them."

Charity continued to regard him rebelliously.

"Their market price is really quite low," he added brutally.

White-faced, Charity jumped up and ran from the room. She kept to her room the next day until he had breakfasted and left the house. From the kitchen she filched some meat and cheese and bread and wine and carried them up to her room. That damned pirate with his insulting ways could dine without her tonight!

She flung back the fine linen sheets, plumped the soft down pillows, attired herself attractively in a sheer nightdress of lawn and lace—cool and comfortable in the warm evening—and settled back in her bed with a book she had borrowed from the chart room.

Before she had read a chapter, the sound of footsteps climbing the stairs three at a time reached her. Heart pounding, she put down the book, then picked it up again as the door flew open.

Court stood there, eyes blazing. "Tis time to sup," he declared.

With studied insolence, Charity put down the book. "I'm not hungry," she said.

His eyes fell on the trencher with its remnants of broken meat and bread. "Tis easy to see why," he said sternly. "Still, hungry or no, you will sup this night. And with me. Unless you prefer the consequences."

She settled herself more comfortably against the pillows, aware she made a fetching sight in the revealing gown. "And I suppose the consequences are that you will seize me as you did at Daarkenwyck and half tear my clothes off?" She made to get up. "Faith, I'd rise willingly rather than endure that again!"

His wintry eyes played over her. "I have willing mistresses," he said coldly. "I have no need of trumped-up affection. Up." And turned on his heel.

With a scream of fury, Charity threw her book at him. It missed his head. Its heavy leather binding

429

crashed against the door, and it fell open, its pages crumpled.

Jeremy Court turned. His face had a dangerous look, the face of a man who had lost patience. With two swift strides he had reached her side. Shaking with wrath, Charity regarded him balefully, her eyes wide and angry.

He stood looking down at her. Then very deliberately his hand shot out and he yanked her from the bed. She cried out and kicked at him, but found herself turned over his lap, her head down, arms and legs flailing. She gasped as his large hand landed a stinging blow on her buttocks, almost bare in the thin lacy gown. Screeching with fury, she redoubled her efforts to free herself. He held her like a vise and rained several more blows upon her already smarting bottom.

Finally, he stood up, spilling her to the floor, where she lay, watching him venomously.

"If you behave like a child, I will treat you like one," he said. "If tomorrow your temper has not improved you will feel my palm again."

Almost stifled by rage, Charity lay on the floor and watched him sweep out the door, heard the clatter of his departing boots on the stairs. She brought her fists down on the floor and would have wailed—but stopped herself in time. Downstairs Court might very well hear her outraged cries and mistake them for despair.

She would not give him that satisfaction.

To her fury, after his having insisted she be present, Court did not come down for breakfast the next morning.

After a while she went up to his room and flung wide the door, determined to say a few words of her own. He stood with his back to her and at the sound of the door flying open he swung about, hand on sword-hilt.

Charity stopped in astonishment to gaze at him. Dressed as he was in snowy white linen shirt, lace cuffed, in dove gray satin kneebreeches, a silver brocade waistcoat and wide-cuffed charcoal velvet coat trimmed in gold, he might have been an English gentleman standing on the steps of Whitehall.

"Where is your Spanish wardrobe that gives you such glee?" she asked.

His dark brows drew together. "I have put it aside for the while. Do you make it your practice to enter rooms without knocking?"

Her lip curled. "Since you were so hot to breakfast with me, I came up to see why you had not joined me."

"Your wish to dine alone is now granted for a time," he said. "You will keep to your room for the next few days."

She felt dashed. "Is—is even the courtyard denied me?"

"Yes," he said. "Even that. Ravenal will take you for a stroll through the town once daily so that you may exercise. Do not attempt to escape him again. My temper has grown shorter and I will not brook it."

To be exercised! Like a dog on a leash! She was so upset she could not speak.

"Close the door as you leave," he said. "Unless you prefer to watch me change these trousers to a pair less tight. I am going to the quay to meet a guest and I have no intent to split them as I make a leg."

A guest! So that was it! She glowered at Court as he tossed his coat and waistcoat to a chair. He was about to strip off his breeches, when she turned and left the room.

Curiosity piqued her and she stayed close to her upstairs window watching for this guest whose visit meant confinement for her. Her patience was soon rewarded for shortly afterward a little procession approached the courtyard. First came a litter carried by two husky men still in the uniform of Spain. And on that litter a lady, richly gowned in black. The folds of a heavy black lace mantilla concealed her face and head. She might have been in mourning. The wind blew the mantilla back a little, and Charity saw for a moment the gleam of white skin.

Beside the litter walked Court, meticulously

groomed as any court dandy, his black periwig catching the sun, a jeweled ring flashing red on his sun-bronzed hand. That hand rested on a tall beribboned ebony cane. Under his arm, most correctly, he carried a wide-brimmed charcoal-gray hat with dove-gray plumes, and from time to time he bent down courteously to say something to the lady.

Behind them toiled two men with trunks and after that a small crowd of the curious, whispering and giggling. One could plainly see that Tortuga found the arrival of Court's mistress titillating.

As Charity heard them coming into the house, she ran and shut her door—hard. And then sat down on her bed to think. She was very curious about this "lady in the black mantilla." Was she the Spanish mistress Court had kept for a while and then returned—now choosing to live a double life with her buccaneer sweetheart as well as her new husband in Havana? If she were close enough to visit she must have forgotten the man waiting in Spain and remarried in Havana. Charity was eaten up with desire to see her. Would she be a blinding beauty? Or merely some woman on whom his affection had fastened for curious reasons of his own?

It seemed she would have no chance to find out. Her food was brought to her in her room and although no attempt was made to guard her closely, Ravenal being presumably still on guard at the front door, dour cook at the back, she felt hemmed in. That evening, she watched from behind a pillar of the gallery and when she saw that Ella had served the couple in the dining room, she tiptoed downstairs and sped on bare feet across the courtyard to the closed door.

Inside she could hear the clink of glasses, the mutter of voices. She pressed an ear against the door but could not make out any words. Suddenly, aware that someone was standing behind her, she whirled. Ella stood there with a bottle of wine. Putting a warning finger to her lips, Charity glided just out of sight along the wall as Ella took in the wine. When she came out, Charity reached out an arm and gently prevented the door from closing. With it open a crack she could hear what was said inside.

A woman's low laugh floated out to her. Silvery, musical—a light, seductive, almost malicious laugh.

Charity clung to the doorjamb for support. Surely there could be only one laugh like that in all the world. The "lady in the black mantilla" was Marie Bellingham!

CHAPTER 38

Heart thudding, she forced herself to listen.

"Is there still a price on my head in Charles Towne?" Court was asking.

"Yes, Jeremy." Marie's voice beyond a doubt!

"I've learned who put it there—Captain St. Clair, flying under my colors. I ran him through for it, that I did."

Charity could hear Marie gasp. "You . . . killed him?" she asked in a faint voice.

"Nay, though I should have! My intent was to kill him, but my foot slipped and my blade pierced a hand's breadth from where I had aimed it."

Marie gave a little sob. "Oh, Jeremy, Jeremy, I cannot bear to think of you taking these wild chances. Must you live this desperate life?"

Court's response was moody. Charity could imagine him in the candlelight, dressed in his English grays, watching Marie across the table with his light wintry eyes. "I think that together we have made an unendurable situation for ourselves. You write me, you arrive, you are here for a few days, and then you go back to your unsuspecting planter in Charles Towne."

"But—it is the only way," she cried softly.

"At first I thought so. It seemed to me that a kindly fate had restored you to me—if only on occasion. Then it came to me that I was placing you in great danger. Not only do you constantly chance the seas to reach me—certainly there is danger there, from the Spanish and from pirates who do not observe the rules that govern the Brethren of the Coast—but at any moment you may be recognized and your whole life blasted."

Charity's hands clenched in fury as she heard Marie's eager, "Ah, Jeremy, tis a chance I take gladly!"

"Nay, but consider. You have told me this Carolina planter has built his life around you. What if he learns of me? What happens to you then?"

"My sister suspects," Marie admitted tremulously. "She considers it strange that I come to her so often and stay so briefly. She has threatened to write to Alan and ask him if he mistreats me that I am always running off to Barbadoes."

"So there you have it. And if she does write and Alan reads the letter, what then of your stories that you are off to Barbadoes at your sister's behest?"

"Alan would believe me against all the world," Marie said simply, and Charity felt the blood rise to her head and beat in her temple.

"He cannot be a complete fool," insisted Court. "Perhaps we should have done with these visits once and for all. It ill becomes you to go running off to seek a lover in some pirate's hole like Tortuga."

"Ah, Jeremy, how could you say that!" Charity grimaced, knowing Marie's large violet eyes with their dark-fringed lashes would be turned on him imploringly. "How could you hurt me so!"

"I did not mean to hurt you," was the grim rejoinder, "but perhaps to save you the pain of being found out. It's for your sake, not mine."

"Then say no more of parting!" cried Marie tremulously . "I cannot—I cannot stand it, Jeremy!"

Charity could not stand it either. She turned and fled on silent feet, in her heart a tumult greater than she had ever known.

Marie, *Marie Bellingham,* was here! Sleeping tonight in the notorious English buccaneer's bed, sharing his embraces, just as she shared Alan's husbandly embraces in Charles Towne. A pulse throbbed in Charity's forehead. She yearned to go down and confront Marie, to shout, "Why aren't you in Charles Towne with René?"

White-faced, Charity stared out at the uncaring

moon as it drifted over the pirate's stronghold, at the white stars blazing down upon Cayona Bay. Even the trade winds could not cool her hot face. And once she brought her fist down so hard she almost broke her wrist. She would confront Marie, she decided. Tomorrow morning!

But her anger wore her out and she fell asleep in her clothes. Limp as a rag doll she sprawled in a chair and when she woke the tropical sun was blazing. Quickly she dressed in fresh clothes, not caring what she wore, and ran downstairs.

At the foot of the steps Court met her.

"I was on my way to fetch you," he said. "My guest has departed and I would have your company at breakfast." Lean and dark, he towered above her. He looked tired, and his voice was conciliatory. He might have been speaking to a rebellious child who had been forgiven.

Charity was surprised. "She is gone?"

He nodded. "With the tide, early this morning. I thought it best."

So, she had lost her chance to confront Marie. Charity rose to her full height and her voice was wild. She seemed to see Marie on all sides of her, wherever she went—beautiful, mocking, glamorous Marie, beloved by all men.

"That woman is Alan Bellingham's wife!" she cried.

"I am well aware of that," he said.

"But—but if you know that, then—"

"She is the woman who was lost to me in England," he said quietly. "On a hill in Devon we plighted our troth long ago. I have not forgot. Nor has she."

"But she *married* Alan."

"Against her will, and under pressure from her father. A tyrannical old man who was against me from the first; I knew him well." His voice was bitter. "Do not condemn Marie too much. She was young and beautiful and she believed me dead." He stared into the courtyard, seeing not the palm fronds or the hibiscus swaying in the scented tropical breeze, but another lovely land—fair Devon far away. "And dead I was

437

while I pulled an oar for Spain. But—" he turned and gave her a twisted smile—"I came back to life, as you can see. Shipwrecked on the Irish coast, my chains were snapped by a mocking God who thought to amuse himself by my writhings."

"You blaspheme," she said softly.

"I do indeed," he sighed. "Gods and devils, they are all one to me. What are gods to galley slaves, toiling ceaselessly at the oars, naked under sun and rain, fainting beneath the lash, until at last death plucks them from their misery and their bodies are hurled to the sharks and barracuda for one last plundering?"

His bitterness struck her like a blow. As did the realization that the fabled "lady in the black mantilla" of whom all Tortuga whispered was his lost lady of Devon. Never, in her wildest flights of imagination had she dreamed that woman would turn out to be Alan Bellingham's wife.

"And you are faithful to this woman?" she murmured.

"I have been. In my own fashion."

His bitterness had washed over her like a flood, but now a bitterness of her own rose up to match it.

"Then you are a fool," she cried, "for she has had many lovers!"

He gave her a stern look. "That was before she knew I was alive," he said. "We all seek surcease where we can, Marie as well as I."

Charity's lip clenched in her soft lower lip. She would bring down this goddess! She would topple this statue of purity he had created and reveal her feet of clay!

"She has a lover *now!*" she snapped. "Did you not know it?" Her voice mocked him. "Your Marie loves a Frenchman named René du Bois. I have seen them together—I have seen her lie moaning in his arms amid the trees at Magnolia Barony!"

Court towered above her. Both his height and breadth seemed to grow so that she quailed in fear at this storm cloud that advanced upon her. His eyes, gray and deadly, stabbed at her like the rapier in his belt.

"We will have no more of this," he said slowly. "Do not speak her name again, or—" he raised his arm and she shrank back—"I will cleanse her name from your lips!"

For a moment Charity stared up at him. So tall and haughty and fearsome, standing there in his calm terrible defense of the unworthy Marie! Then, with a sob, she turned and ran back up the stairs.

She sent word she would not be down to breakfast. But, from the courtyard below, through her open door, she heard Court's voice rumble upward. "Tell Misstress Charity that if she does not appear *at once,* she will feel the flat of my cutlass on her winsome bottom the whole of the distance to the table!"

Charity rose with alacrity. There was no mistaking the deadliness of his tone. Sullenly, she approached the stairs and dawdled down them, moving more slowly with each lingering step, turning an insolent face toward him.

He watched her descent grimly, standing with his long legs spread well apart, his trousers drawn tight over his lean thighs, his hard gray eyes considering her. As she reached the bottom step he gave her a mocking bow and offered her his arm. Ignoring the arm, she marched toward the dining room and flounced down on the chair he held for her.

As they were served, he considered her across the table.

"I had thought to send you back to England," he said musingly.

"Good!" she cried. "I cannot leave here too soon! The place is hateful, you are hateful! When do I sail?"

"You do not," he said. "I have reconsidered."

Charity put down the piece of bread she had just broken. "You have *what?*"

"I realize now that I cannot let you return. You are a danger to Marie. You know that she comes here to visit me and—you have shown a vengeful spirit toward her. You might seek to harm her."

Rage warmed Charity's blood. She sat trembling,

her eyes sparkling savagely. At the moment she wanted nothing so much as to be revenged on them both.

"So, I have brought you downstairs to tell you that you may consider this house your prison."

"Am I not to be allowed out?" Her voice shook.

"Only in my company, or in the company of Ravenal, whom I trust."

"And all this because I was employed at Magnolia Barony?" she challenged.

"No, although that was the reason I kept you here at first. I wanted news of her."

She had not thought of that. She had thought the reason was a more personal one . . . a liking for her company, perhaps. Now the words went through her like an arrow shaft. *He had kept her with him only because he wanted news of Marie.* So overcome was she that she felt herself sway in her chair.

Then common sense reasserted itself. She must trick this buccaneer somehow, she must get away from him and regain her freedom.

"You would not have to send me back to Charles Towne," she said when she could speak again. "I could give you my word that I would stay in England if you sent me there."

His eyes roved over her face thoughtfully. "You would not keep it," he said at last. "You would return to him."

"To whom?" Her voice shook.

"To Alan Bellingham," he answered angrily. "It is plain you love him. Else why so bitterly attack his wife?"

"Would my word mean nothing?" she asked.

He gave a short laugh. "The word of a woman in love means little."

"And of a man in love even less!" she cried, rising so abruptly she knocked over her chair. "You promised to return me to England!"

His eyebrows raised as he considered her lovely outraged face. "And when did I promise you this, pray?"

"Why—why—you always send the women you buy back to England!"

"Not always. Did they tell you there was a Spanish lady?"

"You sent her back! Leeds Kirby said so!"

"Ah, but not to England—to Havana. And in my own good time. Kirby talks too much," he added humorlessly.

She stood, her hands clenched. A whole torrent of wails would not deter him in his firm purpose, she realized. No . . . it would take something else. She must find where the tender spots were. She would learn this man—study him, discover his weaknesses, she told herself grimly.

And thereby find a way to free herself from him forever.

She reached down and with some difficulty righted the heavy chair she had knocked over and sat back down upon it, trying to compose herself.

"There are ugly stories in Tortuga about you and this Spanish lady you kept here and then returned to Havana."

"Faith," he returned equably, "there are ugly stories in Tortuga about you and me. That does not make them true."

She tried again. "It is said she too was another man's wife."

"A widow, soon to be rewed. It is my misfortune to seek solace with other men's wives, as you have discovered."

"Do you not feel . . . jealousy, to know the women you hold dear lie in other men's arms when you are not with them?"

An imperceptible shiver went through his large frame although his face remained expressionless. Ah, she had thrust home, she thought in triumph.

When he spoke his voice was calm. "I have held only one woman dear. And she—through honor— could throw me only the crumbs from her table. With that I have had to content myself."

Charity glared at him. And transferred her anger

441

to her trencher. "I am not hungry," she declared, pushing it away.

"You will eat," he commanded. "It is no part of my intent that you should starve yourself and so become ill."

"Why?" she challenged. "Why should you care if I died even?"

He studied her. "That is difficult to answer," he said. "I suppose I feel a certain guilt that I hold an Englishwoman against her will. But—I have done worse." He shrugged.

"*Your* guilt! *Your* feelings!" she raged at him. "What about mine? Am I to be kept here eternally away from decent people, always in the company of sea robbers and buccaneers?"

She thought he winced at that. "You are right in what you call me," he said. "Although it was none of my making in the beginning, it has become God's truth. I am indeed a sea-robber and I am a buccaneer. But—" his voice hardened—"I am also your host, and as such you will pay me the respect that is due me. Or I will rip that handsome damask dress from your white skin and set you naked at the kitchen table eating scraps!"

A sob caught in her throat. She knew he would not do it, of course. But oh, how she yearned to hurl her goblet of wine at him and see its heavy silver lip strike his forehead making a dark bruise while its red port stained his face like blood!

"Am I excused?" she demanded fiercely, rising. "I would go to my room."

His cold eyes flicked over her. "No, you are not excused. Since we are to be penned up here together, we will eat our meals together and sit together in civilized fashion drinking our wine after dinner. We will speak of other and better times and we will make the best of what we have."

"By what right do you command me, Captain Court?"

A wry smile played over his dark face. "By right of purchase. I bought you in the marketplace."

442

She brought her fist down hard upon the table. "God's death, you're a villain!"

"Perhaps, but I ask you to consider your position. We are trapped here by circumstance, you and I. Life was none so good to you outside this island, was it? Nay, I have it from your own lips that it was not. Would you rather be in Massachusetts then, waiting for the fire? Or in New York trudging through the forests with four lusty trappers? Or perhaps in the patroon's blockhouse awaiting his pleasure?" His words lashed her, and she looked away for she could not meet his eyes. "So I think that you and I must come to an understanding. We live in hell, Charity—an earthly hell that was not of our own making, but we must dwell in it nonetheless. But in that hell we might reach out a hand to each other and make the days more bearable."

"You should have been a preacher," she mocked. "Next you will chide me with my sins!"

"No," he said soberly. "I will not do that. My own are too black to contemplate, and I find yours pale and restful by comparison."

She studied him, calmly now.

"Try to understand me," he said suddenly. "I am pledged to protect one woman, her to whom I plighted my troth—"

"On a hill in Devon," Charity finished woodenly.

"And so I must protect her honor too," he finished silkily. "She takes a long chance by coming to me under cover of her visits to Barbadoes."

Charity recalled Marie's other ruses to gain better access to her various lovers and yearned to tell him of them, but she thought better of it. He was a man of towering rages. To drive him too far would be dangerous.

"If she loves you so much, why does she not leave Alan and come here and live with you openly?"

"In honor she cannot," he sighed. "And she is a woman of honor, even though in your anger you would cast shame upon her. She gave her hand to Alan when

443

she thought me dead, and now she cannot lightly cast him aside."

Charity digested that. Marie had done her work very well, she realized. It would take a deal of undoing. Best to play along with him now, so she could strike later.

"I see that she cannot in honor leave Alan," she said, and sat back down.

He brightened. "You can see that? Ah, then you understand why I cannot let you go? Because even though you promised—and truthfully meant to keep your word—that you would not reveal what you have learned here, there might come a time when in anger or in confusion you might speak her name—and cost her all that she holds dear. Her husband's love, her peace of mind—"

"Her honor," added Charity, trying to keep the irony out of her tone and almost succeeding.

He gave her an uncertain look. "I think you mock me," he said slowly. "But no matter. It is not a thing to concern us much. Twas only that I wished you to understand why I have this great need to keep you here. It is not that I have anything against you, but—"

"I am a danger."

"To her," he finished.

They sat a while in silence.

"You could fare worse," he pointed out. "Here you will be well housed, well served."

"Like any captured bird," she said bitterly and rose. "Have I your permission to leave the table now? I would retire and leave you to your thoughts."

"They are dark ones today," he said and nodded.

She crossed the courtyard, white-faced, her teeth clenched. She had not known it was possible to hate a man so much.

The next day, when Kirby came by looking for Court, who was out, Charity turned on him accusingly. "You knew Marie Bellingham was Court's mistress and that I'd been employed at their plantation!"

"I knew." He paused. "You'd best not tamper with Court, Charity. You'll find his relationship with the

444

lady from Charles Towne has all the force of a marriage for him."

"But—Marie's already married," gasped Charity. "To Alan Bellingham."

"Jeremy doesn't really see it that way," said Kirby, frowning. "Marie was his first, you see. And they were torn apart. A few words spoken over her head by a minister didn't change things in his view. I think he stays out of Charles Towne to avoid killing Alan Bellingham."

Charity ignored that. "Why didn't Marie wait for him?"

"She thought he was dead. A reasonable assumption, when you come to think about it. He was gone a couple of years. When he finally returned, he found himself in the middle of Monmouth's Rebellion. But he went looking for her right through the thick of it. They caught him, of course, but they couldn't hold him. And he has never stopped thinking of her as his only love." Kirby's mood changed and he grinned. "So you'd better stop mooning over Jeremy and turn your face toward me. He's taken."

Charity tossed her head and bade him goodbye. She heard him laughing as he went out through the courtyard.

CHAPTER 39

At dinner that night Charity tried another tack with Court. "I will *buy* my way out of here," she told him. "I will earn money and pay you back for the money I have cost you. Surely you would not hold me then!"

"Earn money? In Tortuga?" Court's eyebrows shot up quizzically.

"Certainly," she said. "I will teach. I am proficient in French and Spanish. Surely there are many here who—"

His laugh interrupted her. "Teach? D'you not know these sea dogs come from France and Holland as often as England? And Spanish most of them know, either from service in the galleys or from Spaniards they've taken prisoner. Teach?" He laughed again.

She tapped her fingers, rebellious.

"Come," he said humorously. "We've finished our meal. Let us play whist and forget your desire to leave me." He rose.

"I do not play whist," she snapped, but rose and followed him.

"Then I will teach you. We can play two-handed." He drew a pack of cards from a drawer and pulled up a chair at the table in the center of the comfortable room she called the English room.

Sulkily she joined him, her eyes striking lights as brilliant as her topaz and diamond necklace in the candlelight as she watched him deal the cards.

She won the first game. And the second. He was watching her kindly and his very forbearance irritated her—this man so lately from Marie Bellingham's languorous arms! In the back of her mind she could hear Marie's tantalizing laugh and it galled her.

447

"I will wager you for my deliverance," she said recklessly.

He studied her thoughtfully. "And what do you wager?"

She straightened and touched the jewels around her throat. "This necklace, my silver comb—all that you have given me, against passage to Charles Towne."

"Passage to Charles Towne?" he growled.

She leaned forward, anger making her eyes even brighter. "Surely you must pass near it as you sweep the seas for prey. All I ask is that you take me near to shore and set me in a small boat—I will *row* to shore."

A cold expression passed over his lean dark face and something she could not fathom, that might have been anger, burned for a moment in his light eyes before wintry shutters closed down over them leaving them murky.

"I was ever a gambling man," he said. "All that I have given you, you say, against passage to Charles Towne? Faith, should I lose I'll sail you into Charles Towne harbor!"

She was taken aback at the controlled fury of his tone. Somehow, she had expected his usual mockery.

"Then deal the cards," she said stiffly.

He did, with consummate skill. As the game went swiftly against her, it came to her with sudden force that she was a novice up against a master. Before, he had merely allowed her to win. Now he was her adversary—crafty, skillful. She was overmatched and with a sinking feeling she realized it. She bit her lips, played recklessly, and lost.

Court swept the cards up in one hand and leaned back in his chair, a hard little smile playing around the corners of his mouth. "It seems you have lost your wager, Charity."

With all the dignity she could muster, Charity rose. In her mind she was recounting all the things he had given her—the scent from France, the small ornate mirror, the delicate ivory fan.

"I will pay my wager," she declared ringingly.

"Here." She undid the necklace and tossed it in a glittering heap onto the table. "I will go up and get the silver comb and other things."

He ignored the jewels that skittered toward him.

"Silver combs do not interest me," he said, and she did not like his expression. "But it has occurred to me that you did not come to me in a dress of yellow silk or in a chemise with silver lace spilling from the sleeves."

She caught her breath. "I will go upstairs and remove these clothes," she said, "and henceforth wear my old ones."

"That will not be necessary." Even as he spoke, he rose and in two long strides had reached the door and locked it. "All that I have given you—the words were yours. Yours will surrender to me, and at once!"

Too late Charity realized the trap into which she had fallen.

"No," she said, backing up a step. "No, I—"

His expression was bleak indeed. "Would you go back on your bet?" He took a threatening step toward her.

In panic she moved around the table, but he reached across suddenly and seized her wrist. In an instant he stood before her, holding her wrist tightly.

"So you see, you will not be required to row to Charles Towne—nor I to take you there," he said softly. "But I will have these clothes which are mine again!" With his other hand he thrust down into the soft cleft between her breasts, his big knuckles forcing her breasts apart, and firmly grasped the material of both her dress and her chemise. Giving a sudden wrench, he ripped the material straight down the front and sent the hooks flying.

Charity felt the material fall away from her breasts and torso. "Damn you!" She struck at him, but he seemed not to notice. His strong bronzed hand ripped the sleeve from her right arm and then from her left. As the material fell to the floor, she kicked at his shins and he suddenly scooped her up and wrested her skirt and petticoats from her. As she writhed in his arms, her chemise went. She fought him and her shoes fell

449

off. She felt her stockings ruthlessly torn from her legs. Panting, gasping, clawing at him, she heard him say coldly, "I will view what I have bought!" And felt herself dropped to her bare feet on the carpet, her naked figure spun around as if she were dancing, held by one arm high above her head.

She saw his hard eyes heat up as he looked at her and a smile spread over his dark face at the sight of her flushed angry countenance. The rosy flush spread down to her gleaming white shoulders and trembling breasts, to the silky skin of her stomach and rounded hips as she stood, naked and lovely before him.

When he swung her toward him, Charity screamed and pummeled him.

Outside the locked door she heard Ravenal's heavy footsteps and deep rumbling voice.

"Tis all right, Ravenal," called Court, his eyes never leaving the sweet lines of Charity's figure. "Mistress Charity is demonstrating to me how she would fight off the dons should she be so unfortunate as to fall into their hands."

With a cry of rage, Charity struck with her free hand at his mocking face and he moved forward and closed with her. From outside the locked door she heard Ravenal's grunt, heard his footsteps depart. She was being held so tightly in Court's sinewy arm that she could not move. The buttons of his coat pressed bruisingly into the soft flesh of her breasts and stomach. She could feel the sharpness of his belt buckle as her trembling legs were pulled against his hard thighs. His hands explored her naked back, sending shivers down her spine. Smiling now, his head bent, he sought her lips, luxuriously.

Enraged, she bit him.

His head drew back sharply and his eyes were colder than she had yet seen them. With what seemed only a reflex gesture, he picked her up and, flinging her on the velvet couch, stripped off his coat and tossed it to a chair.

He was in the act of unbuckling his belt when Charity leaped up and seized the poker from the hearth.

450

In two long steps, he reached her side and, with a lightning gesture, he snatched the poker from her and threw it across the room. Unsmiling, he seized her and pushed her back upon the couch. Staying her flight with a large firm hand, he lowered himself upon her while with the other hand he ripped off his belt, tore open his trousers. As Charity stared up into his dark face, she made one last wild endeavor to strike at him, but was thwarted by a sudden movement of his hand which captured both of hers.

Beneath his weight her legs were leaden, almost numbed. With ease he found purchase between them, the heavy rough silk of his knee breeches over his hard muscles lightly abrading the silky skin of her inner thighs. She writhed, trying to wriggle free from beneath him, and gasped as she felt his manhood suddenly thrust forward and enter her.

But if she had expected savagery from his earlier anger it was not forthcoming. Although he held her in an unyielding grasp, so that she remained firmly fixed beneath him, her back and buttocks pressed down uncompromisingly into the thick red velvet of the couch, his hands on her body were surprisingly gentle and his entry was that of a lover, silken and caressing.

As he drove home, straight and true, she felt a wild tremor go through her slight frame, and her face flamed as she heard a soft low triumphant laugh well up in his throat. She burned with shame that he had recognized her vivid response to him and reveled in it. Her treacherous body yielded recklessly to his embrace, against her will, and she found her back arching toward him in tune to his rhythmic pressure. The force of his will seemed too great to bear, her very being seemed bent by his powerful hold upon her body, her mind, her senses.

With a sob, she surrendered herself to him and her arms entwined themselves around his neck. Her breasts pressed upward toward him and her parted lips murmured soft broken sounds as her breathing quickened. Her whole being raced thrillingly up steep

451

inclines of desire to revel shamelessly in a world of glowing delights. She felt transported, and divined that he too shared this feeling as wordlessly they climbed the heights of passion together until, spent, they drifted back to reality.

She kept her face averted, aware that he was studying her with a long searching look, but sighed as his hands for a moment fondled her breasts and wandered over the smooth silky skin of her stomach.

She could not look at him, shamed as she was by her own wild response to his ardor—a response so desperate, so turbulent that she could not imagine what he must think of her now.

"Have you done with me?" she asked in a hoarse shaking voice, as he rose from the couch. "I will go to my room!" and she, too, stood up.

He began fastening his breeches, but paused to survey the beauty of the pale tense girl before him, her gleaming hair disheveled, her soft breasts rising and falling.

"I will take you there," he said softly, and unlocked the door. "But not naked through the courtyard in case Ravenal is still about. Here—" With a caressing gesture he put his coat over her shoulders, pulled it around her still throbbing body and picked her up lightly. He carried her, her bright hair streaming, her long lovely bare legs dangling, up the stairs from the courtyard and into her bedroom. There, he set her down upon the bed and gently removed his coat from around her shoulders. In the white moonlight from the window, her breasts were silvered, pink-tipped, her eyes dark and luminous. Shrinking back from his touch, she stared up at him.

"I will bid you goodnight," he said shortly and left the room, shutting the door softly behind him.

Charity stared at that closed door, turbulent feelings warring within her. What of tomorrow? she asked herself. How could she face him at breakfast and see in his eyes the full knowledge of how complete had been her surrender, how passionate her response to his lovemaking.

At breakfast she dressed herself in her old clothes. As if to warn him off.

She had no need to fear his presence. She ate alone.

He was gone all day. By dinner, worn out from raging inner fires, she was no longer in a mood for old clothes. Rebelliously she put on a pale blue silk dress trimmed in silver lace and went down to dinner with her head held high.

Although she waited dinner for him an unconscionable time, and sat there long after, sipping her wine, he still did not appear.

She began to wonder if something had happened to him, some altercation on the quays. Perhaps he lay even now in Kirby's infirmary—bleeding from a cutlass wound. No. . . . Kirby would have come to tell her.

She sat in the courtyard a while and then went upstairs to her room. By now the swift-falling tropical night had descended to blanket Tortuga in velvet.

Below, Charity heard the front door open and, soon, footsteps ascending the stairs. She stiffened, and turned as the door opened. Court stood there, smiling. He was dressed rakishly in a white shirt with ruffled cuffs and black silk knee breeches. He must have discarded his rapier downstairs, she observed.

His light eyes flickered. "I see you have decided to be sensible."

"No, I have not decided to be sensible," she flashed.

"In the matter of dress," he amended.

She sniffed, turning her head away from him—then swung it back as below in the courtyard there was the sound of strings. Someone down there was playing a *viola da gamba.*

"I have brought home a musician for your entertainment," he said. "We can hear him well enough through the door."

He closed it behind him.

A sensation she thought to be anger passed through her body. "It matters not," she said. "I have no mind to go to bed yet."

"Oh, have you not?" He tossed his sash and pistols

onto a chair. "And what is so entrancing at this hour that you prefer it to bed?"

"I prefer to view the ships at anchor in the harbor from the window of my prison," she answered. "And imagine them taking sail and flying out on the tide with me aboard them."

"Ah, is that what you dream of?" he murmured.

She did not answer, but turned back to the harbor, her brooding gaze seeking the moon-kissed tall-masted ships that rode at anchor beneath the forbidding shadow of the mountain fortress.

She heard him cross the room and knew that he was standing just behind her. She tensed but she did not look round. The scent of the pimento trees drifted in through the windows and a lingering aroma of roses wafted up from the courtyard. Softly the trade winds blew across her face, ruffled her silken hair. Tortuga spread like a magic carpet below her while behind her the proudest and most dangerous of Tortuga's buccaneers was but a breath away.

The music in the courtyard continued, lulling the senses. A mellow voice was singing now, rich and low, a haunting Spanish love song.

As the song began, Court's arm went around Charity, holding her possessively so that she leaned against his hard chest. She could feel the powerful beat of his heart. Under the magic of the song she relaxed against him, for the moment not thinking of the lean body her back pressed against or the arms that held her, but of the words of the song, a lament for a lover lost and gone. Court held her lightly, without passion, and the thought pierced her consciousness, *We could be friends,* and was as swiftly gone. She could never be friends with this embittered buccaneer who kept her here against her will.

The song ended and, with a sigh, Court buried his face in her hair. She suffered him to do it, stiffening as his hands roved down along her breasts, sliding down around her waist, gently turning her around and lifting her to her tiptoes.

Below them in the courtyard another song had be-

454

gun. The singer's voice drifted up again, but Charity did not respond to the music.

"Why do you fight me?" Court asked dreamily. Instead of letting her answer, he pressed his lips down upon hers, and his right arm tightened about her, while the other eased her dress down so that it fell around her hips.

As her naked torso was pressed against him, she fought a rippling surge of desire. She would not allow this, she told herself hysterically. She would resist him. She would be cold, unresponsive, a stone to his touch. But even as the thought surfaced in her consciousness, she felt the blood course through her veins and every sense came vividly alive.

With an indrawn breath, she felt her breasts flatten against his chest, the soft nipples rubbing against the material of his shirt, as even that fine linen sent soft little stabs of electricity to jar and tingle against her rib cage. A terrible sweet languor stole over her as he deftly slid her dress and petticoats down her hips. The world seemed far away and fighting him seemed difficult and unrewarding. She felt a shivering thrill as the silky lawn of her petticoat glided around her knees to fall softly around her ankles. With a swift gesture, he lifted her up and out of her clothes entirely. Cupping his hands beneath her softly rounded buttocks Court carried her to the bed and laid her gently down upon it. Sweeping her legs apart with a probing knee, he lowered his body, then closed with her and thrust in straight and sure, so that she gasped and her eyelids fluttered closed, her lips parted, her breath grew shallow. He turned lightly from side to side, moving inside her with the smoothness of silk, thrusting forward with a stubborn obstinacy against her yielding softness.

She did not resist him. She closed her eyes and was transported to a place beyond reality. She rose eagerly to heights and plunged recklessly down into valleys, she soared with the eagles and when she fell to earth, she fell softly, her fall broken ever by his warm strong arms. Rhythmically, passionately, he moved within her. His touch had a terrible fierce tenderness that would not be gainsaid.

On that wave of bright passion, she was his— utterly, completely. Again he had taken her as no other man had ever taken her, and made her his own. Gasps of breath came from her parted lips. Her eyes were closed, her expression blissful. For a moment, he looked down on her and smiled. It was almost a loving smile.

In a tumult of emotions, she kept her eyes closed and finally, hearing his rhythmic breathing beside her, drifted off to sleep herself.

Even the troubled sleep.

In the days that followed, Charity came to terms with life in Tortuga in the arms of her buccaneer lover. She no longer fought him. A wild sweet recklessness had come over her, a new feeling that she had never before known; a willingness to take each day and live it, forgetful of yesterday, heedless of tomorrow. She did not ask herself why this should be, but though she was still a captive and as closely guarded as ever, somehow she had forgotten to hate her captor. Instead she enjoyed a summertime of passion, with lazy days spent supervising cook or strolling in the market behind the quay with Ravenal, and long lovely nights of wild embraces and broken murmured endearments as her heart beat together with Court's and their burning flesh was caressed by the soft scented trade winds that blew through the shutters. A moon that was old and wise in the ways of lovers looked down on them, but it shone no brighter than Charity's eyes smiling up into Court's dark countenance. His hard face seemed to soften when he looked at her.

Other men were forgotten. Marie seemed far away. Here beneath the shadow of the grim mountain fort, Charity felt the law could never touch them. It was as if all other lives before them had never been.

She told herself she did not love Court but . . . even when opportunity presented itself, as it often did when

she visited Dona Isabel in the afternoons, Charity
made no attempt to escape.

She was happy here. She had found a new life in
Tortuga.

CHAPTER 40

Charity found there was much to occupy her days. She and Ella busied themselves sorting linens, mending torn sleeves, sewing on buttons. Charity found more attractive clothes for Ella, although the girl steadfastly refused to wear shoes. Court gave Charity the keys and she sorted things in his "treasure room," marveling at the variety of goods. It was a disappointment when Kirby would not allow her to visit the sick at his infirmary, refusing to expose her to fevers and other maladies by insisting that his own assistant was more than adequate. But she did call there regularly with baskets of fruit. On her way home, she usually dropped in to see Isabel, who had settled into domesticity with a vengeance and was redecorating her pleasant house in the severe Spanish style.

Never having been allowed to ramble about, Charity was surprised when Court showed her a stable half hidden in the vines and pimento trees some way from the house. And in that stable two handsome Arabian horses, cared for by a smiling one-armed buccaneer.

"Hal can't swing a cutlass any more," Jeremy explained, "but in better days he was a groom in Dorset."

Charity nodded to Hal, who proudly displayed his prancing charges, two magnificent horses, one black, one white, both with thick waving manes and tails.

That morning Jeremy took her riding with him over the wild rough land. As she watched the lean centaur before her, Charity marveled at his strength and control of his spirited mount. It was all she could do to

459

stay aboard her own horse, but she set herself to follow him, and follow him she did across the rocky trails.
On a high point he reined up.

"Hispaniola lies there." He waved across an empty
stretch of blue water. "A lovely island."

She knew it had once been the home of the buccaneers and looked where he pointed with interest.

He dismounted and lifted her from her horse. At
the contact of their bodies his eyes kindled and she
felt his body grow taut. Instead of setting her on her
feet, he held her against him and gently explored her
mouth with his lips and tongue. She felt herself grow
hot in response as her soft breasts pressed against
his hard lean chest.

They stretched out on a soft patch of grass and
Court swiftly undid the hooks of her bodice, slipping
his hands beneath the material. As he undressed her,
his hands explored her body so that she shivered
against him and her arms wrapped fiercely around
him as, triumphantly, he entered her. His arms about
her were firm, his hands and voice as steady and gentle
as they had been on the reins of his nervous steed, and
the spirited woman relaxed even as the spirited horse
had. Soon she found herself clinging to him in a wild
embrace and moaning his name.

Once their passion was spent, they lay side by side
in the sunlight, and talked of many things. He told her
of his boyhood in Devon. As he told her of his past—
of his schooling, of his love for the sea—he stroked
her breasts and kissed their firm pink nipples, so that
her blood roared in her ears and sang in her veins and
she only half heard him.

His mother, he said, had died at his birth and he had
been brought up in an almost womanless household in
a tall half-timbered Tudor house on the coast. His
older brother had been killed in an engagement with
the Spanish—here his voice rang with his hatred of
Spain. And his father had lost heart when Jeremy, the
younger son, had decided not to follow the sea but to
become a trader in the Colonies and had set sail with
that in mind. From that unfortunate voyage with its

460

resultant capture and slavery in the galleys, Court had returned to find his father dead. He blamed himself for his father's death—grief and despair at the reported loss of his second son had been too much for the elderly man. Had he stayed in Devon, Court told her bleakly, his father might be alive today.

Charity turned and caressed his face with a gentle hand, smiling up into his eyes. "Twas not your fault, Jeremy, that you were captured. But for that, you would have returned in good time and your father would have taken heart again."

"Ye're good for me, Charity," Court said huskily, and again enfolded her in his arms.

After that, on nice mornings, they often rode out together to their own secluded spot that looked out across the diamond-blue water. And their lovemaking on those mornings was wondrous for Charity, casting a rosy glow over her whole day.

She had found a life in Tortuga with her lean buccaneer lover.

She enjoyed running his house. Mid-mornings she did the marketing at stalls behind the quay, accompanied by the impassive Ravenal and Ella. There she selected carefully from among the baskets of plump silvery fish and piles of fresh mangoes and avocadoes and breadfruit and oranges and limes. Ravenal, always somewhat abashed at this duty, carried home baskets of fruits and vegetables, while Ella proudly carried special items such as a plump fish wrapped in green palm fronds.

Patiently, Charity gave the cook her instructions and the food, which was already good, improved. Court, who enjoyed a good dinner, complimented her on her culinary achievements, and she flushed with pleasure, feeling personally responsible for the succulent roasts and delicious soups and meat pies and pastries that emerged from the kitchen. Their conversation at mealtime was vivacious, sprinkled as it was with small housewifely triumphs that she had stored up to amuse him, and countered with items from him about the refitting and provisioning of the *Sea Witch*.

Sometimes they discussed politics—Court hated King James almost as much as he hated the Spanish—and sometimes the future of these islands over which so much blood had been spilled. There always seemed so much to talk about. *Almost like husband and wife,* she would think, as she regarded him across the table enjoying his roast.

In the afternoons, she strolled down along the quay with Ravenal, enjoying the medley of languages, the laughter and excitement as traders and buccaneers bargained for laces and rum and furs. Rarely did Court accompany her on these strolls, and never to market, for he was busy by day with matters to do with provisioning and reconditioning the *Sea Witch.* Charity had learned that he cared for his ship almost as tenderly as he cared for his horses.

But once she paused wistfully beside a shipment of stringed instruments from a galleon some buccaneer had intercepted and studied the guitars. Guitars were very popular in England and were to be found on many ladies' dressing tables. Stéphanie, she remembered, had played the guitar occasionally. Charity found herself plucking at the strings and wishing she owned one.

"It is yours," said a resonant voice behind her, and she looked up to see Court who had emerged from the crowd and now stood beside her.

"But—I know not how to play it," she admitted. "Even though I've always longed to."

"That can be arranged," he said crisply, and she waited, as he bargained for his purchase with a heavy-set swarthy buccaneer.

After that Charity had a new interest to occupy her afternoons, for Court found a Spanish prisoner who could give her music lessons. Soon, she could pick out simple tunes, and she played and sang for him in the courtyard on warm scented evenings.

Once as she sat practicing "Greensleeves," he said, "I sang that as a heedless lad, running along the cliffs, dreaming I'd have my own great fleet and be an admiral of my country." He laughed shortly.

She learned that Jeremy too, pursued studies. His chart room had many well thumbed books on mathematics, and he was studying navigation, which was why he spent hours with Timothy Hobbs both at sea and on land working to improve his skill and knowledge.

On one memorable occasion, Court took the *Sea Witch* out for Charity, and cast anchor on the lee side of a small uninhabited island. He rowed her in a small boat across the silvery phosphorescent water to a sparkling beach.

She leaned back and trailed her fingers in the water as he rowed. The night air so pleasantly scented with spices was soft and warm, and above them hung a low pale yellow moon, like a slice of lemon in the black velvet sky. A romantic night, a night for lovers. . . .

On the secluded white beach beneath that wanton moon, he took her in his arms and held her through the long night. Their naked bodies were wrapped in close embrace, now straining in passion, now spent and resting. Court caressed her breasts, her stomach, her hips, touching her lovingly, making soft explorations across her unresisting flesh that tingled delightfully at his touch. Charity sighed and gave herself up to the seductions of this luminous night—and to her lover.

Morning found them lying in the sand exhausted as the white surf lapped at their toes and raucous gulls screamed overhead. Charity opened her eyes to see Court already sitting up and watching her with a wonderful smile that softened his dark face. She sat up and stretched luxuriously, tossing back her tangled hair to free it from the sand, and as she did he reached around her and gently touched both pink nipples with his lips. She sighed, and he laughed and picked her up and ran with her into the surf where they lolled lazily, letting the warm water suds up around them. They dried themselves in the sun while sea birds swooped and whirled overhead and brown pelicans fished the shoals. As she dressed, Charity dreamily considered the palm fronds that swayed in the trade winds, the big green turtle that came lumbering out of the sea to trudge through the sand, and wondered if ever a place was so seductive . . . a trap to maid and man.

When she turned, Court was already dressed in leathern breeches and white shirt opened to the waist. He stood before her, buckling on his rapier belt, thrusting into that belt a pistol.

"We'd best away," he said. "We're near to Spanish ports and it will not do to linger here by daylight. We could be surprised by a strong force and I've only a skeleton crew aboard. Tis not the gold of the dons I seek today but the gold of a lady's shining hair."

Gravely, Charity nodded to him, her eyes deep and mysterious. Her world seemed to have changed in these last weeks. Gone was the shadow of Marie, gone was the shadow of Alan. No ghosts came back to haunt her on these fair islands sprawling in the sun. She reached out and took his hand—trustingly. For a moment Court looked surprised, then very pleased. With a jaunty stride, yet careful to match his steps to her shorter ones, he brought her to the spot where the rowboat waited. Again he bent his broad back to the oars and rowed her over the glittering water back to the *Sea Witch*.

As they boarded, the crew watched their captain and his captive beauty with envy in their eyes and a certain wistfulness. Then at Court's orders they made ready to sail and, gray sails billowing, scudded back to Tortuga with the wind freshening and a squall in sight.

But no squall appeared on their private horizon. That night in the big house in Tortuga, Charity, clad in a gown of delicate gold lace that drifted over petticoats intricately wrought of embroidered cream satin, ran lightly across the courtyard in the rain, a big silk shawl protecting her carefully dressed hair.

At the gleaming table in the dining room she sat and faced Court across the silver trenchers. Flickering candlelight played over the gleaming white skin of her upper breasts, tantalizingly revealed in her low-cut bodice. Candlelight caressed her throat and flushed cheeks, wrought miracles of depths in her topaz eyes shadowed by their dark gold lashes.

As sudden gusts of rain struck the shutters and rattled them, the candle flames wavered and danced in Court's gray eyes. In her honor he had dressed in the Spanish style tonight and he was a miracle of rich black silks and silver braid and buttons. Ignoring fashion, he had tied a wide red silk sash about his waist. His rapier was tossed onto a chair, and his periwig came down around his shoulders and framed his saturnine features.

"I prefer your own hair," she said. "For all that you hack it off with a cutlass."

He laughed and, sweeping off the wig, tossed it aside. "Cursed thing that it is," he said, "I wore it only to please you. But we're at home, so we are, and can do as we please."

At home. . . . Just as a husband might, he had said they were at home. Here in Tortuga, in what the world considered a vile den of iniquity, Charity *felt* at home.

"Yes," she said, studying his thick dark hair that fell gleaming to his shoulders. "I do prefer you this way."

"For myself," he said, eyes narrowing humorously, "let me say that glass of fashion though you may be, I prefer your hair tumbling free around your shoulders."

"Then—since we are at home. . . ." Charity reached up and, loosening her carefully coiled hair, let it tumble down in a silken mass.

"So you should always look," he said.

"But . . . then I would not look like a lady," she protested.

"You are a lady, Charity. You have no need of fashion."

She was surprised at the richness of his tone and gazed at him uncertainly.

"Were we in England now," he said, "I would be

hard put to keep the county bucks from cutting me out."

"I think . . . you would have no trouble, Jeremy," she said in a soft tremulous voice.

"Can it be true?" he murmured. "I always believed I took you against your will—and felt shame for it."

"I—I was unwilling at first . . . but not later."

Holding her gaze, he rose and offered her his hand. Forgetful of their wine, they drifted out into the courtyard and up the stairs. There he undressed her, caressing her as he did so with his lips and hands. Then he carried her to the big square bed and pressed her to him so gently that she felt fragile and precious. As his ardor rose, Charity yearned toward him, her body arching upward, a low moan rising from her throat at the sheer ecstasy of being held in his arms, of being one with him.

Charity's life seemed an idyll now, filled with wonder and love.

With Jeremy, she explored the craggy rocks and far shores of Tortuga. Together they sat beneath the pimento trees, the lemon trees. Together they found avocadoes and, once, he pulled her back from the dangerous manchineel tree that hung over the water with its poisoned apples.

"Even the fish that eat those damned things become poisonous," he muttered. "Touch it not."

Laughing, Charity ran away from him toward a far height of rocks where he caught up with her. She thought of Eden and the forbidden fruit as they sat and looked out to sea . . . a pirate sea where resolute men in wooden ships sent nine-pound shot tearing into each other's hulls . . . a world of death for all its brilliant beauty, while here in this reputed sinkhole of the world, they lived as if it were paradise.

CHAPTER 41

Marie's letter, when it came, was a terrible shock to Charity.

Somehow she had forgotten Marie. Lulled by what seemed an endless summer on this buccaneer's island, Charity had put Charles Towne and Magnolia Barony from her mind. Here on Tortuga she was suspended between worlds, idyllically becalmed on a great wild ocean full of sawtooth rocks and shoals. She had lingered here, content. Then the letter arrived.

Charity, who was standing in the hall near the chart room, went to the door as Ravenal flung it open and greeted the messenger.

"I'll take it, Ravenal," she said as she reached out a slender hand. Her fingers shook when she recognized the mannered handwriting with its big flourishes. How often had she seen that flowery script at Magnolia Barony! Marie . . . she was holding a letter from Marie in her hand.

She was still staring at it when Court, who had come up behind her with surprising softness, took it from her hand. "I believe that's addressed to me," he said coldly.

With an angry look, Charity flung away from him. Unperturbed, he went into the big room she thought of as his English room and closed the door. In the courtyard Charity stormed about, suffering. He had shut himself away to read Marie's letter. What a fool she had been to imagine that he cared for her. He cared only for Marie. Her own body was a mere convenience for him; to be used and enjoyed—and forgotten.

... the English room a long time. When he ..., he strode out looking formidable and left ... house. Of the letter, when Charity rushed in to look for it, there remained only a tiny pile of ashes in the stone fireplace.

Her lascerated feelings were rubbed entirely raw when at dinner he inquired as to her unwonted silence.

"I shall write you a note later," she answered woodenly. "Like your other whore. The one in Charles Towne."

His face whitened under his tan, and he leaned forward. "You have my leave to go," he said evenly, "before I thrash you!"

Shaking with rage, Charity got up and ran to her room.

The menacing and seductive shadow of Marie Bellingham had returned to hover over her. One day Marie would be coming back to Tortuga—perhaps the letter had been notice of an impending visit. What then? Endure the humiliation of being shoved into a corner, confined to her room, be the woman whose body he used while his heart roamed with someone else back on a hill in Devon?

When, much later, Court came up to bed, she sprang up tensely and announced in a mutinous voice, "I have a headache! Why are you disturbing me?"

Without a word, he turned on his heel and was gone.

He was gone all the next day and she dined alone.

Dusk had fallen when Kirby dropped by, ostensibly to see Court. Still simmering over the letter, Charity spoke bitterly of Marie. Kirby said reflectively, "You might call it a marriage. Court's married to the woman Marie was, his memory of her. Better for you if you'd left him alone. Now you're mired deep in his problems, Charity. You'll never get out."

"I'll get out," she muttered grimly, studying the courtyard tiles.

He gave her a thoughtful look. "If it's Charles Towne you want to see, I could take you there."

468

She looked up, startled. "But you've a price on your head there, Leeds."

He laughed. "Aye, but I go there from time to time nonetheless. None recognize me in a fiery red periwig, dressed as a mincing gentleman and speaking only French."

"Would you really take me there, Leeds?" Her eyes grew dark with entreaty and she moved toward him.

For answer he put an arm lightly about her shoulders, lifted a lock of her hair. "Charity . . ." he murmured. "A sweet name for a sweet lady. And have you other virtues? Such as compassion?"

She pretended to misunderstand him, but he was not to be put off. From her hair, his hand slipped to the back of her neck, caressed her white throat.

"Court . . . would kill you if you took me away," she warned.

He laughed. "Aye, we'd cross swords over it. Ah, the sweet touch of you, Charity. You're a fire in my blood." He bent to kiss her throat and began unbuttoning the top of her bodice.

She slapped his hand away, and her eyes darkened as she turned to stare into his wicked green eyes which were very close, only an inch or two away—and smiling.

"Court's spending the evening out, didn't you know? I saw him leave," he said in a steely voice, and before she could draw away he clasped her to him with a light exultant laugh.

"No! No, Leeds!" Heart pounding, she tore free of him. "I—I will find my own way from Tortuga," she cried wildly. "I will not sell myself for it!"

There was anger in his voice as he said, "Then you'll not leave it soon," and stalked from the house.

Across the courtyard there was a sound and Charity saw a shadow move toward the downstairs gallery. Ravenel or cook? Suddenly frightened, she turned and fled upstairs to bed.

The next morning her door was swung open and Court advanced upon her, unsmiling, his eyes very hard and steely. She paused in the act of combing her hair and drew back a step, lifting an arm as if to ward him off, for his whole manner was menacing. She would have said something about his spending the night out but his hand closed around her wrist in an iron grip and he dragged her, protesting, to a chair and flung her down in it.

Glaring down into her frightened upturned face, he growled, "What's this I hear about last night?"

"I do not know what you mean," she answered sullenly.

"I understand that Kirby made love to you in the garden."

"Who would say such a thing?" she cried, real terror consuming her now.

He smiled and it was not a nice smile. "You are a liar and a cheat," he said softly.

That stung her. "I have never cheated you!" she flashed indignantly. "I never gave you anything—you have only taken."

He gave her a sudden narrow look. "That is not what you told me."

She took a deep breath. "I lied," she said flatly.

For a moment his gaze was bitter. "It is true you are not here by your own will," he murmured. He turned away from her and paced toward the window. "Apparently, women are to be the death of me," he said morosely. "You and another."

"I am not to blame for her either!" shouted Charity. "Do you wonder that I find it tiresome to be held in the arms of a man who only uses me to dream he is holding another!"

"That is not true!" He swung around and his gaze scorched her. "I never dreamed I was holding another. She is lost to me."

"Be damned to you both!" Charity leaped up out of her chair.

Court did not try to stop her as she stormed down to the courtyard and paced about. Later she heard him go out, and she was asleep when he returned. He did not visit her room. Kirby came by the next afternoon and told her that he had made up with Court, but even

470

so, he had never seen Court get that drunk before. Court had challenged half a dozen men while barely able to stand, and had had to be carried away by his friends, protesting all the while he'd slit their gullets for them. Court was sleeping it off, she presumed, and dined alone, going up early to bed.

She awoke to Court's arms closing about her in the moonlight. Before she could protest, his firm mouth came down over her own. His hands turned her flesh to ribbons of fire as he caressed the length of her, causing her to twist and turn in her effort to elude him. The blood pulsed and sang in her veins. Against her will, she felt her body yield, move softly, luxuriously against him. Her world swayed and tumbled at his touch. She could feel a kind of triumph in him, a masterful sense of possession as his long leg moved between her own, and with a sudden thrust he took her.

Her breath drew in sharply and all her senses seemed to reel. All her defenses tumbled down and at this moment Marie's letter was forgotten, Charles Towne seemed far away and unimportant. All that mattered was the lean dark buccaneer who held her in his arms, and she strained against him now, glorying in his body, becoming one with him as together their passion mounted and seemed to explode in a wild sweet frenzy.

But when Charity woke to find him gone and saw the impress of his head on the pillow beside her, it all flooded back.

Marie, he loved Marie!

Charity sat up and beat the pillow in her rage. Damn Court! Damn him! She looked down at her own treacherous body and damned it too. She struck her thigh an angry blow, winced, and came to her senses.

It had become frighteningly clear to her that Jeremy Court might always have this power to bring her to heel, like a bitch in heat.

Now she calmed herself and somberly considered her situation.

She must find some other way to be rid of him.

CHAPTER 42

Deliberately now, Charity set about her plan. Dressed in her most alluring clothes, she strolled about the streets of the town with the impassive Ravenal beside her. When she saw a man who looked bold and dangerous, she smiled in his direction and turned archly away. More than once the giant Ravenal had his hand upon his sword hilt, and he gazed on her in wonder, amazed by her new behavior.

Nor was it lost on Court.

"You walk overmuch about the streets, Charity," he observed dryly. "And wear rather less than is prudent. Ravenal is more than a match for most men, but if you inflame these buccaneers they might set upon him in a pack—and if he falls, the pack would be on you."

"And you would be my protector?"

He nodded gravely.

"I don't want your protection!" she stormed. "I want to leave this place. You will not use me as your whore!"

His eyes narrowed. "If you must disport yourself like one, then what follows is on your own head. Many would offer me a fair profit for you. Mend your ways, or I may be tempted to take it."

She sniffed.

He smiled, and said, "I met a friend of mine upon the quay today. His ship had just anchored. He has been long at sea and will require the attentions of a woman. I think you would suit him admirably."

Goaded, she leaned forward. "I hope to find a man who will set upon you and kill you!" she cried between clenched teeth. "Kill you for keeping me here! For forcing yourself on me against my will!"

Their eyes met fiercely, locked. She saw leaping devils in his, but she did not flinch.

"Forcing myself on you against your will . . ." he said. "So you find my lovemaking distasteful, my body offensive? By heaven, you shall have others to compare me with!"

As he strode toward her, she became aware of the handsomeness of that body she was rejecting. But she was more aware of the leaping evil in his eyes as he looked down at her. She did not flinch, but she backed away a little, conscious suddenly of the power in him.

Suddenly he bent down and put his hands around her white throat. "I could break you so easily," he said in a low deadly voice. "Do not tempt me too far."

She stared up at him, her eyes wide, her breath coming fast. All the hatred she felt for him was reflected in those wide, furious eyes, in the pent-up fury of the words that burst forth.

"I would rather have these—these others!" she cried recklessly. *Than a man who prefers someone else,* was the rest of that remark, but she did not voice it.

He let go of her as if he had been singed by fire.

"You shall have them," he said in a hoarse bitter voice. "Beginning tonight."

He went out, slamming the door, and she heard him bawl an order to Ravenal as he left the house.

White-faced, still furious, she stared at the door he had slammed. He had sounded as if he meant it. Tonight—possibly in this very room—she would be taken like a whore by another man, this friend of his whom he had met on the quay.

Then why had she fended off Kirby?

Her soft lower lip caught between her clenched teeth and the leaping fury in her own eyes was a reflection of the fury she had seen in Court's.

God's death! She would not be so used! She threw a pillow at the wall and sat down trying to calm herself. Then slowly, very slowly, an angry smile hardened her lovely face.

She would show him! She would woo Court's friend

as he had never been wooed before and she would turn him against Jeremy—she would plant seeds of poison and hate! She would turn them on each other, these men who dared to use her for their own passions. She would make them kill each other!

The hours passed and, gradually, the rage died within her. It was all bluster, she told herself. Court would be back tonight, tumbling her about the bed as usual.

She had just set her foot upon the top step, planning to go downstairs and see if the dinner being prepared was to her liking, when she heard the front door open.

"It's glad I am ye can sup with me," she heard Court say. "And glad that ye can stay the night before ye sail. We'll talk over old times."

Charity swayed in shock. Court had made good his promise—he had brought a man to her!

The two men walked into the courtyard below, and Charity could see the man with Court was big and tawny-blond with a flowing mustache and—

"Tom!" she cried in joy. "Tom Blade!"

And ran the length of the stairs to fling herself into his arms.

"Charity!" cried Tom, swinging her around. "What are you doing here?"

Charity hesitated only a moment. "I'm Jeremy's houseguest," she said, and cast a challenging look at Court. "But not for long. I'll soon be going back to Charles Towne!"

"It's a rare sight you are, Charity," Tom cried, and she saw that he was looking very fit. His walk was jaunty and his tawny hair swung to the shoulders of a sky-blue velvet coat. He was sporting gray silk knee breeches and gray silk stockings and red-heeled shoes.

"It's a French fop you've become, Tom," she teased, "In these clothes."

"For your sake," he said wickedly, "I'd shed them all."

She looked again at Court, who was watching them

475

silently. She could not fathom the expression on his saturnine face.

All through dinner she endeavored to charm Tom, bending toward him so that her breasts showed to fine advantage in her low-cut emerald gown. All through dinner she watched Court from the corner of her eye, enjoying his discomfiture. They sat long after dinner drinking wine while Tom and Court reminisced about life in Devon.

Talking about Devon irritated Charity. It was as if Marie's beautiful seductive shadow had drifted into the room. Recklessly Charity matched drinks with the two men, and as the wine warmed her, she grew even more reckless.

When finally the last glass had been drained and they rose to say their good nights, she leaned forward, touching Tom's arm lightly. "Wilt stop by my room before you go to bed, Tom? I've need of your advice tonight. . . ."

His eyes kindled. "Faith, I'd go with you now, love, but—" he turned and looked questioningly at Court.

She had never seen Court look so fierce. "Charity is her own mistress," he said shortly. "It seems she fancies you, Tom."

"But you—"

"Never mind about me. I've a wench in town waiting."

Airily Charity took Tom's arm and led him up the stairs. From the top she looked back at Court, who had paused and was watching them.

He had hell in his eyes.

Then he whirled and in two strides was gone from her sight. She heard the heavy front door slam, and laughed softly to herself. She knew that he had not intended this, had never intended it. Nor had she when she was baiting him downstairs. But now the vision of Marie rose up before her. *To Court it's a marriage,* Kirby had said. And had Court not admitted he kept her here because she might unmask Marie's relationship with him, destroying her reputation? Well, tonight he would be repaid!

Seductively, Charity smiled into Tom's devil-may-care face and swung wide her bedroom door.

CHAPTER 43

Charity told herself fiercely that she was glad, glad to be back in Tom's arms again. He was again the light-hearted lover, laughing and merry, tickling her, causing her spirits to rise even as her passion mounted. She told herself she was getting back at Court, making him suffer.

"Your mind's elsewhere," chided Tom, biting her ear. "You'll be telling me I've lost my touch!"

"No," she said, feeling her body tingle in response to his caressing hands. "You haven't lost your touch, Tom. Never that."

"I've missed you, Charity," he said. "After I'd mended, I met some fellows of like mind and we stole a small ship. We used it to take the one I'm now captain of. And I thought of you often, Charity, wondering if you'd forgotten me, if maybe you'd come to prefer Bart."

Bart . . . Bart who'd tried to sell her to the trappers, whom Ben had shot and she'd buried in a makeshift grave. . . . Dark thoughts coursed suddenly through her mind and cooled her ardor.

"You talk too much, Tom," she said, and wound her arms about him and waited, lips parted, for his kiss. She heard his low laugh and found forgetfulness for a while in his arms.

They were wakened by a banshee wail from the street.

Charity sat bolt upright and, beside her, Tom lurched awake. He jumped up and ran to the window, peered out through the casements into the bright sunlight burning down like a torch over Tortuga.

Curious, Charity followed him.

"Now how did she find me?" he muttered.

Below them in the street stood the woman making all the noise. She was attended by two huge black islanders clad only in baggy knee breeches, red sashes, and rakish hats, and armed with heavy machetes used for cutting cane.

The woman had wild red hair, which tumbled in confusion as if strong winds had blown it, a sumptuous figure, tall and statuesque. She stood with her bare feet apart, her hands on her hips, and glared up at them. Her clothes were ripped to shreds and hung in ribbons about her, allowing bare skin and voluptuous curves to show through.

"Oh, no," Tom moaned. "She's rent her clothes again!"

Charity looked dismayed. "You . . . know her?"

He nodded irritably. "Ah, the new clothes she's cost me!" He turned with a sudden grin and said in a low intimate voice, "Of course hers have cost me but money —the new dress I got for you in the north near cost me my life!"

Charity continued to look down upon the scene in the street below. She was not to be seduced this morning by blarney.

"Tom!" came a ringing voice from below. "Get you down here this instant!"

"Go back to the ship, Daisy, I'll join ye later," called Tom.

"I'll not go back! I'll not! I'll stay right here till you come down, Tom!" howled the tempestuous woman below, stamping her bare foot.

"Get ye back!" roared Tom. "You—Eben and Ephraim—take her back. Now!"

In silent obedience, the black islanders converged on the woman. Each grasped an arm and, swinging her feet off the ground, they conveyed her kicking and screaming down the street, their big knives flashing in the sun. Although a little crowd had gathered to stare at this strange spectacle, the heavy knives kept them at a distance. Charity had a feeling that Daisy frequently made her exit being carried from the scene like a spoiled child.

"Does she do this often?" she asked in a thin voice.

Tom shrugged. "Whenever she gets the notion I've a new wench. Tears her clothes to shreds, she does. Breaks anything that will break. All the plates in the cabin are bent from her hurling 'em against the walls."

"I'd forgotten how faithless you are," murmured Charity, turning away with a frown. Last night she had told herself fiercely that she was happy to be back in Tom's arms again. Now she remembered the hurt that had struck through her at the sight of Tom clad only in his shirt in the hay, his buttocks gleaming against the fairer skin of a servant girl's hips. At the time, she had thought she would die of it.

"Ah, now, Charity, that's unfair!" he cried, taking her by the shoulders. "I'm always faithful to you *here*," he said, striking his chest in the area where she guessed his heart was supposed to be.

"Faithful . . . in your fashion," she murmured, turning away.

He came up behind her and reached around her and cupped her breasts in his hands, cradled them as he explored the back of her neck with his lips. "'Tis the only fashion I possess," he said.

She turned and embraced him absently, but this morning there was something between them besides the tall shadow of Jeremy Court—there was also Daisy who "rent her clothes" when Tom left her for another. Poor Daisy, following him about. Perhaps for Daisy it had the force of a marriage. . . .

Pensive, Charity dressed in a pretty yellow muslin dress and, picking up a delicate ivory fan, she hurried downstairs to join Tom for breakfast.

Court came in as they were eating. He was wearing the same clothes he'd worn the night before and he looked as if he'd slept in them. His face was haggard but his eyes blazed as he saw them there.

"A night well spent?" he asked.

Charity stiffened.

Tom's grin was enough reply.

"I'm speaking to you, Tom," growled Court. "I'd appreciate a civil answer."

"A grand night," said Tom, surprised. "Tis a delight to meet up with old friends."

"I like not your tone," said Court silkily. "Nor your use of the word friend."

At Court's tone, Tom came alert. "Sure now, ye've no cause—"

"No cause?" Court's voice was harsh. "Tell me ye did not take her! Tell me that!"

In consternation, Tom leaned forward. "But, Jeremy, ye said—"

"Said? Bother what I said! Did ye take her or not?"

"I did, but when I looked at her, ye said—"

With lightning swiftness, Court's rapier snaked out. "By heaven ye'll look at her no more! Defend yourself!"

Unsheathing his sword in haste, knocking over his chair as he did so, Tom leaped up and eyed his opponent. "I knew her before," he cried indignantly.

It was the wrong thing to have said.

With a roar Court was on him, driving him around the heavy table and into the courtyard. Charity screamed in terror as they lunged and parried, leaping about over the tiles. She could see that although Tom was a good swordsman, he was no match for Court. With muscles hardened to iron from his days as a galley slave, and driven by the pent-up rage that was in him, Court drove his opponent back and back. Suddenly Tom slipped on a loose tile and fell hard on his back. In an instant Court had flicked Tom's blade from his hand and stood over him, the point of his rapier at Tom's throat.

"Tell me why I shouldn't kill you," he said in a low deadly tone.

Tom stared up at him. "Ye'll not kill me for a girl who prefers you?" he cried.

"Prefers me?" echoed Court bitterly. He drew a deep breath, but kept his rapier tip at Tom's throat. "Is this true?" he challenged Charity.

White-faced she stood raging inwardly, but knew

480

she must agree to save Tom's life. "Yes," she said shakily, "I *do* prefer you, Jeremy."

For a long time he stared at her, and she could not tell what was behind the gray devil's mask he wore.

Suddenly he sheathed his sword. "Up, Tom," he said. "I'm behaving like a fool this morning. If you can overlook it?"

Looking vastly relieved, Tom scrambled to his feet and brushed off his velvet coat. "I must get back to my ship. Wilt walk with me?" Court hesitated. "Ye said she was her own woman, Jeremy."

"That I did," said Court in a weary voice. "Twas a lie, but I said it. She is mine."

His! Once again anger swelled Charity's breast. "I prefer Alan Bellingham to you both!" she screamed after them. And ran up the stairs to be free of the sight of them.

On the small table beside her bed she saw that Tom had left her a gift—a pair of heavy gold bracelets. She stared down at them.

Oh, God, she asked herself, *what have I become?*

Tormented, she flung herself down at her dressing table and gazed at her face in the mirror.

She must get back to Alan, she told herself almost hysterically. She must not live with this devil of a buccaneer who could make her flame up at his touch, who had the power to hurt and degrade her, who would use her and cast her aside as callously as . . . as Tom had done.

For a long time she sat with her head in her hands. Court did not return.

From Ravenal she learned that the *Sea Witch* had sailed.

Charity brooded on that. Another foray . . . another return to her waiting arms. Another battle. She told herself she hoped he never returned.

Still she watched the bay.

And into that bay sailed a ship she knew—the *Marybella* on which she'd come from New York to Charles Towne; its captain must have decided to trade with the buccaneers. The *Marybella*'s captain wouldn't have a price on his head like Court and Kirby—and she knew him. He'd take her with him!

At the marketplace behind the quay, with Ravenal in attendance, she learned that the *Marybella* was indeed bound for Charles Towne—and when she would sail. Minutes before the *Marybella* was due to leave, Charity sat at table and called angrily for the cook, complaining of the meat. With cook tasting her product in puzzlement, Charity flounced from the room and once out, sped by Ella and out the kitchen door. At the quay she quickly contrived her passage with the captain.

She boarded the ship in her old green dress that Alan had bought for her, carrying only Megan's shawl as luggage.

All that Court had given her she'd left behind. She paid for her passage with the golden bracelets Tom had left. Bitterly, Charity told herself that she had earned her passage.

She looked back at the fast-retreating Mountain Fort that guarded the luckless and the lawless. And then up at Court's house, growing small in the distance.

When he returned, he would find her gone. Somehow, the satisfaction she expected to feel from that thought was missing.

BOOK V

Charles Towne 1688

CHAPTER 44

Aboard the *Marybella,* Charity found herself looking back and feeling sorry that she had not been able to say a proper goodbye to her friends in Tortuga. She loved Ella, the dainty little mute girl who had befriended her; it was not right that she had had to run past her in that fashion without so much as a word. And Kirby . . . cynic though he was and bargainer for her body, Charity felt that in his own way he loved her; she should have told him goodbye also. Yet in her frenzy to avoid the giant Ravenal and so escape Jeremy Court forever, she had not been able to do so.

It was one more score she chalked up against Court. How glad she was to escape him. Charity's hands clenched till the knuckles whitened as she remembered her treacherous body's wild response to his lovemaking.

Oh, damn him, damn him . . .

When she arrived in Charles Towne at last, Charity set out immediately for Magnolia Barony. Luckily, on the crowded docks she spied Josh, one of Alan's trusted slaves, come to town with a cart to pick up supplies. His black face lit at sight of her for she'd often been kind to him; he was the first to welcome her back. She spent the time waiting for him to load the cart walking about, breathing the free air of Charles Towne, and comparing it with Tortuga.

Here no frowning fort loomed over the city, its fixed guns pointed out to sea. No wild crowd of swarthy cutlass-clanging buccaneers laughed and jostled and bore away with them bright-eyed women with whisky voices. No medley of foreign traders bargained for stolen Spanish goods at the quay. It was not so colorful but . . . it was safer. Here people led steady, placid lives, made homes, bore children. She told herself that was what she wanted.

Overhead pelicans and black skimmers wheeled, competing with the gulls for a chance at the fish and other seafood piled in baskets below. Ships unloaded West Indian rum and loaded indigo and rice. Tar and pitch went by in wagons and down the sluggish river in pirogues floated big cedar logs on their way to be sold. Around her were piles of beaver skins awaiting transshipment. Josh soon had his cart loaded, and as they jogged down the muddy cart-track through the green walls of lush vegetation, beneath an overarching roof of tree branches and dangling vines, Charity rehearsed her story.

To her delight, the first person she saw at Magnolia Barony was Alan, returning home from the rice fields astride his big roan. She leaped off the cart before it stopped and ran toward him, green skirts flying. With an exclamation, he dismounted and hurried toward her.

They met in mid-lawn and his hands clasped her shoulders. He regarded her in wonder. "But we thought you lost!" he cried. "Dr. Cavendish returned and told us that you and another young woman were captured with him but had disappeared in Tortuga."

"I was bought at a slave auction by a tavern owner," she explained. "He was very fatherly, and allowed me to receive tips for my services—and when I had saved enough for passage money, he let me go."

Alan's smile was bright and believing; it should have warmed her more than it did. But she noticed that he looked drawn and tired. And thinner.

"You'll need rest after your journey," he said. "Brought your luggage?"

"All was lost," she said, looking down at her worn green dress and thinking of all the lovely things she had left behind in Court's house in Tortuga.

"Never mind," he said gently. "We will provide." And led her inside the house.

As they entered, Marie was descending the stairway

486

in a rose-pink silk dress. She paused at sight of them. It gave Charity a grim satisfaction to see the look of astonishment on her face.

"See who has returned from the dead," smiled Alan.

"So I see," murmured Marie.

She is asking herself if I could have seen her on Tortuga, Charity thought, and wondered that Alan did not remark her pallor. He seemed abstracted, indifferent almost, to his beautiful wife standing there.

"We heard you had been swallowed up in the sink-holes of Tortuga," said Marie, regaining her composure.

Charity yearned to say, *We shared the same sink-hole!* But she did not. Instead she glibly repeated the story she had told Alan. That Marie could not gainsay it, she was certain. Court, she felt, would hardly have mentioned her presence in his house, and who else would the cloistered "lady in the black mantilla" know in Tortuga?

With her usual disdain, Marie drew her skirts aside as Charity passed her. But when Charity looked back from the stair landing, Marie was still standing there, gazing up at her with a puzzled expression. As if she had expected Charity to be scarred and contaminated from her Tortuga experience and was surprised to find her looking as fresh and lovely as ever. Resentment flamed Charity's cheeks and she yearned to fling at Marie, *I was as well treated there as you were —though not for the same reason.*

Biting her lips, Charity hurried on to the stuffy little room upstairs with its broken washbowl and hard bed. After her recent luxurious surroundings, it looked worse than ever to her.

Of all those on the plantation, Megan was most joyful to see her. She came running up the attic stairs and, bursting into the little room, flung her arms around Charity and hugged her. "When I heard ye was taken, I cried for days," she said. "Sure and you're like my own daughter to me, Charity."

Charity's throat closed up and she hugged Megan

silently. The gray-haired Irishwoman was a true friend.

Megan pushed Charity away and stared at her in wonder. "It's a miracle!" she cried. "To be taken by pirates and come back looking none the worse for wear! I'd been thinkin' you'd end up in a brothel and that would be the end of you."

And well I might except for Jeremy Court, thought Charity grimly. And wondered where the *Sea Witch* was tonight. . . .

The account books gave a clear explanation of why Alan looked so troubled. Her second day back, Charity had no sooner settled herself on the high stool and opened a ledger, than he appeared. Although he cut a handsome figure in his cream brocade coat and silk knee breeches, his face was very sober.

"A word with you, Mistress Charity," he said, and Charity turned to him, glad that McNabb wasn't present. He cleared his throat. "As you'll see at once, from the books, Magnolia Barony is in trouble. We had a storm in Charles Towne while you were gone. Lashing seas and high winds that knocked down many trees. There was a high tide, one of the flood gates was carelessly left open—in short, the rice crop was ruined."

Thunderstruck, Charity stared at him. "But you were counting on that—you needed it to pay your debts!"

"Aye," he said grimly. "So now the money won't be forthcoming and unless there's new money from somewhere, my creditors will be closing in. All the planters around here were hurt by the storm; none can advance me what I need—many in fact are as lost as I am."

"Never say you're lost, Alan," she said softly, touching his arm, and in the heat of the moment forgetting that she had never before used his given name. "There must be a way."

He looked away as if he could not bear the sympathy in those topaz eyes. "Nay," he muttered. "Not this time. Each year I've got in deeper, spending more, ever more than I have earned."

"Your wife's jewels," she cried. "What of them? Would they not hold off your creditors until you can bring in another crop?"

He looked astonished. "She has but a set of amethysts, some coral and seed pearls—some jet she has worn for mourning for her father. All trifling, compared with my needs."

But what of the diamonds and emeralds and rubies Charity had seen spilling out of that coffer Marie had once so angrily shoved out of sight, Charity wondered silently. Were they all gifts from Court and therefore to be hidden from Alan?

She kept silent, her heart aching for this troubled man, unwilling to so grievously hurt him by telling him of his wife's unfaithfulness.

"Then there is no way?" she asked sadly.

"I see none." He turned to her in misery. "They'll be selling Magnolia Barony away from me." He looked so hopeless that she touched his arm again. At her touch, he turned and with a sob enfolded her in his arms.

She stroked his hair, murmured soothing words and let him hold her thus, his head resting on hers. After a time his dry sobs ceased and he stepped back from her, embarrassed. But his voice was stronger and he seemed to have gained strength from her.

"I ask your pardon," he said humbly. "But this land has meant so much to me. The thought of losing it wounds me deep."

"There is no need to ask pardon of me," she said gently. "Had I but the power, I would give it back to you."

A shadow of a smile passed over her face. "I am sure you would, Mistress Charity. For the kindness of your heart, I am grateful." He paused, embarrassed. "I came to ask you to say nothing of this state of affairs to my wife. She does not know and McNabb is sworn to silence."

"But will she not know when they come to sell the place?" Charity asked.

He gave a nod. "But until then I would preserve her

happiness. Bad enough that I must drag her down with me—let her be happy yet a little while."

Charity promised to say nothing to Marie and watched him walk back to the house, his handsome shoulders drooping in his brocade coat.

There was a time when his last remarks about his wife would have cut her to the quick, but now they left her oddly unmoved. How often had she wished that Alan would take her in his arms and yet, when at last those arms had enfolded her, she felt only pity. In her mind Alan seemed not a desired lover but a lost unhappy child. She felt oddly dissatisfied by his behavior. Court too had suffered grievously, but he had not let life down him, he had continued to fight. Why could not Alan do the same?

It was all very strange and it puzzled her. With a sigh she went back to trying to figure out McNabb's scraggly writing. Before the day was done she realized the depth of Alan's debacle; it would take a small fortune to bail him out.

Magnolia Barony would soon be breaking up, but for the time Charity was back in Alan's household, back in her old job on the plantation—and back combing Marie's lovely ash-blonde hair.

"I am curious," Marie said next day, watching Charity's face intently in the mirror as she wielded the silver comb. "You must have seen many pirates in Tortuga."

"Many," said Charity, combing impassively.

Marie's shoulders moved a little in her lace combing jacket. "Did you, for instance, see the notorious Captain Court about whom all Charles Towne is talking?" she asked casually.

Charity could not resist giving a strand of Marie's hair a sharp pull. "Oh, did I hurt you?" she cried.

Marie winced and her lips compressed. "We were speaking of Captain Court," she said.

"Yes, I saw him."

"And did you find him well-favored?" pursued Marie.

For a moment Charity remembered that lean strong

body with its great breadth of shoulder, the way he strode and took stairs three at a time, his deep resonant voice and arresting hawklike face. In the mirror she met Marie's violet eyes and shrugged. "'I saw him but once by the light of guttering candles. He is very tall and dark. It was not I who served him rum but another girl. Many buccaneers are well-favored. Many bear deep scars from their engagements with the Spaniards.'"

Those violet eyes were watching her keenly. Apparently pleased with her answer, and relieved that she professed not to know Court, Marie asked lightly, "Was it he who took your ship?"

Charity's hand trembled ever so slightly. She managed to control it. "No, a French pirate named St. Clair."

"Under Court's direction, no doubt," said Marie complacently. "'Tis said he is behind all these attacks on shipping from Charles Towne."

You know better than any other that is untrue, for you've had it from his own lips! thought Charity stormily. She stepped around to comb the other side of Marie's hair and in her rage knocked some powder from Marie's dressing table. With an angry exclamation, Charity bent over the spilled powder.

It was well she did so for her expression would surely have given her away. With a madly beating heart, she bent her head and addressed herself to cleaning up the spilled powder. Was Marie so prone to treachery, she asked herself, that she must needs cuckold her husband and then blacken her lovers? Charity's hands shook with fury. But her anger was not so much for Alan as for Court. Alan had long been played for a fool by this violet-eyed temptress. But Jeremy Court—ah, he deserved better. He had come through hell to reach this woman's side. And when Marie had come to him in Tortuga at last, how easy for him to have kept her there, his helpless prisoner! But he had held himself in check to preserve Marie's honor. Her honor! Charity was near bursting with rage.

With as placid an expression as she could muster,

491

Charity straightened up and resumed combing Marie's hair. But having finished her combing at last, Charity could not resist saying, as she removed Marie's lace combing jacket, "Captain Court is known to have a mistress who comes by ship to visit him. She is always veiled in a black mantilla."

She was touching Marie's head as she said that and felt the woman's body freeze for a moment before Marie regained her self-control.

"Oh?" Marie turned her head this way and that to consider her coiffure in the mirror. Her voice sounded strained. "Do they say what she is like?"

Charity gave a contemptuous shrug. "One who saw her face when the wind blew back her mantilla said she was not so much for looks. Light hair but a hard face, as if she were a woman used by many men. He said he'd seen better in the brothels of Tortuga." She laid down the comb and regarded Marie with insolent eyes.

Marie's voice shook as she fought for control. "I would advise you to say little about your experiences in Tortuga. There are those who will wonder how it is that you, without money, managed to make your way back. They will speculate that you may well have earned your passage in those very brothels you speak of, and it will weigh against you in securing a husband."

"I had not thought of that," said Charity, and took herself off to McNabb's office. As she entered, the gray-haired Scot smiled at her. Although he had greeted her gruffly on her return, she knew he was glad to have her back.

She was sitting on the stool struggling with the accounts when Alan came in to speak to McNabb. He looked strikingly handsome in his lavender satin coat and as he turned to leave, he said something to McNabb about conditions at Cavendish Landing. Cavendish Landing, Charity knew, was the name old Dr. Cavendish had given to his upriver plantation. Her words arrested Alan.

"Dr. Cavendish was kind to me on board the *Gull*,"

492

she said. "I should like to see him and thank him. Do you think he will be coming downriver soon?"

"He rarely goes out since his return from Tortuga," said Alan thoughtfully. "Still . . . I have a pirogue going upriver tomorrow morning. You could ride along and return in the afternoon. I think Dr. Cavendish would like to see you; he asked several times if we had heard from you."

So the old doctor in the huge ridiculous pantaloons had thought enough of her to inquire as to her safe return. She was touched.

The next morning Charity waited at the landing and soon found herself gliding up the lazy river via pirogue toward Cavendish Landing. The dark mirror-like water was almost black and along the banks, amid clumps of palmettos and olive and evergreen laurel, great cypresses rose, festooned by the gray funereal Spanish moss. The silence was broken only by the call of birds, the chatter of gray squirrels, and by the occasional burst of deep-throated melodious song from the slaves manning the pirogue. Charity fanned herself with a palm-leaf and watched as a white-tailed deer darted away, startled at their approach. She waved to another pirogue as it went by carrying an upriver planter. She remembered the man from the ball at which she had discovered Marie's affair with René. It seemed so long ago. . . .

She was surprised to find that Dr. Cavendish's house—although everybody referred to him respectfully as "quite rich"—was not nearly so impressive as Magnolia Barony. Built of black cypress on a brick foundation, it was squarish and rather awkward, but its owner came forward with great cordiality and welcomed her.

In a big cane chair on the verandah, Charity sat and sipped a glass of wine. The old doctor was much thinner, more fragile. His Tortuga experience had aged him, she decided.

He brightened when she told him that Polly, too, had managed to leave Tortuga bound for England. She did not say how, but he seemed satisfied.

"I did so worry about you," he told her earnestly. "You were placed in my safekeeping by Alan Bellingham, and I felt I had not taken proper care of you."

She smiled into his eyes and thought how nice if this kindly old man could have been her father.

"And once I thought you had sent me a message," he said, "when I overheard St. Clair's pirates talking about a woman sending a message."

She was not listening very intently, allowing herself to relax after her journey upriver, feeling drowsy in the afternoon heat.

"But twas not you," he added regretfully. "Twas some Spanish lady."

"Spanish lady?" murmured Charity from her luxurious languor. She was thinking of Dona Isabel.

"Well, I would presume she was Spanish. Twas someone called 'the lady of the black mantilla' that they spoke of."

Slowly that sank in. Charity's fingers tightened on her glass and she sat up. "What . . . what did you say, Dr. Cavendish?"

"What? Oh, I was just speaking of some message that devil St. Clair was expecting, that did not come. His quarters were close to mine, you see. I could hear him cursing—though rather weakly, since he'd had a fight with another buccaneer and near lost his life."

"A lady . . . in a black mantilla? You are sure they said that?"

"Aye, tis what they said. They were most fussed over it. Some more wine, mistress? You've had a fatiguing journey upriver."

"Yes, please," murmured Charity, sinking back in her chair. "Most fatiguing." She held up her glass, but absently, for her heart pounded and her mind was flooding with thoughts. Like the jagged pieces of a broken mirror, they fit together one by one and on that shattered reconstructed surface one face was reflected . . . *Marie.*

Why had she not seen it? *Marie*—Marie Bellingham was behind these attacks on the shipping. Marie was *using* Court. Under cover of her visits to her lover in Tortuga, Marie managed—probably at quayside—to slip information on sailing dates and ships' manifests to Captain St. Clair.

Charity was sure that she had stumbled on the truth. It explained everything: Marie's insistence that Charity sail on the *Gull*—she had wanted Charity to be captured so she could not tell Alan about René. Marie had *known* the *Gull* would be captured, that Captain St. Clair would be out there waiting for them. And old Dr. Cavendish with his false-bottomed chest—St. Clair had expected the doctor to have more than five thousand pounds; had Dr. Cavendish not told Marie last April he would be carrying ten? Marie's coffer of jewels so hastily and angrily put away when Charity had come in without knocking—perhaps Court had not given them to her. Were they Marie's commission, her share of the loot for furnishing information to Captain St. Clair?

The revelation almost overcame Charity.

But why? she asked herself. Why would Marie do it?

René! The answer stabbed at her. Neither Marie nor René had any money of their own. But inventive Marie had found a way to get some, by visiting Tortuga and selling information to the French pirate.

Money Marie needed in order to run away with her lover René. . . .

That was why Marie had been so willing to villify Court, why she had been so eager to make Charity think he was behind the attacks on Charles Towne shipping; she wanted to protect her source of illicit income—the French pirate St. Clair!

Charity's teeth clenched through her soft lower lip and her face grew so pale and set that Dr. Cavendish regarded her anxiously. No, no, she insisted, she was quite all right; it must be the heat. But her head was reeling from her discovery, and she found that she could not concentrate on the kindly old doctor's conversation.

It seemed an eternity before the pirogue came to take her back to Magnolia Barony.

CHAPTER 45

As soon as the pirogue reached the landing at Magnolia Barony, Charity hurried ashore and went looking for Megan. She found her in a guest bedroom, tidying up.

"How were things between the landgrave and his wife while I was in Tortuga?" she asked Megan.

Megan turned from plumping a pillow and rolled her eyes. "Terrible," she said. "Just terrible. M'lady came back from her last trip to Barbadoes in a furious temper and stormed about. Then she became very reckless and rode about so fast she was thrown and sprained her ankle. As soon as she could walk again she gave a ball. Something must have happened *there* because she locked herself in her room afterward and cried and cried. And *drink!* Bottles, that woman consumed! That's been some weeks ago, and she's still not recovered. Don't you think she looks bad?"

"Not so bad as Alan—as Mr. Bellingham."

"True, the landgrave looks worse than she does but it's business worrying him, I think. Tis something else upset her. She's not been slipping out o'nights lately. Something must have gone wrong twixt her and whoever she was meeting."

Trouble with René . . . René, the foppish Frenchman Marie loved so much. *French . . .* and St. Clair was French. Could there be a connection? Could René be a—a sort of agent of Captain St. Clair's, here to spy out Charles Towne? Could he have cultivated the landgrave's amorous wife to gain information about her wealthy friends, to learn in advance who could be held for ransom? *Could Marie have been conveying ship-*

ping information that René gathered? And had she—
now that St. Clair was laid up and no longer aprowl—
lost her value to René?

If Marie's cheeks were pale over that, then René
must have thrust Marie aside rather than the other way
around. . . . That ball, after which she'd cried so miserably, might have been her attempt to see him again
without making herself conspicuous, her attempt to
win him back.

It was pleasant to think that Marie might have been
used by René, even as she herself had been used by
Court. For reasons other than love.

Suddenly Charity's eyes narrowed and she smiled
a wicked smile. She would go to Tortuga and confront
Court with this evidence of Marie's perfidy. This time
she would have facts—he would have to believe her.
Ah, to see his face when she told him! She might
have been bought and sold but so, just as surely, had
he been sold—his trust in Marie had allowed it.

The great Captain Court had a price on his head
because a woman willed it!

"Ye look like a cat eating cream," said Megan dryly.

"Perhaps I am," laughed Charity, and she strolled
away humming.

She would go to Tortuga . . . but who would pay her
passage? Her wicked smile deepened. Of course!
Court's enemies would pay it! With sparkling eyes she
went up to her room and, leaning on her elbows in the
window, stared out at the beauty of the countryside
as she conceived her dangerous plan.

First she must find René. . . .

Fortune was good to her. She did not have to look for
René—he came to her. The next afternoon as she
was walking across the lawn from McNabb's office,
she saw a pirogue glide up to the landing and a colorful party disembark. Across the lawn they strolled, the
big-skirted laughing women in bright silks, the gallant
gentlemen in knee breeches and wide-cuffed coats
aglitter with silver and gold.

Charity paused to watch them and her heart gave a
leap—René was with them! Thin and smiling and

498

clad in peach satin, he walked alongside an upriver planter's wife, his plumed hat under his arm, his plum-colored velvet cuffs rolled wide.

From the front door Marie, dressed for riding and carrying her own plumed hat, came out in a rush, her face alight, and hurried forward to greet her guests. Charity thought, had René not been with them, she'd wager Marie would have let them come to her!

As they strolled past her, Charity heard René blandly explaining that he had not been well—a distemper of the climate, no doubt; indeed it had kept him much in bed of late. Charity caught Marie's face as he said that, saw hope spring up in her violet eyes. Marie wanted to believe him, Charity was sure, and indeed René did not look too well, nor was his step as spry as usual.

They could not stay long, one of the women said. They were on their way to Dr. Cavendish's plantation. Poor thing, he had not ventured out since his devastating experience of being captured and held for ransom in Tortuga. Her gaze flicked over Charity with sudden interest. Was not this the woman servant who was captured with Dr. Cavendish? she asked Marie. Marie frowned and shrugged an assent, and René looked at Charity with interest shining in his dark eyes.

He is wondering what I know, divined Charity, and was reinforced in her belief that René was an agent of St. Clair's.

Well, well, said the woman. Imagine being captured and taken to Tortuga . . . Her bright gaze and the sudden titter of the other women told Charity they were imagining black-bearded pirates pouncing on her, tearing off her clothes, ravishing her. She gave them back a defiant look.

"What think you of Tortuga, having been there?" prodded René.

Charity's chin lifted. "It is much like Charles Towne," she said bitterly. "Full of low gossip and well-dressed women of easy morals."

The tittering ceased.

"It is warm," Marie's cold voice cut in. "I need my

499

fan. Charity, you will find it on my dressing table—the ivory one. Bring it to me."

At Marie's command, Charity flushed and hurried away. When she returned, Marie snatched the fan, gave her a black look and turned her back on her. With deliberate casualness Charity wandered through the guests and paused by René.

"I would speak with you," she whispered.

He looked up alertly.

"Alone," she said.

"In the trees beyond the garden," he muttered.

Charity thought, as she turned, that Marie might have noticed them speaking together, but she kept her expression as bland as René's and headed toward the garden.

It was not long before he joined her, moving swiftly, casting his eyes about to find her.

"Here," whispered Charity. "I am here." And came out from the shadow of a big magnolia.

He smiled, his dark eyes kindling at her beauty as she moved toward him. He swaggered a bit and postured as if confident his irresistible charm was responsible for this meeting. Charity regarded him scathingly.

"Shall we sit?" he asked.

"I have not the time," said Charity. "It's long enough you took getting out here," she snapped. "Until I saw you in the pirogue, I was about to look for you in Charles Towne where I'm told you have rooms!"

René blinked. "I do. But what concern is it of yours, that I do not favor Magnolia Barony with my presence?"

"Not *my* concern," said Charity in a voice pregnant with meaning. "Captain St. Clair's concern."

Shutters seemed to come down over his liquid dark eyes, making them murky. "St. Clair?" he mused. "Now where have I heard that name?"

"In Tortuga you have heard it," said Charity boldly. "And elsewhere."

"Ah, yes, and you have been recently in Tortuga. You must tell me about this St. Clair."

"Do not fence with me, Monsieur du Bois," said Charity impatiently. "Captain St. Clair sent me here with a message for you. He's well recovered now from his fight with Captain Court and eager to be aprowl again."

René's eyes narrowed. "And what has St. Clair to say to me?"

"He doesn't trust Marie any longer. He thinks she's conniving with Captain Court to get him hanged."

René laughed contemptuously. "Madness! She is in the palm of my hand."

"Is she? It is well known in Tortuga that on her last visit to Barbadoes she slept at Captain Court's house and did not go near Captain St. Clair. She is playing you for a fool, Monsieur du Bois, and Captain St. Clair sends you word to beware of her or you'll end up dangling on hemp."

René's face suffused slowly with dark color. "The lying baggage," he muttered. He turned to Charity sharply. "But that cannot be the only reason you were sent?"

"No, I'm to take the information to him. He's ready to set sail again and would appreciate some information from you."

"I'll have it. By what ship do you leave?"

Now came the delicate part of her negotiations.

"I'm in some difficulties," she frowned. "I had money when I left Tortuga but I—I diced it away."

He gave a sudden laugh. "That's easy mended. Bring me a handful of Marie's jewels, and you'll have passage money and plenty to spare—that last lot St. Clair gave her is enough for a dozen passages."

"But . . . suppose I'm discovered?"

"It's a chance we all must take," he shrugged. "Did you think I could help you? *Merde,* I'm always in debt to my ears. This coat I'm wearing—haven't yet paid the tailor."

Charity bit her lip. She had expected he would rise to the bait and finance her. "She . . . she watches me," she said defensively. "She is suspicious of me since I've returned from Tortuga."

He shrugged again. "The *Flying Fin* leaves five days hence for Barbadoes. It's carrying nothing of value, but from Barbadoes you can reach Tortuga by the same route Marie did."

Charity nodded, pretending to knowledge she did not have.

"Bring me the jewels and I'll turn them into ready cash. I'll arrange for your passage and you can be on your way before Marie realizes her loss."

Near them a twig snapped, and René's head went up alertly.

"Were you followed?" whispered Charity.

"I don't think so," he muttered.

Laughter from the garden reached them, voices coming their way.

"We'd best part," he said. "Bad to be seen together, although . . ." he reached out and touched her bosom familiarly, "I'd prefer to linger."

Charity stiffened. "Take your hands from Captain St. Clair's property," she said coldly, and he gave a low laugh.

"I can wait," he said. "St. Clair's not a man of hot blood—you'll soon tire of him."

With a very realistic sniff, Charity made her way back through the trees to McNabb's office. As she reached it she looked back and saw that René was just coming out of the trees to join the laughing group in the garden. She spent the afternoon working on the books and when she left the office the guests had already departed, their pirogue was gone.

As she passed the dining room on her way to eat supper in the kitchen, Charity saw that Marie's face was very white and set. She guessed that René had been cool to her advances. Charity smiled with satisfaction. It was time that Marie suffered a little!

The next afternoon Charity looked out the window of the dining room, where she was counting spoons with Megan, and saw Marie, dressed in a handsome green riding dress, mounting her horse. Alan, already astride his horse, waited.

"Where are they going?" Charity asked Megan.

Megan replied that there was a nightdress in Marie's saddlebag. A woman in the group who came by pirogue yesterday had told Marie that one of the Chanceneaux sisters was ill, and Marie was on her way to Charles Towne to see her. She planned to spend the night at the Chanceneaux home while Alan returned to the plantation.

She's going to slip out and see René, thought Charity, studying Marie's straight back and fine horsemanship as the woman headed down the cart track beside her handsome husband. Charity wondered if René would see Marie.

At dinner Alan was jumpy. He did not invite Charity to dine with him, but once when the door to the kitchen swung open she saw him drop his knife with unaccustomed awkwardness. She wondered if Alan had some inkling of Marie's affairs. Perhaps he knew about them and loved her anyway. Somehow that thought had never occurred to her and a little shiver went through her.

"Need your shawl, you do," observed Megan. "You'll be getting a fever. I'll go up and get you mine."

"Nonsense," said Charity. "It's a fine warm night."

And as if to prove it, she took a turn around the lawn before going to bed.

It was her undoing. As she strolled down beside the river on the soft grass a snake suddenly slithered toward her. Turning in panic to run, she fell, landing on a fallen branch, and cut her arm. There was another sound as the snake slid into the water and Charity scrambled up and ran toward the house. When she reached it, she discovered that her hand was wet. Blood had dripped from her chemise sleeve down onto her hand.

Not wanting to bother Megan, who might already have gone to bed, Charity hurried to her room. There, she bathed the cut in water from her cracked washbasin, then sat down wearily to think.

She did not really like the idea of stealing Marie's jewels.

503

It wasn't taking them that disturbed her, for they represented Marie's commission on what had been stolen from others with her connivance. But . . . suppose René failed her. Suppose in spite of his apparent acceptance of her story, he had not been quite sure. Suppose Marie saw him tonight and in his arms convinced him of her loyalty. Then Charity might deliver the jewels to René, who would simply keep them . . . and she would be trapped in Charles Towne, having committed a criminal offense.

She paced about, feeling a deep unease, and finally decided tonight was the night she must strike. Tonight, she was sure of Marie's absence. If she waited until the day the *Flying Fin* sailed, she well might not have access to Marie's room. No, it must be tonight when Marie was gone. She would take some small piece that would not be readily missed. To that end, she did not undress, but only loosened her bodice and lay down on the bed in her green dress, waiting for the house to become quiet.

Outside a vagrant breeze rustled the leaves of one of the big live oaks, whispered through the magnolias. Lulled by the rustling and the soft breeze, she fell asleep.

She was awakened by the sound of her door opening. Her first confused thought was—Alan?

She lurched to an elbow to find herself looking into the muzzle of a gun—held in Marie Bellingham's shaking hands. And in the bright moonlight that flooded the room, Marie herself was a startling sight. Still wearing the green riding dress she had worn to Charles Towne earlier in the day, she swayed on her feet, her eyes wild, her hair now covered with a black mantilla. From her left shoulder blood seeped through her sleeve, ran down her arm to her elbow, and dripped on to the floor. Speechless, Charity stared at this apparition.

"Damn you," Marie said in a low venomous voice. "Damn you!" And swayed, falling like a graceful lily to the floor. Her black mantilla floated free as she fell and the gun dropped heavily from her nerveless fingers.

Charity started up and stared down at the fallen Marie. She tugged down the shoulder of Marie's dress. It looked to her but a flesh wound, but it was bleeding freely.

Suddenly Charity straightened. This woman had staggered up these stairs to kill her—let Alan help her! *She* would not!

Alan was just coming out of his door as she reached it. "I heard a noise," he said. "Something thumped above my head." Seeing that she was white-faced and fully dressed in the middle of the night, he grew silent.

"Your wife needs you," she said harshly. "She is in my room. I think she has been shot."

Alan gave her a horrified look and rushed past her, running down the hall. She heard him take the attic stairs two at a time. Now was her chance! Seizing a candle from Alan's room, she ran to Marie's room, threw back the covers of the bed and took the coffer from the lower drawer of the chest. Careless Marie had left it unlocked. Quickly Charity ran her hands over the tumble of necklaces, brooches, rings—a ring, that would pay for her passage and its loss not be noticed in such a jumble. She seized a ruby ring and replaced the coffer.

She was just in time. Alan appeared in the doorway with Marie's limp body in his arms. "Get bandages, hot water," he cried. "And send for a doctor!"

In his arms, Marie stirred. "No doctor," she murmured. "'Tis not deep."

He looked down at his wife in consternation. So pathetic was the expression on his face that for a moment Charity wanted to laugh.

"Hurry," he said.

She sped to her room, slid the ring under her mattress, then rushed downstairs and seized a handful of linen napkins from the dining room. Rousing the old black woman who was sleeping soundly in the kitchen, Charity told her to heat water and bring it upstairs quickly.

When the wound was bandaged and Marie lay back on the pillows looking dazed, with Alan beside her, Charity crept away. Unable to bear the hot stuffiness of her room in her jangled state, she sat in the dark dining room. It was there she heard the thunderous knock on the front door. She peered out the window. Outside she could see several horsemen. The earth was soft from recent rains and she had not heard them come up. She was certain that this visitation had to do with Marie's unexpected return. Charity waited while Alan answered the door and ushered his late-night visitors into the hall. From the darkness of the dining room she watched and listened.

The men who had ridden from Charles Towne to Magnolia Barony were terse in their explanations. A Frenchman named René du Bois had been murdered in his rooms—poisoned by manzanilla in his wine. The odor from the contents remaining in the glass was unmistakable. He had, it was presumed, shot his murderer. The woman who lived below him, roused by the shot, had rushed out and seen a woman in a green dress and black mantilla run into the street and leap onto a horse. Others had seen the horse take the cart track leading to Magnolia Barony. Would the landgrave be good enough to summon the women of his household, they asked gravely.

The landgrave saw no reason to disturb the women of his household, who had all gone to bed.

Then it must be added, said the leader of the deputation with a sigh, that the landgrave's wife was said to have been in Charles Towne this very day, riding a horse and wearing a green dress.

The landgrave stiffened and said he would call out and shoot down any man who cast slurs on his wife's reputation.

"No need, Alan. I will speak to the gentlemen." Marie's voice floated down to them. Looking up, Charity saw her standing at the head of the stairs, clad in a handsome white satin dressing gown frothing with lace. She was very pale, but there was nothing about her to indicate that she had fainted in her own blood a short hour before. Charity had to admire Marie's courage as she drifted languorously down the stairs, clutching her satin robe about her with her left arm—which, Charity realized, gave her a chance to favor it without seeming to.

"What is the matter, Alan?" she asked. And when he had explained, she paled a little more. The deputation's leader interposed to add there had been a trail of blood across the verandah leading to the front door. And here too! cried his companion—here in the hall leading upstairs, see it? Excited, they made for the stairs.

With his body, the landgrave blocked their way.

Ship's manifests had been found on this man du Bois, he was told sternly. It would appear René du Bois might have been the man who supplied information to those damned buccaneers who lay in wait a few miles out. If it should turn out du Bois had had a female accomplice—

Alan's face was gray.

"You are not looking for my wife," he said grimly. "But for me. I am the man you seek." Amid the general gasp he added, "I killed René du Bois."

Charity chanced to be looking at Marie at that moment and saw hope surge up in her eyes. Suddenly Charity realized how she could refute Alan's confession, and as she edged toward the kitchen door yet another member of the party burst in to announce breathlessly that only one horse in the stable had been recently ridden. As Charity pushed open the kitchen door she heard Marie's contemptuous rebuttal. Josh had taken her horse, curried and fed him, and doubtless turned him out to pasture. With this cool lie echoing in her ears, Charity raced up the back stairs to Marie's room. The jewels were gone. And the gun. And the green dress—which was probably ashes on the kitchen hearth by now. But she did manage to find the black mantilla.

Back downstairs she ran, and rushed in before they could take Alan away. "He must not make this sacrifice!" she cried. "It was Marie—his wife. Examine

507

her! You will find she is wounded in the left shoulder! And here—this is the mantilla that she wore."

Alan's pallor deepened but Marie, perfectly self-possessed, stepped forward.

"Nor can *I* let my husband make this sacrifice," she declared proudly, and Charity paused, as did the others, to look at her. Was Marie ashamed that Alan had so handsomely taken the blame for her, she wondered, and thus thrust his neck in a noose?

Marie's next words cut through any doubts she might have had.

"Arrest this woman!" Marie insisted, pointing toward Charity. "For it is she my husband shields with his false confession. A green dress, you say? Is she not wearing a green dress? A mantilla, you say? Has she not found one readily to hand? I have known of her affair with this Frenchman—that she slips out to meet him—for some time. Eagerly has he sought invitations here to Magnolia Barony in his attempt to be near her. But she is a stray, a woman my husband rescued from pitiable circumstances, and he does feel responsible for her—but not for this! Nay, I will not let him shield her from this—the murder of her lover!"

For a moment Charity stood speechless with rage. Then a torrent of accusing words burst forth from her. She leaped at Marie and one of the men caught her roughly. She struggled with him and her exertions opened the cut on her arm. Blood stained her sleeve and he looked startled, staring down at it.

"The wound. . . ." murmured Marie, smiling. "Come," she added, "we will see where this trail of blood leads."

Too late, Charity realized that it led to her room in the attic, where Marie had come to confront—and possibly to kill—her. There too they found René's gun, which had been fired—and the ruby ring. Manzanilla they all knew was readily procurable in Tortuga, where Charity had so recently been.

When the law men came downstairs, their case against Charity was complete.

Argument was useless.

Hands bound, she was dragged roughly away, and sat in front of one of the men on his gray horse as they plunged into the low ground fog of the cart track to Charles Town.

With a sense of doom, Charity rode in silence, head bowed.

Marie had won.

CHAPTER 46

Friendless and alone, Charity stared around her at the dark little jail cell into which they had thrust her. Still dazed by the rapidity of the events that had brought her to this state, she sank down on the narrow cot. Her situation, she knew, was hopeless. The case against her was too clear. Even Alan, looking at her in horror, had believed it. Though what lies Marie had told him, she could only guess.

Oddly enough, the fact that Alan believed her guilty did not disturb her so much. All the way through the fog she had seen before her another face, lean and hawklike, with wintry light eyes.

Restless, she got up and paced about.

Finally—now that she had not long to live—she faced the truth. Like a terrible explosion in her brain, she saw herself in a bright pitiless light.

She had never loved Alan—*she loved Jeremy Court*. Dear God, she had loved him from the first!

The force of that knowledge weakened her and she sank trembling to the cot again.

All the time I loved him I told myself twas only my body responded to him, not my heart—I could not bear to admit that I loved a man who didn't love me. Twas why I worried so when he was gone, why I tried so hard to enrage him—I wanted to strike at him, to make him feel something for me other than naked lust! Oh, God, I wanted his love and I could not admit it—even to myself.

And when . . . when he took me, when his hands caressed me, when he held me close in his arms, I could fool myself for a little while that he was truly

511

mine and would always be mine. But when our love-making was over, I realized it could never be . . . never. And it made me monstrous uncivil to him. My pride could not stand it, knowing I'd always be second, that another woman would always be first in his heart.

Perhaps tis better I hang, she thought wildly. *I have nothing left to live for. All the men I loved have either not loved me or turned out badly. And Court . . .* her eyes grew tender. *Ah, Jeremy, I left you . . . when all I wanted was to stay in your arms.*

She covered her face with her hands and rocked with misery. Had he not once said he'd had to be content with the crumbs from Marie's table? Oh, why could she not have been content with the crumbs from *his?*

On her prison pallet, she writhed in dry-eyed grief, for she had learned the secrets of her own heart too late.

Only Megan came to see Charity at the jail. She looked old and tired and her gray hair was not neatly combed as usual, but flew about. It hurt Charity's heart to see her so, for Megan had become a second mother to Charity.

"Ye must plead your belly," Megan insisted.

"I won't do that," frowned Charity.

"Sure and tis the only way to be sure of another nine months of life! All accused women do it!"

Nine more months of this torment. . . .

"Perhaps I'm tired of living," murmured Charity.

"Ah, now, that's no way to feel," chided Megan. "Your trial's been postponed. Dr. Cavendish interceded for ye."

Charity laughed shortly. "He needn't have bothered."

"Tis not because of that spineless planter that ye feel this way," mused Megan. "What is it makes ye want to die, Charity?" She gave her a shrewd look. "What really happened on Tortuga? You weren't in no tavern there, were you?"

"No," said Charity, taking a deep breath. "I was mistress to a man you may have heard of—Jeremy Court."

Megan looked startled. "La!" she cried. "The buccaneer!"

Charity nodded. Suddenly she wanted to tell someone, and she poured out the whole story into those kindly old Irish ears, about Court and herself and Marie and St. Clair and René. "And worst of all," she finished, "after all the hell Court went through to get back to her, Marie was just using him. So she could get her share of the prizes St. Clair took—she has a whole coffer full of jewels, rubies, diamonds, emeralds. It was in the lower drawer of her chest, but she must have hidden it somewhere else before she came downstairs because I couldn't find it."

"*That* must have been what she was doing the night you was taken!" exclaimed Megan, her eyes widening. "The voices downstairs woke me and then I heard someone creeping up to the attic. Funny sounds came from that little room over her's—like someone was moving boards in the floor."

"That's probably where she put them," Charity agreed in a weary voice. "But she'll have moved them again by now, in case I alerted the authorities."

"*I* could alert them for you," said Megan sturdily.

"No." Charity put a dissuading hand on Megan's arm. "I'll not drag you down with me. You need your job, Megan."

"Then won't nothing dissuade you, Charity?" cried Megan, leaning forward. "Plead your belly. Sure there's no harm, and in nine months maybe things will have changed."

Charity shook her head. "I've made a mess of my life," she said quietly. "It's best over now."

Her gaze was resolute. Megan's shoulders sagged as she said goodbye. They both knew it was for the last time.

All the dark night Charity lay awake, staring at the moon through the iron bars. Morning found her haggard-eyed and tired, but she had come to a decision.

She would not "plead her belly." She would not grovel, she would not lie. She would go into court and

513

—if they would let her, for she remembered how the magistrate in Massachusetts had cut her off—she would tell them all the truth. About Marie, about Jeremy, everything.

Marie would have to leave Alan then or . . . he would throw her out. She would no longer be accepted in polite society—and a woman as proud as Marie could not stand that. Marie would either have to find her way to Tortuga and live there as Jeremy's mistress, or sink into some nameless backwater and be forgotten.

So Jeremy would at last have the woman he wanted or . . . she would have set him free.

As the days passed, Charity's face took on a set purposeful look. She knew she could not get a message to Tortuga, but . . . gossip found its way there. A colorful story like hers would be repeated, and would warn Jeremy of Marie's treachery, in case Marie found another pirate who wanted to fly under the famous Captain Court's colors.

If they would not let her say these things in the courtroom, she would ask to make a last statement on the gallows. Prisoners were permitted to do that, indeed encouraged to do so, before they were hanged. Usually they were pious exhortations to others not to fall into evil ways, but she would give the waiting crowd the facts before the tightening hemp choked off her words.

It was little enough to do for him. . . .

Oh, God, she loved him so much. She put her head in her hands and wept. Wept not that she must die, but for what might have been. The life they might have had together that now would never be. Wept for her foolishness, the pride that had blinded her.

If only . . . if only for a little while he had loved her, not just taken her body and enjoyed its wild response to him, but loved her . . . she could have taken that with her into whatever hell the hanged were tossed.

But now it was too late and she must do what she could.

Hot tears scalded her cheeks and ran down into

her mouth. She sat up and dashed them away with the back of her hand. Her jailer would soon be bringing her breakfast and he would find her calm. And calm she would stay to the end.

Though the jail food was poor, consisting mainly of gruel and odd-tasting stews, she ate it, determined to keep up her strength. She wanted her voice to ring out clearly in the courtroom, and clearly once again on the gallows. She wanted its echoes to carry all the way to Tortuga. . . .

Then she began to fear the jail food. Suppose Marie guessed that she would speak out and managed to put manzanilla in her food? Jailers could be bought like other men!

She put down her spoon and stared at her gruel in horror. One day she drank only water and the kindly old jailer looked at her, worried.

"Tis good," he insisted, and to prove it took a spoonful himself.

Thereupon, Charity seized the bowl and ate it all. He went out shaking his head.

During the long days she reviewed her life and thought pensively of all that had happened in her short lifetime. Too short, but she would not plead, she would not wallow in self-pity, she would not beg and whine. She would stand up proudly and face them down and tell the truth. And then they could take her out and hang her.

For her folly, life had presented a bill. And she would pay it.

She did not know it was her father's wild Irish spirit that glowed in her now, that spirit that when he lay dying had made him think of the woman he had so lately held in his arms. In his fashion, he had paid his bill.

So would she.

CHAPTER 47

She had no warning when it came. She was sitting dejected in her dark cell when the door creaked open. She blinked at the lantern the old jailer carried and shielded her eyes from its light.

"Ye're free," the jailer said and she looked up at him dully, not comprehending. "I said *ye're free*," he repeated. "Captain Court traded his body for yours."

Charity came to her feet. "Court's—here?"

"Aye, chained in the jail. The *Sea Witch* came in with the tide and he offered to trade himself for the woman accused of killing René du Bois—and that's you, mistress. Out ye go now."

Charity felt suffocated. Jeremy had come for her! She swayed on her feet, her heart bursting. Only a man in love would trade his life for a woman. . . . Jeremy loved her, must have loved her all along! He had been hers—and she had deserted him.

And now he would dangle on hemp for her sake and be buried between the high tide and the low. . . . To this cruel end had her folly brought him.

"Where is he?" she cried. "I must see him. I must speak to him."

"Ye can't. Nobody can speak to him. He's been put in the deepest hole we've got so's he can't escape us."

A great sob escaped her as she ran out past the jailer.

"Wait," he cried. "He's asked that the price on his head be paid to you and that you—"

Charity did not hear him. She had rushed from the jail, sobbing, into the crowd that had gathered outside.

517

"'Tis Captain Court's woman!" cried someone. Heads craned to look at her and Charity came up short, confronted by an evil grinning face. She brushed aside the man who blocked her way and ran past. Still sobbing, she raced down the street until she found a lonely gatepost where a horse was tethered. Without hesitation, she untied the reins, flung herself onto his back and galloped down the cart track toward Magnolia Barony.

Jeremy Court would hang as a pirate because of the lies René and Marie had spread—but not if a confession could be wrung from Marie!

Skirts flying, branches slapping her face, Charity's horse thundered the four miles and more to Magnolia Barony. Nearly there, she stopped, dismounted, gave her horse a pat and stole across the lawn and through the trees. The kitchen door was seldom locked. One of the house slaves was usually on duty there, dozing through the night on a chair. So, she stole through that door, past the sleeping servant and into the house.

A brace of dueling pistols were kept in the dining room. Quietly, Charity found them, loaded one and crept up the back stairs. Once she paused, thinking she had heard a step behind her, then deciding she had not, and moved on. She opened Marie's door and closed it softly behind her. Marie did not stir. She slept soundly, Charity noted. Swiftly Charity found pen and ink and paper—and sealing wax. From the guttering candle by the bedside she lit another taper and then prodded Marie's back with the barrel of the long dueling pistol.

Marie rolled over and saw Charity. Her violet eyes flew wide and so did her mouth—to scream. Charity thrust the pistol almost into her mouth.

"If you say a word," she said in a low voice, "I'll blow your head off." She added, "I would *like* to blow your head off."

White-faced, Marie subsided, shrinking back into the bedcovers.

"You will get up," ordered Charity. "You will sit down at that desk and write a full confession—everything, how you schemed with St. Clair and with René to blacken Court's name. Up!"

Shaking, Marie got up, edged away from Charity toward the desk where pen and paper awaited. "How—how did you get out?" she demanded in a shaky voice.

"Jeremy came for me," said Charity grimly. "He exchanged himself for me." To Marie's open-mouthed astonishment, she waved the barrel of the pistol. "Be about it," she said.

As if mesmerized, Marie sat down and began to write with long flourishes across the paper. Her confession covered several pages. Reaching carefully across the front of the desk, Charity read it with one eye on her prisoner. It was all there—names, places, dates. Surely any court would accept that!

"Now sign," she directed sharply. "There's sealing wax. Imprint your signet ring in the wax beside your signature, and the same to seal it together. Address it to the magistrate. We'll be dropping it off at his house."

"We?" Marie looked up.

"You and I," said Charity with a note of finality.

"No, the three of us," came Kirby's cool voice behind them. Startled, Charity looked around to see his tall lean frame lounging against the doorjamb. Held negligently in one hand was a very large pistol. He smiled at Charity.

"I was in the crowd outside the jail when you were released, and I followed to see where you were going so hotfoot. It's been an interesting conversation I've overheard, that it has, and I'm as eager to read that as any magistrate." He took the letter from Marie, scanned it rapidly. "Very nicely put—and it puts a rope around your pretty neck, m'lady." He gave Marie a mocking bow. "Jeremy will be pleased to know your love for him was so great it moved you to write a confession to free him." He turned to Charity. "We'd best away. I wouldn't want to be here come daylight."

"I'm not dressed!" protested Marie, looking down at her filmy nightgown.

Silently, Charity tossed her a dressing gown.

"Ah, wait—my jewels!" implored Marie.

"They'll help console Alan—and pay his debts," Charity said brusquely, and pushed the wild-eyed Marie from the room. Downstairs they trouped, the confession in Kirby's pocket. This time they left by the front door and moved silently out to the stables where Kirby hitched up the carriage while Charity kept the gun pointed at Marie.

Down the cart track they headed, the women silent, but Kirby keeping up a bright monologue. Had they heard? A general amnesty had been offered to the buccaneers. One had only to go in to obtain the king's pardon. Many would do it.

"Will you?" wondered Marie.

He shook his head, "Tortuga suits me."

"Then they cannot hold Jeremy in jail!" cried Charity. "They'll have to release him!"

"Nay, this is Charles Towne justice," Kirby told her. "'Tis Charles Towne put a price on our heads, and they're a resolute people here. They'll hang him first and ask the king later."

Charity shuddered, hardly listening as he went on to other subjects. Finally, Kirby told her that while aprowl in the West Indies the *Sea Witch* had come upon an English ship aground on a sand bar and Court had ordered it tugged free with ropes. While this was being done, the ship's captain had come aboard the *Sea Witch* for a glass of port. He'd come directly from Charles Towne harbor, this captain, and he brought the latest news. Twas the very night Charity had been taken, Kirby told them brightly, that the captain had left Charles Towne. Of course Court set out—"

"Stop," Charity interrupted. "We're here. This is the magistrate's house." She jumped out of the carriage as they pulled up before the house, grasped the heavy knocker and hammered on the door. A sleepy servant opened the door, told them resentfully the household was asleep and took the letter, mumbling he'd give it to his master next morning.

Charity was near tears; she wanted Marie's confession read *now*.

As they pulled out onto the road they heard a

spattering of gunfire from the direction of the jail, and the heavy roll of guns from the *Sea Witch*. Kirby laughed recklessly. "Court didn't wait for you," he said. "Sounds like he's arranged his own rescue. Probably had the jail taken by part of the crew he thoughtfully landed down the coast before he sailed in."

"What—what will happen to us?" cried Marie.

"I'll signal the *Sea Witch*," said Kirby. They dashed through the town, which was full of people running about so that their careening progress seemed only natural. When they reached the narrow trail by which Kirby said he had walked from the coast, he got out and unhitched the horses. "Charity can ride alone, but you, m'lady, will ride with me—just in case you decide to escape and inform on the way we've gone," he told Marie, and pulled her up in front of him on the horse.

"You were never so ungallant in Tortuga," she pouted.

"Ah, but there Jeremy stood between us," he said humorously. "Now it's my own dainty hide I'm protecting!"

Down the narrow path they hurried—it was an Indian trail and some parts of it were barely negotiable by their horses. Charity could hear Marie cursing as the thorny vines reached out their sharp tendrils and tore at her arms and legs. As for herself, Charity scarcely felt their pricks. *Sounds like he's arranged his own rescue,* Kirby had said. Dear God, let it be so! Let him be safe aboard the *Sea Witch* at this moment! She found herself sobbing brokenly into the wind, *let him live, let him live* . . . when Kirby at last reined to a halt by the shore.

"There she is," he cried, peering out across the dark water. "Can you see her?"

Squinting, Charity saw across the black glittering water the dull gray sails of a dark-hulled ship moving away from the Charles Towne quay.

"Now if the moon's bright enough," Kirby muttered, "this ought to do it." And took from his pocket a piece of steel rubbed mirror-bright. He stood there flashing it at the ship.

Suddenly from the ship a light appeared—a lantern swung back and forth, back and forth.

"They've seen us," Kirby said with satisfaction. "We'll be on our way to Tortuga soon, ladies."

"Let me go back," pleaded Marie. "Jeremy's in no danger now. Charity is safe. I can get back the confession—I can say it was taken at gunpoint. Let me go back and lead my life, Kirby."

"That's for Jeremy to say," he told her shortly. "If that's what he wants for you, he can set you ashore as easily as he picks you up."

"The *Sea Witch* wouldn't have sailed away without him, would she?" asked Charity, afraid.

"Not likely," grinned Kirby. "No, Jeremy's buccaneers would still be back there contesting the guns of Charles Towne for their captain—they'd have ended up tearing the town apart. His men swear by Jeremy, or hadn't you noticed?"

She knew they did, but she was so afraid for him, so afraid. . . .

When the longboat picked them up, the first thing she asked was a faltering, "Is—is Captain Court—?"

"Safe aboard, mistress," Ravenal answered, and Charity slumped against the side of the boat, weak with relief.

Across the dark water the long sweep of the oars took them toward that ship of which she had such memories. . . .

Marie was first to clamber aboard with a flash of white legs and filmy nightgown, quickly covered by her robe. And then Kirby helped Charity up the side. He regarded her narrowly; then, like a man who'd been waiting for just the right moment, he turned to Marie with a laugh. "Ye'll be interested to know that Jeremy thought he was trading himself for *you,* not Charity." he said. "The English captain had reported only that the law was on its way to Magnolia Barony to arrest someone for the murder of René du Bois. Naturally, Jeremy assumed that Marie had been arrested!"

So Jeremy had come for *Marie,* not for her! Charity

found it a stunning blow. She sagged against Kirby, who gallantly threw an arm around her.

She was standing thus, half wrapped in Kirby's embrace, when Court, striding through a crowd of buccaneers, reached them. He frowned.

"I've brought the ladies," said Kirby blithely. "They've just heard that there's a general amnesty offered to our lot. So, some will be for England—or Barbadoes or the Colonies, but not Leeds Kirby! I'm for the free life in Tortuga—what say ye, lads?"

There was a general cheer and Court's frown deepened.

"Does this mean . . . you can go home, Jeremy?" Marie asked.

Court nodded sternly. "Those who wish to."

"Then . . ." Marie swayed toward him. Ever the complete opportunist, eyes sparkling, she threw her arms around Court. "We are back where we started, Jeremy!" she cried. "We can go back to England together!"

Standing there, braced by Kirby's strong wiry arm, Charity reeled from this bitterest blow of her life. She wanted to die.

To her astonishment, Court reached out his arms and put Marie firmly aside.

"But you offered your life for me, Jeremy!" cried Marie, confused. "Kirby said so."

"Kirby was mistaken," said Court coldly, his eyes raking Charity. "My information is better than that. I sent two lads ashore to spy out the town. I knew what woman was held in the jail. I came to save the woman I love." He cast a brooding look at Charity, who was reeling with shock a second time. Her knees almost buckled and Kirby had to hold her up.

"I realize she does not share my feelings," Court said dryly. And before she could protest, "But she is not bound for Tortuga with you, Kirby. It's no life for a woman there. Mistress Charity." He now addressed her formally as she clung to Kirby, stunned. "It is my intention to put you on the first homeward-bound English ship we sight and return you with all speed to England. As I should have done in the first place. Twas a wrong that I did you, to keep you against your will. A wrong I'll now make right."

With a frown, Kirby took his arm from around Charity's shoulders and took a step forward. His voice rang out hard. "The lady should decide where she goes and with whom."

So savagely did Court swing on him that Kirby stepped back a pace and rested his hand on his sword hilt.

Charity had never seen Court look so reckless or so resolute. His dark face was stern and his keen light eyes were narrowed and exceedingly evil.

"As you love your life, Kirby," he said softly. "Do not cross me in this." His hand moved toward the hilt of his rapier. "Friend or no, ye'll feel my blade between your ribs if you try to take her. Ye've no mind to quit this bloody trade and ye'll end your life swinging on hemp. And then where would she be? Weeping in Tortuga and having the others draw lots for her!"

Though the other buccaneers watched uneasily, feeling that surge of electricity that sweeps through the air just before the storm breaks, Charity felt it not. She was only aware of a blind, wonderful, unreasoning joy that lifted her up and up. Court loved her! He had seen Marie for what she was and flung her aside! He loved *her*. He had challenged Kirby for her!

So many terrible things had happened, so often had she been cast down into despair, and so recently had she thought him lost to her forever, that on this, the greatest moment of her life, she found herself standing speechless, with tears sparkling on her lashes.

Charity felt a touch of fear as the two men—redoubtable swordsmen both—studied each other.

Then Kirby gave a smiling shrug and offered his arm to Marie. "Sure, I'll have my hands full escorting this lady, who knows not the ways of Tortuga."

Marie, who knew the ways of Tortuga very well indeed, shook him off impatiently. "If you don't want me, Jeremy, you could at least let me go! Set me ashore that I may find my way back to Charles Towne!"

Court's wintry glance played over her lustrous body in its filmy nightgown, which was only partially concealed by her carelessly tied robe. "As for you, madam," he said coldly. "I'd a mind to take you to your friend Captain St. Clair, who deserves your scheming ways."

Marie caught her breath. "Ah, Jeremy, you wouldn't!"

"That's right," he said softly. "I wouldn't. Though by heaven it's what you deserve. Ashore you shall go."

"Ah, now, Jeremy," Kirby chided, "the lady's signed a confession absolving us all. You wouldn't want her to swing for that!" And to Marie, "Tis doubtful in their rage that they'll let you go. You know that, don't you? Mobs need someone to wreak their vengeance on and you'll be handy—condemned by your own words in your own handwriting! And who's to say you were forced at gunpoint? They'll think you merely missed the *Sea Witch* as she left and are forced into new lies to save your pretty neck!"

Marie winced, seeing the truth of what he said.

"Didst ever ponder that a surgeon's share of the loot taken is second only to the captain's?" Kirby asked impudently.

For a moment Marie seemed to waver. Beautiful, voluptuous, she stood there weighing her chances. Suddenly she smiled at Kirby and their glances locked —two handsome, cynical opportunists, a perfect match for each other.

"I'll take my chances in Charles Towne," said Marie. She shrugged. "They are but men who'll decide my fate there and—" she glanced coldly at Charity— "I'll wear a green dress."

Only Charity caught the allusion. She knew that Marie would trust to luck, and felt she would win out. And for the first time Charity could not pity Alan. He'd wanted Marie, he'd married her, he'd shown himself willing to die for her—perhaps he deserved her.

As Marie was helped over the side, she flung one last tantalizing smile at Kirby. "Perhaps I'll grow bored and come to visit you in Tortuga," she murmured.

His eyes kindled. "Do that and *I* will visit *you* in

Charles Towne," he said. "If they decide to hang you, send me word and I'll persuade this grim-faced captain here to come and sack the town!"

"They'll not hang me," Marie called out and her light seductive laugh floated back to them as she climbed into the longboat to be swiftly rowed to shore.

Charity turned to Court. He stood watching her, and for a moment she saw the deep hunger in his face and the spasm of pain that crossed it. Then it was gone, leaving his dark countenance haggard and stern. He turned on his heel.

"Get her from my sight," he ordered in a thick voice. "Ravenal, take her to my cabin."

There was no love lost between the crew of the *Sea Witch* and Charity, who had nearly cost their beloved captain his life on two occasions. Before she could recover herself, Ravenal had seized her and hustled her away.

She glanced back once and caught Kirby's gaze. *I can wait,* that gaze told her. *There'll be other nights.*

And then she was in the captain's cabin, Court's cabin. Surely once he came through that door his heart would soften, he would not send her away. . . . She touched the bunk with tender fingers. Remembering his touch like liquid fire, his hands moving over her soft quivering breasts, the hard feel of his thighs. How often she had fought him! She laughed to herself. But never again, never again . . . now, together, they would sample all the delights of love. Her heart was full of plans as she waited for him, but the sun pinked the sky and still he did not come.

Tired, she pounded on the door and Ravenal's laconic voice answered her. No, she was not to be allowed on deck. Not to be allowed out at all until an English ship was sighted.

"And suppose none is sighted?" she flashed.

"Then we take you with us to Tortuga, I suppose," rumbled Ravenal.

To Tortuga . . . ah, there she would have him. Let Jeremy keep his rage on board this rolling vessel. Caressed by the spice-scented winds of Tortuga he would find it harder to keep his footing.

Gloomily, she ate the breakfast the cabin boy brought her.

An hour later she received a rude jolt when Court knocked on the door of the cabin and told her coldly to make ready, an English ship had been sighted and she would soon be transferred.

"Aren't you going to tell me goodbye?" she asked wistfully.

"I told you goodbye in my heart when you ran away from Tortuga," he said through the closed door. "You let the letter from Marie turn you against me without even waiting to find out my reply. No, I'll not give you another chance at me."

"But you came for me in Charles Towne, Jeremy. . . ."

"That was to save your life," he said crisply. "The like will not arise again."

Anger rose in her.

"Are you a coward then?" she taunted the closed door. "Afraid of a woman? Faith, I always thought so!"

With an oath the door was flung open and Court strode into the room. His boots held the deck squarely and his rapier clanged against the doorjamb behind him. His eyes were steady and cold but his face was haggard and at sight of her he paled under his tan.

Charity laughed. She was at the moment taking a bath. Standing naked at the washstand. Tossing back her damp pale-gold hair, she held out a cloth. "There was a time," she reminded him, "when you'd have washed my back for me."

Court groaned. "You drive me too far. If I touch you, I'll carry you back to Tortuga—and hold you there against man and God!"

He tore his eyes from her and turned to go.

With speed she had not known she possessed, Charity made it to the door first, leaned her naked back against it, holding a towel almost to her chin.

"If you put me off the *Sea Witch,* when I get back to England I swear I'll take the first passage back to Tortuga," she warned, her eyes gleaming.

"What do you mean?" Court demanded hoarsely.

"That I love you, Jeremy," she said, and dropping the towel, walked naked into her lover's arms.

From the deck, the voices of a group of buccaneers singing drifted down to them. . . . The songs were of lost, of hunted men, lonely and forever damned to roam. Someone had a stringed instrument and plucked at it softly, and the twanging notes mingled with the words that told of homes they'd never see again, of lips they'd never kiss. Like the wind over the water their lonesome music cast its own spell.

"Ye'll be the death of me," Jeremy muttered. "Against my better judgment I held you before, and against my better judgment I take you now." He turned his head toward the door. "Ravenal," he shouted. "Forget the English ship. Tell Tim to come about and resume course. The lady's coming with us."

Later, much later, after a silken joining that was all she could have wished for, she lay spent and naked against his broad chest and asked drowsily, "Are we for Tortuga then?"

"Briefly," he said. "To pick up Ella and then, with the king's pardon in hand, I thought to make for the James and buy me a plantation there. I'll be needing a wife. Will you come with me, Charity, and share in this venture?"

Wife . . . his wife. Tears shimmered on her dark-gold lashes and wet her cheeks.

"I will go with you, Jeremy," she said huskily. "To Tortuga, or the James—or to hell. Wherever you're bound."

At the richness of her tone, he lifted his head and looked into her eyes, looked deeply, smiling into their topaz depths. The words would be said over them later but their troth was plighted then. With that long word-less look they had given themselves to each other for all time, whatever fate held in store for them.

Then his arms tightened about her again and she moved luxuriously as their bodies locked together and together they sought the farthest shores of desire—and fulfillment.

THE END